Planet Urth: The Savage Lands (Book 1 & 2)

A novel
By Jennifer and Christopher Martucci

This book is a work of fiction. Names, characters, places, and incidents either are a product of the authors' imagination or are used fictitiously. Any resemblance to actual persons, living or dead, events, or locales is entirely coincidental.

PLANET URTH (BOOK 1)

Published by Jennifer and Christopher Martucci

Copyright © 2012 Jennifer and Christopher Martucci

First edition: October 2013

Chapter 1

Wind howls through the trees and rushes in the cracks of the cave, whistling shrilly. I bolt upright, startled. In the bleary moments just after waking from a deep sleep, I worry that they've found us. When my eyes adjust, I see that we are alone and our defenses have not been breached.

I sigh and feel the panic begin to leak from my body as my eyes sweep the familiar surroundings. The sun has not risen yet. Eerie, iridescent light trickles in with streams of air that carry the sweet, pungent zing of ozone. Sharp and fresh, the scent fills the cave. I wonder if my sister, June, smells it. It is one of her favorite scents, the way the atmosphere smells before it rains. But she is still asleep, her small body curled in a ball beside me. I am tempted to wake her. She does not like to miss any opportunity for joy, as joy is a rarity in our world. But she looks too serene to disturb. With her eyes closed and her features relaxed, she looks her age: eight years old. Her brow is not creased in concern. Her eyes are not narrowed as they usually are. Her face is smooth, innocent. She looks at peace. But I know that when she finally wakes, favorite scents or no favorite scents, peace will seep from her. Daylight will appear to age her. It always does.

I watch her for several moments. The familiar ache begins in my chest and quickly tightens my throat. I swallow hard, gulping in vain against the lump of dread stuck there. I don't know why I bother. It never moves. I doubt it will ever leave.

Thunder rumbles and shakes the cave's stone walls. Rain patters at first then drums loudly, the shriek of the wind accompanying it. A violent storm is underway. Still, June remains asleep, unbothered and unaware of it. I almost envy her.

Her eyelids flutter and a small smile tilts the corners of her mouth upward. She must be having a pleasant dream. I have forgotten what pleasant dreams are. My dreams are never pleasant. They are usually filled with dreadful images, and running, always running, without a destination in sight. The veil between nightmares and reality is thin. Some days, I have trouble distinguishing between the two. I would have ended it all long ago were it not for June.

June is my reason to live, the *only* reason I still live. She is my purpose. I exist to keep her safe, for she needs protection from many things in this world. It has been eight years since I've seen another human being that wasn't my father or my sister, June. I'm convinced we are the last human beings on what was once called *planet Earth*. I would never tell June that. I tell her every day that I believe someone will find us, that we will one day feel safe instead of scared all the time. But I know that is not true.

I force a smile on my face each day, in defiance of the truth, in defiance of the ache in my heart, and tell June that one day our lives will be filled with calm and order. It is a sharp contrast to the jumbled chaos of our day-to-day existence. Most days the madness of it all weighs on me so heavily I contemplate scouring the forest for berries my father warned me against, and filling my belly with them. Once, I came dangerously close to doing just that that.

A few weeks ago, I leaned against a tree trunk, mesmerized by the yellowish-orange fruit, and picked a handful. I brought my hand to my mouth and parted my lips, tears of relief slipping down my cheeks as I envisioned an end to it all, to the never-ending tightness in my throat, the constant worry, the suffering. I was about to eat several berries when my sister called out to me in the distance. She was cheering excitedly about catching her first squirrel, which turned out to be a skunk. I froze. The gravity of what I was about to do hit me like a fist to my gut. The berries fell between my fingers and dropped to the ground below. "In a minute, June," I yelled. I needed time to collect myself and breathe through the swell of emotion crashing over me. I had intended to take my life, had come dangerously close, in fact. The actuality of it staggered me. I was angry, scared, and grateful all at once. I sprang to my feet and paced for several moments, panting like a wild animal, before I calmed down enough to plaster a tight smile on my face. I returned to June and did not speak of what I almost did. She never asked, and I never told. I haven't done anything that reckless or stupid since. I don't have the luxury of doing such things.

Now, as I watch the rise and fall of June's chest as she takes deep, even breaths, I realize I was selfish weeks earlier. I am selfish every time I entertain the idea of ending the yawning pit of sadness inside me for good. She needs me. She would not survive without me, especially since our father died a little more than a year ago. He lived what I guess was a much longer-than-average life and passed away peacefully at the age of fifty. In the days before his death, I promised him we would stay safe, and I would keep June out of harm's way and never give up. He showed me how to do it, how to survive. The rest, namely living, is a bit more complicated.

I lie back down and close my eyes, remembering all my father taught me. I curve my body around June's sleeping form, comforted by her stillness. She does not feel me there. She continues to sleep. The storm rages outside. And the lump in my throat balloons to the point that I fear it will strangle me.

But in spite of the turmoil outside and the havoc rattling around inside me, exhaustion takes hold and pulls me on a dark and velvety tide. I sleep until the chirping of birds wakes me.

Sooty shadows still stretch across the cave I've called home for the last six years, but the light filtering in is considerably brighter. My stomach clenches violently, rumbling and growling, and I know it is time to hunt. Food has been scarce the last few days, leaving only small animals to trap and eat. I have only caught rats. They taste terrible, have very little meat on them, and always leave me feeling sick. I crave the filling sustenance of boart meat, but haven't seen one recently, not in the last three days, at least.

The thought of filling my stomach with tender, succulent boart flesh forces me to sit up. My back complains and my neck aches. Too little sleep and positioning myself oddly conspire against me. Regardless, I push myself to stand, shoving my palms and heels against the hard, rocky floor. I scrub my face with my hands, then stretch before pulling out the logs that are lodged between the wall and the boulder at the mouth of the cave.

Six years ago, my father found a stone to cover the cave's opening. He spent months etching it, chipping away at its surface little by little, until it fit, rounded and able to roll bumpily. With an assortment of wood stuck all around it, the boulder conceals June and I and keeps creatures of every kind from getting in. The beings that roam the land after dark are deadly. We cannot go out once the sun sets, not even in the event of an emergency. No human being can, should any exist. The others are long gone. And together, the boulder and the logs safeguard June and I from Lurkers.

The thought of Lurkers makes my skin crawl, as if thousands of insect feelers are scuttling across it. The need for fresh air and light becomes urgent. Large logs wedge the boulder into the mouth of the cave to keep it securely in place. The logs extend from the boulder to the far wall. I frantically clear them, working so hard I am winded. When the last log is cleared, I rest my hands on my knees and gulp air greedily. I brush my brow with the back of my hand and my eyes immediately go to June, still fast asleep. I regret having to wake her, but the next task is too difficult to be performed by only me. The boulder is heavy, and while I'm at my prime at age seventeen, my strength is no match for the stone.

Reluctantly, I move toward her and sit. I brush a lock of golden hair from her forehead.

"Good morning, sleepyhead," I say.

She stirs and slowly opens her eyes. Her eyes narrow and focus on my face, erasing the smoothness of youth. She suddenly looks all of her eight years, plus some.

"Time to move it." I thumb over my shoulder to the boulder.

June groans and scrunches up her face.

"Come on, lazy bones," I tease her. "If you want to get outside and enjoy the long, warm day, I suggest you quit moaning and help me." I poke the tip of her small nose with my index finger. She smiles, an expression that lights her entire face, then sits up and hugs me tightly. The gesture loosens the tightness in my chest and I am reminded of what, or who, I am living for.

"I do want to go outside," June murmurs into my hair. "I hate nighttime."

Her words resonate in my bones. She loosens her grip on me and sits back. "We need to do a lot today, but if we have time left, we will go to the meadow."

Her face lights up and her pale-blue eyes sparkle. "Oh, Avery, you promise?" she squeaks, and her eyebrows nearly disappear into her hairline.

"Promise," I say.

She mumbles something about having the best sister ever and my cheeks grow hot. I do not deserve her compliments.

June scrambles from her sleep sack and stands. Her long limbs are thin, her elbows and kneecaps prominent. Our recent diet, reliant on rats as a source of protein, is taking its toll on her. I curse myself under my breath for not doing a better job, for not taking care of her properly as I'd promised my father I would.

"Let's move this thing out of the way," I say more cheerily than I feel.

We must crouch to walk through the narrow, tunnel-like structure that leads to the mouth of the cave. It is a tight squeeze, but we do whatever is necessary to secure ourselves.

June follows, placing her hands beside mine. A crisp breeze blows, cooling my skin just before we pull the stone until a thick rim of light appears all around it. We continue until a brilliant glow pours into the cave. I squint and shield my eyes with my hand as they adjust to daylight.

"Wow," June comments, her eyes round with wonder. "Look at the sky. It's so blue."

She's right. The sky is bluer than usual. It looks as if it has been scrubbed clean. Not a cloud mars its perfection.

"You know why it looks like that, right?" I ask.

"No, why?" She looks at me quizzically.

"We had storms a couple hours ago, and someone slept through all of it," I comment playfully and elbow her lightly in the ribs. She frowns and knits her brow as if she's done something wrong, not quite the response I'd hope for.

"Were you scared?" she asks, her eyes pleading pools of crystal-clear water.

"Nah, not at all," I lie. "The only reason I woke is because you snore." I elbow her again. This time, a wide, goofy smile spreads across her face that makes my chest temporarily release the stranglehold on my heart.

"Yeah, well, it's better than drooling like you do," she teases me back.

"Hey!" I say with exaggerated annoyance.

"Come on, drool-girl, I'll race you to the river!" She arches a pale brow and twists her mouth to one side before darting off into the woods toward the fresh-water river where we start our days.

"No fair!" I call as I dash after her.

The air is cool, refreshingly so, when it rushes in my face as I race after June. She is small and thin and quick as lightning as she streaks between trees and bushes, dodging vines and creepers. Birds flit from tree to tree and chipmunks peep in annoyance. All around us, the woodland wakes. A new day has dawned. Storms have passed and the grass is wet, but the mugginess is gone, the air is lighter, as if the world has sighed away a heavy burden. But I know the Lurkers still exist. I wish it were that easy.

When I reach the river, June is there already. Her hands are on her hips, and her chin is tipped upward, a sly smile rounding her cheeks.

"I thought you'd never get here." She tries to sound smug, but she is incapable of conceit or arrogance of any kind. She is better than that.

"What can I say? You're fast, too fast for me," I reply.

Her smile broadens. It reaches her eyes and makes them dance with pride.

"Come on, let's wash up and hunt." I splash my face with water warmed by the summer sun.

June follows my lead and scoops handfuls of water and scrubs her face and underarms. Once we are clean, I turn to her.

"We are going out a little farther than the perimeter today," I say. June's brow furrows deeply and her eyes narrow to slits. She folds her willowy arms across her chest and listens intently. "Do you feel comfortable going off on your own out there? Do you think you'll be okay?" I ask, fearful that she is not ready yet.

She nods resolutely and says, "I'll be fine."

I place a hand on her shoulder, giving it a firm squeeze as I smile. I do not hide the pride I am feeling, or the relief. Going beyond the boundaries we've observed for years is crucial. The knobbiness of her shoulder is a painful reminder that if we do not push our boundaries, our food supply will continue to dwindle.

"Great," I say. "I knew you were."

June's eyes widen at my words, gleaming with satisfaction, and my heart swells.

"I'm going to get us a couple of rabbits for dinner tonight," she says with steely determination.

I admire her grit and wish grit alone were capable of snaring a pair of rabbits. But it is not. The sad fact is that June rarely catches anything, and has never caught an animal substantial enough to feed us more than once. I feel confident today will be no different, but I respect her more than words can say for waking up every single morning and trying. She is undaunted by failure, unsullied by it.

"Good," I tell her and wink. "I look forward to it."

"Count on it," she says. Her posture straightens, so full of optimism and hope.

I wish she would learn to hunt. I hope she reaches her goal today. She needs to be able to kill and prepare her own food as a precaution. We live in a dangerous world. If something were to happen to me, I want to know that she will not starve.

"All right, let's get going before the sun is overhead and the animals seek shelter from it," I tell her.

She realizes it is time to separate and a strange look clouds her face. Without warning, she closes the distance between us and wraps her arms around my waist. "Be safe, Avery," she says. "You are my sister and my best friend."

My throat constricts around words that are jammed there. I swallow hard and try to talk, managing just a hoarse whisper. "I'll be fine, sis. Don't worry," I tell her. I hold her briefly, then gently push her away. Our eyes lock, and I hold her gaze. "We'll go to the edge of the woods together. Stay nearby." Nearby means that she is not to wander more than a few hundred spear lengths from me. "I will signal when I get something. Okay?"

June nods in understanding and we move through the woods.

The forest is awake and humming with activity. Birds dart from tree to tree, rustling leaves and branches. Intermittently, a chipmunk scurries across the needle-covered ground and chirps loudly. June is silent as we walk. I watch her from the corner of my eye. Her expression is concerned. I reach out and take her hand.

"Everything is going to be okay," I say.

She clutches my hand for a moment, then releases it. "I know," she says and smiles. But I'm unconvinced. She is eight years old, a child by most standards, yet she must shoulder adult burdens. It's necessary for her survival, a point that I regret with every fiber of my being.

When we reach the edge of our safety zone, the trees grows farther apart and the area is brighter. We are not as concealed.

"Don't go too far," I tell her.

June's eyes plead for a moment, shining with emotion. "Love you," she says.

"Love you, too," I reply.

Her demeanor haunts me as I watch her crouch low and move cautiously between spiny ferns and brush. Why was she so worried? Did she sense something I'd missed? My mind starts spinning questions, rolling around in my head like a ball of barbed wire. But I need to force them to the dark recesses of my brain. I cannot worry or speculate about intuition or what-ifs. Too much is at stake. Eating takes priority.

I walk for several minutes until I find fresh boart droppings. My father once told me that long ago, before the war, boarts were called boars. But like every other animal on the planet, the boars changed. They mutated into a different species. I quickly look all around, scanning the low growth for the pot-bellied beast responsible for the droppings. I do not see one, but know it is near so I decide to seek higher ground. The massive oak beside me is the perfect lookout point.

With my knife sheathed at my thigh and my spear and sword in a scabbard at my back, I grab hold of the lowest branch and hoist myself up. I climb from one to the next, scaling the tree cautiously, gently. I do not want to disturb anything or make a sound. I do not want to scare the beast and send it running. I continue, gingerly navigating the dovetailed branches and only stop when the limbs above me become thin and fragile-looking. I do not want to risk resting on one that cannot bear my weight and settle into a squatting position where I am. I crouch low, balancing. Unsheathing my spear, clutching it securely in sweat-slickened hands, I watch as nearby growth stirs and a boart comes into view.

Minutes tick by and the boart does not move. The sun beats down through limbs and leaves. Sweat stipples my brow and trails between my shoulder blades, but I do not dare brush it away or shift. I must remain still, poised to strike when the moment presents itself. The snorts and chuffs of the beast grow closer. I do not move. I barely breathe. My muscles ache and tremble, and my knees protest holding the same position for so long. My pulse hammers against my temples. The beast continues to inch forward, creeping at a leisurely pace. Hunger gnaws ceaselessly. My belly rumbles, a sound so loud I worry it will frighten the boart and ruin any chance of eating for myself and June. But it does not. I have it in my sight, my gaze zeroed in on it. It disappears for a moment behind a dense thicket, so close to me I can smell its pungent stink.

It reappears after several painstaking seconds. Up close, it is enormous. It must be nearly three hundred pounds. Not that I would know that for sure. The last scale I'd seen was when my father was alive and we'd stayed at a camp with other humans. Then, I'd been weighed and told I was one hundred five pounds and five foot one. Years have passed and I've grown since then. But the beast easily triples my girth. Massive shoulders and hindquarters are connected by a generous belly, and small eyes sit atop a generous snout. Pointed tusks bulge from its lower jaw and saliva drips from its wide mouth as it sniffs a tuft of blossoms near the trunk of the tree I am perched in. It continues to snuffle and grunt, and I grip the handle of my weapon so tightly my palm aches.

When it is just below me, I jump.

The ground hurtles toward me. All breath leaves my body and needle-sharp stabs of pain claw my legs as branches lash my thighs. Bruises and cuts will result, but I do not care. All I can think of is feeding my sister, and me.

My spear drives into the base of the beast's neck before I land atop it. I hold the spear steady with one hand while I unsheathe my blade and slice its throat. It squeals, a tortured, awful sound, and thrashes. Warmth gushes over my hand, covering my blade, but I do not let go. And I do not let go of my spear either. I hold fast and plunge it until the entire middle section of the spear is no longer visible.

My chest heaves and every part of me quivers. The world around me has gone quiet. All I hear are my own ragged breaths and the fading shrieks of the stuck animal.

Before long, the boart stops flailing. Blood is everywhere–on my hands, on my arms, my legs, and my face, even feels like it's coating my tongue, but it's not. It is just the heavy, coppery smell, so thick and overpowering, tricking my mind into believing blood has entered my mouth. The boart's weight begins to shift as it topples to one side. I must keep my dagger from becoming trapped beneath its massive body. *I* must keep from getting trapped beneath its massive body.

I flick my knife to the side and hear it land with a soft *thud* in the grass, then yank as hard and fast as I can to pull the spear from the boart's body. I dive to the ground, reaching and stretching with every ounce of strength I have to throw myself clear of the beast's fall. I land hard just in time to avoid being a squashed blob underneath it then whistle loudly for June.

The faint swish of wet grass and leaves sounds and before long, my sister appears. At first she sees the blood covering my hands and splattered across my face. She gasps and her hands fly to her mouth. She cries out words that are unintelligible.

"Oh no, no, no," she sobs.

"June, no, I'm okay," I assure her and point with a trembling hand to the boart carcass.

Her eyes widen. "You got one!" she squeals excitedly. "Oh wow!" She bounces on the balls of her feet, clapping her hands, and I am reminded of her youth, of her innocence. I suddenly wish she did not have to see the boart's carcass. But one day she will have to gut a boart on her own.

"Come on, let's prepare this boart quickly before the scavengers come out to play," I say, referring to the buzzards and other winged predators that could announce our position.

June assists while I carve enough meat to stuff ourselves for the day, as well as the next morning. The boart is robust, its flesh plentiful, but we cannot take all of it. It would spoil by midday the next day. Wastefulness of any kind pains me, particularly when it concerns food. If it were winter, every bit of its meat would be taken and packed in snow, then eaten for weeks. Today's kill is just for the day.

We return to the cave with our haul and cook it immediately. Cooking after the sun sets is off-limits. The smell of roasting flesh would frenzy the creatures of the night and all but guarantee our deaths. The thought makes me shudder.

As soon as the meat is fully cooked, I offer the first piece to June. She devours it immediately. I nibble a chunk and watch as she reaches for a second then third serving.

"Be careful not to stuff yourself," I warn her. But it is hard not to. The salty taste and the tender texture of the meat are irresistible. Before long, I find myself ignoring my own advice and helping myself to more.

"I have to stop," I moan, but a full belly is blissful. "We have to train still," I say more for my own benefit than June's benefit.

"Aw, do we have to?" she asks and frowns.

I level my gaze at her and do not say a word. I do not need to. She knows better, knows that it is imperative for us to train each and every day, to keep our senses sharp and our reflexes swift. I never allow a day to pass when we do not train. That is what our father taught us. And June needs to become as good with a sword and spear as I am. Her life depends on it, and so does mine. Room for improvement always exists.

"Can't we just relax for a little while?" June begs.

I look to the sun, my mind warring with my heart, and realize there is plenty of daylight hours left. June deserves a reprieve. I owe her that, at least.

"Okay," I concede.

Her head whipsaws from me to her food then back to me. "Are you kidding?" she asks suspiciously. "'Cause if you are, it's not funny."

"Nope, I'm serious," I say. "Let's go now."

June does not need to hear me say it twice. She is on her feet before I am. We make our way to the meadow quickly. The clearing is overflowing with wildflowers that perfume the area. I would love to run through the field and pick as many as my arms could carry but I am not permitted such an indulgence. Instead, I settle for sitting on the outskirts of the meadow.

June plops down then flops backward. I sit for a while then lean back on my elbows.

Warm, buttery sunlight heats us from overhead. A tangy, earthy scent infuses the air as we lay in the tall grass gazing at the sky, a vast blue canvas scrubbed clean by the early morning storms. A butterfly flits past June before landing on her nose. She giggles as the floppy-winged insect stops for a second then flaps and flies away. The sound is sweeter than anything I've heard in a long time. I turn to face her. Light washes across the top of her head, highlighting the natural gold of her hair. It makes her appear almost angelic. She closes her eyes and dozes while I fight the exhaustion that follows the adrenaline rush I had from killing the boart. A full belly assists my physical fatigue.

Before long, my eyes grow heavy and my body feels as if it is being rocked, cradled in warm arms, a sensation I barely remember but yearn for nevertheless. I fall into a deep, dreamless sleep.

Chapter 2

My eyes snap open, and immediately my heart batters against my ribcage. I scramble to a sitting position, my eyes surveying the clearing. Tears burn and blur my vision as I squint at the blindingly bright light all around me. The sun is high in the sky, the heat blazing. I realize I have slept for hours not minutes, and a sense of deep regret fills me. A good portion of the day has been lost, wasted really. Time spent sleeping that should have been spent training. I exhale loudly, pinching the bridge of my nose as I do so. This day has been marked by squander; first the boart meat, and now this.

In my periphery, I see that June is still sleeping. I am grateful she is okay, that she is still by my side, despite being annoyed that time, a precious commodity, has been lost. I take a deep breath, calming myself before I wake June. I do not want her to see my frustration. After all, it is not her fault. None of it is her fault.

I twist my body and look at her. Her hair is fanned out all around her, a riot of golden tendrils coiling around flower stems. I hesitate for a moment then tap her arm.

"June. June, wake up," I say as I jiggle her shoulder. "June," I try a bit louder.

June whips her head in my direction, her eyes wide and bloodshot. "What, what is it?" she asks concernedly. She looks dazed, still half-asleep.

"We both fell asleep," I tell her, and she looks at me strangely, as if to say, "No kidding." I shake my head then add, "We slept a *long* time."

She sits up quickly and I follow her gaze as it sweeps the meadow. Little by little, what I have said registers. A frown creases her face.

"Oh no, I'm so sorry," she starts to say, but I interrupt her.

"You have nothing to be sorry for, June. This is my fault. I shouldn't have fallen asleep."

"No, it's not your fault. Please don't blame yourself," she says, and touches my arm lightly. "It's a beautiful summer day and you were tired." She tries to excuse my negligence, but I have made a mistake and cost us valuable hours of daylight.

I ignore her attempt to let me off easy, "Half the day has been wasted. We never should have rested in the meadow in the first place," I do not temper my aggravation. "And now, we need to hurry to our spot and train," I raise my voice, allowing some of the irritation I am feeling to slip out.

Her face wilts and her eyes glaze with tears.

"June," I start. "I didn't mean to sound so angry. I am not angry with you, just the situation, okay?" She seems unconvinced. She tips her chin up and swallows hard, blinking feverishly. "Come on, please don't be sad. I am a jerk," I say, and know it is true. I have hurt the one person in this world I share my life with, the one person I love.

Regret and self-loathing knot in my stomach. June is only eight. I should not have taken a sharp tone with her. It does not matter that my anger was not directed at her. I should know better. My father always did. He was calm. He would be disappointed in me if he knew I upset June.

A cool hand on my hot skin yanks me from my brooding. "I am sorry I'm such a baby, that I cry when I'm upset. I wish I were more like you," June says.

I clamp my eyes shut. "No, you don't," I say. I want to tell her she is perfect, that she is better than I could ever be, but my voice chokes when I try to speak. I open my eyes then look away from her and chew my lower lip, gulping hard against the stinging pain in my throat. But thin arms encircle my shoulders.

"You're not a jerk," June says into my neck as she squeezes tightly. "I love you."

I hug her back and tell her I love her too. I do not let go until her grip relaxes. I don't know why she forgives me, but I am grateful for it. She is the only thing that keeps me going. I stand and offer my hand to help her up; the time to leave is upon us. She follows me wordlessly, away from the field and back into the denser part of the forest. We walk for several minutes, passing our cave, and continue until we reach an area my father constructed years ago, where trees have been stripped of their branches and trimmed, their bark removed so that the hard, inner wood is exposed. Targets have been fashioned out of stretched animal hides and stained with berry extract for spear-throwing practice, and wooden swords have been designed so that June and I can spar without hurting each other. This is our training area, where we prepare to fight for our food, to fight animals; to fight for our lives.

A quick look at the sky reveals the sun is sinking fast. Little time is left to spar. I move toward our weapons. The swords are hidden. A large boulder sits in front of a thicket of thorny bushes. Under the thorny bushes, our swords wait, wrapped in an animal pelt. They are left in the woods, concealed by the bushes. To any creature roaming about, the pelt and swords would go unseen. But June and I know better. I drop to my knees and reach for the skin, scraping my forearm as I hurriedly drag it. I unroll it and toss one sword to June and keep the other for myself. June catches hers clumsily, and then clutches it in her hands.

Though the weapon is light in my hands, the small muscles in June's upper body bulge as she wields the wooden sword, taking several practice swings. I know she is straining, but I must see beyond what is in front of me. I must look into the future, a future that requires her to be able to defend herself.

I advance several steps and June and I begin. June uses a small sword I practiced with when I was little. I now use the one my father did when he was alive. It feels different in my hands than the one I keep on me at all times, perhaps because it lacks the heft of its metal counterpart or, the finely honed tip. Either way, these swords suit our purpose, which is to exercise.

The wood of our weapons makes loud clacking sounds as they collide with each other. When sparring with my sister, I exercise a degree of restraint. Our sessions are for her benefit only. After we finish, she rests, and I must sharpen my skills with the poles my father made.

My father designed all that we see before he died. I practiced with him throughout the years for more hours than I could count. I loved sparring with him. He trained me, fostering what he called my 'gift' until I could best him in a match. Of course, the gift he referred to was my ability to swing a sword. He said I was born with it. I think it is a result of hard training. Perhaps it is a combination of the two. Whatever it is does not matter. All I am certain of is that I must continue practicing, keep my muscles strong and my reflexes quick. The poles are helpful, but lack where instinct is concerned. Subtleties are missing. A being must be read when fighting; at least that's what my father always told me. I was able to beat my father by the time I was fifteen, always anticipating his next move, sidestepping it before acting faster. He was a great warrior and was proud that I would win. He never held back and he was never embarrassed. I miss having an adult to spar with, someone stronger than me. I miss sparring with my father. I wish he were still alive. But he is gone, and I am responsible for June's survival, as well as my own.

I keep that important point in mind every time I train with her. My goal is to build her endurance and strength, her speed and instinct. I need to build her confidence. The way she hefts and swings her sword screams that she is not comfortable doing so. I worry about her. We have been working for months and her improvement has been minimal.

In my heart I believe she should have existed centuries ago, back when children her age played with dolls and went to places called schools to learn about all kinds of subjects. Sometimes I think a cosmic joke of some sort has misplaced her here instead of an era when she could have been safe and healthy and happy.

The tension in my chest pulls, tightening painfully, when I look at her and imagine her wearing dresses the color of wildflowers.

My insides feel as if they are coiling like a snake readied to strike. I focus the pain, focus the anger, and take it out on the poles. Extending my arms, I swing the wooden blade, slicing through the air with a *whoosh* before it strikes wood, scoring it. I continue, repeating the motion, but alternating between my left and right arm, swinging high and low, until my skin is slick with sweat and my throat burns. My entire body throbs to a single rhythm and I feel alive, truly alive.

Blood rushes through by body, drilling against my skin so hard I feel I could burst, but I do not stop. I swerve and twist as I cleave the air. I must be prepared in case they find us. Other beings live beyond the woods we call home. They rule the world and will kill us if they find us. If they knew humans were living deep in the forest, that June and I exist, they would come for us.

They used to be human, but have evolved into something far different. They now call themselves Urthmen, and they hate us in a way I do not understand. They want nothing more than to drive humanity to extinction. They may have already been successful for all I know, except for me and my sister. I watched them kill hundreds when I was younger, my neighbors, my friends, my mother. Back then, we lived in a village with others like us. My father, sister, and I were the only survivors. My father fled to the forest with us, knowing that the Urthmen do not venture deep into the woods, for they are not the most dangerous species roaming the planet. Lurkers are. They live in the forest. They only come out at night. And Lurkers would feast on the flesh of Urthmen as quickly as they would humans.

The Urthmen live in the cities that used to be inhabited by humans, before our kind fell at their hands. They rarely enter the woods by day. Doing so at nighttime would mean certain death. Even Urthmen fear the forest. The only reason they would ever leave the comfort of their communities would be to hunt humans.

I used to ask my father why the Urthmen hate us so much. He said they fear our intelligence and they resent that we are unchanged by the War of 2062. Recalling tales of the War of 2062 sends a shiver down my spine. My father explained to me what happened to our kind, that we had brought this misery on ourselves. Humans from different countries had warred with one another. A powerful chemical virus had been created by a Middle Eastern country, and released on the people of North America. The attack caused the leaders in America to launch nuclear weapons in retaliation, destroying much of the world.

North America, where I live, is the only place where life is thought to still exist. It has been ravaged by chemical warfare, but life has continued. I do not know for certain whether the rest of the world is inhospitable, but judging from the stories I've heard, I do not see how it would be possible. The only reason many humans survived the war in the first place resulted from the mass underground shelters that had been created when the threat of war seemed imminent.

Bomb shelters, as they were aptly named, were created for important people and rich people to take refuge in. Hundreds of thousands of the rich and important people lived there for decades until their supplies ran out and forced them to come aboveground. By then, they figured the diseases had cleared and that they were safe. The diseases were gone, but something much worse awaited them.

When they surfaced, they were met by grotesque, distorted versions of human beings, abominations, who had gone mad from the chemicals and diseases. Those abominations butchered any humans they came across, who had hidden and were unaffected by illness. Some humans managed to get away, and they hid.

Two hundred years later, the offspring of those affected, the abominations, have evolved. They look much as they had then. They are grotesquely distorted versions of humans, and their intelligence is far lesser than a human. They call themselves the Urthmen. They now rule the world. And even after all these years have passed, after watching the fall of humanity and the rise of their kind, the Urthmen's hatred of humans remains.

I haven't seen Urthmen since the massacre at the village I used to live in. Thinking of them makes me pause and look at June.

"Come, let's go again," I say between pants.

"But we just finished a little while ago," she protests.

I beg her with my eyes to stop and she does. She reluctantly stands and picks up her wooden sword. We spar again, only this time I push her harder, challenging her, demanding with my weapon that she defend herself more intensely. Her posture becomes more rigid, her strikes more purposeful. Her lip curls over her teeth, and in her eyes there's a steely resolve I've never seen before. She is suddenly focused, pushing herself to her limits. She is using her speed and agility to her advantage, darting all around me as she attacks unrelentingly. Pride mushrooms inside of me.

I smile broadly when she lowers her weapon to catch her breath. "I am proud of you, June," I say, and her spine lengthens. She is barely able to stifle the grin creeping across her cheeks. "Oh, go ahead and smile," I tell her. "You should be happy. You have made tremendous progress."

June's eyes crinkle with her smile. "Really? You mean it?" she says, and cannot keep the excitement from her tone.

"Absolutely," I nod. "Maybe we should goof off more often," I add, and arc an eyebrow at her.

Her lips part briefly before snapping shut, as if she is not sure of the correct response. I was being sarcastic, making fun of myself, really. But she is uncertain.

"Come on, give me your sword. We are done for the day," I tell her.

She hands over her weapon and I wrap both in the animal pelt and return them to the space beneath the bush.

As we walk back to our cave, June comments on the sky. "Wow," she marvels. "It's so pretty."

The sun has just about set and bands of pink and lavender streak the sky. June has only seen a handful of twilight skies. We seldom stay out this late. Danger prowls when the sun goes down.

With that threat in mind, I link my arm through June's and pull her close, quickening my pace. She rushes to keep up with me, and we make it to the cave just as darkness falls.

As soon as we are inside, we roll the boulder in place and secure it with brush and logs. We eat some of our cooked boart meat, then I light a small candle made from beeswax. June settles into her sleep sack for the night.

"Avery?" she calls as I roll out my bedding.

"Yes?"

"Will you tell me some stories Dad used to tell us at bedtime?"

"Of course," I answer as my mind's eye produces an image of my father sitting right where I am, tucking us in for the night and sharing stories of years long-passed, stories his father told him that his grandfather had shared.

I lie beside her and place the candle between us. "Once, long ago, people like us, human beings, lived in big, sprawling structures made of wood and brick. They were called *houses*. Usually, only one family lived there, parents and children." I pause and look at June. Her sack is pulled up to her chin, her fingers curled around the edge. Her eyes are fixed on mine as she waits for me to continue. "Inside the houses, they had little rectangles on the walls with knobs at their center. When they moved the knob, lights would turn on."

June laughs at what I've just said; the idea so far-fetched it is funny.

"The rectangles were called *light switches* and they were pretty much what their name stated: switches that made light shine."

June covers her eyes with her hands and shakes her head.

"And the light switches were not alone. There were other rectangular things called *outlets*. People would plug tools into these outlets and they would work by themselves."

"Like the picture boxes?" June asks, and drops her hands, her eyes lighting up with interest.

"Yes, people plugged their picture boxes into the outlets. Picture boxes were like magic. They would show miniature people inside of them that could speak loud enough for everyone to hear. The people inside would perform and tell stories."

June claps her hands over her face again and laughs. "That can't be true," she says through giggles. "There wasn't any such thing!"

"No, there was," I say. "Dad's father told him, and his father before him. It is all true."

She lowers her hands and rolls her eyes. "Wow," she breathes.

"Oh, but there's more," I continue. "There also used to be friendly animals that lived in people's houses and they were treated like family."

"No way! Now I know you're making that up!" she snorts and is overcome with silliness again.

"I am not making it up," I say and can't help but chuckle softly, mostly at her delight. "They were called *dogs* and they would lick people's faces and let people pet them. They would even sleep with the people they lived with in a big, cozy bed. Great-grandpa told Dad that some people had clothes for their dogs." I watch as June doubles over clutching her belly in hysterics.

The notion of an animal living with a person is preposterous. Mammals are ferocious creatures to be avoided. Most only come out at night, as their eyes are no longer able to handle daylight. The thought of one licking anyone's face is inconceivable.

When June's laughter calms, I continue telling stories until her eyes struggle to stay open. After her eyes close, I blow out the candle. The cave is plunged in darkness, but I am not afraid. The dark of our cave is familiar, it is safe. Beyond our stone walls is another story entirely though, one that does not include friendly animals, magic picture boxes, houses, or families. It is a world of violence and chaos; a world of danger.

I fight to push the never-ending risk surrounding us to the back of my mind. I know it will be waiting for me when I wake. But right now I need rest. I close my eyes and feel sore muscles relax before all the terror stills and sleep takes hold.

Chapter 3

The constant rumble of my stomach wakes me. Four days have passed since I caught the boart. In those four days, food has been scarcer than usual. Yesterday was the worst so far. Typically, eating rats indicates a severe shortage of available food, but yesterday, I couldn't even find any of them. June and I were forced to eat insects, mostly crickets and grasshoppers. I roasted them over an open fire and wrapped them in leaves to mask them. But the distinct crunch when I bit down, along with the irreversible knowledge of what I was actually eating, surpassed what a thin green leaf could do. I gagged on them, and so did June, barely able to keep them down once I swallowed.

My body is demanding heartier nourishment, something more than crickets and grasshoppers. Physically, I am exhausted. Emotionally, I am in agony. I turn and look at June. She looks thinner than usual, gaunt. The few days of meager food have taken their toll on her. I roll onto my back, looking at her makes pain blaze behind my eyelids. I am failing her. Today I will venture past our safety zone to hunt. It is a risky endeavor, but it is one I must take for June's sake.

I twist onto my side. All energy has deserted me, even though I slept the night through. I am barely able to push myself up to a sitting position. When I finally do, my limbs tremble and a dull ache at the base of my skull persists. I rub my eyes with the heels of my hands then force the corners of my mouth to lift. I must keep a brave face for June. I must smile even though I would like nothing more than to scream and cry.

I give June a gentle shake. Her eyes open and I immediately notice that the silvery sparkle in her blue irises has clouded to gray. Her expression is bleary and her cheeks have hollowed further.

"Hey, sleepy girl," I say. My voice is chipper and I smile.

"Is it morning already?" June asks me.

"Yep, time to rise and shine," I maintain my put-on cheerfulness.

June tries to sit. I see that she hesitates. Her hand goes to her forehead.

"June, are you okay," I ask and cannot hide the panic in my tone.

"Whoa, my head is spinning," she says and closes her eyes. Her thumb is rubbing one temple while her fingers work the other. "I must not have slept well. Did I toss and turn a lot?" she asks.

She did not toss and turn. Movement of any kind wakes me. June was still all night. Hunger is what is exhausting her.

"Hmm, maybe," I lie. "I slept like a rock, so I can't be sure."

"That must be it," June bobs her head slowly.

"Listen, why don't you stay here and skip going to the river. I'll bring back extra water and you can just stay here while I hunt."

June's sunken eyes search the stone floor as if considering my suggestion.

"Besides, I am going out beyond our perimeter today. Staying in the cave, or close by at least, would be the best thing for you to do."

Her head whips in my direction as soon as the words have left my lips. "What?" she asks and is clearly shocked. "You're going to go out where dad told us never to go?"

I sigh and feel tremendous weight bear down on my shoulders. "I have to, June. We need to eat. *You* need to eat. We cannot live on grasshoppers and crickets."

Just the thought of either causes a wave of nausea to quiver through my stomach.

"Those things are disgusting," June shivers and wraps her arms around her body.

"I know. And they are not enough," I say somberly. "So I have to go out there and get us something more, a turkey or squirrel."

"I see," June says thoughtfully then adds, "I will come too. We will go together."

"No!" I reply snippily. June's face withers and I immediately regret my tone. "June, I'm sorry, but you cannot come with me. It is too dangerous."

"If it is too dangerous for me, how come it isn't too dangerous or you?" she asks as tears well in her eyes.

I take my lower lip between my teeth, measuring my words carefully. "June, I love you. You are my family, my only family. I will not bring you to an unsafe area and risk anything happening to you."

"The same goes for me!" she protests. "You are my only family, the one person I have in this world. What will I do if something happens to you?"

Her question catches me off-guard. I am unprepared for how adult she sounds. She has a valid point. "June, you are staying here and that's final," I say and hate myself just a bit for treating her as I am. "I am in charge and I say you must stay, okay?"

"Okay," she says feebly. Crimson ribbons streak her cheeks. She is sad. I have hurt her feelings yet again. I cannot tell her that I value her safety over my own. She wouldn't understand. Also, in her weakened condition, she would slow me down. I have a long hike ahead of me and limited hours of daylight to do so in. I do not have time to spare. Hunting and cooking must be finished before the sun sets. I try to appeal to her sense of duty.

"I have to hunt. The animals in this area have scattered for some strange reason. I need you here, ready with a fire going when I return so that we can cook and feast before sundown."

June's stomach growls as if on cue. "I am so hungry" she says softly.

"Me too," I whisper.

"Have the animals around here learned to stay clear of us?" she asks.

My muddled brain entertains the notion for a brief moment before dismissing it as ridiculous. "No, some have probably just moved on to other areas to eat. Maybe some have found a lush meadow filled with sweet clovers."

"Rabbits like clovers," June says and licks her lips.

I swallow hard. My mouth is watering for tender, juicy rabbit. My empty stomach rolls under and over itself like a wave, snarling anxiously.

"Yes they do," I say. "Hopefully I will get us a nice fat rabbit."

"I am still worried about you going out there alone," June says and her voice falters.

"I will be fine," I promise. "I will come back, and with dinner." I smile broadly until I notice a thin rivulet running down June's cheek. My smile capsizes immediately. "June, what is it?" I ask and grip her shoulders.

Her eyes lock on mine. "I don't know. I'm just so scared, all the time I am so scared."

I want to tell her I am too, that she is not alone in feeling as she does. I live in perpetual terror right alongside her. But I can't. I need to be strong for her. I need to hold us together. "Everything is going to be okay," I tell her as I draw her close. "I will take care of you, I swear. And I will come back. I will never leave you. I am coming back, always coming back." I blink back tears that brim and threaten to spill. My throat is too tight to say another word. So I stay where I am and just hold her.

Before long, June pulls away. She wipes her face with her hands and tells me to go. I race to the river with a small bucket my father left us and return with it filled. June is grateful. After a little more reassuring, I set off and begin my journey past our area of safety.

The sun has just risen and it is not hot yet, but it will be soon. The air is balmy and the grass is coated in dew. My skin feels clammy but I am oddly cold. I grip my spear tightly and use it as a walking stick as I navigate creepers and vines that slink along the forest floor. My weapons and canteen are heavy and I hope I do not have to go too far to find an edible animal.

Hunger has heightened my sense of smell. The forest is thick with the scent of evergreens and musty earth. My eyes alternate between scanning the low-growing brush and the ground below. I look for pinecones stripped of their seeds, for torn bark or bite marks of any kind. I do not see anything but thickening vegetation. I am also looking for impressions in the earth or droppings. Either would indicate that I am on the trail of a mammal. But I see neither. Most would be active when the sun is positioned as it is. Boarts eat all day long. I hope I will be lucky enough to cross paths with another boart. But I do not see any signs of wildlife whatsoever. I continue to press on despite feeling discouraged.

The sun is beating down from overhead, penetrating the treetop canopy with blazing shafts of light, when the terrain becomes so crowded with growth it is difficult to continue at my brisk pace. Earlier, I began pulling large flat leaves and twisting them before tying them to trees as markers to follow back to the cave. My dad always told me I was a good tracker with an excellent sense of direction, but I do not want to risk breaking the promise I made to June. I will not take any chances that involve a return to her after sunset. I do not want her to worry.

I still have not come across so much as a trace of a creature other than the occasional chirping of small birds perched in treetops. I am about to turn and head back, to give up, when I hear the distinct sound of moving water, the gentle hiss and rustle of it rolling over land and rock. I notice that winding vines and undergrowth are giving way to more stony terrain underfoot. The heavy brush thins considerably and sudden thirst grips me.

My body feels overheated and the back of my throat burns. I want nothing more than to spear an animal and wade out into cool water. But neither seems possible at the moment. I continue for a bit longer and do not see rushing water. I decide to sit, depression crushing my chest like lead. Hunger gnaws in my gut and I am forced to scoop a beetle from the dank soil and eat it. I close my eyes and slip it between my lips. All the while I suppress the urge to retch. I chew fast and try my best not to think about what I have just eaten. I chug the last of my water from my canteen, but still feel as if I may vomit. I breathe deeply several times, willing myself to hold it down, until the feeling passes.

After a brief rest, I stand again and hope to find food to feed June, and myself. I am about to begin walking again, when a high-pitched laugh slices through the silence. I freeze in my tracks and my stomach plummets to my feet. I hold my breath, listening intently, waiting, hoping my hearing is playing tricks on me. The laugh sounded as if it came from June. Who else could it be? She must have followed me, putting us both at greater risk. My heart thunders in my chest.

I whirl around, half-expecting to see her, but find that I am still alone. The laughter sounds again, persisting this time. I follow it, wondering why she would draw attention to herself. She knows better.

I sheathe my spear on my back and I plow through bushes dotted with prickly balls, feel them scratch and scrape my skin, but do not stop. I must get to June before she gets us killed.

Suddenly, the laughter I believe belongs to June is interrupted by another, slightly deeper laugh; a boy's laugh. I move faster. Blood rushes behind my eardrums and my heart has lodged in my throat. I shove forward, the ground beneath my feet pebbly, until I reach a gentle slope that leads to a narrow river. The river snakes and winds until it ends finally at a lake. And what I see in the lake makes every hair on my body rise.

I see a girl about June's age flopping and floundering about. She is laughing, delighted. Next to her is a boy. He looks older than the girl. He, too, is laughing happily.

I stand, hidden by more hostile bushes loaded with burrs. My mouth is agape as my mind whirls in lopsided circles, struggling to make sense of what my eyes are seeing. Human beings, children, are swimming in a lake just hours from where June and I live in our cave. Other humans are alive! My entire body begins to tremble.

The children continue to caper about and I find myself smiling naturally. I hear a splash but do not see where it came from. Are there more? I wonder. The idea is almost too much for my brain to handle.

The water beside the boy stirs before a large form becomes visible. And then I see him. He breaks from the surface of the water and surprises the smaller boy, grinning wide and greeting him with a growly "Argh!" The boy flinches then squeals in delight, but I cannot even look in his direction. My eyes are fixed on the larger of the two, the one who emerged from the depths and is standing now, his waist covered by water, while droplets trickle between the swells of his chest to the hollows of his stomach. His skin is tanner than mine, bronze almost, and his eyes are so light they stand out and seem to glow.

I know I should look away, scan the area and see if there are more, but cannot. My gaze is pinned and I realize I have not yet blinked. Part of me is afraid that if I look away, he will be gone; that all of them will be gone, and I will wake from whatever dream or hallucination I am having.

I take a tentative step forward, toward a thin tree. My heart is drilling my ribs and my belly feels as if it is filled with butterflies fluttering and flapping at once. I rest my shoulder against its trunk and inch closer still, wanting to lean all of my weight against it. But a branch snaps beneath my foot unexpectedly. My sprinting heart stumbles and the boy in the water with the glowing eyes looks in my direction.

Though I am concealed by tall plants, bushes and the puny tree, my breathing hitches and heat burns up my neck until it reaches my cheeks. I know he does not see me, cannot possibly see me, but I see him, and not just his profile either. I see his entire face. A strange tremor vibrates through my belly that has nothing to do with hunger. He rubs his hand through his thick, dark hair and I am riveted by the cords of rippling muscles that intertwine and gallop down his arms.

I am suddenly lightheaded and realize I have forgotten to breathe. My tongue is stuck to the roof of my mouth. I am overwhelmed by thirst. I reach a trembling hand to my canteen and remember it is empty.

A sweet female voice calls out, and the boy with the pale, radiant eyes looks toward the sound.

"Come on, guys. Let's eat," the voice says.

The children groan and I watch as the boy whom I cannot tear my eyes from begins to shepherd them out of the water. He guides them to the shore of the lake. I follow him with my gaze. It is trained on him as if acting separate and apart from my will. He steps out of the water and, seeing him stand beside the others, I see that he is taller than I thought, and stronger looking.

He shakes his head and water cascades from his hair and sprinkles the children. They screech, their joy evident in their expressions, and I feel my own surge of glee rocket from a part of me I never knew existed.

I watch as a woman approaches and embraces the children. For a moment, I think she will embrace the older boy as well. In those seconds, I feel a hot tendril spark inside of me that is anger and fear fused. The sensation is completely irrational, but I am powerless to stop it. She says something to him that I cannot hear. He laughs, and the flame is replaced with an odd sense of loss. But when he speaks and says the word "mom" loudly, I am heartened. The woman turns and faces the woods, where I am, and I see that her face is creased, and that she looks similar to the boy I have been watching.

She continues to focus on the spot where I stand. I think about going to them. My muscles twitch as I debate. But something inside me keeps my feet rooted where they are. Just envisioning myself approaching them, speaking to them, to the older boy in particular, makes my breathing become short and shallow and my stomach free-fall. I try to slide a foot forward, but my muscles are tense, too tense. They begin walking toward an opening in the craggy shore and opportunity slips from my grasp like grains of sand. I am left standing, watching the lakeshore and feeling a pang of remorse.

But my regret is quickly trumped by pure excitement. I have seen human beings, others like me and June! I turn and press my back against the tree trunk and close my eyes. I clinch my mouth with my hand and curb the elated yelp begging to be released. I have not killed a meal for us and the sun is dipping fast. I need to head back to the cave right away. The hike here was long. The hike back may be longer if I lose my way. A potentially risky situation is looming, yet I am almost giddy.

I spring to my feet and bound back, deep into the forest.

As I walk, I am lost in thought. The older boy's face is imprinted on my brain, and no matter how hard I try I cannot seem to focus on anything but it. I make a lame attempt at focusing, at surveying the riot of tangled bramble all around me, and see something that jumps out at me.

A tuft of glossy, russet fur catches my eye. My concentration shifts from the boy at the lake and grinds to a razor-sharp point. I train my gaze on it, watching it, stalking it. The fur jerks then bounces, edging out of concealment. That's when I see a puffy tail, downy and round, popping from a cluster of weeds. I unsheathe my spear as silently as possible, and then creep toward it slowly, clutching my weapon, careful not to spook my dinner. I move in to kill the rabbit.

I am just seven or eight paces from it, poised and prepared to skewer it when it turns on me unexpectedly; whipping its small head so that I swear it is looking at me. Large eyes, more forward-facing and predatory than I have ever seen, watch me. A deep growl rumbles from it and its thin, black lips snarl back and reveal oversized, pointed teeth. It hops away from me, a small cautious move that is not in keeping with its threatening demeanor. I remain where I am, holding fast to my spear. Its nose tics then it is perfectly still for a moment. I prepare to strike, but am caught off-guard when it leaps into the air without warning. It is lunging at me with its jaw wide. I do not delay and launch my spear at it. The spike lodges right into its open mouth and pitches it backward until it sticks into the trunk of a tree.

The rabbit does not move, and it is no longer growling. A small flash of triumph flickers inside me. June and I will eat well tonight. I walk over to where it is impaled and pull my spear, with the rabbit attached, from the tree. I slide the carcass from my weapon and toss it into a satchel made of animal skin then toss it over my shoulder. I continue my journey to the cave, to June and the only home I've known, hiking at an energetic pace. Tonight, I will sleep well. My belly will be full, and for the first time in as long as I can remember, I feel hope.

Chapter 4

When I reach the woods near the cave, my cheeks ache from smiling. I cannot recall the last time a smile born of genuine joy made me feel as I do now. My insides hum and buzz with a trembling sensation that gives me a weird, jittery energy I have never felt before. I have forgotten how hungry and tired I am and do not feel as though I have hiked the entire day, but I have. I am practically bouncing, my stride is springy. I spot June just beyond the opening of the hollow. One arm crosses her waist while the other is raised. I see that she is chewing the skin around her thumbnail. She is pacing, lost in worry.

"June!" I call out to her; perhaps a bit too excitedly as she instantly spins toward my voice, her face a mask of fear.

"Avery!" her voice pitches up an octave. "Oh gosh, are you oaky? You're bleeding!" she exclaims and rushes toward me.

I forget I have not washed since slipping the rabbit from my spear. Gore still coats my hands and likely my face as well. I am sure I have absently wiped sweat from my brow and temples and have smeared blood there. Judging from June's reaction, I look frightening.

June descends on me and is plucking at my arms. Her lips press together firmly and a crease marks the space between her eyebrows.

"I am okay, June. No worries," I assure her. "I killed a rabbit and did not have time to stop and clean up."

Her features smooth and she exhales noisily. One hand splays across her hairline while the other clutches her belly. "Thank goodness," she breathes.

I rub a hand on her back then pull it back quickly, remembering the blood. I have been so distracted by what I saw at the lake, I cannot seem to concentrate. It is a wonder I was even able to catch the rabbit I am carrying in my satchel.

"You were gone so long. I've been worried sick," she begins saying. Emotion causes her voice to crack.

I am tempted to tell her about what I saw, to tell her about the children and the woman, and the older boy. The words bubble inside of me before they are on my tongue, but I hold back. She will ask why I did not approach them. She will ask why I did not make my presence known. I do not have a legitimate reason for not, other than panic.

I panicked, and I am embarrassed. I promised her that when I found others like us, I would embrace them, join them. Strength exists in numbers, at least that is what I heard when I lived in the village years ago. She would consider finding one human being a gift. Four would be too wonderful to be true. Yet it is true. Four humans live a quarter of a day's walk from where we stand. And I froze. I did not go to them as I said I would. My cheeks burn with shame briefly, but I recover when the weight slung over my shoulder reminds me of an important aspect of my trip.

"I got this," I say and pull my satchel from my shoulder. "We're having a fat rabbit for dinner," I add with a smile.

June looks at me quizzically for a fleeting moment then smiles along with me. "Rabbit," she says and nods. "That sounds *so* good."

I roll down the opening of my bag and pull the plump rabbit from it, showing her what is in store for us. A grin lights up her entire face and for a moment, I do not feel so bad about freezing back at the lake.

"Is the fire ready?" I ask. "I want to cook this up right away."

"Yes, I did just as you told me to," she says proudly.

I tip my head to one side and my smile widens.

"Something is different about you, Avery," June comments and eyes me suspiciously. "Something happened that you're not telling me about."

"What?" I say and stall. "That's crazy. Nothing happened." I sound so absurdly dubious I don't even trust me at this point.

"Hmm," June murmurs. Her eyes bore into my skull.

I shift uncomfortably. My skin feels too hot, too tight for my body. "Come on!" I say and start to walk toward the fire. "I can't take another minute of being as hungry as I am."

"I know. I'm starving," June says and reminds me of the direness of our food shortage.

My smile shrivels. I have been preoccupied with my outing. I have been selfish. While I was out, delighting in the realization that we are not alone, June was here, very much alone.

"Well, let's remedy that," I say brightly before I skin and prepare the rabbit then place it on a spit to cook over the open flame.

"My mouth is watering," June says as the mild, almost sweet scent of roasting rabbit meat infuses the air.

"Mine too," I admit.

Once the rabbit is cooked, I serve June first. She gobbles it quickly and I immediately hand her seconds. Her appetite seems insatiable as she wolfs down the meat I have just given her. She gulps water and it dribbles down her chin.

"Do you want more?" I ask.

"I do, but my stomach hurts already," she reluctantly confesses. "It just tastes so wonderful, and I don't know when I'll eat something this good again."

"Hey," I say and place a hand on her forearm. "You don't have to make excuses. Eat up. And there will be more like it tomorrow."

"There will?" she questions and her brow rises.

"Yep," I say confidently.

"How?" She leans in and her voice is just above a whisper.

I lean in too and lower my voice conspiratorially. "I am going back out tomorrow, going past our boundaries to hunt again. We will feast for a second time tomorrow."

"What!" June shouts. Her features are screwed up, horror marking them. "No! You can't! I can't handle it if you go again! I just can't!" She is shaking her head and waving her hands in front of her body to punctuate her point.

I am not sure what prompted this outburst but am eager to end it, to calm June. "Whoa, whoa, hold on, June. Calm down," I say in a soothing voice. I reach out and take one of her frantic hands in mine. "It's okay. Everything is okay." I whisper. "Talk to me. What is going on?"

Tears begin streaming down her cheeks, carving streaks through the dirt that has accumulated on her face. She sniffles and turns her head away from me, as if embarrassed. "It's just that, well, it's just that," she stammers. "I was so worried about you, worried you would not come back, that you'd be killed." Sobs beset her. Her shoulders shake and she cries.

"Oh June," I say and wrap an arm around her shoulders.

"I don't want to lose you," she manages and is barely able to choke out the words. Her face is still angled away from me.

I reach out and hook my index finger under her chin. "Hey, come on, June, look at me," I say gently.

She turns toward me timidly.

"You are not going to lose me," I try to comfort her by saying.

Her eyes drop to her feet. "Humph," she mutters and makes plain her doubt.

"Listen to me, June; I am not going to leave you. I am a warrior, just like dad was. He trained me and I am even better than he was," I tell her and do not feel as if I am bragging. I am stating a fact. "I only take risks that are necessary and make sense. We need to eat so I need to hunt, and if there aren't any animals nearby, I have to move out farther to hunt. Do you understand?" I hold her gaze and wait to see if the gravity of my words sinks in.

June nods and bobs one shoulder halfheartedly.

"Good," I say calmly.

I drop my finger from beneath her chin then stand. The sun is about to be swallowed by the horizon line. We must hurry and clean up and get inside right away.

June, as if reading my thoughts, stands too and begins poking the logs and embers with a long stick, breaking them apart. I race to the river with our bucket and fill it with water. Every branch that cracks makes my pulse rate spike. It is late, later than I have ever been out in the woods alone.

Water sloshes from the container and I run with it, stopping only when I make it to the fire. I dump half of its contents first. The fire hisses and smoke billows as soon as the water touches it then June rakes over the debris left behind. We repeat this a few more times until we are confident the fire is out, and any remnants of it ever being there are gone. We scurry inside and secure our boulder and brush.

I light our beeswax candle and June and I chat for a little while. I tell her more stories our father used to tell me about the world before the war. She listens carefully and laughs as she always does when I tell her of gas-operated vehicles human beings used to use to get where they needed to go rather than walking. The absurdity of it all makes her howl with laughter. But soon, her eyelids droop and her yawns become more frequent. She dozes just as I begin telling her about handheld devices that people used to use to talk to each other from great distances apart.

I blow out the candle then lie back with my arms folded over my head. I reflect on the day, and my thoughts center on the boy at the lake. I close my eyes and picture him, picture his sun kissed skin, his dark hair and pale eyes. I find myself wishing I knew the true color of his eyes, whether they are blue or green, or a color in between. I would like to see his face up close. I would like to see all of him up close, to stand beside him and see how much taller he is than I am, to see what he smells like. I imagine he smells like grass and sunshine. The thought makes my heartbeat quicken and my stomach cartwheel. The boy at the lake was very pleasant to look at. I hope to watch him again soon and plan to return to the spot tomorrow. I will hunt, too. But watching him is what I look forward to most.

As I think about him, I begin to wonder whether I am pretty. June tells me I am, but I have only seen my reflection in water, and even then, it mattered little. My appearance has never been something I concerned myself with; until now. At the moment, my looks, or more specifically pondering what the boy at the lake would think of my looks, is all I can think of. Would he like the sandy color of my hair? It tends to get streaks in it that are nearly white by midsummer. His hair is so dark. Maybe he would find mine unappealing. And my eyes, my dad told me they are hazel just like my mom's eyes were. He used to say I look just like her.

I remember my mother's face. I remember her eyes, the way her irises looked, a light-brown palette speckled with green, gold and blue flecks. In sunlight they would lighten in color, the green and blue eclipsing the soft brown and gold, always changing, always unique. They were so pretty. She was so pretty.

Reminiscing about her nearly knocks the air from my lungs. I would love to see them again, just once. But I know I cannot. She is gone forever. The best way to honor her memory is to look to the future, to live. And living requires survival. The cornerstone of survival is food. I will hunt again when I wake. I will return to the spot I went to today, far past the outer bank of the forest June and I have explored, where a river winds to a lake and four others just like us live. I will indulge in watching the oldest boy and silently envy that the woman I assume is his mother still lives. Perhaps I will work up the courage to make my presence known, to go to them. I owe it to June, to all the people that we have lost, to do it. And meeting the boy with the tan skin and pale eyes would not be such a bad thing either.

His face is the last image my mind produces before my eyes close and a tide of darkness sweeps me away.

Chapter 5

I wake with a start, struggling to catch my breath. My heart is racing, hammering as if trying to break free of my body. My hand flies to my forehead. The skin there is slippery to the touch, coated in sweat. I look all around me. It takes a moment for complete consciousness to return to me, for my brain to register that I am awake now. I realize I am in the cave I share with my sister. Beside me, June is sleeping, snoring softly, swathed in inky shadows. Just a thin stream of predawn light streams in and I know it is not time to rise, yet I cannot imagine going back to sleep.

I comb my fingers through my hair and discover that the front is wet. I am not surprised though. I have had a nightmare, the same nightmare I have had almost every night for the last six years. None of what I am experiencing is new.

I push myself up to a sitting position. The act requires effort, more than I feel capable of using. I exert myself against a rushing current of emotion that crashes over me, intent on drowning me. Once upright, I can feel that my clothes are clinging to my skin. I run my hand down my neck then over the top of my covering. My body and sleep sack feel damp. Though I am sweaty, tremors rack my body. I draw my knees up and hug them to my chest, still haunted by the vivid images that flashed through my mind's eye.

When I sleep, a mere dream does not plague me. It is so much more, so much worse. They are memories, horrible, violent memories that replay in my head with striking clarity over and over again. I relive the day my mother was killed.

I rub my eyes, wishing to purge all of it from my brain, but know it is useless. I cannot rid myself of the memory any more that I can rid the sky of the sun. And just as night surrenders to day powerless against the rise of the sun, I am powerless against recollections that are branded into my brain. They are always with me, always lingering at the surface of the dark ocean of my heart I keep it in. Each time it surges forth, it feels as if I am experiencing that day all over again.

I was eleven years old and on the dirt floor of the hut I shared with my parents, playing with June who was just two. I was making her laugh; crawling around on all fours, grunting and snorting like a boart. My father sat on a tattered piece of wood and fabric he said had survived the war. He told me it was called a couch and that people used to spend hours at a time sitting or lying on them. I couldn't imagine anyone wanting to do either. The few times I'd sat on it, I found that it smelled strange, like decay and smoke. Regardless, my dad did not seem to notice and rested on it, beaming each time a fit of laughter overtook June. My mother sat beside him, her head nuzzled against his shoulder. Every so often, she would rub her round belly and sigh. My parents looked so content, so happy.

I remember that moment. I remember that it was the last time in my life I felt safe. That moment ended abruptly.

Screams ripped through the peace we'd been enjoying, piercing the very air we breathed, and echoed outside our hut. My father jumped from the couch, a look of concern etching his features as he crossed the small space and went to the door. I sprang to my feet and my mom leaned forward to the edge of the couch. My father turned and leveled a serious gaze our way. He told us to stay put; that he was going to see what was happening.

More screams rang out followed by a flurry of inhuman sounds. My father glanced over his shoulder with his hand perched on the doorknob. A look unlike any I'd ever seen flashed across his features; one filled with dread and fear, of awareness that life as we knew it had just changed.

As soon as he opened the door, he was met by one of the men from our village. The man's face was pale, his demeanor horror-stricken.

"They're here, Gerald," he told my father. "The Urthmen have found us."

As soon as the word "Urthmen" was uttered, I felt my stomach lurch before it nosedived. We had spent our entire existence either fighting them or avoiding them, but never at our camp. We'd always encountered them out in the forest when we'd wandered too far, but never near our camp, never close to home. They'd never made it into our village; not until that night.

"How many are there?" my father asked and the urgency of his voice raised the fine hairs on my body.

"It's hard to tell," the man replied.

My father did not wait for the man to speak another word. His look of worry was replaced with steely resolve. He drew his sword and clutched it in one hand. With the other, he reached out to my mother and helped her up from the couch. Her belly was swollen and pulling herself to her feet from a seated position was a challenge as she was eight months pregnant. My mother scooped June from the floor and followed my father as he led us out of our hut and into another, one that had a tunnel burrowed beneath it that led deep into the woods as an emergency escape route.

"Wait here," he told us once we were inside. "If I am not back soon or if you hear voices close by that aren't human, leave, take the tunnel and get out of here as fast as you can."

My entire body shook when he gave us his instructions, when I realized there was a chance he would not be with us, that he was preparing for his death.

"Gerald, no," my mother started, her voice smothered by emotion. One hand flew to her belly while the other clutched June. "We need you. We can't survive out there alone, if we even make it out there. Please," my mother pleaded. "Please, come with us."

"No," he replied, his tone firm. "I will not run and leave our people to die. I am not a coward. Besides, surviving the night with or without me will be next to impossible," he said, grief lacing his words. He looked between June and I then said, "Hopefully there aren't too many Urthmen and we can fight them off."

My mother's gaze locked on my father's face, holding him there for a moment before she hugged him and whispered something in his ear that I did not hear. When he said good-bye to her, his voice was a hoarse whisper. He kissed June's forehead and my mother's belly then the top of my head before he walked out. He left us there and went to join the others in their fight against the Urthmen.

The hut we waited in was one of many that comprised a community. Nearly two hundred humans lived there. We were lucky to have found them. The complex was tucked in the woods, deep enough within its protection that we were hidden from the Urthmen that patrolled, but far enough from where the trees grew close together and the terrain became too difficult to navigate. A high stone wall had been built and was heavily guarded. Lurkers shared the woods with us. We needed protection from them as well as Urthmen.

No one wanted to lose the only sense of belonging they'd ever had. No one wanted to lose the complex, or each other, but they did.

As time passed, more men from our community placed their families in the hut with the tunnel beneath it and gave them instructions similar to the ones my father had given. Many of the people left behind were women, children and villagers too old or too ill to fight. Some of them cursed and expressed outrage, but most of them just stood where they were placed, clinging to whichever family member they'd been left with. We all wore the same expression. We all looked equal parts terrified and confused. I felt as I looked. But I was anxious too; worried in a way I'd never been before about my father.

My mother rocked June, cradling her tightly in her arms with their cheeks pressed together. I felt pressure build in my body with such force it strained against my skin. Tortured cries rang out; the sorrowful sounds of life ending brutally, of suffering, shrieked through the hollows of my core as they grew closer, and I thought I would explode. All around me, women and children wept. June wailed and even my mother cried. I held my tears in, balling my fists so tightly my nails bit into the tender skin of my palms and drew blood. I wanted to help. I hated not knowing exactly what was going on, being incapable of playing a part in my own fate.

When finally, I'd reached my breaking point, I moved to the door. With my hand on the knob, I turned to my mother and said, "I can't take it anymore. I need to know what is happening out there. I have to know what's happening to dad."

My mother's face contorted. "No!" she hissed. "Come back here now and wait for your father."

Until then, my mother had never raised her voice at me. I never remembered her even being angry with me. But she did and she was.

For a moment, my hand recoiled from the handle as if it were on fire. Then I placed it there again, and ignoring my mother, I twisted it and pulled it toward me.

"Avery! You heard what your dad said!" I heard my mother say, but I had already taken a step outside.

My eyes swept the area just beyond the hut. I saw nothing, not one person, so I took several more steps, venturing further. And when I did, my brain was unable to process what my eyes were seeing all at once. Urthmen were everywhere, flooding our village in a tidal wave of frenzied violence. Many were atop fallen men, rearing their misshapen heads and baring their oversized teeth savagely. The metallic stench of blood hung in the air like mist and I fought the urge to gag.

"Avery, come back here this instant!" my mother called. But her voice sounded muffled and distant, as if it were echoing from the end of a long tunnel.

My feet felt as if they were being swallowed by quicksand. I was unable to move, paralyzed by fear, by shock. The carnage before my eyes held me hostage. I tried to breathe, but each time I inhaled, my senses were assaulted by the smell of bloodshed. I looked around for signs of survival, of any of my fellow villagers, but only saw countless mutant Urthmen sacking and slaughtering everything in their wake. My gaze zeroed in on an Urthmen who hefted a club high overhead. The man beneath him was one I knew, in fact, I'd just seen him not long ago. It was the man who'd come to our hut to warn us. The Urthmen was about to bludgeon him. I wanted to scream, to shout for the beast to stop, but my voice was strangled somewhere deep in my throat. I watched in horror as the Urthmen brought his club down hard against the man's head. The fiend raised it again and hammered the man's face until his features were pulverized. When the Urthmen had finished, gore had splattered all over his distorted face.

I turned from the massacre, from what must have been thousands of Urthmen butchering our village, and ran back to the hut.

Once inside, I leaned my back against the door and immediately said, "We need to leave *now*!"

"Avery, your father," my mother began but I interrupted her.

"He's dead, mom. They are all dead," I said to her.

My mother's face paled then collapsed. She nodded slightly, agreeing that the time to leave had come. "We have to leave," my mother informed the others in the hut, but none of them were willing to accept what they'd heard. They refused to leave and said that they would wait for their husbands.

"There are thousands of Urthmen out there!" I screamed. "All of our men are dead! If you want to live you have to leave!" But the others refused. No one would follow us. So we went alone.

After opening a hatch in the floor, my mother handed June to me, and I climbed down a long ladder that led to the start of the passageway. My mother followed and came down right after me.

A yawning pit of darkness stretched before me. It smelled of wet earth and lime. The only light I saw was feeble and came from the hut above us. But it did little more than create a weak beam of light that crawled across the floor and revealed a narrow swath of glistening, gray stone. The pitch-black shadows seemed to continue endlessly.

The tunnel was huge, about ten feet wide and eight feet high. It ran underground, beneath the stone wall and out deeper into the woods. Years had been spent constructing it. I never understood the true purpose of having it, after all, I'd enjoyed the security and safety of the village for so long, I'd come to almost take it for granted. But all that had changed. Reality had come to call.

I began to run, holding tight to June. I could not see clearly what was ahead, but heard my feet slapping against the hard ground as I raced as fast as I could and as far as I could from the hut we'd just left. My heart contended with the sound and I swore it echoed along with my footfalls down the tunnel.

I looked over my shoulder, though I could not see my mother, when a loud thump rattled overhead and rumbled like thunder, shaking the walls all around me.

"Oh no," I muttered and June began to cry.

"Just go!" my mother urged. "Keep running, Avery, and don't stop!"

Suddenly, a high-pitched whistle filled the air all around me, clawing at my eardrums, before an unearthly din howled out and resonated through the endless hollow. The sound beat against my skull with such force I thought the bone would crack. Urthmen had arrived.

Bloodcurdling screams immediately followed their call, the sound of women and children dying. I covered June's ears with both hands, trying desperately to shield her from their cries. The people we'd just left, all of them, were most certainly dead. I wanted to scream, to cry, anything, but could not. I had to keep running.

I pushed myself harder, faster, until my lungs burned and my muscles ached as I rushed headlong into the blackened abyss. I peeked over my shoulder to see my mother's dark form behind me and saw something that made my breath catch in my chest.

Behind my mother, the tunnel was lit. I saw that four torch-wielding Urthmen made their way toward us, gaining ground fast. In the firelight, I could see their faces clearly. The closer they progressed, the more horrific they became. Nearly transparent skin did little to cover the expansive, vivid entanglement of veins that webbed their malformed heads. Lidless eyes shrouded in a thick, milky film darted wildly, bloodthirsty. They did not have noses but did have two asymmetrical holes that appeared to serve the purpose of nasal openings. Lips were also missing from their faces, though lines gave the impression that mouths may reside beyond them. They were monstrous, my worst fear realized at the time.

With my heart threatening to beat out of my chest, I pressed on, testing my muscles as they'd never been tested before. But I was small and weak, and carrying June was hard.

My mother caught up to me and said, "Keep going and don't look back! Don't turn around!"

She slowed down and I did not see her beside me anymore. Then I heard her footfalls stop altogether. I looked back at her and saw that she stood with her arms out in surrender.

"Run, Avery!" she yelled, but I stopped moving. I could not believe what I was seeing.

Panic seized every cell in my body. "Mom!" I cried out. "Mom, what're you doing?"

She did not answer me, though. She spoke to the four Urthmen that approached.

"Please don't kill me," she begged. "I am pregnant."

But her pleas fell on uncaring ears. The Urthmen did not care that she was pregnant. In fact, in hindsight, they probably saw the unborn child she carried as a bonus kill.

While my mother raised her hands and submitted, one of the Urthmen hoisted his club high in the air and whipped it forward until it crashed against her skull. My world went completely still and my heartbeat ground to a near halt. I could not believe what had happened. My beautiful, kind mother, pregnant with my next sibling, had been hit. She sunk to her knees, a thin rivulet of blood streaming down her temple. Another strike followed and she collapsed to the tunnel floor completely. And then the Urthmen swarmed, all beating her feverishly.

I tried to scream, to shout at the beasts to stop, but I could not breathe. My lungs refused to fill and remained frozen, like blocks of ice so cold their chill burned.

"No," I tried, but the words came out as a raspy whisper.

Pain radiated from the center of my chest and branched out, throbbing and aching as my heart shattered into a million jagged pieces. My knees threatened to collapse beneath me. The woman who gave me life, the one who protected me and taught me, fed me and cared for me, was dead, murdered by monsters.

I wanted them dead; all of them. I wanted them to suffer for what they'd done to my mother.

When finally I was able to draw a breath, I heard a female scream tear through the chaotic grunts of the Urthmen and soon realized the scream was mine. And I wasn't the only one to realize this.

The Urthmen spun to face me. "Get the humans," one pointed at June and I with blunt, stubby fingers as his voice scraped like metal against metal.

But before he could say another word or make a move toward us, his head was lopped from his body. It tumbled from his neck and landed against the ground with a thud. Two of the others with him turned and were carved at their waists. They dropped to the earth below, eviscerated like the animals they were.

When they fell, I saw my father square off with the last of the Urthmen in the tunnel with us, and for the first time in my life to that point, he looked like a fierce warrior. He looked deadly.

The Urthmen swung his club recklessly several times. My father dodged his attack with the calm and poise of a predator. The next swing the beast took was met with my father's blade. His sword glinted in the glow of the fallen torches right before it cleaved the Urthmen's arm. The arm fell to the ground and my father immediately veered and decapitated the monster.

For a moment, my father just watched the fallen Urthmen, his chest heaving. Then he bent to his knees, to where my mother's body lay still, and released a guttural cry of agony so profound, I felt as if my bones shook.

I wanted to go to him, to crumple into his arms and cry until my body was emptied of tears. But the sound of footsteps approaching kept me in place, still holding June. My father stood and ran to me. He ripped June from my arms then flung both of us over his shoulders. He took off, away from the looming Urthnmen, and sprinted faster than I thought was humanly possible.

Each step he took punished my ribs and back as I jerked and flopped against him. But none of the physical pain I felt compared to the heartache I was feeling. I had just seen my mother murdered.

When we reached the end of the seemingly endless tunnel, my father stopped and began kicking a thick log.

"Come on," he spat as he continued to kick what I quickly learned was a support beam.

"Dad, put me down. I'll help!" I shouted above the ferocious cries of the Urthmen echoing down the passageway.

He placed me on my feet and I helped him. We kicked until the rafter gave way and he gripped my wrist. We ran several yards then stopped again. We climbed out of the tunnel. We were in the forest. It was dark and damp and there was a nip in the air. Bare tree limbs gashed the night sky, black and skeletal against the navy heavens. The musky, slightly moldy scent of fallen leaves that I would usually find pleasant now terrified me. I knew that Lurkers waited, their movement muffled by the hoots and calls of nocturnal hunters. My father placed June in my arms then dug with both hands through leaves and brush until he pulled a length of thick rope from it. He leaned back, pulling it with every ounce of his weight, until the sound of wood splintering snapped through the night. Another beam toppled, only this time, it was followed by a low growl, deep in the bowels of the dirt. The growl rolled and shook, and I understood in that instant that the tunnel had been booby-trapped. The passageway was collapsing on itself.

Chunks of soil sprayed as it caved in. Pebbles flew in every direction and pelted us. Confused shouts turned to wails of agony as the Urthmen were buried alive. But we did not stay to hear them go silent. We ran.

That was six years ago.

Six years have not dulled the pain I feel each time I dream of that night.

I swipe beneath my eyes with the tips of my fingers to clear the tears there. I do not want to risk June waking and seeing me like this. She does not remember what happened. She is lucky.

Each day since my mother was killed, I regret that her body was left behind, that she will rest for eternity alongside Urthmen, monsters. She deserved better than that. I also regret that I spoke harshly to her and disobeyed her when I left the hut. I never got to ask for her forgiveness. Now it is too late.

A silent sob shakes my body and I hug my knees to my chest as tight as I can. I breathe deeply, trying to calm myself until it passes, until the knot of pain inside me loosens enough for me to breathe. I must hold myself together. I must be strong. I concentrate on relaxing every muscle in my body and breathe through my nose, sucking in air until my belly puffs out. I blow it out in a thin stream through my lips, repeating the process until I feel more in control of myself.

I glance at June and see that she is still asleep. She is unbothered by my crying seconds ago. I am thankful for that.

I force myself to lie back down. My eyes burn and I am thirsty, but I close my eyes and push both discomforts to the back of my mind. Neither is of any consequence. I remain still and rest until threads of light slip through the cracks of the boulder and another day of hunting begins.

Chapter 6

I doze on and off until light begins to spill through the openings around the boulder. I am still shaken by the recurrent nightmare I had, by the past. Time has not dulled the pain, and it has not ended the dreams. They continue.

My mother is still on my mind. Her death weighs on me with untold heaviness. My throat constricts around the sadness that has collected there. I sit upright, not wanting to be still a moment longer and risk crying. I kick the covering from my legs and stretch. My movement causes June to stir. Her eyelids flutter then open groggily.

"Is it morning?" she asks, her voice thick and tired.

"It is morning," I say and my own voice surprises me. It breaks.

June scrunches her features. "Avery, what is it? Are you okay?" she asks.

I hate that I have alarmed her. "I'm fine," I lie and clear my throat. "Must be the way I slept or something. I sound like a frog, you know, a little croaky I guess."

"Are you sure?" June asks and looks at me with eyes so wide and vulnerable I almost feel guilty for lying.

"I'm fine," I say and smile. "But if it keeps up, I might be forced to leave the cave and find myself a sweet, deluxe lily pad," I narrow my eyes and tease her.

She laughs. The sound is just what I need. Her laughter is delightful. "Hmm, that might work. But I am sorry to say you wouldn't cut it as a frog."

"I wouldn't?" I ask with pretend surprise. "And why not?"

June's eyes sparkle mischievously. "Well for starters, you hate the smell of pond scum," she begins counting on her index finger and says.

"You've got me there," I lick my teeth and confess. "I do find it extra stinky."

"Second, you hate eating bugs," she marks her comment with her middle finger, tallying the second reason, then grins, proud of her clever remark.

"That is a fair comment. I find bugs as meals revolting," I nod somberly as if she has clobbered me with her points.

"And lastly," she starts.

"Sheesh! There's more!" I throw my hands in the air then clutch my head and bow it with feigned defeat.

"And lastly," she says again. I raise my head and she looks at me sternly. "You don't even like frogs. You can't be something you don't even like. You have to like yourself." She blinks and shakes her head. She looks satisfied with all that she has said. "So no lily pad for you," she concludes.

I clasp my hands together and interlace my fingers. "Well that settles it," I say gloomily. "I guess you're stuck with me. Lily pads are not in my future."

June throws her head back and giggles. Her laughter is contagious and I find myself smiling just before a small laugh slips past my lips.

"Come on, silly girl. It's time to get up and start our day," I tell her.

I stand and stretch and feel as if every muscle in my body is complaining at once. June copies me and even adds a groan for good measure. Together, we move the boulder blocking our cave and head to the river to wash.

As we dab ourselves with water, I inform June of a decision I've made.

"So June, I am going out again today, out past the perimeter. I need you to do something while I'm gone," I say.

"What?" June asks. "What do you need me to do?"

"I need you to hunt on your own today."

June freezes where she wades and looks at me, her eyes round with surprise. "Really? You want me to hunt by myself?" she asks. "I thought you said it is too dangerous when you are not close by, that I am not ready," she adds.

"Well, now that you remind me of what I said, maybe you should stay put and hang around the cave," I toy with her.

"No!" she exclaims quickly. "Uh-uh! There's no way you're making me stay inside the cave by myself!"

"Oh, so you do want to hunt on your own?" I ask as if I don't already know the answer to my question.

"Of course I want to, and don't you dare think about changing your mind, Avery!"

"Okay, fine," I say as if she's somehow convinced me. "You win. You can hunt. But you need to be careful. Be aware of your surroundings."

"Yes!" she claps her hands and bounces up and down.

"Calm down there, Miss Springy," I tell her teasingly. "I am not sending you out there so you can bounce and play. You have to try to kill something for dinner, and you have to stay close to the cave."

I meant to sound playful, but June stops bouncing and frowns. She straightens her posture.

"I know I am not going today so I can play," she says quietly. "I am going so I can help. I am going to hunt for us near the cave while you hunt farther out in the woods."

Her cheeks are pink. I have embarrassed her.

"June, there's nothing wrong with playing and bouncing around. I love that about you," I tell her. "I was trying to joke around with you. I guess I didn't do a very good job of it because you are hurt." I reach out and place a hand on her shoulder. "I never want to hurt your feelings."

I am surprised when she shrugs off my hand. "I'm fine," she says. "You don't have to keep treating me like a baby 'cause I'm not a baby anymore. I'm eight, remember?"

She is eight. How could I forget? I was just a little older than her when I held her minutes after she was born. I remember twirling and bouncing when I first met her. I remember what the magic of littleness feels like. I do not want her to lose it. I do not want her to feel pressure to grow up faster than she has to. I am the adult, not her. I am here so that she can enjoy as much of her youth as possible while learning to survive in the hostile world we live in.

On a whim, I decide to do something I have not done in a long time. I begin bouncing and splashing, scooping handfuls of water and slapping my palms up before the water returns to the river. When my hands collide with the water and smack it, droplets spray in every direction.

June watches me from the corner of her eye. I can see her strain to see what I am doing.

I use both hands to ladle a generous amount then toss it up and whack it as hard as I can. Water cascades over June's hair. She whips her head around and looks at me, rolling her eyes. She is being stubborn.

I ignore her stubbornness and continue to caper about, splashing and jumping and laughing. At first, I fake my enthusiasm for June's benefit. But after a few minutes, my silliness becomes genuine.

Before long, I am not alone in my frolicking. June joins in. She is splashing, stomping and flopping in the water, splattering me with as much as she possibly can. My hair is dripping and my clothes are soaked, and I laugh so hard my belly hurts. June is laughing too. She laughs so hard her eyes tear. I guess she needs to see me let loose once in a while.

"Ah, Avery," she gasps but does not say anything more. She does not need to. I can see the relief in her features. I can see that she is not mad at me anymore. "I am going to catch a boart today," she says.

I am shocked and proud at the same time. The odds of June actually finding and killing a boart are slim at best. I do not wish to sell her short or undermine her intention, but tracking and killing a boart is not an easy feat. Regardless, trying will be good for her, even if it means we will eat a rabbit or squirrel I catch for dinner and not boart for three meals.

"I would love to have boart for dinner tonight," I encourage her and rub my empty stomach.

"And breakfast and lunch tomorrow too. I am going to get a big one," she says and sets her jaw. Determination radiates from her.

June looks at me then unexpectedly says, "I can do it, you know. I am ready."

"I know you are, June. I believe in you," I say with certainty. "Go for it," I smile and say to June.

She does not smile but her eyes shine with satisfaction.

We play a little longer then I am forced to remind her that my trip will be a long one, and that I must leave now if I want to make it back before the sun sets. We return to the cave and I collect my gear. I reinforce the fact that she must be extremely careful then set off toward the lake.

I walk through the forest hurriedly. The rustle and stir of leaves keeps me alert. I continually scan trees and brush for any sign of movement, for danger.

The sun has just risen and already the air is warm and sticky. The woods are rich with the smell of decomposing leaves and logs. I walk for hours. The air quickly becomes stifling. I stop to drink for a moment, and when I do, I look down and notice large, tubular droppings, boart droppings.

I notice a section of weeds that has been overturned. A small hole has been dug.

I narrow my eyes and press my lips to a hard line, and stalk past the uprooted earth. I follow and watch the low-growing brush as I clutch my spear. I lower my body when I move, my head moving from side to side. I see more droppings ahead. I continue until I find another patch of ripped up growth.

The faint swish of water in the distance distracts me from my trail. My heart rate hurries. I realize I am fast approaching the edge of the forest where the trees begin to thin.

I look to the trail then toward the direction of the sound. The rush of water calls to me as if singing my name. I know who lives near it. I know I should stick with following the boart. But I don't. I follow the strange flutter in my belly, the extra beats of my heart. I move away from the trail and toward the lake.

I pursue a different animal entirely. I find myself moving toward the rim of the woods. Thin trees are spaced farther from one another and lower growing shrubs offer little shelter. But I cannot stop myself from shuffling closer. I want to see the other humans again. I want to see the boy I saw yesterday.

I keep inching, creeping slowly until I can see that the younger children are out of their cave. They are dunking clothes in the water and swirling them around. The woman comes out and wrings what they've washed and lays them on flat rocks to dry. The children watch and listen as she explains what she is doing.

I see the silhouette of another person at the mouth of their cave. It is taller and broader. My pulse picks up speed. He steps from the shadows, out into the bright, golden sunlight, and I have to remind myself to breathe. He is even more beautiful than I remembered. His bronze skin glows in the sunshine and his short, almost-black hair sticks up on end and looks shorter than it did yesterday. He must have just gotten it trimmed. I am suddenly envious of whoever was lucky enough to run his or her hands through it, close enough to stare into his pale eyes.

Mesmerized, I move closer. I stand behind a sickly looking bush and poke my head out from beside it. I am sure I look like an idiot but cannot imagine leaving. I want nothing more than to march right over to the family and introduce myself. I want to be close to the older boy for reasons I cannot explain. But the idea of it seems much easier than actually doing it. In fact, when I picture myself going there and speaking to him, when I try to build my courage, my stomach squeezes and I feel nauseated. I feel shaky and cold despite the sweltering heat. Still, I know I must go there. I know I must overcome the intense nerves.

I take another step closer, away from the bush. As I do, a man comes up behind the boy that makes my legs feel spongy. He is about the same height and has identical coloring. He claps the boy on the back then rubs his hand on top of his head playfully, messing it further. If it is possible, his mussed hair looks better still. He turns toward the older man and gives a lopsided smile. I find myself smiling along with them. I cannot hear what they are saying to each other, but the exchange seems playful, loving even. I assume the man is his father and I am struck with a pang of jealousy so sharp I clutch my chest. The boy, the man and woman and the children are a family; an entire family intact. I did not know such a thing was possible. June and I were not as lucky.

I shift my weight from one leg to the next. But when I do, a branch snaps loudly beneath my foot. Everyone near the lake looks up. Blood rushes to my cheeks and burns there. Then it gets worse. I see the boy take off and run toward me. He is charging for the bush I am standing behind.

For a moment, I cannot move. I am utterly frozen. But his fast-approaching footfalls force me to act, to move. I stumble backward then scramble behind a young spruce tree. The boy stops at the bush I was just at. My heart is hammering so hard I worry he can hear it. I can see him clearly now. He is close, too close, a fact that steals the air from my lungs. I watch him, body trembling with unfamiliar nervousness.

His eyes are a brilliant blue-green, pale, like tropical water I once saw in a picture, and his hair is as dark as a raven's feathers. He is near enough for me to make my presence known to him, and him alone. I know I should, that it is what needs to be done, yet all I can think about is that I am dirty. My clothes are filthy from the hike and sweat coats my skin. But he is sparkling like a gem and I am a grubby stone.

The knocking in my chest stutters before I feel my heart sink. My shoulders curl forward. I realize I do not want to be seen. I feel something I have never felt before. I feel self-conscious, ashamed of the way I look.

When the boy moves from the bush back toward the lake, I take off. I run away from him.

"Hey come back!" I hear a voice call out that makes goose bumps emerge on my skin. It is him. It is the boy. He has seen me. "Why are you running?"

Heat blazes up my neck and sets my face afire. Hot tears burn down my cheeks and blow back into my hair. I do not know what I am more embarrassed about, the fact that I chickened out and ran from him, or the fact that he saw me looking as I do.

I hear fast footsteps gaining on me and think he has started chasing me. But I do not stop. I am humiliated. I wish I were braver. I wish I were cleaner. But I am neither. And I do not want to meet him like this. I push myself and move quickly, disappearing into the woods.

I run toward the cave, back in the direction I hiked from, until the landscape becomes too tangled to run. I slow then stop and listen. I do not hear the rustle and crunch of footfalls atop brush and feel confident I am not being followed. I crouch and catch my breath, and silently scold myself for running away. Finding other human beings is everything June and I have ever hoped for. I failed her. I failed myself. I have no idea what came over me. I have faced off with boarts and other wild animals. I have seen death and destruction that haunts my days and nights, yet talking to the bright-eyed boy with the suntanned skin terrifies me in a way I cannot explain.

I rest for a moment until my breathing becomes less labored. I stand, still feeling the effects of shame prickling my insides. But when I turn, my prickling insides stop stinging and crash to the soles of my feet. In that instant I realize my failure to talk to the boy with the bright eyes and tan skin is the least of my problems.

Standing a fallen tree trunk's length from me is an Urthmen, glaring at me with lidless, pits of blackness, the murderous eyes of a slaughterer.

Chapter 7

Murky black eyes the color of sludge are locked on mine, yet I do not move a muscle. I cannot move a muscle. My mind screams for me to reach for my sword, to run, to do something, *anything*. But my limbs are suddenly made of stone. The forest has gone still. I do not hear a thing, not the crackle of dry leaves, the buzz of insects or the chirp of chipmunks. Even the birds are silent. The forest is scared stiff, too, holding its breath and willing the beast gone. All I hear is the rush of blood behind my ears, and the frantic beat of my heart.

The Urthmen opens his mouth, an oily pit of blackness, and a dark, vile tongue slithers out. It slinks over his pointed teeth and I feel as if I might puke. I force my eyes from his rotten mouth to the hand that clutches a club, just in time to see his arm tense. In the space of a breath, he swings his weapon and I draw mine. I raise it and block his blow just before it connects with my skull. Still, the impact is powerful. It knocks me back a few steps.

I struggle but regain my footing. The rhythm of my heart has passed panicked and is now wild, dangerously so. He swings again. But this time I dodge it entirely and launch an attack of my own. I swipe my blade, slicing the air horizontally, and carve a gash below his chest.

He howls out angrily. I have hurt him. He looks down at the wound and sees that it is bad. Glee tiptoes down the length of my spine. I hoist my sword to shoulder height and summon all my anger, all my fear, and use every ounce of my strength as I swing. The blade whistles through the air and meets with his neck, cutting through flesh and bone until his head falls from his shoulders.

The Urthmen's body collapses to the ground in a heap and his head rolls into a bush loaded with burrs. I am panting. My entire body trembles. I cannot believe what I have just done, that I am not sorry for what I have just done. But movement in my periphery demands my attention. I snap my head toward it and see that just two spear length's away is another Urthmen.

He looks to me. His misshapen head shakes quickly, horrified by how easily I have slain his friend. He turns and runs, afraid he will suffer the same fate. I panic and take off after him. The notion seems absurd. Urthmen are what I have spent my life avoiding, yet here I am chasing one. But I know I cannot let him go. If he and the one I just killed were the only two scouting the area then he will return to his base and tell the others. The rest of the Urthmen in the area will know that there are human beings living in the woods. They will return with hundreds more and scour the terrain until they find us. They will kill the family by the cave. They will kill me. They will kill June. I cannot allow any of that to happen. I will stop the Urthmen running from me.

I see him not far ahead of me. He is fast. I push myself hard, testing not only my speed but my agility too. Exposed tree roots arise like gnarled knuckles of underground beasts, and vines snake and snag at my feet while thin branches whip at my legs and body. Still, I pursue him. I pump my arms and push my legs to their limit. But no matter how fast I run the Urthmen runs faster. He seems to be putting more and more distance between us.

Hungry and exhausted, I am running out of energy fast. I have just one option left. I reach my hand to my back and pull my spear from its sheathe as I continue to run. My muscles are spent and the weapon feels heavy in my hand—heavier than usual. But I hoist it level with my shoulder and aim it as best I can while moving. When the center if the Urthmen's back is in my sight, I launch my spear with every bit of power I have left in my body and fall to the ground just after I release it. Fortunately, my knees and hands hit the earth before my face does, lessening the impact somewhat.

My palms and knees throb and I have a mouthful of dirt, but I force myself up onto my hands to see if my spear landed anywhere near him.

I am shocked when I see that I scored a direct hit. I see the Urthmen slumped against a large boulder with my spear sticking out of his back. He is still moving, but barely.

I slide my feet beneath me and stand. I slowly begin walking over to the boulder on aching legs. When I reach him, I place my hands on my weapon and yank it from his back. He groans loudly then rolls onto the ground on his back.

My hands, which shook moments ago, have stilled. I hold my spear tightly. Its tip is poised just above the Urthmen's heart. Black eyes rimmed in cherry red stare up at me.

"Please human, don't kill me," he grinds out his words as he begs.

His voice scrapes like knives inside my ears. I want to shout at him to shut his filthy mouth, that he is not worthy of sympathy, but the words get stuck in my throat around the emotion jammed there. A memory flashes in my mind. I see my mother, my kind, beautiful, pregnant mother, with her hands held out in front of her in surrender, begging for mercy, begging that her life and the life of my unborn sibling be spared. But the Urthmen did not show her mercy. They took her pleas as an invitation to beat her to death.

I feel my lip snarl up over my teeth and a dangerous emotion winds inside me tightly. I squeeze the handle of my spear so hard the wood bites into my flesh. My chest is heaving and my breaths are short and shallow. My body is drenched in sweat when I pull the tip away from his chest.

The Urthmen's face relaxes and his stubby fingers touch the area just above his heart.

"I will tell them you spared me," he says.

I watch him for a long moment. I know I ought to feel compassion for him, pity of some kind. I search my mind, the hidden hollows of my heart. But I feel nothing for him. I feel only hatred. I raise my spear high in the air and stab down with it, burying the tip in his throat. His final expression is complete shock as life leaves him. A wave of satisfaction washes over me. But I do not have time to celebrate. I look around carefully to see if there are more. I scan the immediate area, searching tall weeds and brush, shrubs and small trees. I do not see any movement, and I do not see any more Urthmen. I need to get back to the cave and see if June is all right.

As I run, I realize I should return and tell the family at the lake about the Urthmen. I need to warn them. But it is getting late, and Urthmen are not the only threat to us. Lurkers will be out as soon as the sun sets. And even Urthmen know better than to be out when Lurkers are out. I hurry my pace even though my legs feel as if they will collapse beneath me at any moment. Rest would be nice, but is a luxury I cannot afford. I have a considerable distance to cover before I am home. I will go to the family in the morning. I will steel my nerves and approach them despite the wobbly-kneed feeling the oldest boy gives me. I will not chicken out this time. Lives are at stake.

Images zoom through my mind in a hazy jumble as I approach the woods near our cave. I relive my mother's death. I relive the experience of claiming the lives of the two Urthmen. In the moment, I felt as if her death was being avenged. But in the calmer time that followed, I realized that until every Urthmen falls, justice will never be served. The score will not be settled. And even if that moment ever comes to pass, I still won't have my mother. The thought makes my eyes as blurry as the pictures in my head. I try to think about something else. I immediately picture the family, the mother and father, the two young children. I see him, the boy with the aquamarine eyes that shimmer like fish scales. They make me feel better, happy almost. They make me feel something else, as well, something dangerous. They make me hopeful.

I cling to that hope even though I fear it will slip through my fingers like the silk of a spider's web. It keeps me going.

I am overheated and drained and want nothing more than to wash and sleep. When I reach the cave, June is nowhere in sight and worry worms its way into my brain. I examine the woods immediately in front of the cave. I do not see her. Panic floods every cell in my body.

"June!" I call out against my better judgment. If we are not alone in these woods, I have just alerted the enemy to my presence. But June is my sister, the only flesh and blood that is mine on this planet. I will risk my life to find her.

She does not answer so I call out to her again. "June! Where are you?" I say louder.

After a moment too long, warning is shrieking through my body and I am about to charge into the woods and not return until she is with me.

"Avery, over here," I hear June's voice echoing strangely.

I search the bushes, but do not see her.

"Avery!" she cries.

Her voice snares me like a lasso then pulls me. I run in the direction of her voice and do not stop until I am deeper in than I'd like to be and standing before the base of a tree.

"Avery!" she calls and sounds as if she is right beside me, yet I still do not see her. "I got one," she says and it sounds as though she is speaking to me from the treetop.

I look up and see her sitting on a thick branch. I start to walk around the tree to see if there is an easy way to get her down and am met with the angry grunts of one of the largest boarts I have ever seen. It is brown with an enormous patch of jet-black fur on its back, and its angry gaze is locked on me.

"Oh my gosh," I breathe.

The boart is scuffing its hoof against the dirt. When I look down, I see a boartling, small and plump, with a narrow spear through its neck.

With my eyes never leaving what I presume is the boartling's very angry mother, I kneel and grab the largest rock I can find then wing it at her. "Get out of here!" I threaten through my teeth. The rock knocks her in her hind quarters and sends her scrambling.

"See, I told you I'd get a boart today!" June squeals excitedly from the tree. "See it? See the boart?" she points to the boartling she skewered.

"Yes, I do," I say proudly. "Excellent job!" I make no mention of the fact that she is hiding in a tree from the baby boart's mother. That detail is not worth bringing up.

June climbs from the tree limb and clambers down the trunk. When she is on her feet, I ask, "When did you learn to scale a tree like that?"

She shrugs then marches up to her kill. "Our dinner," she says and splays her hands out to her sides proudly.

"I am so glad. I wasn't so lucky today," I say and weigh whether or not I should mention my run-in with the Urthmen. I do not know what to do. I do not want to scare her. But not telling her could be more dangerous than telling her.

"Why? What happened?" June asks the question that opens the door to our discussion.

But I decide that if I tell her, I will tell her after we eat. I want her to have her moment to celebrate. She deserves a victory.

"I didn't track as good as you did I guess," I frown and say. "You are the hunter today, Miss I-speared-a-boart-for-dinner!" I wrap an arm around her shoulders and bring her in close. "You did a great job," I tell her again.

She collapses into my arms and hugs me tightly. "Thank you," she murmurs.

"Don't thank me." I nudge her with my hip. "You're the one who did all the work. My hunting trip was a flop," I say.

June laughs. "I don't know about you, but my belly is rumbling. Let's eat already," she says.

I pull the spear from the boartling and hand it to June then carry the carcass by its feet. We bring it back to the cave and prepare a fire. I roast the boartling and slice the meat from its bones. We will have enough for dinner tonight, as well as breakfast in the morning. I am very proud of June.

We fill our bellies then put out the fire and wash up for bed. After several stories, June falls asleep. I did not tell her about the other humans and I did not tell her about the Urthmen. I will tell her in the morning, right before I set out to warn the family by the lake that Urthmen have been in the woods, and that others may know of our existence.

Exhaustion seizes me and grips me in a warm dark embrace. I fall asleep as soon as I close my eyes.

Chapter 8

As soon as my eyes open, the realization that today is the day I not only meet the boy by the lake, but tell June everything as well, makes my insides curl into a heavy knot. Both are tasks I desperately want to fulfill, yet at the same time am terrified of fulfilling.

Beside me, I feel June stir. She typically sleeps later than I do. I am the one who wakes her, but not today. On this day, she rises with the sun.

"Avery," she whispers softly. "You awake?"

I close my eyes and do not answer right away, stalling. I know it is foolish of me, that there is no way around the things I must do today. Still, I wish to buy myself a bit more time. I wish I could roll over and pull the cover of my sleep sack over my head and hide from both, hide from the always-chaotic and scary reality that is my life. But I cannot.

"Avery?" June tries a little louder.

"I'm up," I startle us both by saying in a strong, clear voice.

I feel June jump.

"Sheesh, you scared me!" she gasps.

"Sorry," I say.

"Why didn't you answer me the first time?" she asks a question I do not care to answer.

"Sorry," I say. I take a deep breath. "Let's get ourselves together here and have some breakfast. There are some things we need to talk about."

"Talk about?" June asks and a worried expression clouds her sunny features. "Am I in trouble for yesterday, for being in the tree because of the whole boartling thing?"

"No," I start but June talks over me.

"Because that mother boart was huge! I mean did you see the size of her head? Her head was bigger than the two of ours put together! I got scared. Anyone would have. Well, not you. But most people, if there were any people," June rambles.

"There are other people," I say.

But my words do not register with June right away. She continues thinking aloud. "You are like a boart expert, a boart slayer," she laughs at her own joke. Then her face goes blank briefly. Her brows gather and she looks at me. "Wait, what did you just say?"

"I said there are other people, other humans," I say.

I did not plan to tell her like this. The words just fell from my lips like rain. I do not know who is more surprised by what I've said, June or me.

June bolts upright and twists her body so that she is facing me. Her jaw has unhinged and her eyes are round. "Other human beings," she says and her eyebrows rocket to the middle of her forehead. "As in more than one person?" She can barely get the words out.

"Yes," I reply.

"Oh my gosh!" she exclaims and explodes from her sleep sack. "Where? Where are they? When did you see them? How many are there?" The questions fire from her in rapid succession.

"I saw them two days ago. There are five, a family. They live past our perimeter, out where a river and lake meet," I say and hope I have answered all of the questions she has asked.

"Two days ago!" she nearly shouts. "And you're just telling me about them now?"

June's cheeks are a deep shade of pink. Her eyes have narrowed to slits and her hands are on her hips. She begins pacing.

"Please don't be angry," I begin, but she cuts me off.

"Don't be angry? Are you kidding me? I am angry!" she stomps her foot and shouts. "The one thing I have been waiting for my whole life, to find other human beings, and you wait to tell me? It should've been the first words out of your mouth when you saw me!"

I have never seen June so angry. She is livid, in fact, and with me. I am not sure what to do.

"June, calm down," I say. "Please I did not mean to upset you."

"But you did upset me!" she fumes.

"I am sorry, June," I say feebly.

A long moment passes between us. June simmers. But after a while, she takes her lower lip between her teeth and a small smile rounds her cheeks. "I am not as angry as I seem, just disappointed. I mean, really, how mad can I be? I just found out we are not alone!" she squeals suddenly.

I am impressed by how maturely she is handling my misstep of not telling her right away.

"So what are they like? You said they are a family. Are there any children, any children that are my age? I can't believe this, Avery! I can't wait to meet them! Tell me all about them!"

She is exuberant. She bounces and twirls and smiles from ear to ear. I am afraid of what she will say when I tell her I did not speak to the family by the lake.

"Well, uh, let's see," I fumble. "How do I say this?"

"Just spit it out already! I want to know everything!"

"I don't really have much to tell," I say quietly.

"Huh? Why?" she asks and looks at me. She is puzzled.

"I didn't exactly, you know, go up to them and, uh, you know, talk to them," I admit embarrassedly.

"What?" June shrieks. "You didn't talk to them! Why? Why in the world wouldn't you talk to them?"

I lower my eyes to my feet. "I chickened out," I say and my cheeks blister with shame.

"You were scared?" June asks. Her tone is softer, gentler. I feel undeserving of her understanding.

"I-I don't know what happened to me," I confess. "I saw a little girl. She's probably your age, and a boy who looked about twelve, but then the older boy came out, and I don't know, it was like I couldn't breathe or something. I choked. I wanted to go talk to them, but my legs were shaky and my belly felt all wobbly and squishy and I just couldn't," I say and feel so ashamed I wish I were a turtle with a shell I could tuck myself into. I cover my face with my hands. "I probably sound crazy right about now. I'm not making much sense."

I feel a warm hand on my shoulder and drop my hands from my face. June has knelt and is beside me.

"You don't sound all that crazy," she says soothingly. "I can't say I know what I would do if I came across another human. I would probably chicken out too."

She wraps her arm around my shoulders and pulls me close. She does what I do to her when she is feeling insecure.

"I should have gone anyway. I should have gone even though I was scared out of my wits," I say. "I guess I am not as brave as I think I am."

June shakes her head. "You are the bravest person I know," she says.

"I am the *only* person you know," I say.

"Not for long," June smirks. "And you are still brave," she adds with a wink.

I shake my head. "No, I am not. I chickened out twice. I saw them again yesterday, and I think the older boy saw me. But like an idiot, I ran off. Trust me, I am not brave. I am a coward."

June considers what I've said and I expect her to erupt and scold me. I deserve it. I had a perfect opportunity to meet one person from the family, to not be outnumbered or overwhelmed, and I blew it. I ruined my chance by running away.

"You were scared. So what?" she shrugs and says. "I don't blame you. I probably would have done the same thing. Besides, we need to be careful, even with other humans. What you did doesn't mean you aren't brave."

"I don't know, June. Being brave doesn't mean you aren't scared, that you do things without fear. I always thought being brave means doing something *despite* being scared."

She is quiet for a moment then *tsk*s at me and smiles sadly.

"You are mean to yourself, you know that, Avery," June says and rests her head against my shoulder.

"And you are too kind to me," I say and kiss her forehead lightly.

She flashes a lopsided grin at me. "Okay, so when are we leaving to meet them?" she claps her hands together and asks.

"I am going to them as soon as we wash and eat," I say and emphasize the word *I*.

"I am coming too, right?" June asks with a smile.

"No, June, you can't," I say matter-of-factly.

"What? Why?" she asks and her smile collapses completely.

"June, the family is not the only discovery I made in the woods when I went hunting," I tell her. Remorse swirls in my gut. I am about to stab a dagger through the heart of her hope.

"What do you mean?" she asks and I can see fear flicker in her silvery eyes.

I fill my lungs then blow out a breath through pursed lips.

"Yesterday, on my way back from watching the family, I came across two Urthmen," I tell her and watch her features drop like a stone.

"Oh no," she breathes. "Oh, my gosh, no." Her hands fly to her mouth, covering it.

"I killed them both, but I think more are coming," I say.

June looks as if she's been punched in the stomach.

"You fought them?" she asks. Her complexion is pale and her bottom lip quivers.

"Yes, I did," I say. "They are dead now. But where there were two, there will be more."

June throws her arms around my neck and I feel a small sob tremble through her body.

"You should never doubt your bravery," she says, her voice a strangled whisper. "I am so sorry that happened to you." She weeps.

"June, hey June, no, no, please don't cry. I'm okay. I'm right here. I got them," I try to reassure her.

"But you were out there alone, and could've been," she says but her voice trails off. "You could've been killed."

June's words send a chill racing down my spine. She is right, of course. I could have easily been killed. There were two of them and only one of me. What if there had been more? What if there had been a dozen? The what-ifs rattle through my brain, through my bones, and any semblance of safety I ever had in these woods is stripped from me.

True, something primal, something animal and ferocious overtook me when I faced off with the Urthmen. But I don't know if that was a one-time occurrence. I may not be so lucky in the future.

"I have to warn the others. That is why I am going out there today. That is why you can't come. In fact, I want you to stay in the cave while I am gone. Keep your spear at your side and don't leave it for a moment."

June's entire body is trembling. She doubles over and clutches her belly. I rub her back.

"I-I-I can't do this. I can't be alone all day wondering if you are dead, or if Urthmen are coming for me, or both," she says.

I understand how she feels and wish there were another way. But she is much safer tucked in a cave no Urthmen would bother to look in than out in the open with me. No, that cannot happen. I will go as quickly as possible and warn the family. Then I will return to her. And when I do we will decide whether or not we will leave.

"June, the Urthmen were right by their cave. They must know about the family. Why else would they be there?" I say. "I have to help them."

June nods in agreement then adds, "Get them out of there. Bring them here."

As much as the idea of sharing our tight space with the older boy makes my stomach flop like a fish on dry land, the fact of the matter is our cave cannot accommodate five more people.

"We don't have enough room for five people," I tell her.

"We can make room if they want to come, if it will save their lives," she says and levels her sharp gaze at me. When she stares as she is now, she looks so much like my father my heart clenches. She has his fire, his commitment. I see it plainly now.

"Okay. I will invite them here," I agree. "You're right. We cannot leave them to die."

"Good," she says and somehow, she looks as if she's aged in the moments that have passed.

"You will stay here and ready this place for our company. After we wash and eat, I need you to help me move the boulder to cover the opening so that you are as concealed as possible," I tell her. Her spine lengthens at news that she has a job. "I will leave enough room for you and me to get in and out of the cave, but that's it. When the family gets here, we can open it further. But while I am gone, I don't want to take any chances," I say firmly, then add, "You are too important to me."

My voice falters at the last sentence I speak. I do not like entertaining the possibility of ever losing June. I am sickened by the idea of leaving her, but taking her is not an option.

"I will be fine here," she says. "And I will get everything ready. You have nothing to worry about. Our new guests will feel welcome and comfortable."

I want to tell her that I highly doubt any of us will ever feel welcome or comfortable in these woods after knowing Urthmen were here. But I keep that grim thought to myself. She is calmer, and that's all I care about. If I am to fight for my life, I must preserve the one who is most important to me, the person I fight for, the person I live for. My sister must remain as safe as possible, as healthy as possible, and as happy as possible in this sinister world we live in. June must live for me to live to fight another day.

Chapter 9

My heart pumps frantically and echoes the hurried pace of my footsteps as I journey through the forest toward the outer banks to warn the family near the lake. My insides quiver and my mouth is dry, but I know the option to chicken out does not exist. I must overcome the overwhelming anxiety I'm feeling and go to them. Lives are at stake, five to be exact, and that's not including June and I.

Despite the direness of the situation, the thought of crossing the thin strip of woods between the spot I hid in during my last two trips and coming face to face with them makes the contents of my full belly somersault endlessly. For once, having breakfast seems to be working against me. Every time I picture myself approaching the family, my food threatens to launch up my esophagus. I take deep breaths to calm myself, but they are of little help. I am still a nervous wreck. But I must warn them. I must warn the boy with the shimmering eyes.

Just thinking of him sends a jolt from my stomach to my feet. My knees feel weak. I realize my fear is less about the mother, father and younger children than it is about the boy who looks close to my age. Thinking about standing arm's length from him makes me lightheaded. Speaking to him might make me faint.

What if I faint? The question whirls through my head. What if I see the boy with the aquamarine eyes, faint and never even warn him and his family that they are in danger? I will make a complete fool of myself and fail to accomplish the task I set out to achieve. The worry joins the multitude of other worries swimming around in my brain and worsens the tumbling in my belly. The last thing I need to do right now is play out possible scenarios in my mind, especially ones that involve me failing, fainting, or falling. Imaging any of those possibilities works against my waning courage. I will get there in one piece, still standing, and I will warn them.

I continue repeating that sentence in my head over and over. It becomes a rally cry as I slip through the forest. But with each step I take, the challenges to my self-confidence are replaced by the sensation that I am not alone.

I quiet my racing thoughts and focus every bit of my energy on the space surrounding me. Every twig that snaps, every shuffle of leaves and stir of treetops sets my heightened senses on even higher alert. I lower my stance and am nearly crouching, clutching the hilt of my sword as I dash through the woods. I swear I feel eyes on me. But what I believe are the sounds of footsteps following me is what finally makes me stop dead in my tracks, unsheathe my sword and spin around, ready to fight. I expect to see the deadly, milky-eyed stare of an Urthmen, but I do not. Instead, I see a plump rabbit watching me with oversized eyes that sit unusually close together on its face. I take bold step toward it, warning it off. It hops away, but not before unhinging its jaw, showcasing its impressive fangs and hissing at me.

I contemplate running after it and adding rabbit to our boart feast later, but know that I do not have time to do so. Each moment I am not moving is a moment wasted. I slowly turn from the rabbit's path and head to the lake.

My run-in with the Urthmen the day before has shattered my feeble sense of safety. Now, as I tread in unfamiliar territory, I feel an added element of fear. I believe these woods could be overrun with Urthmen. I quicken my pace and jog, thankful for the boart meat I ate this morning, that June had killed a boartling yesterday. It supplies me with enough energy to continue until the sun is high overhead and the twisting vines underfoot become so dense and tangled that I must slow down. As I do, I hear the river and know the lake is nearby. My moment has come.

When I reach the edge of the woods where the trees grow farther apart and the brush thins, I see them. The family is out of their cave and sprinkled around the lake. I must go to them. It is the reason I came.

I slide one foot forward and it feels heavier than usual, and unstable. I am dizzy and nauseated. I feel cold though it is warm. My palms are damp and base of my throat throbs in time with my racing heartbeat. My mind wills my body to move, but my body is reluctant to cooperate. I am a quivering bundle of contradicting signals. I do not understand what is happening to me. I have slain wild animals, have fought and killed mutant beasts known as Urthmen, but those tasks generated less of a physical response than my current undertaking. I feel as if I may need to vomit. I pull in a sharp breath of air in hopes it will have the same effect as before. To my surprise, it does not. Instead, my legs are shaking violently. So I do what has become typical of me in recent days. I duck behind a hostile looking bush that looks in need of saving and has become somewhat familiar to me. I stay there and try to build my courage.

My cheeks are in flames. I am embarrassed of my behavior. The family's safety depends on me alerting them that a threat is on the horizon. I cannot let them die because I am a coward. I will not live with more blood on my hands.

I stand, emboldened by the knowledge that lives depend on me. I close my eyes briefly then take a step forward, then another, and another. I keep going, putting one foot in front of the other, until I am at the shore of the lake. I see all of them, the entire family. Each of their heads whips in my direction. I quickly raise my hands in front of my body, my palms facing outward, in surrender. I do not want them to feel threatened. I want to communicate that I will not do them harm.

"Hello," I say because I do not know what else to say. I have not seen another human being in a long time. My socialization has been limited to June in the last year.

Glances volley from one person to the next, and though I have been consciously avoiding looking at the boy with the aquamarine eyes, I turn my head and am met with his face. He is looking at me, a small smile playing across his lips.

My breath catches in my chest. I wonder if he is smiling at me because he is happy to see me, or if I have done something stupid. Thankfully, his mother's voice yanks me from fretting about it.

"You can put your hands down," her clear voice says. "You are not a threat."

I am not a threat; to them at least. But if they only knew of my hunting and sparring skills, that I killed two Urthmen by myself just yesterday, the woman might have thought twice about counting me out in the threat department.

"My name is Avery," I begin, but my words are suddenly smothered by the woman's shoulder which rams into my mouth when she wraps both arms around me and brings me in for a tight hug.

"Avery," she says my name aloud. "You have a beautiful name befitting your beautiful face."

I wonder how she could possibly know what my face really looks like. It is buried in the space between her neck and elbow. But I keep that detail to myself. She sounds as though she may cry and I do not want to upset her further. Especially since I do not know why she is so upset. I am perplexed by her words and actions, in fact. She hugged me and complimented me, yet she is sad. I do not know what to do. I stiffen a bit and she releases me.

"Oh, gosh, I am so sorry," she sniffles and says. She brushes back tears with the tips of her fingers. "It has been so long since we've seen another," her voice falters.

"We haven't seen another human being in a few months," the man I presume is her husband speaks. "Kate is just so happy to see you. We are all so happy to see you."

I awkwardly shift my weight from one foot to the other as I blink back the hot tears that threaten unexpectedly.

"Oh dear," Kate says and shakes her head. "You've introduced yourself and here we are not doing the same. I guess that's what isolation does to people," she says.

I smile tightly. I know all too well about isolation. But I do not speak. I do not trust that my voice will hold up. I feel eyes on me, and if they belong to whom I think they belong to, I do not want to risk breaking down in front of him.

"I am Kate and this is my husband, Asher. And these are our children," she begins and starts with the girl first. "This is my daughter Riley and my sons Oliver," she points to the smaller boy. "And Will," she concludes and gestures to the taller, older boy I have watched the last two days.

Will. The boy's name is Will. I say his name in my head and each time my stomach flutters. I inexplicably feel like twirling. I don't, of course. I look from face to face and smile at the new people I've met. I mutter something about being pleased to meet them as my dad instructed me was proper to do if or when I ever met another human. But when I get to Will, my smile capsizes. He looks directly into my eyes and heat creeps up my neck and spreads over my cheeks. A boy has never looked at me the way Will is looking at me right now. Probably because the last time I saw a boy my age was when I was eight and lived in the village, and even then, I had not seen many boys at all.

"Glad to meet you, Avery," Will says.

My heart sets off at a gallop. I wonder if he can see it bashing my ribs, if it is causing my shirt to drum visibly. I take my lower lip between my teeth and look at my feet. I am grateful when his sister Riley starts talking.

"Avery, I'm so glad you're here. Another girl makes things even. You can be my sister," Riley's eyes light up as she speaks and she is bouncing on the balls of her feet the way June does.

"Uh, thanks," I say self-consciously.

"Who says she's staying?" Oliver asks unexpectedly.

Kate and Asher's glances shoot in Oliver's direction.

"Oliver!" his mother says with obvious embarrassment. "Say you are sorry."

"No, don't. You don't have to be sorry," I say quickly. "I am not staying. And neither should you. That is why I am here actually." I dive into my purpose of coming without thinking.

Five sets of eyes land on me.

"What? What are you talking about?" Kate asks. Her soft brown eyes are fixed on mine. She is crestfallen. "Why would you want to be alone?"

I look between her and Asher then to the smaller children. "Maybe we can talk somewhere else," I say when my gaze returns to them.

"Oh, I see," Asher says and takes my rather obvious hint. Then to the children he says cheerfully, "Can you two go to the cave and collect the clothes? We need to start our chores and need your help."

Both faces droop and they take off toward the mouth of the cave before their father utters another word. I smile at Asher and he smiles back, but it does not reach his eyes. Worry seems to be weighing down his face.

Kate folds her arms across her chest and Asher places a hand on her back.

"So what is it you need to speak with us about?" Kate asks with concern.

"Urthmen are here," I answer and watch as my words transform their demeanors.

"Urthmen?" Will repeats what I have said. His voice makes my scalp tighten and tingle, even though it should not. The circumstances are grave but I am powerless to stop the effect his voice has on me from happening. His hands rocket to his hips, fists balled. "How do you know?" he asks.

"I saw them," I say. "I killed two in the woods right beyond this lake."

Will cocks a brow at me as if he does not believe me. A quick look at his parents tells me he is not alone in his doubt that I could kill not one, but two, Urthmen.

"You killed two Urthmen?" Asher asks. I hear the disbelief in his voice and feel my temper flare ever so slightly. I am not used to proving myself to anyone. I am what I am, and that is not up for debate or question. If I say I did something, I did it. In the world we live in, exaggeration does not possess a benefit. If any other human beings exist in other areas, they either have the skills to survive, or they do not. The ones who do not are likely dead.

My spine lengthens and my shoulders straighten. "Yes, I did," I say in a strong, clear voice.

"But, uh, you are so small," Kate says and looks embarrassed by her words.

"My size means little. My father trained me well. I hunt each day for my sister and I, and have killed boarts as well as the two Urthmen yesterday."

Kate, Asher and Will look at me skeptically.

"Believe me or don't believe me. I know what I saw and I know what happened. The Urthmen are dead. I would show you their bodies but am pretty sure Lurkers took care of them as soon as the sun went down last night. I came here to warn you and I did," I say as annoyance blisters inside of me. I am not accustomed to this kind of interaction, the exchanges of secret glances, and the subtle facial expressions that doubt my integrity. "I also came to invite all of you to stay at the cave I share with my sister. It is a quarter of a day's walk from here, so I suggest you gather your things and come along. Do not waste any time. We need to go right away."

I look to the three of them expecting them to begin moving and getting their belongings, but they don't. They stand perfectly still as if they're made of stone.

I clear my throat, wondering whether I imagined what I just said to them.

"Uh, you guys heard me just now, right?" I ask quietly.

My stomach feels like a bag filled with snakes slithering and rolling over one another.

"Yes, we heard you," Kate says and tilts her head to one side the way I do when June is melting down. "But I think I can safely speak for all of us when I say thank you for the invite, but we will be fine here."

Her words do not register in my brain right away. I am dumbfounded by what I have just heard. "What?" I ask and hope I was wrong, that I did not just hear her say she and her family plan to risk their lives and stay where they are with Urthmen afoot.

"We are not going with you," Asher says and I feel as if I have just been punched in the gut. "We are safe here."

His face is so smooth, so calm, as if what I've just told him is so absurd, he cannot not even react to it. But it is true. Two Urthmen had been close to their camp, too close. I want to shake each of them and shout in their faces that they were being ridiculous, that they will be found and killed. But I think that if I did that, I would solidify any ideas they already have about me. The best thing I can do now is walk away, leave and put Kate, Asher, Oliver, Riley and Will out of my thoughts.

"I see," I say and do not mask my disappointment and shock. "I hope you are heavily armed," I say as I turn to leave.

I stalk off toward the woods. Scalding tears stream down my cheeks. I know their names, I have met them, but I wish I hadn't. Now I know more people who will die.

I am just past the area where the anemic bush I hid behind twice is located when a voice calls out to me.

"Avery! Hey Avery, wait up!" Will exclaims.

"Quiet!" I hiss. "Do you want to announce where you are?" I ask heatedly.

His features rumple and he stops walking for a moment.

"What do you want, Will? Did you come to mock me as I leave?" I ask and do not hide my frustration.

"No," he says. "Nothing like that. I just want to talk to you."

He stops arm's length from me. This close, I can see every detail of his face, the brilliant blue-green of his pale eyes, the dip of his upper lip just below his straight nose, and the smooth, even quality of his skin. It looks as if it would feel like a rose petal. Still, I am angry that he and his family treated me like a liar then chose to stay and face certain death rather than listen to me.

"What do you want to talk to me about?" I ask huffily. "Didn't you and your parents say everything that needed to be said back there?"

"Why did you run from me yesterday?" he shocks me by asking. "Why did you run away?"

I want to tell him I was afraid, that the thought of talking to him made me so nervous my legs froze, that I am still nervous, but the words die on my lips.

"Turns out it was the right thing to do," I say. "I should never have come back."

A pang of hurt flickers in his eyes. I regret being so harsh.

I open my mouth to tell him I am sorry, but he speaks first.

"I am sorry about how my parents were, how I was, back there," he says.

I am too surprised by what he has said to respond right away. My mouth is agape and an uncomfortable silence fills the space between us. I consider bolting out of sight. But my legs are leaden once again.

"You are?" I mumble.

"Yes, I am," he says and reaches out. His fingertips graze my forearm and send a euphoric shock of bliss racing straight up my arm and down my back. "You put yourself in grave danger to do the right thing, to come back here and warn us."

"So you believe me? You believe what I told you?" I ask and am mesmerized by the pastel azure and emerald in his eyes that undulate like waves in water.

"I do," he says and holds me with his gaze.

"Then you need to talk to them. You need to get them to leave as soon as possible. It is not safe here. The Urthmen I killed were here, just past where we are now, in broad daylight. And if they were here, others know about the area, they know about you."

A crease forms between Will's brows as the weight of my words settle on him. I see a small muscle by his jaw flexing.

"Please," I continue. "Get your family out of here."

"I will. I will convince them," he says. "I do not want to be like the others we've met over the years.

"Others?" I can't help but ask.

"Yes, the other humans we have met."

"You have met other humans?" I feel my eyebrows rocket toward my hairline.

"Yes, we traveled for a long time before we settled here and saw many like us, colonies, in fact. But the ones we found hid and kept to themselves for the most part. They are killed off regularly." Will frowned. "I think that's why my parents are so hesitant about leaving. This is the first real home we've had, and it's close to the river and lake. We have everything we need here. It's much better than what most have."

"I understand," I say. I want to tell him about the village I lived in, about my mother and father, about June. There is so much I want to say, but time is ticking. I need to hurry back before night falls. My journey is long. I wish I could stay here for hours, gazing at Will, and exchanging stories. But I can't. I must leave. "I have to leave. I have to get home before the sun sets."

Will's shoulders sag. I would have missed it if I weren't so focused on everything about him. But I am. And I saw the small change in his posture. I wonder whether he is disappointed that I am leaving. The idea makes my insides teem like a full beehive.

"Oh," Will says. "So this is it? This is the end of our, uh, you know, meeting each other?" he says and seems as nervous as I am.

"No," I say and surprise both of us. "I will come back tomorrow and see what they've decided," I tell him. "I'll see if you've convinced them to go. If they decide to come with me, they will need me to lead the way to the cave I share with my sister."

Will's lips collapse to form a hard line. "Is it safe for you to come back?"

"According to your family, yes, it is," I say bitterly, and as soon as the words leave my mouth I regret them.

He stares at his feet then I see him glance at me through a thick fringe of dark lashes.

"I will be as cautious as I was today," I say. "I am always careful. My sister is young. She needs me. I am all she has."

"And you risked yourself to come here and warn us," he says and his voice is thick with apology.

"Yes," I say honestly. "I did." My words hang in the air between us for several beats. "I must go." I tell him again.

I turn and begin to walk away from Will.

"What is her name?" he asks.

"Who?" I twist and ask.

"Your sister, what is your sister's name?"

"June. Her name's June and she is about the same age as Riley," I say with a half-smile.

Will's face brightens. "Tell June I say hello, okay?"

"I will," I reply.

I turn and resume walking. I sense Will's eyes on me and feel my cheeks flush. My trip was not a success by the standards I set forth when I left, but I am pleased, nevertheless. In fact, I smile so broadly my cheeks hurt. I replay every word he spoke, how he looked when he talked, and most importantly, the moment when he touched my arm. Though brief, the contact was like lightning bolting beneath my skin, exhilarating and delightful. My entire body shivers like leaves in the wind as I remember it. I have no recollection of ever being touched by another human being who was not related to me. Will was the first. I wonder what it would feel like to touch him back, to run my fingers over the lean cords of muscle that twine up his forearm. I hope to find out, and that hope twists in my chest.

Hope is dangerous. Humans are an endangered species. Still, I find myself indulging in it, imagining a future, a life with Will in it. Even if my hope is futile, I enjoy it while I walk. The distance seems smaller and time passes quicker as a result. I have not prepared for how I will tell June about the family's rejection of my offer. I do not know what I will say or how I will tell her that I plan to go back there for a fourth day in a row, knowing fully that Urthmen have infiltrated our safety. I am certain of only two things: I will pass along Will's message; I will share his greeting with her. And I will go back to him in the morning.

Chapter 10

I walk along and feel as if my feet are barely touching the earth as I make my way back to the cave, back to June. A smile continually tugs at the corners of my mouth. I keep picturing Will, the way his eyes glowed against his tan skin and nearly black eyelashes, the way his lips moved when he spoke. Just remembering the sound of his voice sends a wave of tingles from my scalp straight down my neck to my arms. Goose bumps appear on my skin though the midday sun is sweltering. I am happy in a way I have never been before. I cannot wait to return to the lake, to Will, in the morning.

Despite my happiness, though, I remain vigilant. My eyes continue to scan the surrounding woods. And the sensation that I am being watched returns. Only this time, it is more than just a paranoid concern. I *feel* eyes one me. Someone or something is drilling their gaze right into me. I am sure of it. The realization drains any excitement I've been feeling.

I slow my pace and examine the area before me. I see nothing, not even the slightest movement stirs the leaves. I turn and look toward the direction I just came from. I study the dense bushes for any sign of disturbance, but again, I see nothing. Everything looks as it did. I begin to wonder whether I am imagining things. For a moment, I try to convince myself that I am, that my overwhelming excitement has sent my senses into overdrive. But no matter how hard I try to tell myself that, I still have the feeling, the heaviness of being a target. I feel as if I am being stalked.

Awareness slinks down the length of my limbs and the fine hairs on my body stand up at attention. I am being hunted.

My hand reaches behind me slowly. The rustle and swish of branches causes me to grip the hilt of my sword. I stop walking and listen. Above the caw of birds and the chirp and scurry of chipmunks,

I hear it. I hear heavy footfalls. I silently unsheathe my sword and hold it out in front of me, gripping it with both hands.

My heart is banging against my ribs and a rivulet of sweat trickles between my shoulder blades and slips down to the small of my waist as I wait for whatever or whoever has been tracking me to make an appearance.

"Come out!" I shout as the stress of waiting to be confronted takes its toll on me. "Come out and face me! I know you're there!"

I do not get a verbal response, but hear a throaty huff instead, and every cell in my body floods with adrenaline. I am under attack. Urthmen are undoubtedly positioned and poised to ambush me at any given moment.

I squeeze the handle of my sword. Every muscle in my body is tense. I take two wary steps on the path I've been on, but halt when the sound of twigs crunching echoes through the ether. I stiffen and look in the direction of the sound. Low-growing bushes part. I see prickly fronds shift, and I move in for a closer look.

Cautiously, I approach the cluster of spiny plants. As I do, I see it is a large snout jutting among the tangled mess of branches. The snout is connected to a boart, but not just any boart. This one looks familiar. I saw it just a day earlier, the one I assumed was the boartling's mother, the boartling June had killed. I recognize the unmistakable swath of black fur that interrupts the otherwise all-brown coat.

Small, closely set eyes glare at me and saliva drips from its wide mouth, over pointed tusks that protrude like deadly spikes. A bristly tuft of fur at its nape stands on end and quivers like quills and it grunts first then emits a sound that can only be described as a wail. The sound freezes the blood in my veins and I clutch my sword, ready to act. But before I do, the boart bursts from the brush, charging at full speed. I do not have time to stab it so I take the only other option I am left with. I dive out of the way, narrowly avoiding being gored by her lethal teeth.

I nearly lose my sword when my body meets with the hard ground. I roll to my side and scramble onto my hands and knees then spring to my feet.

I see the boart stop abruptly and turn. Her eyes lock on me and suddenly, the feeling I had earlier and then again a moment ago gels. I was not being hunted by Urthmen. I was being stalked by an angry mother boart. She is avenging the death of the boartling, *her boartling*, June killed yesterday. Though the notion seems farfetched, it is the only likely one. Boarts do not simply attack unprovoked. At least they never have before. I also thought that rabbits did not attack. Apparently I know less than I thought about the new, ever-evolving animal kingdom.

The boart rotates her bulky shoulders and scuffs her hoof against the earth. Her eyes narrow to gashes then she lets out a guttural cry and charges me again.

I sheathe my sword just before I turn and put my head down and take off. I push my legs as hard as I can, demanding they run faster than ever before. Thin branches whip me in the face and thorny vines lash my legs. But I do not care. A boart is after me, hoping to impale me with its massive tusks.

I glance over my shoulder and see her hefty form barreling down on me. Her back is almost as tall as I am and her tusks match the length of my arm from elbow to wrist. If she sticks me with one of them, I am dead.

The terrifying reality of my predicament propels me forward. But my speed is no match for the boart. She is faster, stronger. Out of desperation, I dip behind a tree and watch her blaze past me. But the moment she becomes aware of what I have done, she skids to stop. I do not waste a second of precious time and bolt in a different direction. I attempt to dart through thick, interlocked growth. But the patch is closely packed and makes running difficult.

I hear the grunt of the boart and see that she is tearing after me, plowing a path through the solid foliage. I cannot fight the boart as it charges me. Even if I stab it, I will be hit and killed for sure. Without any other choice, I run from her.

I hear my feet slapping against the dirt as I sprint. But my effort is useless. She is gaining on me. A quick glance over my shoulder confirms as much. And when my gaze returns to the path I am headed on, I see I am at the top of a steep ridge. I do not remember climbing a hill as I traveled to the lake. But then I also did not have a boart that probably quadrupled my weight and nearly matched my height on my heels. I try to turn and avoid the sharp descent, as well as getting hopelessly lost in the forest, when my foot snags on an exposed root that pokes out from the soil. I stumble and find myself tumbling down the embankment full speed.

Pain erupts across my flesh, blasting against my body like hot coals, as I plunge faster and faster. The ribs on my left side topple over a sharp stone. I scream, unable to harness the agony, and still, I am falling. I clutch my head in my hands to protect it and feel my forearms being shredded by rocks and sharp branches. At the base of the mound, the terrain lips and hurls me into the air. I expect to smash into a boulder or tree trunk and break every bone in my body, but am surprised when I land against a spongy surface that absorbs my weight and rebounds it so that I bounce, springy and in midair.

I look up, grateful that I did not, in fact, crash into a boulder or tree trunk, only to see the boart careening down the ridge. It is heading right for me. Suddenly, I think I would have been better off having my bones shattered by the boulder or the tree rather than being demolished by the largest boart I have ever seen. I squeeze my eyes shut and grit my teeth, bracing for the impact. All the while, images of June and Will and the life I would miss flash in my mind's eye.

I am shocked when the boart lands just a leg's length from me. It sticks to the flexible material I lean against, hovering above the ground. It squeals and flails and appears to be stuck. But I can barely hear or see its tantrum. I am panting and crying and mumbling all at once, tears blurring my vision. I try to move my hand to my face to rub my eyes, but feel resistance. My skin is being tugged. My arm is stuck. I begin wriggling and twisting, trying to free my arm, but learn my entire body is stuck to the squishy net-like structure that prevented me from launching into the woods. I feel my sword sliding around at my back. I want to be still but can't stop the panicked squirming of my body. I attempt to kick my legs and use my heels to free myself, but my movements are a waste of time. A loud clang, the distinct sound of metal clashing with rock, and the immediate loss of weight at my back means my sword has dropped to the ground below. Held by the gummy meshwork and stripped of my sword, I am frightened. I frantically search all around me. My head is not connected to the tacky substance so I am able to look beneath me and above me.

Sunlight filters through treetops and illuminates the odd pearlescent threads that crisscross intricately between two sizable trees. When it does, it reveals I am trapped in a net of some sort, a web. Overhead, I see bones, many bones arranged neatly, that resemble the skeleton of a boart.

My mind struggles to think of what could have created the sticky snare I am caught in. Urthmen come to mind immediately. Perhaps they'd fashioned this to capture humans. Maybe this is what the two I killed yesterday built and I just caught them as they were leaving. Thoughts spin in my brain, burrowing into murkiness faster than a grub burrowing into soil. If that is true, if Urthmen built the web then June is in danger. My eyes are wild as they roam the web for weakness. But the extra, terrified glimpse of the complexity involved in its construction makes me think the Urthmen would not be intelligent enough to make something so elaborate.

I curl my torso forward and pull with all my might, trying to separate from the sticky mesh. But all that happens is that I feel the skin on my back stretch and pull, hopelessly stuck. I cannot budge. Angry shrieks and protests from the boart remind me that it is trapped with me. It flails and fights but is not strong enough to free itself. It is a powerful beast, much tougher and much stronger than I am. Yet it, too, is ensnared. My situation is far worse than I ever dreamed possible. I will either die at the hands of whatever has me trapped or I will die at the hands of a Lurker. Either way, I will die this day. And what's worse is June will not be able to roll the boulder in place and cover the opening of the cave. She will not be able to secure herself. She will be wide open, a midnight treat for Lurkers. She has been issued a death sentence.

Tears rain from my eyes and stream down my cheeks. I cannot bear the thought of June being butchered by a Lurker. I twist and pull again, and this time it is not the boart's cry that pierces the forest. It is mine.

I remain bound to the web until the sun sags low in the sky. One arm has lost feeling. It has been perched over my head since I first landed here. The rest of my body aches from the fall and holding my awkward position. But none of that even matters now. If I make it out of the web alive by some stroke of luck, I will never make it back by nightfall. I will be dead before sunrise one way or another. I allow my chin to fall to my chest and close my eyes. But a quiver on one of the strands I am stuck to vibrates. My eyes open and I see something moving at the base of the web. The bushes shimmy. I strain my eyes to see what is coming, to finally meet my awful fate, and when I do, I learn that nothing I have seen in either reality or my worst nightmares has prepared me for the sight before me. Shock prevents my gaze from leaving the creature that slowly scuttles onto the lowest fiber of the web.

Armed with eight leathery looking legs with prominent joints that bend and flex as it creeps, and a fleshy body sectioned into two defined segments, both coated in tawny fur, the being makes its way up the silken thread. The closer it looms, the clearer my vision of it becomes. An insect face with five amber, feline eyes watches the boart. Its body is as long as mine only much thicker. I can see bulky, pronounced muscles flexing as it walks. I want to scream, but the sound is smothered by my heart, firmly wedged in my throat. I am thankful for that, because the boart is shrieking and carrying on. All the sound and motion seems to be encouraging the beast.

The spindly legs of the creature reach the lower half of the boart. The enormous boart thrashes again, but like me, it is attached solidly. All the while it cries and screeches as the creature reaches its head. The creature perches its colossal form atop the boart and rears the upper sector of its body. Each of its five eyes is a bottomless pit of doom. Its mouth opens and two huge fangs, glistening with a thick, iridescent substance, extend from the roof of its mouth. It lowers its mouth to the boart's neck then in one lightning-fast motion, it buries its fangs into the boarts throat.

The boart yelps and cries. It is the most awful, anguished sound I have ever heard an animal make. I am sickened as small whimpers pass through my lips. The boart is in agony. But the more the boart howls, the longer the creature's fangs seem to grow. My eyes widen in horror when I see their tips poke through the other side of the boart's neck coated in red. The boart stops moving and the fangs retract suddenly. The creature backs up slowly. But I see that its golden eyes are now on me. It scurries off the boart unhurriedly, watching me with the eyes of a skilled predator. It takes every bit of restraint I have to keep from screaming. I know screaming will not help me any more than the boart's cries helped it. Instead, I feverishly try to free myself.

My entire body trembles. I see the milky filaments all around me quake. I pull my arm, wrenching my shoulder until it feels as if it will separate from my body altogether. But I do not care. Anything will be better than enduring what the boart endured. I tug and yank. Skin stretches to its limit, but I ignore the pain. I continue to pull with strength I never knew I had as the beast draws nearer. My skin starts to tear from my forearm and I am flooded with a sick sense of relief. The stinging is torturous. I can't stop though. If I do, I am going to die. And I don't want to die, not like this. I will die fighting.

With a sickening rip, my skin breaks free of the sticky web.

My forearm is raw and bleeding when I feel the first of the beast's legs begin to make their way up my body. With a shaking hand coated in my own blood, I reach for the dagger I keep sheathed at my thigh and wield it just as the beast's face is at my chest. I thrust the tip of my blade upward and lodge it deep into the lower section of its torso and twist. I cry out the primitive cry of a warrior and it screeches as well. I feel warmth gush over my hand. I look down and see bright-yellow goo pouring over it. I withdraw my dagger and stab it again in one of its golden eyes. It howls out again and I see the points of its fangs begin to lengthen. If they appear fully, I will not survive the speed and deadliness of a strike.

My body is slick with sweat and I am panting and crying at the same time, gore and the pus-like substance covering me. It is lowering its mouth closer and closer to my face. With every inch of space that is closed, my mind centers on thoughts of June, sweet, innocent June who will die because of me. I pull the blade from its eye and, with no room left to shove it, I am trapped, waiting to have my throat pierced by the razor-sharp incisors suspended just above my jugular.

"I'm sorry, June," I sob as the creature drops against me.

"Oh, oh my gosh," I am gasping and wheezing as the beast collapses so close to me its blade-like teeth nick my shoulder.

I laugh and cry and feel a spurt of warmth saturate my torso. I have killed it.

Covered in sludgy gook and with the creature atop me, I use my dagger to slice the web that my upper body rests against. The spongy mesh immediately gives way and I begin to plummet. But before I plunge to the ground with the creature on my chest, a crushing death for sure, the sticky network of threads clings to my legs and the massive beast rolls from my chest and tumbles to the ground below. I am left, suspended upside down, knowing that I must cut my legs free, that I will drop on my head. I curl my aching body forward and slash at the web to free the rest of me. I go down hard and hit a branch before my head and upper body takes the brunt of my fall. My neck and back complain. A patch of my skin has been torn from my body and my entire body feels banged up. I also smell fouler than anything I have ever smelled. But those are the least of my problems. The pinkish-orange glow of the setting sun surrendering to twilight is. I am far from home, off any path I have ever traveled to make it to the lake, and darkness is almost here.

I scramble to my feet and race for my sword before taking off in a full sprint toward the cave, toward June and the only home I have ever known. I race against my battered body. I race against time itself. I hope against hope that I win. My life and June's life depends on it.

Chapter 11

The muscles in my legs ache as I challenge them and clamber up the steep embankment I fell down earlier. I must push off with my toes while I use my hands to stabilize myself, digging into the loose earth with both. I am hungry and thirsty as well as drained of all strength, but I cannot stay where I am. I cannot let myself die. I need to get to June.

I move as quickly as I can and make it up the ridge. I do not slow as I glance quickly from one direction to the next. I must assess my position fast. Time is running out. I am uncertain of my exact location and am forced to choose without true consideration. I cannot survey the area and find my tracks to follow back. I am left to guess. I think of my father and wish he were with me. His face flashes in my mind's eye along with June's as I turn and race in the direction I hope is a familiar one, the one that leads back to the cave.

Day is surrendering to dusk and the sky is a pale shade of violet. It is a lovely color I have never seen before, and never want to see again, not alone in the middle of the woods as I am now.

I pump my arms as I run. Wind rushes in my face and is the only relief I feel. There is not a part of me that does not hurt. My heart is beating so fast I hear it echoing in my ears. Branches slash my arms and legs and vines tug at my feet as I run for my life. A stitch stings my ribs and demands that I slow, but slowing is not an option. I continue, my feet pacing my heart.

I pass a clustering of poisonous berry bushes and feel confident I have seen them before, that I saw them on my hike to the lake. The sight is welcome. It means I am heading in the right direction. Time still remains a problem though. The last rays of sunlight bleed around the horizon line as it is devoured by the landscape. As the sky deepens in color, the likelihood of me being swarmed by a pack of hungry Lurkers increases with it.

Panic has me in its grips. Trees reach with darkened, skeletal arms. I cannot tell which limbs belong to trees and which belong to something else entirely. I have slowed. So much time has passed, too much time.

I am getting close to home. I am approaching the small clearing at the outskirts of our cave. I try to run faster. Home is so close I can almost smell the mossy, piney scent that hangs heavily just outside the opening of the cave, the same scent I breathe in every morning. I want to breathe it again. I want to survive this night and many after it. I don't want to die.

I am only several hundred paces away from the cave when I see the first Lurker make its appearance. My pulse races frenziedly before spluttering to a near halt and plunging to my feet. It slinks from behind a spruce tree. I see its eyes first; it's deadly, closely set eyes. They are an eerie, iridescent color that glows against the darkening sky. It sees me, I am sure. I feel its lethal gaze trained on me, burning into my flesh. I do not know what to do. Lurkers hunt in large packs. My father told me that long ago, they were called wolves and used to walk on all fours and that their bodies had been shaped differently. Now they walk on two legs. And they are never alone. Their bodies look human in form, only with more muscles than I have ever seen a human have.

As I watch the Lurker, I realize I have slowed. Its glittering eyes are mesmeric, and also the reason it cannot hunt during daylight hours. They cannot handle bright light. I tear my gaze from it, terrified that it may strike suddenly, and look ahead. I see the cave. I see June standing outside it. She is looking at me. Thankfully, she is smart enough to be silent, to not call out to me. She knows they would descend on her if she were to do that.

I turn and run in the direction I just came from. I know it could be suicide, that if the half-formed plot I've hatched fails, I will be offering myself up to them readily. But I need to try. I need to do something to try to save us both. I slide under a bush and hold my breath, waiting, watching for the approach of Lurkers.

Lurkers are not bright animals by any means. They are incapable of speaking and higher cognitive functioning. The only thing that motivates them is hunger, constant and insatiable hunger. My father once said that their brains had not evolved at the same rate as their bodies. They are more cunning than Urhmen, but their intelligence does not compare to that of a human, or even an

Urthmen. I hope what my father has told me is accurate, that I am not just a meal beneath a bush waiting to be feasted on.

When I see ten sets of feet shuffle past me, my spirit is buoyed slightly. They have followed the trail they thought I took. But they will not follow for long. I keep this in mind as I slide from the bush and dart toward the cave.

I do not need to look back to know that they have turned back and are now behind me. I hear the swish of grass and brush beneath their feet as they lope after me with animal grace. Trees and bushes stir and I know more are joining in the hunt.

In the distance, I hear a sound, a low rolling that echoes through the trees. Faint at first, it grows louder fast, and more distinct. Like innumerable hooves beating the earth beneath it, the noise thrums through me in time with my heartbeat, a pounding that sounds as though hundreds of boarts are racing toward me. But I know that a stampede of boarts is not headed my way. I would welcome a herd of angry boarts over the bloodthirsty packs of Lurkers determined to tear me limb from limb.

I am afraid to turn and look behind me. I keep my eyes fixed straight ahead. I see June.

June is within my reach. I get to her in time to watch her eyes widen in terror before she dives inside the cave. I am squeezing through the narrow opening when I look up. My breath catches in my chest as I see them. Dozens of menacing shapes are visible, dozens of eyes glowing hungrily. Manes of golden hair that match the paleness of their gleaming eyes billow in the breeze and impressive paw-like feet with long, lethal talons tear at the ground with each stride they take, rushing toward the cave. They are monstrous, hideous beasts. And they are racing toward June and I.

I shove myself through the tight opening and begin shouting.

"Help me! Hurry up! Help me roll it now!" I bark orders at June.

She is as still as a stone for a brief moment.

"June!" I shriek.

Her body jars into action and she springs to her feet and begins pushing the boulder into place.

The beasts are so close I can see saliva dangling from their sizable jaws as I push the boulder with every last drop of strength I have. Terror rockets through me, jolting my system as if lightning has passed through my veins. The thunderous clatter of the Lurkers' approach grows deafening. They emit spine-tingling howls. The sight and sound of them is a nightmarish vision.

"Come on! Come on!" I cry as I clumsily wedge the first of several logs around the boulder. My hands shake violently and my legs feel as if they are made of sponge.

Though the sloped edges of the base of the logs are wedged beneath the boulder and the tops are flush against the wall of the cave, I feel faint resistance on the other side of the rock.

"Oh my gosh," June begins sobbing.

"No, no, no!" I exclaim. I use both feet and every ounce of will to live to hold the boulder still, to prevent the monsters from moving it before all the logs are in place. My back is pressed against the rough stone, straining. "June! Get the last wedged in now!" I shout. My voice is shrill and foreign to my own ears.

June does as she's told. The last log is fixed in place. I am reluctant to drop my legs. They tremble from nerves and effort.

The howling outside gives way to throaty hissing that curdles the blood inside me. The Lurkers are just outside the cave. One is attempting to push the boulder. It is trying to get inside.

My mind spirals in a thousand different directions. I do not know what to do. I know the opening of our cave is only big enough for one Lurker at a time so they can't all push at once. The logs wedged in place would be impossible to break. Still, I do not feel comforted by our defense. But there is nothing more I can do. I lower my knees and bring them to my chest. I collapse to the floor of the cave and take my head in my hands. The fate of my sister and me rests with stars I've never seen.

I feel every emotion I did not have the luxury of releasing well inside me, rising like floodwaters. The first tear that rains begins a deluge that cascade down my cheeks. I cannot remember the last time I cried in front of June. For once, I do not try to hide it. I do not feel weakened or embarrassed by my tears. I simply let them fall. My chest heaves and makes my whole body throb, but I do not deny myself this release. I glance at June and see that her eyes are round. She is undoubtedly stunned by everything she has seen and is seeing. I do not blame her. I am pretty shocked myself. I realize my appearance is likely contributing to her fright. A quick look at my hands reveals they are caked in filth of every sort. Dirt, blood and the eight-legged monster's sludgy gore is caked all over me from the neck down. My cheeks have likely been sliced by more branches and thorny limbs than I want to know about. I am a bloody fright, a fact that is not lost on June.

"Avery, what happened to you?" I am surprised June is not crying. Her voice trembles, but at least she isn't sobbing as I am. I wonder whether she is in shock.

I tell her what happened, about Will and his family, about the mother boart chasing me, about falling down the steep hill, about landing in the web, and about the eight-legged beast. I tell her everything in as much detail as I can remember. The days of withholding information are over.

Several times throughout my recollection, her hands cover her mouth and she gasps. The sounds are muffled, though. The yelping and hissing beyond our cave continues and drowns her out. We both keep looking to the boulder, half expecting Lurkers to burst through at any moment. I am trembling uncontrollably. The day's events have crashed over me with the force of a tidal wave and are pulling me down, sinking me.

When I finish recounting my day, when every last word has been choked out, I see that June is crying softly. She looks more frightened than ever before. Still, she is holding up better than I am.

"Those cuts and bruises look painful," June says gently.

I am surprised by how composed she sounds.

"They are," I mumble through sniffles.

June stands slowly and walks to the far corner of the cave. She moves several bags and retrieves a backpack. She brings the pack over to me then sits and begins riffling through it. She pulls gauze pads, bandages and a tube from it.

"Let's get you fixed up," she says and begins using the supplies my father risked his life to take from the village we used to live in.

He returned multiple times after the settlement had been sacked by Urthmen. He made dangerous trip after dangerous trip to stockpile as much medical supplies and clothing as he could. I am thankful that he did. They come in handy as June squeezes ointment from a tube directly onto the raw flesh of the skinless patch on my forearm.

I wince when the salve touches it.

"Sorry, Avery, I know it hurts," June says soothingly. Her hands shake as the baying beyond the boulder is accompanied by frenzied snarling and scraping. The sound chills me to my bones. "I don't know if this stuff is any good," she continues, her voice is as unsteady as her hands. "But I remember dad saying it used to be used to prevent infections."

"I remember him saying that too," I say and watch as she dresses my arm.

When it is wrapped, she looks up at me and says, "What are we going to do, Avery?"

I take a deep breath. I cannot imagine doing anything at present. Not with packs of bloodthirsty Lurkers howling just beyond our home. But I know I must plan for the future. I must think of tomorrow. The sun will rise again and drive the beasts back to their lairs.

"Tomorrow morning, we are going back to the lake to speak with Kate, Asher and Will. We will see if they have realized yet that they are not safe and hopefully they will come back with us."

"We? Us?" June picks up that I have included her in my plan to visit the lake.

"Yes, June," I say and look directly into her eyes. "I will never leave you here alone again."

"Are you serious?" June asks. Tears spill from her eyes.

"Yes," I reply. "I see now that it's even more dangerous to leave you by yourself. I've been wrong all along, thinking I've been protecting you from what is out there," I say. I am barely able to get the words out. My throat is thick and tight with emotion. "I've left you alone and scared," I say and use my fingertips to swipe beneath my eyes. It is useless to try to clear the steady stream of tears flowing. I don't know why I bother. I guess old habits are hard to break. Keeping my true feelings from June is another major mistake I have made along the way. Maybe she needs to see me for who I really am. Maybe she needs to see my tears, hear of my worries and fears. "I am so sorry, June," I say. A fresh set of sobs rack my body. I am sorry for leaving you here, scared and alone. I am sorry I tried to keep everything from you." I swallow hard.

"No, Avery," June says. "Don't you dare be sorry for doing what you thought was right. You were trying to protect me."

June throws her arms around my neck and squeezes. The hug, though physically painful, is the best feeling in the world. We hold each other for several moments. When June drops her arms, I allow mine to fall too.

The Lurkers continue their loud wailing. The sound claws at my insides like sharpened blades. The threat of violence quivering through the air is simply too much for me to handle.

"We're safe, right?" June asks. Her eyes are wide and pleading.

"I don't know," I answer honestly. "I don't know if we are safe here anymore."

I watch as June wrings her hands in front of her. "I know," she whispers.

"The Lurkers know we're in here now. They know where we are. And they will come back. They crave our flesh and blood," I say and my words make dread unlike any I have ever experienced slither down my spine. "Their hunger is what motivates them. It's only a matter of time before they figure out a way to get in."

Speaking the unabashed truth is harder than I thought it would be. June cries and my gut twists. Seeing her hurt and fearful and knowing I am responsible is difficult. The reality of our circumstances, the gravity of our situation, is harsh. I know now that she needs to be aware of it. I draw her into my arms and hold her tight.

"We may need to find a new place to live," I murmur into her hair. This makes her sob harder, but she needs to know. She needs to be prepared to make a change. She has lived in our cave for most of her life. A move would be a tremendous upheaval. But if it means our lives will be saved, she will have no other choice than to learn to accept it. "Maybe we will find a place with Will and his family," I say and stroke her hair.

"But where would we go?" June asks. "Where is safe?"

"I don't know, June," I reply. I wish I had an answer. I wish I knew of a place free of Urthmen and Lurkers and eight-legged fiends. I can't even imagine such a place. It is the stuff of daydreams, of whimsy. My father told me that once upon a time, the Earth was a place where dreams could come true, where monsters did not roam and Urthmen did not exist, where safety, food and shelter were things most people took for granted. I cannot envision the world as he said it was. But I would do just about anything to travel back in time, to see June safe and free.

I do not let go of June as the night wears on. I rest her head against my shoulder and cup my hand over her ear, trying to block out the awful sound of the Lurkers calls. We doze off and on for short periods of time throughout the night, all the while we wish for the infernal racket to end, we wish for peace.

Chapter 12

I open my eyes and see that sunlight sifts through tiny crevices around the boulder. The sight, along with the silence it brings with it, is welcome. I blink several times. My eyes are puffy and bleary from crying and spending much of the night awake. June is slumped across me with her head on my lap and my legs are numb. I napped lightly while sitting exactly where I am while Lurkers scratched and cried out just outside our cave.

I give June a gentle shake. I need her to wake. We have a long trip ahead of us. We will both be exhausted, I am sure, but we have to go. We have to convince Will and his parents that they are in danger.

"June," I whisper and jiggle her shoulders. "June," I try a little louder.

She wakes with a start and her head rockets up. "They've pushed in the boulder!" she gasps. Her eyes are darting from one side to the next.

"No, no, June," I say and rub her back. "We are okay. It is morning. They are gone," I try to calm her. "The Lurkers are gone for now."

"Oh gosh," she breathes, still rattled. "We made it through the night?" she asks more than says. "Yes, we did," I tell her. "And now we will take our trip."

A slow smile spreads across her cheeks.

"But before we go anywhere, we need to wash and eat."

"That sounds like a good idea. Especially since *some* of us need to wash more than others," she says and crinkles her nose at me.

A hysterical chuckle surges and brims unexpectedly. My nerves are frayed and it takes effort to subdue it.

"Who? Me?" I ask with pretend confusion.

June nods and twists her mouth to one side to suppress a giggle. She seems to be afflicted with the same panic-induced humor as me.

"Are you saying I don't look my best?" I ask and maintain put-on cluelessness.

A giggle slips from June's lips. "Yes, that's exactly what I'm saying," she says just before she doubles over laughing.

"Hey!" I say with exaggerated offense. "How rude!"

"I'm doing you a favor," June says between chuckles. "You can't let that family by the lake see you looking like that," she adds and points at my dirty clothes and matted hair.

"What do you mean? I look fabulous," I say in a silly voice.

June snorts then her laughter starts anew. "I-I don't know, Avery," she says between pants. "Would *Will*, that boy who looks your age, like the way you look right now?"

I do not respond. The mere mention of Will makes my stomach feel filled with insects, all beating their wings at once.

June does not notice that I have gone quiet. She keeps teasing me. "In fact, if he saw you now, he would probably run away," she says and continues to laugh.

I take her words lightly. She is right, after all. I would probably run from me if I were to see myself as I look now.

"All right, wise guy," I shake my head and say. "That's enough. I get it. I'm gross. Now let's go to the river and get clean already."

I stand sluggishly. Movement causes pain in varying degrees of severity to explode throughout my body. I groan involuntarily. The surge of twinges is overwhelming.

June's smile dissolves. "Avery, let me help you," she says and springs to her feet. She cups my elbow with one hand and pulls me up with the other.

"Thanks," I say as I straighten my posture. "I'm okay."

I hobble to the logs and begin dragging them away. Though I know Lurkers sleep during the day, a part of me fears we will move the boulder and come face to face with the wide-mouthed muzzle of one of them. I try to force the worry to the back of my brain. We need to wash, eat and leave as soon as possible. I do not want a repeat of last night. I expect that they will be at our cave again tonight, but I do not want to lay eyes on a Lurker ever again as long as I live. I shudder just seeing their vicious faces in my mind's eye.

June rushes to my side to help. We clear the logs then roll the boulder to the side. I peek out of the cave before taking a tentative step forward. My eyes sweep the surrounding area. I do not see any

Lurkers, but I smell them. The acrid stench of their urine fills the air and replaces the mossy, piney scent that normally greets me when I leave my home. The Lurkers have ruined it. They have marked the territory. I fear the act guarantees their return.

June pinches her nose. "Ugh! It stinks out here. What is that smell?" she asks.

"Pee," I tell her. "The Lurkers have peed all around the cave. They've marked where we are so they can track the scent."

"And come back," June says somberly.

"Yes," I whisper. "I think they will be back."

June's eyes shine with unshed tears. I feel like crying as well. But I do not dare. I do not want my eyes to swell more than they already have. I blink back the moisture feverishly.

"Come on," I say and grip her hand. "Let's go get ourselves clean. I don't want to send the whole family scattering," I say and try to remind her of her joke earlier.

She smiles feebly and nudges my arm with her shoulder.

We make our way to the river. The cool water feels good against most of my cuts and bruises. I begin removing the bandages from my arm. As I peel away the gauze pad, I see how raw and angry looking the tender flesh there is, the part that had skin torn from it when I pulled my arm free from the web. I splash water on it and wince as soon as droplets touch the wound. But I must clean it as best I can despite the agony it causes me. I do not know what poison the spidery beast had running through its veins. I was forced to spend the night with its vile fluid seeping into my pores. I do not want it on me a moment longer. I scrub my skin, all but the wound, with spongy moss until it is a rosy pink. I scrub my scalp with my fingertips then comb my fingers through the knots.

When I feel sufficiently purged of the web ordeal from the day before, I dress and make my way back to the cave. June follows and is carrying an aloe leaf. Before we eat, she cracks opens the fleshy gray-green leaf, careful to avoid its serrated edges and small white teeth. She holds the opened side over my wound and allows its clear contents to trickle over the inflamed skin then wraps it in a loose dressing.

"What about the ointment?" I ask her. "Shouldn't we use it?"

"No. That is for cuts more serious than this," she says and points to my forearm. "Remember, dad said the stuff in the tube is rare."

"Yes," I say and nod. "That's right. You're right."

I am so proud of how calm and mature June has behaved. For the second time, she has bandaged my arm and not recoiled from it. I realize that perhaps I have underestimated her for too long. She is handling the discovery of Urthmen not far from us in the forest and the Lurkers marking our cave with their urine for an all but guaranteed return with more composure than I ever thought she possessed.

"I'll get us the leftover boart meat while you check on the rest of your cuts and scrapes," she says with a tight smile then turns and sets about unrolling the strip of leather the cooked meat is packed in.

The meat is two days old, but June trimmed the thick chunks to thin slices and hung them on a tree branch. When they'd turned dark and wrinkly, she placed them in the leather. My dad once told us about preserving meat this way, but we never tried. The idea of leaving meat overnight seemed too dangerous. That danger seems trivial now in light of all we've been through.

Still, I hope we do not get sick from the dried boart meat as I inspect the gashes and bruises that litter my skin. There are too many to count and range in color from purplish-red to bluish-black. Now that I am clean, their colors are pronounced against my pale skin. I find myself hoping that Will is not revolted by my battered appearance. It should not matter, I know. I am not going to the lake to be on display. I am going to make a final attempt to urge his family to leave, to join us. But a part of me that I do not quite understand can't resist hoping he is not disgusted by me.

After a deep breath, I forego braiding my curly blonde hair that falls to the middle of my back as I usually do. I allow it to cascade over my shoulders in hopes it will hide some of the more obvious welts on my upper body. I turn toward June. She has set out two crinkly, unappealing looking strips of dried meat ready for me to eat.

"Wow, Avery. I forgot how pretty you look with your hair down," June says.

My cheeks warm. "Thank you," I say. "I'm sure I will braid it once the sun is high, but figured I'd take your advice and try to hide some of my ugly bruises."

June's chest puffs out a bit. She smiles wisely. "Good. I'm glad," she says and hands me my breakfast. "Now let's eat and get over there."

The excitement in her voice is obvious. I can understand why. I am feeling as if countless bubbles are bursting inside me. It amazes me that the night we had has not dulled our ability to feel enthusiasm, to feel hopeful. But we do.

We dress in clean clothes and leave.

June is excited as we walk. Her excitement radiates from her brightly and rivals the sun's sickly rays that barely dribble from behind a bank of tattered gray clouds. She has a bounce to her step. She does not seem to want to stop chatting either. She has so many questions about the family, questions I do not have answers for. I find it hard to concentrate and am only partially listening. My focus is elsewhere, preoccupied with every branch that shifts or leaf that turns. I search the woods for Urthmen, for boarts, and for webs made by giant spidery monsters. My hand does not leave my spear at my back. Anything could be stalking June and I at this point. I am nervous, jumping at every snap or crackle of wood. June seems unbothered by my edginess. She is likely oblivious of it. She tells me what she will say when she meets Kate, Asher, Oliver, Riley and Will.

At mention of Will's name, my ears prickle and I tune in. But she only brings him up in passing. My focus returns to the surrounding forest. The trees and bushes are bustling, teeming with critters I never bothered to notice. Sounds of life abound. They could easily dampen the sound of footsteps and I find myself feeling more vulnerable than usual. Perhaps it is because June is with me or perhaps it is because I know that these woods are overrun by Lurkers when the sun goes down. Maybe the presence of Urthmen has destroyed any semblance of relaxed awareness I hunted and hiked with, or maybe it is the fact that there are monsters like the eight-legged creature I was almost eaten by roaming about that I have yet to see. Maybe it is all of the above, conspiring together. Regardless, I am more anxious than normal. I do not feel the least bit safe. And now June is with me, the person I worry about most.

Time passes quickly and we reach the stubby plant I have come to know and kind of like on the outskirts of the lake. I crouch behind it and invite June to do the same.

"Oh Avery, I'm so nervous," June says as she squeezes her hands together.

Her words echo my exact sentiments. Ordinarily I would not say as much. But things are different now. I do not hold back.

"Me too," I say. "Every time I have come here, I feel like I am going to puke. I get so jittery," I admit.

"Really?" June looks at me incredulously. "I didn't know that."

"There's a lot about me you don't know, I suppose," I tell her and feel a pang of regret. "I kept it all to myself for so long."

I lower my eyes to the ground below. June reaches out and takes my hand. She gives it a gentle squeeze.

"You don't have to do that," she says.

"I know," I answer and wonder when exactly it was that she transformed and became this grown-up.

She lets go of my hand and her eyes lock on the lake. I hear a high-pitched voice, the voice of a young child, then see Riley trot out of the cave.

"Get ready, June," I say. "You're about to see humans for the first time, other than me and dad, of course. Well, at least the only people you remember seeing," I qualify my statement quickly. "Take a look," I say and stand up.

June stands beside me. Her gaze travels down the gentle slope of the hill we stand on. The broadest smile I have ever seen her wear stretches across her face when she sees Riley, followed by Oliver and Kate, make her way to the lake. Riley dips her toe in the water and Oliver comes up behind her. He shoves her playfully and her entire leg is submerged. She squeals and a sound catches in June's throat.

I stop watching June from the corner of my eye. I face her. And what I see makes my breathing hitch.

June's eyes are moist. But for once, she is not upset. Her eyes are glazed with tears of joy. They overflow her lower lashes and trickle down her cheeks, glistening like morning dew on the petal of a flower. I hear Will's voice. But I cannot take my eyes off June. She looks so content. I have never seen her look as she does now. I wish she could feel this way always. I wish I could freeze this moment in time. Seeing my sister, the only person I love on this planet, experience joy, pure unadulterated joy, is a gift I will not soon forget.

I continue to watch June then suddenly, I see her smile disappear. Her eyes widen and a mask of terror replaces her blissful features. My head immediately spins toward the family, toward what she is seeing. And when I do, my heart stops beating.

I see more than a dozen Urthmen. They are clutching their clubs. Their thin lips are pulled back over their pointed teeth as they streak with impossible speed toward Will and his family.

"No!" I scream. My voice rips through the forest. "They're here! Will look out! They're here!"

Will looks up. He is watching me and I am pointing to the approaching Urthmen weaving through the trees that border the lake.

Will and the others look up, but by the time they see what I see it is too late. Will starts shouting words I cannot hear over the pounding of my pulse in my head. Asher turns to grab a spear and a nearby rock and Kate unsheathes a blade from her thigh.

"Oh no, oh no," June is repeating beside me.

I grip her by her shoulder. "June!" Her eyes are unfocused. I worry she is in shock. I shake her. "June! Please! I need you to get under that bush and hide. Do not come out until I come to get you. Do you understand me?" I ask. "They haven't seen you. You need to hide while I go help Will and his family." My words come out quickly, quicker than I can think.

"No, Avery," June finally says. "No. Don't leave me. Please, you said you wouldn't leave me again."

She is right. But I have to help. I cannot sit by while another family is slaughtered.

"I have to go," is all I have time to say.

Understanding flickers in June's terrified eyes and I hope I never have to see the look of defeat, the brokenness in her gaze, ever again.

June scurries beneath the lowest branches of the bristly bush and tucks her limbs within it until she is no longer visible. I race toward the lake.

As I rush, all sense of time and space leaves me. My legs feel disconnected from the rest of me and the sounds of the forest fall silent. I only hear the rush of my blood behind by ears and feel the weight of my weapons on my body.

Ahead I see Will hefting a large rock. He is at the perimeter of the lake, where the Urthmen are pouring through, and catches one midstride. He smashes the rock against the Urthmen's misshaped head and sends the unsuspecting attacker reeling backward with his face split open. Will does not waste time. As soon as the Urthmen falls to the ground, he finishes him off with the stone. He then rips the club the Urthmen carried and turns to face the two more that are upon him.

My attention is pulled from Will to the smaller children. Three Urthmen are descending on them. I need to get to them. I need to help. Oliver is only a few years older than June yet he is attempting to defend his sister, Riley. He is armed with only a stick that he just picked up. It is not sufficient to protect himself with, much less his sister.

I am less than fifty strides away but realize I will never make it in time to help. Oliver will be pummeled to death, as will Riley. I make a split-second decision and draw my spear. I launch it midstride and watch without slowing as it pierces the air with a soft whistle just before it plunges in the center of the Urthmen closest to Oliver.

The Urthmen's head whips in my direction and for a moment, he is stunned silent. He sees the lance sticking out of him and wails in agony. He drops to the ground just as I reach Riley and Oliver.

I pull my sword from my scabbard and clutch it with two hands. When the next Urthmen advances, I cleave the air. The metal meets flesh and I see that my strike has landed at his neck. I follow through with the swing, bringing my blade down until it does not move any longer. I pull it free with a grunt. The Urthmen is opened from his collarbone to his navel. But I do not stop to watch him die. Two more are coming at me.

"Run!" I shout to Riley and Oliver, but they do not budge. They are frozen in place. I have no choice but to shield them with my body. I will not let them die.

The pair of Urthmen rushing me swipes their clubs at me. I dodge both blows with dexterity I never knew I had, especially since my entire body trembles so hard it is a wonder I am even able to stand. But I not only stand, I fight. I feel as if the Urthmen are moving at a slower speed than I am, that I can see their actions with razor-sharp clarity and anticipate what they will do next as plainly as if they were my own thoughts.

When the Urthmen closest hefts his club overhead to skull me, I drive my sword through his throat then yank it free and turn on the other alongside him. His arms are at one side and his torso is twisted. His midsection is unprotected, and is now my target. With a cry that comes from somewhere deep inside my core, I grit my teeth and ram my sword straight through his gut then wrench it free. The Urthmen calls out words I have rarely heard; words my dad called swear words. He then drops his club and clutches his stomach. As he falls to his knees, I bring my blade up and slash his throat.

My movements, though brutal, are necessary. I do not regret them any more than I regret breathing or eating. They are fluid and natural. They are what I have trained my whole life for. But despite my training, I realize that the ease with which I can kill and the swiftness of my reflexes are special skills. I understand why my father had always been so shocked by my abilities, why he praised what he called my 'gift.' I always thought he was just complimenting me to get me to train harder. But I know now that he was simply sharing his thoughts about what he saw. Fighting is instinctive to me. It feels as if it is what I was born to do, that ridding the world of the hideous Urthmen is my purpose.

A flurry of movement in my periphery jerks my attention from the Urthmen I have killed to Will. He is battling two that stormed him. I contemplate helping him, but am intercepted by my own set of Urthmen. They both attack simultaneously. I sidestep the first club but am unable to avoid the second. A club catches me squarely in the arm. I cry out and evade a swipe intended for my head. I twist and cut through air and slice open the arm of the Urthmen that hit me then immediately sink my sword into the other's heart. But as I am retrieving my sword, a shadow crowds from behind. My short life flickers before my eyes in quick, disjointed flashes. And in a fraction of a second, I know I am about to meet my end, that it is too late for me to react. I squeeze my eyes shut and brace for the blow of a club to strike my head but snap them open when I hear a scream, the scream of a young boy. I spin and instead of having my skull cracked open, I see a spear tip protruding from the Urthmen's chest, my spear tip.

The Urthmen falls and I see Oliver. He is shaking and his breathing is short and shallow. He pulled my spear from the Urthmen I killed, the one that was about to butcher he and Riley, and used it to save my life.

"Thanks," I say to Oliver. But Oliver's eyes are round and his mouth is partially agape as he looks over my shoulder.

I turn and see that Will has taken down one of the Urthmen he was fighting and struggles with the other on the ground. I look toward their parents and my gaze zeroes in on what has caused Oliver's look of horror.

"No!" I scream as I see Kate on the ground. An Urthmen swings his club overhead and drops it against her head, pounding her skull again and again. "No! Kate!" I hear myself screaming, but my voice sounds as if it is echoing from the end of a long tunnel.

Oliver is crying and mumbling words that, while not entirely intelligible, are familiar. I am sure I have muttered them before because I have lived through what Oliver has just witnessed. I want to hug him, but there isn't time. Asher, Oliver's father, has just killed one, but two more Urthmen are just about on him. I take off at a sprint to help.

"Hey! Over here!" I shout to distract at least one of the Urthmen. But they do not look up at me. Their gazes are fixed on Asher. One wields the knife Kate used earlier in addition to his club while the other circles around, behind Asher. I just about reach them when the Urthen strike instantaneously. One grabs Asher from behind while the other drives the dagger into the center of his chest. Asher falls to his knees, an expanding circle of garnet staining his shirt.

"No!" I hear Will scream, his voice tears through my veins and echoes through my soul. I look to him and watch as he attacks the Urthmen he was fighting against with reckless ferocity, ignoring the possibility of being hit himself and boldly stepping forward, swinging the club ceaselessly. The club smashes the Urthmen over and over until he collapses to the ground in a pulpy heap. Will does not stop though. He charges toward the two that just killed his parents. I meet him there and fight beside him to avenge his parents' deaths inasmuch as any death can truly be avenged.

Will's eyes are wild and his pulse darts at the base of his throat. I feel his fury. I feel his anger and sorrow, the anguish coursing through his body like lifeblood. I remember it. I know it well. It is a dark and ever-present companion of mine. I let it fuel me and drive my sword as I carve the air horizontally and behead the putrid Urthmen nearest. Will waves the club expertly and bashes one of the last two remaining until he is reduced to a bundle of unrecognizable features. But while Will vents some of his overwhelming suffering on the fallen Urthmen, another reaches him before I do and hits him in the back. Will tumbles forward, but before the Urthmen who raided him from behind can strike again, I drive my blade through him. The Urthmen falls to the ground. I have killed the last of them that stormed the family at the lake. But I do not feel satisfaction of any kind that they are all dead. Will parents were lost. There is nothing to celebrate.

Will staggers to his parents' bodies and drops to his knees and for the first time, I hear another human being's heart cry out. Through sobs, Will says over and over, "Mom, dad, no, please no."

My breathing snags several times before I begin to cry too. I know I do not have the right to cry, but I am powerless to stop the tears from falling.

Riley and Oliver join Will. Their small bodies shudder as they weep. No one should have to see what they just saw. No one should have to live through what they just lived through. Through my tears, I silently vow that if I ever find another family, I will do anything and everything in my power to preserve it. The core of humanity is family. Whether they are people we are born to or people we embrace along the way, family is the crux of human life. And I will defend it with every last drop of blood that pumps through my body.

Armed with my newfound resolve, I turn and allow Will, Oliver and Riley time to grieve. I set about checking each fallen Urthmen for any signs of life. I plunge my sword in all of them for good measure. I will not take any chances. I will not risk any of them surviving.

When I have completed my task, I call to June.

"June," I say.

But June does not reply.

"June," I try again a bit louder.

But still, she does not reply. I do not hear her shuffle or see the woods stir. I do not hear a sound, in fact, apart from the soft whimpers coming from Will and his surviving family.

Panic sets in.

I race toward the bush June was stashed beneath, and when I get there, my insides crystallize and my heart stops beating in my chest.

An Urthmen has a handful of June's hair and holds the tip of my spear just below her ear at her throat. Will runs up beside me. I see him from the corner of my eye.

"Drop your weapons, or I will kill her," the Urthmen orders.

"Please," I begin to beg. "She's just a child."

"I said drop your weapons, humans!" the Urthmen shouts.

There isn't a doubt in my mind that he will kill her regardless of whether I drop my weapon or not. He will kill us all if given the chance. June will die no matter what. I must do something. I will not let the Urthmen kill her.

My mind scrambles for a plan.

I look off to the right of the Urthmen, just past him. "What are you waiting for?" I say to no one. "Kill him! Cut his head off!"

The Urthmen turns around to look behind him, and when he does, I only have seconds to act. I pull my dagger from its sheath and hurl it at him. It tumbles through the air end over end, and when he turns back to look at me, my blade lodges into his eye. He releases June and my spear and drops to his knees shrieking.

June dives into my arms. I hug her tightly and mumble, "Urthmen are as stupid as dad said they were."

But June is uninterested in anything I have to say. Who can blame her? Will finishes off the Urthmen and hands me my dagger just before his brother and sister rush to him. They huddle and cry. June is crying and silent tears stream down my cheeks as well.

All of us have seen too much violence, too much death and destruction. We have been left to fend for ourselves and survive against impossible odds. But as I look around at our blended group, I feel an odd glimmer of hope spark inside of me. I don't know when or how, but I believe for the first time in my life that we will someday overcome the carnage and cruelty we were born into.

Chapter 13

I watch as Will transforms before my eyes. I know he is grieving, that he is hurting in a way that cannot be expressed aptly. But I see the change he is undergoing. His posture straightens. He extends his long, sculpted arms to Oliver and Riley. They rush to him, fall into him, and he envelops them. I see cords of muscle bunch and flex as he embraces them tightly. The black sleeveless shirt he wears dampens from their tears. He whisks away his own tears with the back of his hand then turns and looks toward June and I. His light blue-green irises glow brighter than when I saw them the day before. Their color pales further against the reddened whites of his eyes. His gaze locks on me and the air suddenly leaves my lungs. I don't know why I feel as I do and hope I am not falling ill. I give him a small smile and watch as the sun kissed skin at his cheekbones deepens in color. I worry that I have embarrassed him by witnessing the raw emotions flowing between him and his siblings, or that perhaps my smile was misunderstood somehow.

I turn so that I am no longer facing Will and his brother and sister. I do not want to intrude on the very painful, emotional moment he is sharing with them. I also know that he is in the process of assuming a new role, that part of his change includes surrendering any semblance of a childhood or any shred of youth he ever held. He is in charge now. He is the person Oliver and Riley will turn to. And he knows it. He is being strong for them, comforting them and putting on a brave face when he is sadder and more terrified than he has ever been in his life.

I just met Will, but I know him better than he thinks. I know exactly what he is doing, what he is going through. I have done and been through it myself. I wish I could make it easier for him. Losing a parent is bad enough. But watching them lose their life is quite another experience, a horrendous one that will be branded in his memory forever.

"I feel so bad for them," June whispers to me. "What they went through, it's just awful."

June does not recall our mother being murdered by Urthmen while we watched. She only remembers our father's gentle passing. She is lucky. I can close my eyes and relive it all.

I do not share that detail with her. Instead, I reply, "Me too." Then add, "It is a terrible thing to watch your parents die," with sadness so profound it causes my voice to falter. "We will help them though," I say. "We will take them back to our cave with us and figure out a plan. But no matter what, we will help them." I rub June's back softly and she leans into me. But her head whips toward Will and his siblings when Oliver's voice rings out.

"No! I won't calm down! Those monsters killed mom and dad!" Oliver nearly shouts then breaks away from Will and Riley. He races to the Urthmen that just held June and threatened to kill her with my spear and begins kicking the corpse. "I hate you! I hate you all!" he cries. Spittle sprays from his mouth. He is sobbing and yelling at the same time. He turns and picks up a good-sized stone. He hoists it over his head.

But before he brings it crashing against the dead Urthmen's lopsided head, Will closes the distance between them quickly and circles his arms around Oliver, pinning his arms to his waist. The stone tumbles from his grip and lands on the ground by his feet.

"It's okay, Oliver," Will says soothingly. "Just calm down. Everything is going to be okay."

Oliver's lower lip begins to quiver and tears pour from his eyes. "Nothing is okay, Will," he barely manages then turns and buries his face in Will's midsection.

"I know, I know," Will says and holds his brother tightly. Pain is etched in his features. Everything he is feeling is visible just below the surface of his expression. I see it plainly and resist the urge to go to him and throw my arms around him, just as he is doing with Oliver. My muscles twitch, urging me to take the first step toward him without my mind's permission, but a gentle squeeze at my hand holds me back.

June's small hand grips mine firmly for a moment then releases it. I wonder whether she sensed my movement and guessed what I was about to do, or whether seeing firsthand what Will is going through with his brother and sister is giving her insight into what life has been like for me. Either way I stay where I am and wait until the crying subsides before reminding everyone that we need to leave immediately. About a dozen Urthmen stormed Will's family. I doubt they were acting alone. More will follow. I do not want to chance being ambushed out in the open as we are now.

I clear my throat. "Uh, Will, I'm sorry to, uh, interrupt, but we need to leave as soon as possible." Will trains his aquamarine eyes on me and an odd quiver passes through my belly. "They know we're here," I say of the Urthmen. "There will be more. The ones at the lake might even be part of a bigger team that split up. They could be on us at any minute."

Will's dark brows gather. His gaze hardens. "No," he says resolutely.

His refusal throws me almost as much as his expression.

"No?" I feel my features scrunch as they showcase my complete confusion.

"No!" he says heatedly.

Blood rushes to my face and I am certain it is the color of a crimson rose petal. "What do you mean no?" I ask and blink back the hot, unexpected tears searing the backs of my eyelids. Does he have a sudden death wish? And why does he seem so angry with me? Each cell in my body is firing at once. I do not know what he will say next, whether he will shout at me or speak sharply to me again. I do not know why I care if he does or doesn't, but I do.

"I am not leaving my parents here," he says softly. He features have smoothed. He no longer looks as he did seconds earlier. He looks vulnerable.

I feel the color drain from my cheeks.

"I won't leave them here for Urthmen to take and put their heads on spikes," he continues and speaks through his teeth. "Or leave them here to be devoured by the creatures that come out at night."

"The Lurkers," I practically spit when I mumble their name under my breath angrily.

"The what?" Will shocks me by asking.

He heard me. My head feels engulfed in flames. I don't know the technical name for the beasts that roam the woods when the sun sets. I know what they were once called. And I know what my father called them, what I still call them.

I take my bottom lip between my teeth and shift uncomfortably under the weight of Will's stare. "We call them Lurkers," I say and nod.

"Lurkers?" Will asks and I wait for him to mock the name, to mock me.

"Yes," I say and twist the hem of my shirt with the hand that does not hold June's hand. I am waiting for him to tell me how idiotic the name is, how babyish and laughable it is. I brace for it when he parts his lips to speak.

"Huh, makes sense, Lurkers," he nods. "They're always out there in the night, lurking and waiting," he says.

I nod, awkward silence hangs in the air like a bank of fog.

"What do you call them?" June's voice chimes like a bell when she asks. She has not seen or spoken to another human being besides myself and my father in her entire life, yet she has better social skills than I do. "Did you have a name for them?"

Will smiles the saddest smile I have ever seen. His eyes are focused on a distant point. "My mom and dad called them Prowlers," he says with a hollow, cheerless chuckle.

"Sounds as if they thought like our dad used to think," June says with respect in her voice that exceeds her eight years of life by decades.

Will's gaze leaves its far-off focal point and lands directly on June before flickering to me. "Your dad is not with you?"

I am unsure of whom he has asked, but I answer anyway. "He passed last year," I say and feel guilty for the strain in my voice, because while we did lose him, his death was a serene passing compared to the butchery Will and his brother and sister just saw.

"I'm sorry," Will says with genuine remorse. "What about your mom, is she," he hesitates for several beats, "alive?"

I swallow hard. I do not know how to answer his question without upsetting an already sensitive and sore situation. I stare into the distance. I take a deep breath then hear the words spill from me freely, gushing like blood from an open wound. "She was killed by Urthmen. She was pregnant and running with me and June in a tunnel beneath a village we used to live in with our parents and they killed her right in front of us," I say in one breath. I see it again, see the brutality in my mind's eye as if it is happening in front of me a second time. "She begged them not to, *begged them*, but they showed her no mercy. They did not care one bit. She was nothing to them. They killed her. June was a baby and I was holding her. I saw it all. I saw them beat her to death."

I have let go of June's hand. My fists are clenched tightly at my sides and my breathing is short and shallow. I look up and see Will is speechless and so is June. I have never spoken of what happened the night our mother was murdered. I have held it inside me for years, bearing the burden of an unspeakable scar alone; until now. Now was the most inappropriate time ever to suddenly feel the need to share, and I hadn't wanted to. The words rushed from me as if of their own accord. I have had time to grieve. Will, Oliver and Riley have not. Their parents were both just murdered right in front of them and they are reeling from loss and shock. And I had the audacity to blurt out my sad story! Perhaps it has been for the best that I haven't met another human being in some time, for their best, that is. I wish the earth would swallow me whole, or that I could disappear, disperse like grains of sand in the wind. But I cannot do either. I am stuck, left to stew in my embarrassing outburst.

Just when I feel as if I will die of shame, Will says, "I am so sorry, Avery."

I want to shout that I am the one who is sorry, that he does not owe me words of consolation. It is quite the opposite. I have been through what he is going through and because of that, I should have known better than to open my big mouth. I cringe and shake my head slightly. His eyes are on me, and he sees it. I know he does. He sees how mortified I am. June wraps both arms around my waist. My body is slick with sweat and she feels like a hot rock plastered against me. But I do not dare move. I will not take the lead yet.

"We are going to go and bury my parents," Will says solemnly.

"Would you like us to help?" June offers. "Or would you like privacy?"

Again, I am astounded by her poise and tact. She grows more amazing with each minute that passes. I realize I have so much to learn from her.

Will smiles at June tightly. "Thank you for offering to help, but I think Oliver and I can handle it. But if Riley wants to stay with you, can she?" he asks.

"Absolutely," June answers brightly without missing a beat.

Will turns to face Riley. "Would you like to stay here with Avery and June?" he asks. "Oliver and I are going back to the lake. We have to take care of mom and dad's remains," he adds.

Riley's eyes are wide and frightened. "I-I don't want to see them as they are now. I want to see them how they used to look," she sniffles and says through tears. "But I want to stay with you."

"Then I will carry you and cover your eyes and you can wait in the cave while we work," Will says tenderly. "Whatever you need me to do I'll do, okay?"

Riley bobs her head and lifts her arms to him. Will scoops her up. "We won't be too long," he says before turning and going back to the lake.

When he is a far enough distance away and out of earshot, I drop my arms then slap my hand against my forehead. "I can't believe what a jerk I was," I say with a groan.

"Avery, I don't think what you said upset him. If anything, knowing he's not alone will help him."

I hadn't thought of that possibility. I just assumed that my blabbing would have nothing but negative effects all around. And while I am not totally convinced of June's theory, I find it helpful.

"Maybe," I say with the exact amount of uncertainty I feel. "Still, I can't believe I said all that. I mean, talk about terrible timing," I shake my head and add.

"Yeah, well, maybe the timing would have been better if you waited until later or tomorrow, but as I said before, I think you did more good than harm," June says.

I am astounded and impressed by her wisdom. "June, are you sure you're only eight?" I ask in another unfiltered, random bout of blather.

June giggles. It is a sweet sound that reminds me of when she was little.

I smile at her. "After all you went through yesterday, last night and today, I am amazed by how well you are holding up," I admit honestly.

With shining eyes in a powdery-blue shade that rivals the sky on a clear day, she tips her chin and looks directly at me. "I had a really great role model who taught me to deal with what life throws at me."

"Yeah, dad was pretty great, wasn't he?" I say and think of how levelheaded he always was, how calm and in control he remained at all times.

"I am talking about you!" she says and smacks me on my arm lightly. She stomps her foot then places both hands on her hips. "Sheesh, don't you even know how to take a compliment?" she asks me exasperatedly.

I am taken back by what she has said. "Me? I'm the role model you're talking about?"

"Yes, you dope! Who else would I be talking about? I was looking right at you," she says and throws her hands in the air. They land against her thighs with a slapping sound.

"First of all, where the heck did you get your temper from? And second of all, uh, I thought you were talking about dad because I am not half the role model he was. I kept everything bottled up forever, remember? I was too afraid to tell you anything," I say then add, "and I am not a dope."

I wait for June to erupt and unleash the last few days' worth of fear and anger on me. But she does not. In fact, her face is serene.

"You're right," June says. Every bit of fire in her voice is extinguished. "You are not a dope. Not at all, in fact. You are smart and strong and an amazing hunter and an even more amazing fighter. You can do anything you set your mind to, Avery. And you take good care of me. All those things make you someone to look up to, the person I look up to and want to be like."

My throat tightens and my eyes burn again. But this time they are not tears born of sadness or shame, anger or frustration. This time, they are tears of gratitude, and pride.

"Thank you," I say in an unsteady voice.

"No," June says. "Thank you."

I allow a moment to pass between us as I blink feverishly and try to keep from crying.

"My pleasure," I barely manage.

June smiles broadly then turns toward the lake. I take a moment to compose myself and at the same time, scan the woods for any sign of Urthmen. All seems quiet for now, but the day is slipping from us. I did not realize so much time had passed. Will and his brother and sister have been gone for a while and June and I have been talking for quite some time. Time feels as though it is ticking faster than ever. We need to leave as soon as possible. We need to hurry if we want to make it to the cave before the Lurkers come out.

"It looks like they are almost done down there," June says quietly.

I breathe a silent sigh of relief. I do not mean to be disrespectful in my thoughts, but the world we live in does not provide us time for anything. We are always running from something horrible, hoping we are headed toward something that will bring us comfort and solace. Moments of peace are rare and precious. And they do not last long.

Will, Oliver and Riley head up the hill with some of their belongings. Their moment has ended, and a new one begins.

"Are you ready?" I ask Will when he is before me.

"I guess so," he replies after a deep breath.

I want to reach out and touch his arm and tell him he is, that he will be okay, that his brother and sister will make it through this. But now is not the time, and standing in the middle of the woods where Urthmen just struck is certainly not the place.

"All right then you guys can just follow us," I say with a weak smile and wave them on.

We walk and backtrack the trail June and I traveled to get to the lake. Our pace is brisk and I notice that Will is as vigilant as I am. His eyes sweep the landscape continually. The forest is filled with ordinary sounds. Birds flit from treetop to treetop. Leaves rustle, and squirrels and chipmunks scurry across our paths. The only added sound is the pleasant lilt of June's voice as she tries to make conversation with Oliver and Riley.

"Our cave is not huge or anything. It is cozy. And Avery and I have candles made from beeswax that we use at night. She usually leaves them lit until I fall asleep," I hear her say.

I strain to watch Will from the corner of my eye. A tiny smile pulls at the corners of his mouth. His smile becomes contagious. I feel a similar one begin making its way across my lips. June has a charm about her that I never knew existed. And how could I have? We've been isolated for her entire life. Her gift has been kept under wraps. Now, though, as we walk and I hear her working her magic on Oliver and Riley, getting them to respond with tones that are remarkably upbeat considering their circumstances, I am blown away by her. She is my new role model in that regard. I will look to her when hoping for pointers on how to win them over and help them.

We continue at our hurried speed and June continues to captivate Will's brother and sister with her magnetic personality. She has described our cave inside and out, has told them about the river we go to every morning and her incident with the boart that led to my incident with the mother boart. I notice she is careful to leave out the part about me getting entangled and almost eaten by the spidery monster and the Lurkers that we barely escaped. Neither Oliver nor Riley need to hear a story as disturbing as the one that unfolded last night. Even I would prefer not to hear it. The memory is just too frightening to relive.

When we reach what I believe is the halfway point of our journey, I slow and take a quick glance at the children. The conversations have ended and the three of them look tired. I look to Will then them and take my cue from his expression.

"I don't know about everyone else but I need to stop and rest my feet for a minute," I say.

Will watches me then agrees. "Me too. Who else is with us?" he asks.

June, Oliver and Riley raise their hands.

"It is unanimous, I guess," he says to me.

"Okay, how about we rest over there by those big flat rocks," I say and point to a pair of stones that jut from the earth and are surrounded by bushes dotted with plump, yellowish-red berries.

The children do not need to be told twice. They scramble for the opportunity to sit and beat Will and me there. The three of them sit on one rock while the other remains empty.

Will sits first and slips the straps of his backpack from his shoulders. He places it between his feet and looks at me. My feet are throbbing and I want to sit, but the thought of being so close to him makes my insides tremble like leaves in a windstorm. But exhaustion triumphs and I make my way to the rock slowly before sitting.

I notice his scent right away. Unfamiliar but pleasant and welcome, I am suddenly filled with his musk-and-sunshine scent.

"I don't know how to do this," he says and tears me away from the strange joy I am reveling in from simply sitting next to him.

I pause for a moment and need to remind myself what he is talking about. I do not know why my mind feels so scrambled.

"I don't know how to do what my parents did, you know? I don't know what to do for Oliver and Riley," he says quietly.

"You did great back at the lake when Oliver was about to smash the Urthmen," I say and feel as though the sun is blazing down on me from overhead when it is not.

My clothes cling to my body. My skin is suddenly damp with perspiration. My calves complain from trekking all day as I tuck one leg under my bottom. I am suddenly very aware of Will's close proximity. He reaches for his backpack and unzips it. As he does, his forearm brushes mine. His skin is fiery against mine, unexpected and yet so deliciously welcome despite the fact that I am perspiring as though I have been running in midday summer sun. I scoot aside ever so slightly, away from Will, for fear I will burst into flames if his skin touches mine again. I am suddenly parched. I reach for my canteen.

As my fingertips graze the hard exterior, my thirst burgeons. I quickly open it and bring it to my lips. Cold water trickles down my throat as I greedily gulp. It is refreshing and cools me from the inside out. Some dribbles from the corner of my mouth. I try to whisk away the droplets with the back of my hand without Will noticing. I glance at him quickly and see that he drinks from his water bottle, too, but is far more refined about it, sipping rather than swigging as I did. When he finishes, he turns to face me. He bends his leg as he twists his body and his knee rests against my thigh. I feel heat bloom across my cheeks.

"How did you do it?" he asks. "How did you care for June all by yourself for the last year?"

I consider his question briefly before answering. "Truthfully, I have no idea. I know that's probably not the answer you want to hear, but I just woke up every morning and did it. I rarely have a plan for anything. I take one day at a time, and some days, it feels like I can only take one breath at a time," I admit and hope I have made sense and that I have not said too much.

"Yeah, I understand what you mean," he says and looks directly into my eyes.

I am lost in the swells of pastel blue and green as they blend seamlessly and undulate like ripples on a still lake. I have to remind myself to blink, to breathe. The moment quickly becomes one that I can only take a single quivering breath at a time. Words escape me and my heart plucks away at an unsteady rhythm inside my chest.

Will scrubs his face with both hands and the hypnotic spell of his eyes is broken.

"I just," he starts. "I just can't believe they are gone," he says and his voice cracks. "One minute my family was happy and fine and the next," he says and his words trail off.

Sadly, I know exactly what he is talking about, what he is feeling. "I know," I hear myself whisper.

"The hurt," he begins, but his ability to speak is strangled by loss.

My hand darts out, acting without the authorization of my brain, and touches his forearm. His skin looks exactly as it feels: rich, almost velvety. He is hurting, suffering, and I know that my thoughts about his skin and the fact that I am touching him is inappropriate, but I am inexplicably powerless to stop myself. I want to comfort him, but do not know how. Words of consolation do not exist in the

English language for what he and his brother and sister have been through.

He looks at my hand on his arm then to my face. Heat zips like a laser beam from his eyes to my cheeks and sets them afire. I start to pull my hand away and am shocked when his long, slender fingers cover my hand and keep it there. My pulse quickens and a peculiar rush similar to hope gushes through my veins.

"How do you work around it? How do you get through it and take care of June? Right now I can't imagine anything other than how I feel right now."

His grip on the top of my hand tightens and I worry that when I try to speak, my words will come out in one breathless jumble.

"It wasn't easy," I say honestly. "I mean, after seeing my mom," I start but cannot say the word 'killed.' "I still had my dad. But once he passed we were on our own."

Will lowers his head. "Oh," is all he says feebly.

"You will figure it out. You've already started. I saw it back at the lake," I say. "And I will help any way I can," I add.

He lifts his chin and looks at me. "Thanks," he says and offers a small, pained smile. He looks to the sky and I follow his eyes.

"It's getting late," I comment on the position of the sun. "We're only about halfway to our cave."

"I guess we should get going," Will agrees.

He releases my hand. I withdraw mine and delight in the puzzling tingling in my fingertips. He stands and turns to me. Golden light sluices through the forest canopy and kisses his deep-tan skin, illuminating his lustrous eyes, making both glow with unearthly radiance. Even his rich, dark hair has scattered highlights. He offers his hand to me and I take it unquestioningly. He helps me up. I did not need help, but the feel of his hand wrapped around mine again is welcome. Once I am on my feet he releases it, but not before giving it a slight squeeze.

"Okay guys, we need to start walking again," he tells Oliver and Riley.

I nod to June. She stands and we resume our hike back to the cave. I lead the way and Will picks up the rear. The sun is dipping lower with every minute that passes. Dusk will be upon us before we know it. We must hurry if we want to avoid another massacre; one none of us would survive. I am all too aware of the danger threatening all around us, Urthmen, Lurkers, both seem unavoidable. But as I walk knowing Will is behind me, my thoughts remain divided, split between the endless hazards that menace us continually and the endless possibilities of a future with our new friends.

Chapter 14

When finally we make it to the cave, Oliver, Riley and June are exhausted. Will and I killed a rabbit each on the way home and roast both quickly before putting out the fire and settling inside the cave for the night. I show Will the boulder and logs and how the boulder fits perfectly against the mouth of the cave and then is wedged in place by logs that extend to the far wall. He seems impressed by our security system. I used to be. But after the night June and I had with the Lurkers screeching and hissing as they scratched at the boulder, I am not so sure anymore.

June has lit the beeswax candles and served dinner. We eat in silence then the children, June included, lie beside each other. June wants to hear about Will, Oliver and Riley's lives before they moved to the cave by the lake.

"Where did you live before finding the cave by the lake?" she asks. "Are there others out there, other humans like us?"

"Yes, there are," Will begins speaking. "Remember the people we met?" he addresses Oliver and Riley, prodding their memories. His rich, deep voice fills the space. His brother and sister nod.

"We've met quite a few different people along the way," he says. "Remember Calyx?" he says to just Oliver.

Oliver shudders as if bugs are crawling over his skin and says, "Oh yeah, how can I forget her?"

"Calyx was an old woman who lived underground with her daughters. They had survived attack after attack somehow and found us when we were out hunting."

"I screamed. She looked like a girl Urthmen," Oliver adds. His expression is grave. "She had only one eye that worked and it was droopy. Half of her face was like that. The other eye was all cloudy looking and whitish. It rolled around and never focused." Another tremor shakes Oliver and he crinkles his nose as if he has smelled something unpleasant. Will shoots him a stern look and Oliver's features smooth instantly.

"That's true," Will says. "She had an unusual look about her. So when Oliver saw her, he started screaming. My mom and dad came racing out of the bushes they hid in and were ready to kill her, but her daughters rushed to help her. We saw them and realized they were human and that the old woman belonged to them."

I look at June. Her eyes are round and her mouth is shaped like a small 'o'. She looks captivated by Will and Oliver sharing a tale of other human beings living in our midst.

"What happened next?" June asks. "Did anyone get hurt?"

"No," Will answers and rakes a hand through his short hair. "No one was hurt. My parents lowered their weapons and they all greeted each other."

"What about Calyx?" June persists. "Weren't her feelings hurt because everyone mistook her for a female Urthmen?"

A chuckle passes through Will's lips. It is an amazing sound I want to hear again. "I don't think so," he says. "We didn't tell her what we thought. We kept our initial opinions to ourselves, especially after seeing her daughters."

"Oh wow," June says dreamily. "That is so great. What about the daughters? Were they beautiful? They must have been," June says.

A strange sensation washes over me at her words. I feel agitated and threatened for no reason. I feel a blend of anger and sadness at the thought of Calyx's daughters being beautiful, or more specifically, of Will thinking they are beautiful. I do not know what has come over me, why it would matter if he did or didn't. My fists are balled in my lap. My nails are biting into my palms. I am waiting for Will to agree or disagree with what June has said with the same eagerness I anticipate a meal.

"Uh, no, not exactly," Will says uncomfortably.

"Yuck! No way! Tell them the truth, Will," Oliver chimes in impishly. "They looked just like their mother: old and scary!"

"Ollie, it's not nice to speak about people who were nice to you, to all of us, like that," Will says levelly and trains his gaze on his younger brother. The mischievous twinkle that sparkled in Oliver's eyes dulls and his shoulders slump.

I am relieved that Will did not find the women attractive and I am proud of how he handled Oliver's expression of his opinion. He was calm but firm.

"Sorry," Oliver says sheepishly. "And please don't call me Ollie. I'm not a little kid anymore," he adds and sounds exactly like June.

"Okay," Will agrees. "I won't call you Ollie and you won't speak unkindly about others who aren't here to defend themselves. Deal?"

"Deal," Oliver agrees.

"So there are three more humans in the forest?" June says excitedly and steers the subject back to Calyx and her daughters.

A gloomy expression clouds Will's features. "Calyx and her daughters are," he starts then pauses. He clears his throat before he continues. "They did not make it. They were killed in an ambush."

June's hands rocket to her mouth and cover it. "Oh my gosh," she says from behind them.

"We weren't there when it happened. We had left for the day to hunt. When we came back the place had been stormed by Urthmen," Will says the word 'Urthmen' through his teeth. "That's been the case with everyone we've ever lived with," he says and looks at his feet. "I guess we're bad luck or something," he adds weakly. His shoulders hunch forward, he looks defeated.

"I don't believe that," June disagrees adamantly. "You are not bad luck. And besides, we don't need luck. We are all safe with Avery here," she says proudly. "Avery is the best fighter there is."

I feel Will eyes bore into my skull and I am afraid to turn and look at him. A bead of sweat trickles between my shoulder blades when I hear him speak.

"I know she is. I have never seen anyone fight quite like her," he says to June but continues to watch me. I see him in my periphery. His eyes are the sky and treetops combined and bathed in a pale glow of sunlight, and they are on me. He and my sister are talking about me, about something that comes as naturally to me as breathing, yet I am so unsettled by it I could jump right out of my skin. "Where did you learn to fight like that, to swing a sword and throw a spear?" he asks me directly.

I turn to face him slowly. My cheeks are burning but the rest of me feels ice-cold. "My dad," I say quietly.

"Your dad must've been some teacher," Will says. He studies my face. "I have never seen anyone with skill and speed like yours."

I squirm uncomfortably. As June knows, accepting compliments is not my strong suit.

"She was better than our dad by the time she was fifteen," June offers. "Avery has a gift."

I would like to melt into the stone of the walls and floor I am so embarrassed.

Will is still watching me. "Yes, she certainly does," he says then looks to June. "I think you're right. We are safe here." He smiles at June and she returns the gesture with a sunny smile of her own.

"Tells us more stories," June urges him.

"Yes, Will, please tell us stories mom and dad used to tell," Riley says. Tears slip down her cheeks and I slide June a glance. June moves and puts a comforting arm around Riley's shoulders. Riley nuzzles against her and I realize in that moment that June's gift goes beyond bloodshed and violence. It transcends butchery and war. Hers is so much more important, and not just to me, but to the world. She represents all that our present world lacks. She is kind and decent. She has an open heart and a capacity to love that I never even knew existed.

"Okay, let me see," Will begins. "Once upon a time, people, humans, ruled the earth. They lived in houses and the adults went to places called *jobs* and children went to places called *schools*."

I look to June again. She is watching me with a mysterious glint in her eyes. Perhaps it is because she has heard me tell similar stories, or perhaps it is something else entirely. I am too tired to figure it out right now. I am enchanted by Will's voice.

"School was a place where children would gather. They would learn their letters and numbers and sometimes even play together. One grown-up would teach them to read and write and ready themselves for the future."

"Teachers were important people," Riley says then yawns.

"Yes, they were," Will smiles at her affectionately.

He continues telling them about school and jobs and the order that once existed in our disordered world. Before long, I can see June's eyelids growing heavy. Will's voice flows smoothly. His cadence is as soothing as floating on a gently rolling river. It has lulled the children, and one by one, they drift off to sleep.

I am left alone with Will.

We clean up any remnants left behind from dinner and straighten the new gear he and his siblings have brought. Once everything is organized and put away, I unroll my sleep mat next to June.

"You're tired?" he asks quietly more than states.

"I should be, but I'm not," I admit. Having him in the cave with me, so close by, I doubt I'll ever be relaxed enough to sleep. "How about you, are you tired?"

"No, I guess I'm like you. I should be exhausted, but the thought of sleeping right now seems impossible."

"Huh," I say awkwardly.

Will walks away from the sleeping children and leans against the far wall, exactly where I spent all of last night awake. He slides down until he is sitting. I am suddenly self-conscious of the fact that I am now standing alone, hovering over my sleep sack. I do not know what to do. I do not know whether he wants company and wants me to come and sit beside him or whether he wants to be left alone with his thoughts. I have messed up once today, when I blurted out that I watched my mother be killed by Urthmen back at the lake. I do not want to do it again. I do not want to offend him on his first night without his parents, away from home and at our cave.

"Want company?" I ask stiffly and steal a nervous glance his way.

"Yes, please," he answers and sounds sincere.

My heart stutters a moment while my brain commands my legs to move. I walk on shaky legs to where he sits and take a seat beside him.

"Okay," I say as candlelight flickers and dances across the smooth, stone walls of the cave. I am thankful for the dim light for once. My words have made my face flush, I am sure.

When I am seated beside him, he turns his body to face me. As he does, his knee grazes my thigh then rests there, his skin touching mine so lightly it send chills racing over my flesh. "I can't believe that this day actually happened. None of it seems real," he says. "I mean, I know it really happened, but I guess I keep hoping it is just a bad dream, a nightmare I'll wake up from."

I wish I could wake him and tell him it was all just a dream, a horrible, vivid nightmare. I wish I could make it all go away and take away his pain. But I cannot. Life isn't that simple. Nothing is easy in our world.

"I am sorry, Will," I say.

My words are so minimal. They seem so empty on the surface. But I mean them, all of them. I am truly sorry for what he and his siblings have been through.

"Thank you," he says. "Thank you for warning us right before it happened, and for saving Oliver and Riley," he pauses and swallows hard. His voice is gravelly when he begins talking again. "What you did was brave, braver than anything I've ever seen. You risked your life for us. Without you, we would all be dead."

The starkness of his statement strikes me like a slap in the face. He is thanking me profoundly, genuinely, yet all I can think of is the last sentence he spoke. I've only know Will for a less than a day, but the thought of losing him terrifies me.

"You're welcome," I say when I realize an awkward amount of time has passed.

I want to say more. I want to tell him I worried for him and his family for two days, that I am so happy to have them with me, but I cannot. He is suffering, grieving the loss of his parents who were taken from him in the most heinous fashion imaginable. I have lived through it. I know what it is like to feel as if a raw, ragged hole has been punched in my chest. I wish I could fill it for him, heal him. But I do not possess the power to do so. Instead, I smile as warmly as I can and try to silently share the sympathy I feel for him.

Will parts his lips and is about to speak, when a horrible din peals through the quiet of the cave.

I know the sound. The sun has set. Night has fallen and the Lurkers have returned.

Hissing and howling clashes with a snarling noise that sounds like the wet slopping of one animal feasting on another.

Will's face is haunted when he looks from the boulder to me.

"They're here," I say. "The Lurkers are back."

"Back? They were here before?" he asks incredulously.

"Yes, last night," I say.

"You slept though this last night?" he asks and is clearly rattled by the unnerving shrieks and calls.

"I stayed awake all night, afraid they would get inside the cave," I say and look at June. She stirs then opens her eyes. Her head shoots up frantically.

"No, no, no," she cries. "They're back."

Oliver and Riley wake as well. They begin to cry. Between the crying children and the incessant yelping outside, the cave is flooded with hash, discordant sounds. I am overwhelmed. My insides tremble. My nerves are frayed. I feel as if I cannot withstand another moment of the loudness.

Just when the noise becomes deafening, Will shushes everyone.

"Please, be quiet for a second everyone," he says. The children listen and stifle their cries, reducing them to sniffles and small gasps. And when they do, I hear what he heard over their tears.

A clanging sound echoes and grows louder and louder, closer. My head whips toward him and his features mirror mine. Dread drags them down, taking any hope for safety and a good night's sleep with it. The Lurkers not only regrouped before their return, but they'd also formulated a better plan. They were trying to get inside.

"Oh my gosh," Will breathes. His eyes are locked on mine. He is looking to me for answers I do not have, chief among them: What do we do now?

After a moment of chaotic, panicked thoughts, I do exactly what I did the night before. I assume my post beside a log and June joins me. She rests her head on my lap and I cup her ear with one hand, stroking her hair with the other. The act soothes both of us slightly, but I know eventually she will fall asleep. Will watches me then gestures for his brother and sister to follow suit. They drag their sleep sacks to him and place their heads on his legs. He covers their ears and begins humming. I have never heard the tune he hums, or any other tune for that matter, but the sound he creates is comforting. I focus on it and try to block out the cries and clangs of the Lurkers.

Will and I spend the night upright with the people we love closest to us. We do not talk. We do not need to. The glances we exchange at the deepest point of the darkness covey more than thousands of words can express.

When finally I realize the sound has stopped, my ears are ringing. My legs are numb and I feel Will's head resting against my shoulder. I am achy all over, but happy to have had him with me, that I was not alone while in charge and experiencing the awful sounds.

I carefully slide June to the floor in hopes of letting her sleep a little while longer. But her eyes snap open.

"It stopped," she says groggily.

"Yes," I say. "It is morning." I point to the faint threads of light seeping in.

"We made it. They did not get in," she says.

"No, they didn't," I say.

Not this time, they did not, I think. *But they might tomorrow, or the next day. It is only a matter of time.*

I do not share my thoughts. June and the others have been through enough. Besides, I think Will knows as well as I do that we have not heard the last of the Lurkers.

Riley and Oliver stir and Will's head leaves my shoulder.

"Are we alive?" Riley asks.

"Yes," Will answers and smiles at her tenderly.

"Why don't you guys lie down for a bit?" I suggest. "I need to move the boulder and make sure everything is safe before we go to the river and wash, okay?" I tell the children.

Will nods in agreement. "I'll help," he says and stands.

I stand too. My body feels kinked and gnarled as we make our way to the boulder. We both crouch to reach it, a movement that makes every muscle in my body complain. Will is strong, stronger than I am by far. We move the boulder with ease and cautiously step outside. The stench of urine is potent as my eyes scour the once comforting landscape beyond my home of stone. I notice deep holes have been dug all around the entrance and small fragments of rock littered everywhere.

My heart begins to hammer and the situation comes into stinging clarity.

"Will, come with me," I say.

He hears the urgent edge to my voice and becomes alarmed. "Help me," I say as I grip the boulder. "Help me turn it so I can see the side that faces out."

He and I grunt and labor until the boulder is turned enough for me to see exactly what I feared had happened.

An enormous crater has been chipped away on the surface of the rock, the part that faces outside. I know now that the clanging we heard last night was the sound of Lurkers chipping away at the only solid defense we had.

"They've chiseled a hole in the boulder," Will says. Terror creases his face.

"And they will keep chiseling until it shatters. They will be able to get to us in a matter of days," I say. "We cannot stay here anymore. We are not safe."

"Where can we go?" he asks. Desperation laces his words. "We're dead by nightfall if we are still in the woods without shelter."

"Maybe we should leave the woods," I say, though I cannot fathom life beyond the walls of green I have called home since I was June's age.

"We can't. It's not possible. There's nothing for us out there," Will says and points toward the skyline where the sun has just begun to peek over the horizon.

"I don't think we have another choice," I say.

I turn and look at the three small faces that have gathered near us then to back to Will. Oliver, Riley and Will are now mine and I am now theirs. We are a new, blended family, and even though we are not bound by blood, we are bound nonetheless. I know a new chapter of my life is about to begin. I know now that other humans are out there. I feel the need to find them, to band together and grow our numbers. To do that, we will be forced to venture out into a hostile world ruled by beings who seek to end our existence entirely. We will face Urthmen, if we make it out of the forest. And I don't know how we will survive the night. It is likely we will not. We might be ambushed by packs of Lurkers before our feet ever touch asphalt. But I do not see another option. I cannot simply sit passively and wait to be executed, clubbed to death by an Urthmen who's infiltrated our sanctity, or torn to shreds and eaten by a Lurker. I cannot stay and wait to die, not with three new people added to my life, people I will give my life to keep alive. I will not fail. I will not surrender June, Oliver, Riley or Will's life to any creature. It is time to leave the meager safety of the woods and risk creating a life together on Planet Urth.

Chapter 15

"Just keep going," I encourage an exhausted looking June. I whisper the words in her ear and will her body to be infused with strength. My sister turns to me briefly. A look flashes in her silvery eyes. It is laden with steely determination, and utter fear.

"I am," she replies breathlessly.

Her cheeks are beet-red and her breathing is labored. I hate seeing her this way, especially knowing that I am to blame, sort of.

My temples pound in time with my heartbeat, the sound of blood roaring in my ears filtering the sounds of the woods. But they hammer with less ferocity than the anxiety drumming away at my brain.

"How much farther are we going?" June asks between pants.

"I don't know," I answer honestly. I wish I had a better answer. I wish I knew exactly where we were going and how long it would take to get there, but things are not that simple. "But you're doing great. All of you are," I say as I crane my neck and look over my shoulder at June, Riley and Oliver.

Riley offers a weak smile and Oliver just nods. Behind them, Will walks. Rays of light streak through the woodland canopy and kiss his golden skin, causing a wash of chestnut highlights to scatter through his raven hair as he continues along the same dirt path the children and I travel along. His appearance, his rich bronze skin and brilliant aquamarine eyes are a sharp contrast to my emotions. Dark and heavy, I feel none of the vividness and lightness he radiates. To the contrary, I feel every ounce of the weight of four lives resting squarely on my shoulders.

As if sensing my load, Will says, "We'll keep going until we find a safe place to rest."

I marvel at his tone. He is not winded and he does not sound low-spirited. Surprisingly, his tone is almost upbeat.

"I know this is hard on you guys," he continues. "All of us are leaving a place we've come to know and love. It's scary. We've been through scary, horrible stuff. But we're here now, together, and we'll get through this."

"That's right," I agree and wish I felt as certain as Will sounds.

"I'm just so afraid," Riley says. The tremor in her voice is apparent. "Those monsters, the Urthmen, they killed mom and dad and I can't get it out of my head."

"Neither can I," Oliver says.

I slow my pace so that I walk alongside Riley and Oliver. Up close, I realize Oliver looks a lot like Will, only shorter and with rounded, more boyish features.

I place a hand on his shoulder and give a gentle squeeze. "I know what you're going through. Not that it helps at all," I add and mentally kick myself for being so socially inept. I close my eyes for a split-second and try to channel June's fluidity when she speaks to others. "What I mean to say is that what you saw was just about as awful as it gets, but you will get through it. The pain and sadness you feel, you'll get through it, I promise."

Oliver turns his head to face me. His eyes are glassy and bloodshot, making the blue-green of his irises glow. "Thank you," is all he can manage. I hear the all too familiar catch in his voice as his ability to speak is strangled by the tightness in his throat.

Sadly, feeling his throat constrict is one of the many experiences he will endure when he recalls his parents' murder. He will never forget what he saw. None of them will. I haven't. Time only eases a small portion of the initial trauma, but it never erases it. The event will be indelibly etched in his memory. I cannot tell him that, especially since the loss of his parents is not the only challenge he faces.

We are fleeing the forest. Will, Riley, Oliver, June and I are leaving the only shelter we've ever known and heading toward an uncertain destination, one that promises unrelenting danger. But we must go. Urthmen, monstrous mutations of human beings that rule the planet, have infiltrated the area, and Lurkers, bloodthirsty beasts that hunt by night, have discovered our cave, have caught our scent. If we had stayed in the cave June and I called home for the last six years, they would not have stopped until they found a way inside and made us their meal. We did not have another choice. We had to leave. Our lives depended on it.

We continue to walk for what feels like eternity, passing tree after tree, bush after bush. Occasionally, I look behind me at Will. The hike begins to wear on his positive mood, and now, what can only be categorized as a tormented expression plays across his face. Tormented, or perhaps it is an expression of quiet resignation to our fate. Either way, a horrible, sick feeling materializes in the pit of my stomach.

"I'm so thirsty and tired," Riley says and demands my attention. Her voice is as thin as a reed. I can hear the fatigue in it, the desperation. Her words echo my feelings. I wish I could tell her, tell everyone, that we can stop and rest, that another solution exists. But it does not. The sun is slanted low in the sky. The world around us is bathed in waning rays of gold. Dusk is looming. We must keep moving. We must keep going as fast and far as we can possibly travel. I know we will not make it out of the forest by nightfall. But we cannot remain out in the open as we are, vulnerable prey awaiting the predatory advance of ferocious creatures. I search for a place for us to hide as my eyes scan the lush surroundings.

"The day is slipping fast," Will says to me. He peers at me over the tops of the children's heads. His voice is tight and fraught with concern, and his lips collapse and form a dour line. "Time is running out."

He has stated the obvious. As the sun sinks lower, our need to find shelter becomes direr. Once it disappears altogether, so too do our chances of survival if we are not secure somewhere safe to spend the night. I do not know if such a location exists at this point.

"I'm looking," I tell him and do not mask the unease in my tone. "We need to find something fast. Just keep looking."

His eyes narrow and his brow furrows as he nods in agreement. He turns from me and looks out into the forest. I do the same. We are headed in a direction I have never explored before. This part of the forest is heavy with the scent of evergreens and musty earth. Pinecones continue to fall from trees and land with soft thuds and plunks. Overhead and all around us, imposing trees with limbs that sag as if bearing the weight of snow stand sentinel, intimidating with their pointed barbs and rigid appearance. Shadows of tree branches dance along our path as if waving us forward, inviting us deeper into the heart of this uncharted area of the woods. I do not see a craggy rock formation, or anything for that matter, other than towering pines, firs and other green, spiny-leaved trees. A rock formation would suggest a cave, which is what I had hoped to find. Even if it were small, Will and I would find a way to squeeze our group inside, I am sure. But the possibility of finding a cave seems remote at this point.

A thread of doubt begins to weave its way into my brain. But there isn't time for doubt or hesitation, only commitment. I have committed myself, and everyone with me, to making it out of the forest safely. June, Will, Riley and Oliver are all my responsibility.

We push ahead and make our way through the thicket.

Once we are past the point where the pines and evergreens grow side by side closely, I get a better view of what we have to work with: Nothing. We have nothing to work with at this point.

Worry sends an icy chill through me that courses through my veins until it wraps itself around my heart and nearly freezes it mid-beat.

Will casts an anxious look my way. I rub my forehead. My palms are sweaty and my heart has resumed beating. Its rate is now spiked, not from physical exertion, but from panic.

"I don't think I can keep walking," Riley says and rips us from our wordless interaction.

Her color has paled dramatically, a fact that does not go unnoticed by Will. He rushes to her side.

"She needs to rest. We all do," he says to me as I make my way toward Riley.

Will is kneeling and digging in his backpack. We took only what we could easily carry from the cave and left the rest. He retrieves a canteen and raises it to his sister's lips. Before she fills her mouth, I place my hands on her cheeks. They are clammy and cool to the touch, a bad sign considering the heat has been sweltering all day long. I drop my hands and watch as she drinks.

I realize Will is right. I have pushed the children harder than their young bodies are capable of handling. They need to rest. And I need to figure out how we are going to survive the night.

"There," I point to a small clearing with moss covered logs on one side. Will looks up and follows my finger's trajectory. "Let's sit over there," I gesture to the closest one.

Will caps his canteen and slings his backpack over one shoulder. He then cups Riley's elbow with one hand and wraps the other around her small waist. He leads her to the log and makes her sit and drink from his canteen. Oliver sits beside them, but June stays with me.

"Think she's going to be okay?" June asks me, concern lacing her words. She stares at Riley and Will for a long moment.

"Yes, I do," I reply. "She just needs a rest and some water, maybe some dried boart meat, and she'll be fine. I've pushed you kids too hard today," I admit.

"We are running for our lives, Avery," June spins and faces me as she speaks. Small coiled tendrils of her blonde hair have escaped her braid and frame her face. Her complexion is flushed, and a small crease marks the space between her eyebrows.

"I know," I say in a voice that is barely above a whisper. "I need to find us shelter fast, but I don't see anything even remotely suitable."

June chews her lip contemplatively and folds her arms across her chest. She stares off into the distance. "What can I do?" she asks after a moment. "Tell me what you need me to do and I'll do it."

Will approaches and she turns toward him. "How's Riley? Is she okay?" June asks.

"She's fine," Will answers reassuringly. But his expression remains serious. "Would you mind sitting with her and keeping an eye on her for me for a minute while I talk to your sister?" he asks June in a warm, familiar tone.

June nods and says, "Of course," before making her way to the log on which Riley sits.

When June is out of earshot, Will's demeanor transforms from friendly and earnest to tense and cool. "We need to find a place now," he says with intensity.

He is looking to me for a solution, one I do not have. I have led us deep into the forest blindly, and without even the most skeletal of plans.

"I know," I say as my eyes scour the surrounding area. My stomach knots tightly. Four people are counting on me to save them from an encounter with Lurkers. "I just need to think."

Will leans in. "Hey, I'm not putting this all on you," he says. His tone is apologetic. "I'm with you; we are all in this together." He grips my shoulders and looks directly into my eyes. "And we need to get through tonight together." His breath feathers across my face and makes my skin tingle. Our circumstances teeter on the edge of a great precipice of danger, yet Will manages to evoke an array of unfamiliar reactions in me.

"I know," I say quietly. I feel heat bloom across my cheeks and hate that I cannot stop it from happening. I swallow hard and finish my sentence. "But I got us into this. And I have to get us out of it."

Will drops his hands from my shoulders and rakes his fingers through his dark hair, ruffling it so that I nearly lose my train of thought. "I am here to help too. I'm just not sure there's anything to help with at this point," he adds dejectedly.

"Well, we can't just keep walking," I say. "The kids are drained and the day is fading fast. I have to come up with something."

Will's eyes lock on mine briefly before they peek over my shoulder at Riley. Worry etches his features. He has lost so much already. His pain is plain.

"Go," I say to him softly. "Go make sure she's okay. She needs you."

I need him too, but I do not dare say as much to him. His sister is a child, a child who just watched her mother and father be butchered by Urthmen. Riley's needs take priority over me rummaging through my brain for a suitable and safe shelter for the night.

"I'll be right back," he says to me before he darts off toward Riley.

I close my eyes and rub my temples. I think of my own parents, of June and the life we led, of the life we are leading now. I wish my mother and father were alive. My father always knew exactly what to do. He had a gift for surviving seemingly insurmountable odds. I wish he were with me right now. I wish he could tell me what to do. But I know he can't. He is gone; a fact that nearly brings me to tears even though it has been a year since his passing. I shake my head in a feeble attempt to clear his face from my mind's eye and open my eyes. I turn them skyward. And when I do, I spot a massive elm tree. Its branches stretch and seem to reach until they touch the sky, abounding with leaves, full and dense, its top rounded in appearance. As I stare at it, an idea dawns on me. I am reminded of the night we escaped the attack at the compound with my father, the night my mother was murdered by Urthmen.

That night, we burst from the tunnel and, after collapsing it on the Urthmen inside, fled into the forest, into the night. Darkness, thick and sinister, swallowed us whole. Stony moonlight cast a ghostly pallor on the vibrant hues the woodland was usually bathed in and faded everything around us to an ashen silver-gray. I remember it all; remember it too well, in fact.

Standing in the forest in broad daylight as I am now, I swear I can smell the musky scent of molded leaves and seasons changing, just as I did that night. Our lives had just changed, yet the scent struck me, stayed with me. I breathe deeply and hear my father's ragged breathing, the memory of it so fresh it feels as if it happened only yesterday.

The threat of Lurkers was imminent that night, as it is every night, their presence as certain as the blood pumping in our veins. But we had just survived Urthmen storming our village. We did not have time to search for a cave or a decent place to hide. We had just lost everything, my mother, my unborn sister or brother, our home and most, if not all, of the inhabitants of the compound. We managed to escape, but barely. We had a new obstacle to contend with, another deadly one equally as dangerous as Urthmen. We were confronted with Lurkers.

As we dashed among trees and growth, the rustle of grass and leaves plagued our nerves. I remember squeezing my father's hand so tightly, I worried he'd wince in pain. But he didn't. He knew better than to make a sound and alert Lurkers to our presence. He carried June and led us to a tree similar to the one I am looking at now.

Broad, bushy limbs stretched and looked as if they mingled with the constellations. My father slid June to his back and lifted me as high as his arms could reach then told me to climb, to keep climbing until he told me to stop. The urgency in his voice set my feet into motion. I clambered knotted knobs on the trunk until limbs intersected one another like ladder rungs. Once, I craned my neck and looked over my shoulder to check on my father. I realized in that moment how high up I had climbed and remember feeling as if a wave of cold nausea crashed over me. My skin became damp and my brow and palms became slickened with sweat. A whimper attempted to vault from deep in my throat but was seized by the lump of terror lodged there. I couldn't feel my heart beating in my chest and my hearing assumed a muffled quality similar to being underwater and perceiving sounds above the surface that were softened and distorted. Still, I pushed down the anxious reactions raiding my body and climbed. My arms and legs felt as if they were made of sponge and my insides quivered. But the instinctive need to survive won out over my silent panic attack.

When my father's voice whispered for me to halt, I froze where I was and waited for him to tell me what to do next. I did not dare look down again when he instructed me to hoist my leg up onto a limb and sit with my body leaning against the thinner center portion of the tree. He and June joined me and we waited there until a blazing arc of orange crested on the horizon line.

My father, June and I endured the forest at night, teeming with Lurkers, sitting on a tree limb concealed by leaves and branches.

An almost identical tree saved June and I once before. I hope it can do the same for Will, his brother and sister, June and myself a second time. With no other option in sight, the colossal elm tree before me is our only hope.

My eyes remain pinned on the tree when I mumble my thoughts aloud and say, "We'll stay here tonight."

Impossibly, Will hears me. He looks away from Riley and leaves her. His features scrunch in confusion as he approaches. "What? You want to stay here, as in right here where we're standing?" he asks.

My head suddenly feels like the flame on a beeswax candle. "N-no, not, uh, here exactly," I say and trip over my words. My gaze vacillates between him and the elm. I raise my arm and point. "I meant there, in the tree. We'll spend the night in that tree." I stare at the interlinked branches so jam-packed with leaves a creature would be hard-pressed to see us without concentrating hard.

In my periphery, I see Will's head whipsaw from me to the tree then back to me again. He looks at me as if I do not know what I am talking about. He looks at me as if I have lost my mind. "What?" he asks incredulously. "You can't be serious! Oh my gosh! I can't believe this is happening! I can't believe we listened to you and left!" He is gesturing animatedly, his words cutting me with more precision than his hands cut the atmosphere. He takes a few sharp breaths then looks at me. His expression is hard. "We cannot spend the night in a tree," he pronounces each word slowly and deliberately.

"We don't have another choice," I say levelly and match his tone by enunciating each word.

"There's got to be something other than this," he says huffily and slices the air a final time with his hand.

"Oh yeah?" I say heatedly. "Is there really?" I feel the tension of the day spiraling tightly inside of me. "Well then, I'm all ears. I'd love to hear any and all suggestions you have."

I plant my fisted hands squarely on my hips and glare at Will, waiting, daring him to come up with a better solution. I allow several beats before the pressure in me starts to seep. I tip my chin defiantly and purse my lips.

"Hmm, I'm still waiting," I say and tap my foot impatiently.

I know I am being obnoxious, but Will touched a nerve, a raw nerve, when he implied that I don't know what I'm talking about, and that it was a mistake to leave the cave. His top lip curls over his teeth and he looks as if he is about to say something. I roll my shoulders back and boldly maintain eye contact, bracing myself for what I assume will be a venomous retort. I am not about to be bullied or belittled by a boy whose life I've saved, or anyone else for that matter. I don't care that his sparkling aquamarine eyes popping against his tan skin makes my insides swirl. I will not tolerate him grumbling at me or meanness of any kind.

Several seconds pass and he does not lash out at me as I expected. In fact, I am shocked when Will's features soften. His posture relaxes and he stops glaring at me. His gaze flickers from my mouth to my eyes. I wonder why. I wonder whether one of the children is nearby and he is silently telling me to shut my mouth. I did not hear footsteps approaching.

I test my theory and part my lips to speak. He does not flinch or look as if he wishes for me to be silent so I say calmly, "I know the tree sounds like a crazy place to spend the night, but please, just trust me, okay? My father kept June and I safe the night my mother was killed by hiding out in a tree. Actually, it looked just like this one," I say and point to the tree again.

Will nods somberly. "About what I said before," he starts.

"You don't have to say anything. Don't worry about it," I say tightly and hope he does not hear the strangling sensation I feel choking my voice. The backs of my eyelids are hot. His doubt, the thought of him regretting leaving with me, branded itself in my core before he ever spoke the words aloud. Hearing his voice actually say them only served to solidify them. It brought a fear of mine to fruition.

He holds my gaze for a moment, but I look away first. "I'll tell June about my plan. You can tell Riley and Oliver whenever you're ready," I say and turn on my heels. I walk briskly to where June is seated beside Riley.

I watch as my sister rubs Riley's arm and speaks soothingly. She is a natural-born nurturer in addition to so many other splendid things.

"June, can I borrow you for a minute?" I ask.

"Sure," June says and reads my face. She excuses herself just as Will approaches. He sits where she sat and I gather he will tell his siblings what I intend to tell June.

"What's up?" June asks and looks serious.

"I found a place for us to stay tonight," I tell her.

Relief floods her features. "Really! That's fantastic!" she exclaims. Her eyes begin sweeping the area around us. Her features wilt a bit. "Where? Where will we stay?" she asks and is clearly perplexed. "I don't see a cave or any real shelter."

I lick my lips and take a deep breath. "We are going to do what we did the night we left the compound, the night mom was killed," I say.

"What? What does that mean?" June asks.

"You were too little to remember what happened or how we survived, but I do. We fled the village through an underground tunnel and found ourselves in the middle of the forest at night," I say and try to coax a memory from her I know she does not possess.

"Okay, yeah, I vaguely remember dad mentioning it through the years, but he never wanted to talk about that night at all," she bobs her head slowly as she speaks.

"I know," I say solemnly. "But what we did that night saved our lives and I think it is the only option we have now to avoid being dinner for the first Lurkers that find us."

I hear the words leave my lips. They send a shiver down my spine and conjure the sound of hissing and snarling we heard from the night before as Lurkers tried to dig their way into our cave.

June's arms are wrapped around her waist, clutching her midsection. "So what do we do? What's the plan?" June asks.

"We're going to hide out up there," I say and point to the elm tree.

"What?" she asks and her face crumples just as Will's did moments ago.

"I know it sounds crazy, but you and dad and I never would have made it that night if we hadn't gone up into a tree."

June watches me warily.

"We'll climb as high as we can and avoid the Lurkers altogether."

"But Avery, you're forgetting that Lurkers can climb," June adds in a voice that trembles.

"No, I know they can climb, but why would they?" I ask and look toward the tree again. "Unless they see us going up, they'll never know we're there."

June's eyes follow my line of vision. Her lips part slightly and she expels a thin stream of breath.

"Right now, it's our only hope. Hiding out in the tree is all we have," I tell her honestly. "We can stay in the tree for the night then hike all day tomorrow and be out of the woods and not have to worry about Lurkers."

"That's right. We won't have to worry about Lurkers anymore. The worry of Urthmen will replace it, only there is no escaping them, not even in the daylight."

A look I have never seen haunts June's face almost as much as her words haunt her voice. Her words crystallize my thoughts. She is right. We will not hide from Lurkers at nightfall. We will continually run from Urthmen.

"June, the woods are not safe from Urthmen anymore either. You know that. Will's parents were just the beginning. How long do you think it would take before they found us too? No, we are not trading up one threat for another, worse one. We're losing one of two if you ask me."

June closes her eyes and shakes her head. "Oh my gosh," is all she murmurs.

I reach out to her and put my hands on her shoulders. "Hey," I say. "June, look at me."

Her eyes open and slowly meet my gaze.

"It's going to be okay," I say. "I promise. We will be okay."

Her lower lip quivers and I see unshed tears shining in her eyes. She blinks them away feverishly. "How can you be so sure?" she asks in a small voice.

"I-I can't explain it," I say and would rather not describe that I was thinking about our father when the idea popped into my mind and the tree came into view. Whether or not it was a coincidence does not matter. I am sure this is the only way to live through the night. "I just am," I tell her. "It's what dad would do if he was here, and he could survive anything."

Tears spill over June's lower eyelashes and stream down her cheeks. "You're wrong. Dad survived a lot of things but he's not here. So he could not survive everything," she says and refers to the fact that our father is dead.

"He lived a long time. He had fifty birthdays. That's a lot considering all the medicines that kept people alive two hundred years ago don't exist anymore," I try to explain. But June is only eight. Her understanding of life is limited. I do not fault her for that. "Please June, just trust me, okay? Do you trust me?"

A small sob racks her body and she nods. "Yes I do," she manages.

"Good," I say. I draw her against my chest and hug her. I hold her tightly for several moments then gradually release her. "Now let's go see how Oliver and Riley are taking the news," I smile weakly and say.

I take June's hand and lead her toward the log Will sits atop. An expression of confirmation flashes across Will's face.

"So we're all set here?" I ask.

"I think it's cool," Oliver says. "It's a really great idea, Avery." Despite his words, Oliver's expression isn't that of a wide-eyed boy, but a young man, wizened by tragedy.

"Thank you, Oliver," I say to him. "I'm glad you're on board." Then to Riley, I say, "How about you, Riley? Do you think my idea is cool, too?"

Riley does not answer. She twists and buries her head in Will's chest.

"She's a little nervous about being up so high," Will says and rubs his sister's back.

Me, too, I want to say. But my fear of heights is irrelevant at this point.

"You'll be okay," I say to Riley. "Your brothers and I will make sure of it, won't we guys?" I say.

"Yeah, absolutely," Oliver puffs out his chest and adds.

"Of course," Will says.

"So it's settled then. Let's hunt and eat quickly and start climbing before the sun sets."

I hear utterances of agreement and June leaves my side. She goes to Riley. Will approaches me.

"Want to hunt together or should one of us stay here and guard the children?" he asks me.

I would like nothing more than to have him by my side at all times, but I know that it is too dangerous to leave the children unprotected.

"I'll go ahead. You should stay here and watch over the kids."

Perhaps the time alone will be good. Hunting comes naturally to me. I am at home in the woods stalking prey. Maybe I will gain some perspective off on my own and away from the group.

"Oh, okay," Will says reluctantly. His shoulders hook forward ever so slightly and his gaze drops to the ground below.

If I didn't know any better, I would think he is disappointed. I do not know for certain.

"Okay then," I say and work a small tuft of weedy growth back and forth with my foot. "I guess I should get going. Dusk will be here soon," I say and bring up the fast fading day.

"Yeah, you're right. See you back here soon," he says. One side of his mouth tilts upward; stretching his thick lips enough to make the dip beneath his nose almost disappear. I tear my eyes from his mouth and take a fleeting look at his eyes before I stalk off in search of a rabbit or some other mammal that will feed the five of us.

I am able to spear a rabbit and a squirrel for our dinner. We make a small fire and roast the meat once the animals are skinned and gutted. June extinguishes the fire with dirt and is careful to clear any evidence of our flames, just as our father taught us. With our bellies full, the time to retreat to the tree is upon us.

The sky is a faded blue, wan and pallid beside the stunning stretch of brilliant salmon that encircles the setting sun. Day has not yet surrendered to dusk and the sun is making a final appearance, blazing in its entire splendor. Though thoroughly terrifying, the sight of the setting sun is breathtakingly beautiful. I would love to stay and watch it, but more pressing matters demand my attention. We must get up into the tree before the sun disappears.

"I think Riley should go first with Oliver right behind her followed by you," I say to Will when I realize he is standing right beside me, gaping at the sunset.

"Okay," he says.

"Next June will go, and I will go last," I conclude while the children speak to each other quietly.

"Okay," he says again, his eyes fixed on the glowing sphere of orange blazing closer to the horizon line with each moment that passes.

"Okay," I echo his word choice. "I think we should go now."

Will turns to me. His tan skin is warmed by radiant rays of pure gold. His pale blue-green eyes are luminous and watching me intently.

I do not know what to say. All words have escaped me. He reaches out a hand and places it on my cheek lightly. His thumb strokes my cheekbone so gently it makes the fine hairs on my body rise.

I try to inhale, but my breathing snags. He is close, so close to me I can smell his skin, feel his heat. I do not know what he is doing, why he is cupping my face with one hand. All I do know is that I wish he would keep doing it, that we could stay as we are forever.

"Avery," he says my name and my heart sets off at a gallop. He opens his mouth to speak again, but before a sound slips from him, Riley's voice calls out.

"Will!" Riley cries. "Come on! I need you with me before we go!" she says.

His eyes leave my face slowly, along with his hand, and whatever Will was about to say remains a secret only he knows.

I inhale and exhale several times before I rejoin our group. When I do, we make our way to the elm tree. Will hoists Riley as high as he can, and as soon as her feet touch bark, she begins climbing. Oliver goes next followed by Will.

"Don't stop until I tell you to, okay?" I say exactly what my dad said to me the night we sought refuge in a tree just like the one I stand before.

Will and his siblings agree.

"June, it's your turn," I say and give her a reassuring hug from behind. She pats my forearms and places one foot on a knot protruding from the trunk. She begins climbing.

After a quick scan of the surrounding woods, I trail behind her. I ask Riley and Oliver to stop once they are high in the tree branches, nearing the point where the limbs become too frail to hold the weight of a child, much less adults such as Will and me. I sit on a branch opposite Will, Riley and Oliver and watch as the sun melts into the skyline. Darkness descends quickly.

Bloodsuckers swarm my face as I clutch June's waist with one arm and the branch of the tree I am sitting on with the other. I want nothing more than to shake my head from side to side wildly and swat the air around my face. But I cannot. I must endure the onslaught of mosquitos and allow them to feast on me. Being their human buffet table, though annoying, is a welcome alternative to being a midnight snack to a Lurker. I squeeze my eyes shut and repeat that fact in my head again and again. But when I hear the swish of grass below, they snap open. I glance beneath me, through the intricately interwoven network of branches, and see dark shadows, oily and blacker than the pitch darkness. Lurkers, I am certain, are stealing about. They slink by, prowling in the night. I hold my breath. I do not dare look down again and risk my stomach pitching before diving to my feet and silently hope they do not sense us.

When the soft sound of grass rustling passes, I fill my lungs with air and offer thanks to whatever nocturnal animal they were likely tracking. I lower my chin and peek fleetingly at the earth below before returning my gaze to June, then to Oliver and Riley. As I scan their faces, I realize that Riley has dozed off. Will's arms are wrapped around her protectively, but his eyes are locked on my face.

In the weak light provided by innumerable stars dotting the inky-black sky and an anemic-looking not quite full moon, I can make out the lines of his face, the chiseled angles of his chin. And I feel him watching me. A slight breeze whispers through the treetop we are tucked in. My stomach sways along with the branches. Despite being completely sapped of energy and more spent that I can ever remember being, knowing that Will is watching me sends a jolt rocketing through my insides. We exchange a knowing expression that makes my scalp tighten and tingle despite my extremely uncomfortable position, and the fact that I am perched high in a tree with murderous Lurkers stalking in the vicinity.

Another breeze stirs the leaves and thin branches around us. I take a cursory glance in the distance and see that other treetops do not move. Goose bumps prickle my arms as waves of apprehension sweep over me. The stillness all around me is unnatural compared the odd, intermittent whooshes of air that puff toward us. I look at Will. He seems to notice what I observed. He looks from the stillness beyond our tree to the wavering leaves, limbs and foliage around us. His brow furrows and I feel certain something is not right.

I am about to motion to him when a large splotchy shape streaks past us. It is so quick I almost miss it. And as it passes, it sends a small burst of air our way much like the breeze I thought I'd felt. Will's gaze follows the greasy form as it doubles back toward us. It slips in our direction, only closer this time, and I hear the beat of wings flapping against the ether.

A gust of wind wafts in my face and I am tempted to shield myself against it, but I do not. Instead, I remain, eyes wide open, and look on in horror at the winged creature gliding toward us. Its body is easily the size of mine, only it looks nothing like a human, or anything else I've ever seen for that matter. Large ears prick upward, stabbing at the sky and standing at attention, while shining eyes, pitch-black and darker than the night itself, pierce the space between us. But neither its eyes nor its ears are what make the creature terrifying to behold, not even its pale, wrinkled, snout-like muzzle. The most chilling aspect of its appearance lies lower. A broad mouth is opened wide revealing razor-sharp incisors and oversized blade-like canines.

Shockwaves rip through my body and my heart feels as if it will explode.

"Oh my gosh," I breathe as it dives toward us and emits a shriek that curdles my blood.

June startles. Her eyes snap open and she sees the winged creature. She gasps and starts to scream, but I slap my hand over her mouth and remind her where we are in a low voice. "Don't make a sound," I warn her. "Lurkers will hear you."

The beast is close, its beady eyes trained on us. It caws and zips past us. I am certain it intends to circle back.

The sound and the flurry of activity will draw attention to us, Lurkers will come for sure. That is, if the creature does not attack us first. I cannot allow either to happen. I lean close to June and whisper, "Hold tight to the center of the tree. Do not let go. Do you hear me?"

June nods and I let go of her waist slowly. I lift my legs and slide them both to one side then push myself up to a crouching position. I stand carefully and grip a branch above me as soon as it is within reach. I widen my stance then draw my sword. I wait for the bat-like beast to return.

I hear the whoosh of air as the creature swoops toward us, its jaw unhinged. My heart batters my ribcage so hard I fear a rib will be damaged in the process. I am panting when the beast comes within reach. I haul my sword high overhead with one arm and cleave the air. My blade meets with flesh and carves straight through it until it is freed on the other side. I have beheaded the beast. Its head careens to the ground below immediately, followed by the body, and both land with a *clunk*. The follow-through makes me begin to lose my footing and cling to the branch overhead, all the while squeezing the hilt of my sword so tightly with my other hand that my palms burn. I regain my balance just in time to watch a pack of Lurkers descend on the head. They begin devouring the meat that rained from the sky, but not before sniffing the air and investigating the area around them. They yelp and chuff softly. I crouch and sheathe my sword then slide beside June and press us both to the center of the tree. Will and his siblings do the same.

We remain out of sight until the wet slopping sound of feeding returns and we feel confident the Lurkers have resumed feasting. We breathe a collective sigh of relief when finally they finish and move on. June's body shivers next to mine and I hold her tight until her body stills and her breathing becomes even. Several times during the night, I feel my grip on her slacken, feel my body tip forward and begin to fall, but catch myself just in time.

The night creeps at a painfully sluggish pace. I fear I will fall so I do not sleep, save for the intermittent dozing that leads to waking with a terrified start. When day finally dawns, I feel as if I may cry. I am bone-tired; exhausted in a way that surpasses physical exhaustion. But I know a daunting task awaits me. I must climb down from the tree. And I must hike for the entire day.

I groan and June stirs.

"It's morning!" she exclaims as soon as the bleariness leaves her eyes. "You were right, Avery! You were right all along. I'm so sorry I doubted you," she whispers.

"Me, too," Will surprises me by saying. "You saved us again last night from that . . . monster," he adds. "I owe you a debt I'll never be able to repay." His voice is sincere and serious.

"You owe me nothing," I say softly and look him in his eyes. Then to the children I say, "We need to get down from here. I don't know about any of you, but my backside is numb."

A series of chuckles ripple among them and one by one, we make our way down the tree.

I do not know where our next journey will take us and I don't know what the future holds. All I know is that as long as blood pumps through my veins, I will fight to keep us safe. I will fight for our right to live.

Chapter 16

At the base of the enormous elm tree we took shelter in, I stretch the many kinks in my back and shoulders. I feel as if I have been beaten with a stick. Parts of me ache that I didn't know were capable of aching in the first place, namely my backside. I would love to soak them in hot water until the pain eases. I remember stories of hot springs and heated indoor tubs of water that existed before the war. My dad used to tell June and I about them. So many tales had been shared from one generation to the next, tales of comfort and safety, of luxury that June and I will never know.

I roll my shoulders and rub my throbbing thighs and legs and silently wish we would stumble upon a hot spring. I would like nothing more than to submerge my sore body up to my chin and revel in the soothing heat. I daydream about what it would be like to indulge in such an experience, to feel the tension inside me, inside each and every muscle, melt and become one with the water. My eyes burn and feel as if they have sand particles in them. I allow my eyelids to slowly slide shut. I envision myself wrapped in warmth, in soothing ripples of comfort. My breathing becomes slow and steady. Little by little, I feel as if I am falling away from my body, as if my mind has separated from it and is floating away on a lazy river.

The rough, rigid bark of the tree trunk scrapes against my cheek as my temple knocks against it. It comes as a rude awakening in every sense of the expression. I realize I fell asleep while standing and keeled over into the tree.

"Avery, are you okay?" I hear Will ask. His voice is filled with concern.

My vision is blurry for a moment but I see that he is moving toward me quickly. I blink several times in an attempt to clear the haziness.

I am embarrassed beyond words. My head pounds in time with the rest of my limbs and my cheek stings from the scrape.

"I'm fine," I say to Will quickly. "I just, uh, bumped my head," I add and nod stiffly.

My cheeks are blazing. I can practically see the glow from them lighting the space in front of me. I curse my fair skin under my breath. If I were as fortunate as Will and his siblings to have a rich, olive skin tone my shame would be hidden better. But I do not. And skin tone is the least of my problems at the moment. Eating and getting our group moving so that we can find a suitable place for all of us to sleep is.

Will's brows gather. "Are you sure? You look a little pale and your cheek is bleeding. Maybe you should sit for a minute."

I am about to open my mouth and dismiss Will's worries when June approaches and steps between he and I. "Let me take a look," she says to me and sets about inspecting my cheek. "Oh, it's fine. It's just a little scratch. No big deal," she comments casually then changes the subject completely. "I hate to be a pest, but shouldn't we eat and start hiking?"

I am in awe of June's tact, as well as her timing. I'm grateful that she has not only diverted the attention from my humiliating face-first fall into the tree but also appears to have read my thoughts exactly. I want to scoop her up and hug her, but settle for offering her a small, sly grin instead.

"Yes June. You're right. That's exactly what we should do. Thank you." My thanks are more sincere than they seem on the surface. I hope I didn't overemphasize the words as I spoke them. I don't want Will to think I'm unappreciative of his concern. I am thankful. But I'm not accustomed to fusses being made over me. "I'll hunt for some breakfast for us and we can get out of here," I say to June then smile warmly at both she and Will. Animals have been easier to find farther away from our cave so hunting should not be an issue, a point that pleases me. In my condition, I doubt I could handle wandering too far, or worse, engaging in a lengthy chase.

June winks at me. "I'll go see if Riley and Oliver want to help get a fire started so that when you come back, we're ready to cook," she says then turns and heads to where Riley is inspecting what appear to be fangs just a few spear lengths away. I assume they belonged to the bat that tried to descend on us during the night. Perhaps they did not. Either way, whatever creature they belonged to, the fangs are all that remain of it. The Lurkers took care of the rest.

Will stays behind and we are alone.

"Seriously, are you all right? You fell pretty hard," he says softly.

I scrub my face with both hands. As I lower them I murmur, "I don't know if I'm okay."

Will takes a step toward me. "Then why don't you sit. I'll hunt and you can just, I don't know, be still for the first time since I've met you."

"Huh, I don't know if I can do that," I say. "And for the record, I didn't fall exactly. I fell asleep. Is that technically falling? Maybe it is," I ramble.

Will's eyes widen. His expression is equal parts concern and sympathy. "You haven't slept in days," he says. "Not at the cave and not in the tree."

"Nope. And the night before you came was the first time the Lurkers spent the night howling and hissing just beyond our boulder."

"So for three nights you haven't slept," he says.

"Yes, that's right," I admit.

I watch as his lips press together tightly and form a line. I don't know whether he is angry, scared or worried, or a mix of all three. My thoughts are too fuzzy and muddled to identify his expression. I decide to ask him flat out. Frankly, I am too tired to do anything else.

"Will, why do you look so mad? Are you mad or worried or something else? I'm too out of it to tell. Just make it easy for me and tell me, because when you stand there looking like that, it confuses and upsets me."

I cannot believe I just said what I said. I was direct, blunt even. My lack of social skills is glaringly obvious. Candid words haphazardly rushed from me, and I worry I have offended Will. We're linked together now. The last thing I want is to have a tense relationship with him. Allowing the first thing that comes to mind to heedlessly spill from my lips may have done just that.

A nervous moment passes between us, during which I contemplate attempting to smooth matters, knowing fully that doing so would likely be a debacle.

I am relieved when the corners of his mouth bend upward and a slow smile spreads across his face.

"Mad?" he asks. "Why in the world would I be mad?" Will is shaking his head.

I shrug. "I don't know," I answer and shift uncomfortably.

"Well I'm not mad. I'm worried. I want you to be well. You've done so much for me and my sister and brother. I want to help take care of you."

Through the fogginess of my sleep-deprived confusion, I swear I heard him say he wants to help take care of me. I'm not positive, but I think he did say those words. I don't know how to react to such a statement.

"Uh, thanks," I say awkwardly. "That's, uh, nice of you," I add and bob my head. I probably look like a fool and know that my head is little more than a crimson blob with curly blonde hair attached to it. But I'm too tired to care.

"No problem," he says.

A small stretch of silence spreads between us. He looks from me to the woods back to me then the children and back to me again.

"So, I guess I'll go hunt," I tell him when I cannot endure the self-consciousness I am feeling another second longer.

"Oh, no, you should stay here and rest," he says and places a hand on my upper arm.

His touch is warm and pleasant. I want to close my eyes and savor it. I would likely fall asleep immediately again and collapse atop him so I do not dare.

"No, that's okay. You're tired too. You didn't sleep the last two nights either," I say.

"You haven't slept in three nights. You have me beat," he says.

And you watched both your parents die at the hands of Urthmen, I think to myself. The thought echoes in my brain so noisily that for a moment, I worry I spoke it aloud. I glance at Will to gauge his reaction. I see that he is still wearing a small smile and looking at me expectantly. I assume that if I had said what I thought, he would not look so serene.

"Fine. Whatever you say. I'm too beat to argue with you," I say feebly.

"Good," Will says and rubs my arm gently. The act makes goose bumps dot my flesh. His eyes lower to the roughened skin beneath his fingertips, and I realize that he notices them. "Are you cold?" he asks.

I step back, away from him. "No, I mean, yes. I uh, I just caught a chill. That's all," I fumble pathetically. I cannot tell him that every time my skin comes in contact with his I feel as if I am being covered in a blanket of pleasant tingles. Even in my exhaustion-induced stupor I know better than to admit that.

"Oh," Will replies. His features are clouded by an expression I cannot name precisely. It is difficult to read faces when I have to concentrate so hard on not falling asleep or just falling in general. "As long as you're okay," he adds and smiles thinly.

"I'm fine," I say and smile back at him. "I'll go join the kids."

"Okay. See you soon," he says.

I start to walk toward the children when Will calls out to me.

"Avery!" he says my name with urgency.

I spin. The act makes me dizzy. "Yes?" I respond.

Will inhales and opens his mouth to speak but closes it immediately. He waves me off. "Never mind," he says.

"Are you sure?" I ask him and am thoroughly confused.

He is acting strangely. I hope I haven't done something to cause him to feel bad. He has lost his parents and is the sole guardian of his brother and sister. He's come under attack from Urthmen and had Lurkers scratching and clawing to enter the cave June and I took him to. He's had an extraordinarily awful few days. I don't want to make matters worse.

"Yep," he says. "I forgot what I wanted to say."

"Oh, okay," I say and take a step toward the children. I can't shake the sense that he's not telling me the truth, that he wanted to say something to me but changed his mind. I don't know. Maybe it is just fatigue scrambling my brain. I let it go. "Be safe, Will. I'll see you soon," I say.

Will smiles then turns and takes off into the woods.

When he is out of sight, June rushes to my side.

"What did he say?" she asks. A mischievous twinkle sparkles in her eyes.

"Nothing. He forgot what he called me for," I answer honestly.

"Right," June purses her lips and draws out each sound in the word. "And you believe him?"

"Uh, yeah, I do," I say.

"Okay, believe whatever you want to believe, but I think he wanted to tell you something important," she persists.

"Oh yeah? And what might that be, my all-knowing sister?"

"I don't know all that. He just had a look on his face like he had something to say." Her singsong voice suggests she is implying Will intended to make some major declaration. I don't know what ideas are rattling around in her head, but I cannot entertain any of them. I worry what she thinks is right, that maybe Will planned to part ways with us and tell me as much before he went hunting. I don't want to tell her and upset her because I am unsure. Regardless, I can't handle the thought of him finding me, us, so repugnant he'd rather take his chances with his siblings than continue with us.

"Yes, June, he did, and he forgot what it was," I say to try to end the conversation.

"I don't know," June continues. "I think it was something more."

"And I think you're wrong," I say snippily. I catch myself and soften my tone. "Will and I have not slept in days. He watched his parents die at the hands of Urthmen and is now responsible for his sister and brother," I say. "I'm pretty sure all that entitles him to a little forgetfulness."

June's cheeks are streaked with bands of pink. "When you put it that way," she starts. I hear a tremor in her voice and immediately feel guilty for being sharp with her at first.

"I'm sorry, June. I'm grumpy and tired and achy. You don't deserve to have me act like a jerk. You're going through all this with me." I pull her toward me and hug her tightly. "Sorry."

June hugs me back. Her arms wrap around my waist tightly before she drops them and steps back.

"I'd better get the fire started before Will gets back," she says and smiles.

"I'll help," I offer.

The children and I light a small fire. Will returns shortly after and carries two rabbits by their feet. He and I skin and prepare the rabbits then roast them. We eat quickly then sip from our canteens. Once the fire is extinguished and any evidence of its existence has been cleared, we begin hiking in hopes of finding a final place to stay for the night.

As I walk, I feel as if I am slogging through deep mud. My legs are heavy and my muscles ache. Too little sleep in the last several days has caught up with me. Spending the night in the tree did not help matters. We managed to survive, therefore my goal was achieved, but in many ways I feel as if I'm a dead person walking. My arms feel disconnected and leaden, as if they belong to someone else entirely, and my eyelids shutter closed every few minutes. I know that I can't possibly spend another night in a tree. I do not have the strength to climb, much less keep June stable while clinging to branches. There isn't a doubt in my mind that even if I somehow manage to make it high into a treetop and by some stroke of magnificent luck am able to steady June as we perch, I will fall asleep immediately and plummet to my death. No, the tree option is out of the question for tonight. That leaves me with few, if any, other choices. For the time being, however, I cannot focus on trees and places where we can't stay. I must concentrate on getting us closer to the edge of the woods, to where weeds and wildflowers meet asphalt and concrete.

We walk for much of the day, pushing ourselves harder and faster than the day before, and stop only once to fill our canteens at a seasonal stream. The sky is a chalky blue and the sun's rays are weak. A soft breeze stirs tall grasses and treetops. The air carried on it is cooler, less humid. I search the landscape for mossy ridges and rocky formations for a second day. I do not see either. I do notice, though, that some of the leaves are beginning to lose their rich green coloring. When the leaves change from shades of green to shades of red, orange and yellow, I know shorter, colder days will follow. By then I hope we are living in a safer environment, protected from the elements and no longer concerned with Lurkers. I do not know whether my hope will become a reality. I will do everything in my power to see it come to fruition.

In the distance, I see that a stone wall rises from the ground. It encircles a building also made of stone, but with ones that are more uniform in shape and size and colored a faded reddish hue. With steep roof pitches and a bell tower that looks as if it pierces the milky sky above, I feel as if the elaborate sprawling structure is familiar. I feel as if I have seen it before.

"Oh my goodness," Riley inhales sharply then says.

"Whoa, what is that?" Oliver asks and points to the entire setup.

"A stone wall that protects a building," I say absently as my eyes roam the length of the wall that is visible. They search my memory in time with my brain.

"Yeah, a building Urthmen occupy for sure, and one we should get as far away from before something terrible happens," Will says and places a hand on my shoulder.

I turn and face him. His features transform instantly. He drops his hand.

"What is it, Avery?" he searches my face as if he is seeing my mind piece together the puzzle.

"This wall, this place, I don't know. Something about it is familiar to me," I say. I look to the wall again and allow my eyes to travel along its perimeter. I strain them to see a chain-link gate with a giant padlock securing it shut. I lick my lips and my heart rate accelerates. Then recognition lands like a blow to my chest and nearly stops it from beating altogether. I place my hand over my heart and I know. I know exactly where I am. "Oh my gosh," I breathe.

"What's going on?" Will asks worriedly.

"This place," I say breathlessly. "I know this place. This is where I used to live before the Urthmen stormed it and killed my mother and everyone else who lived here."

Images flicker through my mind's eye. Fragmented flashes and disjointed images streak by in a dizzying whirl. I see my mother, pregnant and beautiful, sitting with my father. Then I see chaos, and blood, so much blood. Clips of utter darkness follow, then a burst of light, and after that a club striking my mother again and again. I squeeze my eyes shut and rub my temples. I try to consciously purge my mind of the memories blinking in my brain. But the building, the stone wall and the locked gate bombard my senses. Even the odd scent of musty leaves remains.

I feel Will's hand on my shoulder again. He gives it a gentle squeeze. Reflexively, I reach over and place my hand atop his, just as I would do with June. But the sensation of June's skin never causes me to feel as if a miniature bolt of lightning has passed between us as Will's touch does.

"We need to get out of here," Will says. "We need to get far away from this place."

"I agree with Will," June says. I hear her approaching. I drop my hand from where it rested on top of Will's hand. "The building, the wall, the whole layout creeps me out." Will drops his hand and I turn to face June. Her arms are wrapped around her waist again. She is hugging them to her body. "I don't want to be here. I don't want to be near the place mom died."

Her fear is evident. I am about to speak when Oliver chimes in.

"Yeah, I'm with June. Stumbling on a small fortress loaded with Urthmen is not somewhere any of us should be," Oliver says. There is hardness in his voice, an edge that borders rage and fear. I understand it. I feel it too. But a thought occurs to me.

"Urthmen aren't here," I say.

I feel four sets of eyes on me instantly. I look at each of them then Will's voice captures my attention.

"Urthmen stormed this place. Why would you think they would leave?" he asks.

"What reason would they have to stay?" I counter quietly.

The muscles around Will's jaw are flexing. "I don't follow," he arches a dark eyebrow and says.

"Think about it," I say. "There's nothing for them here in the forest." I search Riley and Oliver's faces then look at June. "Unless you count Lurkers hunting you every day from sunset to sunrise," I add sarcastically. But no one finds my sarcasm amusing in the least, not even Will. His arms are folded across his chest and his features are gathered. He looks serious.

"What about the gate?" he asks.

"What about it?" I shrug and do not quite get where he is going with his question.

"It's locked. If Urthmen don't live there, why is it locked?"

I hold his gaze briefly. He has made a decent point. But I'm still unconvinced that Urthmen live within the walls of the stronghold. "I'm going to see why it's locked. I'm going to take a closer look," I say impulsively. My statement draws gasps and grumbles.

"No! Avery, you can't," June cries out, her voice a hoarse whisper. "Please, don't go. It's too dangerous."

"So is staying out here," I say and cringe at the expression on her face after the words leave my lips. I soften my tone. "It will be dark soon," I remind her. "And we don't have a place to stay for the night yet."

"We can find another tree," she says and tries to persuade me to stay.

"You and I both know I can't spend another night in a tree, not if I want to live until morning, at least," I admit truthfully.

"Then it doesn't have to be a tree. We can come up with something else, anything. Just don't go near that place," she pleads.

I want to shout at her *Look around June! Do you see anything remotely resembling a safe place to spend the night?* But I don't. I know my short temper is just fatigue getting the better of me. So I say nothing. I turn and start walking toward the gate before the stone wall. I ignore the whispered attempts to call me back, even Will.

I streak through the tall grasses and weeds and remain low, crouched. I hide in bushes when I am close. I look back, over my shoulder and see that both June and Will wear similar expressions. They both look furious. Their brows are furrowed and their lips are pursed. June's hands are on her hips and Will's arms are folded tightly across his chest with his fists balled. His is pacing back and forth, shaking his head slowly. When June sees that I am watching her, she gestures for me to come back before tapping Will's shoulder and alerting him to my position. He begins gesturing animatedly as well. I do not heed their calls. Instead, I turn away and dash toward the wall. I press my back to the cool, rough stone and inch my way closer to the gate.

When I am right beside it, I steal a glance and chance being seen. My head darts out then back quickly. But I am able to make out an empty space. No one is milling about, none that I saw, that is. I wait a few seconds and am about to return to Will, June, Oliver and Riley and endure stern lectures when the faint sound of footsteps is accompanied by a shape flashing in my periphery.

I spin and see what appears to be a man. I retreat and pull back, but curiosity nags at my brain. I need to know whether my eyes deceived me, whether I did, indeed, see a human. I poke my head out and look again, only this time I focus on the being's head. I see that it is shaped properly. It is oval in appearance and has hair therefore it is a human being, not an Urthman.

I tuck my head and body back behind the concealment of the wall. My breath catches in my chest. A human is living at the compound I used to call home before Urthmen seized it. I begin to fantasize that Urthmen left immediately after storming the village and that humans happened upon it and repopulated. I know it is a farfetched dream, but it gives me hope in an otherwise hopeless world.

My heart rattles loudly in my chest. I cannot resist looking again. I thrust my head out a second time and am shocked to see two more humans. I can tell both are male thanks to the long shaggy beards they wear. The men are armed and appear to be patrolling the wall. I realize I must make my presence known. If there are more like them, the children and I, along with Will, could align ourselves with them. The prospect energizes me. But before I call them over and share with them my plan, I gesture to Will to stay where he is, to wait and remain hidden. I need to make sure it is safe to proceed. I need to get a sense of how these humans operate without putting my sister and friends at risk.

I take a deep breath and step away from the wall. I place myself directly in front of the gate and say, "Hello!" in a loud clear voice.

The three men startle then freeze in their tracks and turn to face me. They stare, still motionless, looking completely shocked for several beats until one of them makes his way to the gate followed by the others.

The closer they come, the better able I am to see their faces. I immediately notice that they look much older than I do. Their skin is weathered looking and ashen in color. Teeth are missing and their clothing is filthy.

A tall, meaty man with frizzy hair the color of rust smiles broadly at me and reveals his front tooth is missing. "Oh gosh! Wow! Where'd you come from?" he says and does not hide the surprise and excitement in his voice. He does not wait for me to speak either, and continues to rattle on.

"Sorry to react as I did a second ago. It's just that we don't see many other humans around here," he says.

"Oh, yeah, I guess not," is all I can think of to say.

"I'm Ross, by the way. And this is Tal," he says and points to a lanky man with small eyes and a prominent nose, "and this is Jay," he says and points to a shorter, sturdier looking man with stringy hair that falls to the middle of his back and has several teeth missing on the bottom who looks a good fifteen years older than I am. They all appear to be at least fifteen years older than I am. And while they look creepy and in desperate need of a soak in the nearest river, their greeting is warm and welcoming.

"Hi Ross, Tal and Jay, I'm Avery," I introduce myself.

"We're very happy to meet you, Avery," Ross says. He exchanges a sidelong glance with Jay, and a distinct uneasiness scurries across my skin that I cannot quite explain. "It's always good to find another survivor," he continues. "How did you manage to survive out here all by yourself?" he asks.

His question is one I would ask as well, and a harmless one at that, still I can't shake the suspicious feeling scuttling about when I hear his voice and watch the three men interact wordlessly with one another. They seem friendly enough on the surface. And they are humans. The experience of living among humans when I was young has taught me that humans are not out to hurt other humans. We stick together when we find one another. We have shared interests; we all share common enemies: Urthmen and Lurkers. I have no reason not to trust them.

"I am not alone," I say and watch as one of Tal's brows tics slightly.

"You're not?" Ross asks and looks past me.

"The others, the people I'm with, they're hidden," I say.

Ross and Tal's eyes scan the landscape.

Ross' features gather. His concern seems genuine when he says, "I suggest you get them in here before something happens to them. These woods aren't safe. Those hideous creatures prowl these woods at night, and we saw Urthmen not far from here scouting. Out in the open is no place to be if you want to live." He clutches his weapon and his eyes look off into the distance.

His words chill me to my core. They ring with hard truth.

"No, I guess they're not," I agree with a shiver. "I'll get my friends," I tell them.

I step back and check the cluster of bushes Will, June, Oliver and Riley are hiding behind then whistle once, a flat, monotone sound. June's head sticks out first. I catch her eye and her face brightens. I wave my arms and gesture for her and the others to join me. She hesitates at first, but eventually grabs hold of Will's arm and leads him toward me with Riley and Oliver in tow.

Everyone appears skeptical as they draw near. June's eyes round when she sees how unkempt Ross, Tal and Jay look and Riley recoils when they greet her. Their reactions do not go unnoticed by the men. I cringe inwardly when Ross' expression withers and he looks down at his clothes self-consciously. Will nudges me lightly. I am sure there is something we should say at this point, some excuse that justifies the children's reactions. But both of us come up empty. I shift my weight from one leg to the next and consider grabbing the kids and venturing out again when Ross' gravelly voice rumbles.

"You'll have to excuse my appearance, kids. If I'd known I was going to have guests today, I would have cleaned up a bit," Ross says. "We don't have a river nearby so we don't get to wash as often as we should. Just know that Jay smells the worst. I'd be sure to steer clear of him if I were you," he says and bobs his eyebrows before grinning.

Oliver laughs while June and Riley giggle nervously. Hearing their laughter eases my nerves somewhat. The ice has been broken.

"How'd you lose them?" Oliver surprises all of us by asking Ross.

Will flinches and opens his lips to undoubtedly reprimand his younger brother, but Ross speaks first.

"Lose what?" Ross asks with a puzzled look on his face.

An uncomfortable silence hangs in the air and pressure begins to build at my temples. The moment is so awkward I could scream.

"Your teeth," Oliver finally says in a small voice.

Will shoots him a stern look and starts to interject when Ross says, "What? My teeth! I lost teeth? Oh no!" Ross runs his hands through his wiry, shoulder-length hair and frets exaggeratedly. The children look stunned until Ross throws them a sly smile filled with mischief. "Gotcha!" he says and points both index fingers at Oliver then Riley and lastly June.

Tension seeps from my body and I exhale the breath I'd been holding. Will's shoulders lower, and the strain in his posture relaxes visibly. I feel his fingers grip my wrist and give it a gentle squeeze. I take his gesture as a signal of his approval.

"So," Ross claps his hands together. "Who's hungry here?" he asks us.

The children's hands rocket into the air as they mutter that they are starving.

"We haven't eaten since this morning," Oliver says, but Ross does not look at him. His eyes are on June. A small frown drags the corners of his mouth downward. She is thin, painfully so. Our continual hiking and meager food supply has taken a toll on her. She looks frail. Ross reaches out a hand toward her and reflexively my hand flies behind me to the hilt of my sword. It is unsheathed before his fingertips graze her shoulders.

"Whoa, whoa," Ross says and splays his hands out in front of his body in surrender. "I don't intend to hurt the girl," he says and steps away from June with the same caution a person moves away from a wild animal. "Please, put your weapon away. We can't have visitors with weapons within the walls of this compound. We are a peaceful people, and we intend to keep it that way."

My cheeks blaze and beads of sweat dot my brow. Slowly, I lower my sword and watch as the men around me relax then exchange furtive glances. "Sorry," I say halfheartedly. "We haven't come across humans in quite some time," I lie and neglect to share that Will, Oliver and Riley are new to June and I. "June is my sister and it is my job to protect her," I say flatly.

"I understand," Ross says. "But we are humans, just as all of you are. We're not the enemy. We're not who you have to worry about."

His words make sense. I know they are true, but when it comes to June, logic ceases to exist.

"Fair enough," I say and sheathe my sword at the scabbard on my back. Ross watches me do so then his eyes roam my body and rest on the dagger at my thigh. My lips press to a hard line and my eyes are narrow when his gaze returns to them.

"It's just about time for dinner," Ross directs his attention to the children once again. "You are all welcome to join us."

"Thank you. That would be great," I say.

"Yeah, thanks a lot," Will says appreciatively.

"But there's only one problem," Ross says.

"Problem?" Will asks.

"Well, not a problem really," Tal chimes in. "More of a rule we have."

I watch as all three men move in closer. I suddenly feel as if the air around me has thickened, that the temperature has jumped suddenly.

"You see," Ross begins. "We do not allow weapons beyond this point. No strangers are allowed to set foot inside if they have a knife, bow and arrow, sword or any other kind of weapon on them," he says and gestures over his shoulder toward the building.

My stomach bottoms out. I have never willingly parted with my weapons. This would be the first time ever.

"I don't know," I think out loud. "I'm not sure how I feel about that," I say and hear the steely suspicion in my voice.

"I don't know how to say this politely so I'm going to just lay it on the line here," Ross says and smiles almost apologetically. "I have no intention of harming you or any of your friends or kin. I am not a threat. But if you step inside the walls of our compound armed, you are a threat, and I cannot allow it." Ross rubs his hand over his face as if he is truly troubled by what he has said or what he plans to say next. "It's your choice. You can either give me your weapons, or leave."

His words are like a blow to my gut. My eyes immediately go to Will. His expression is unreadable. In my periphery, I see that the sun is about to set and the sky is dimming fast. Ross has not offered us much of a choice at all. He has essentially told us that we can give up our weapons and enjoy food and shelter or keep our weapons and take our chances at twilight with Lurkers waking from their daytime slumber.

"Considering that evening is just about here, I don't have much if a decision to make," I say levelly. "We will be torn to pieces by Lurkers, uh, I mean the creatures that come out when the sun sets, before we're able to find shelter for the night."

"That is true," Ross says with regret lacing his words.

When Will hands over the club he took from the Urthmen who stormed his cave by the lake, I am shocked. He turns to me as soon as it is out of his hands.

"I don't want to die tonight, Avery," he whispers.

Ross hands the club to Tal and Tal leads us to a metal cabinet. Using a key attached to a thin chain on his belt he unlocks the cabinet and places the club on an empty shelf.

"See," Tal says. "All of our weapons are here. Every person who stays here has surrendered his blade, spear or stick."

I scan the shelves and see that knives and bludgeons of every size and shape are arranged neatly on the top shelves. Daggers, spears and swords occupy the lower shelves.

"Come on, Avery," Will's hot breath fans across my neck when he leans in to whisper to me. "I'm not happy about it either, but think about June and Riley, about Oliver and me, about you," he tries to convince me.

Reluctantly, I pull my dagger from the case on my thigh, and with a hesitant hand, I turn it over to Ross. A grin stretches across his face and crinkles the skin around his eyes. Next, I surrender my spear then last, my sword. I feel naked, stripped of any means of protecting June and I.

"Excellent," Ross says as Tal places our armaments in the cabinet then locks it. He twists and faces the children then says, "Now that all that boring grown-up stuff is over, we can finally eat and meet the rest of the people here." He uses a silly voice as he continues to speak to them and leads them inside. Tal and Jay follow.

We continue down a long, narrow corridor and follow the scent of burning brush and cooking meat. I remember that the main area that was used as a dining hall had a fire pit. It is surreal that I have returned to where I spent so many years as a child, to a place where I once felt safe and happy. I feel neither now.

"What do you think?" Will asks and moves so close to me his lips almost brush my earlobe.

I do not know how to express the leeriness I feel. It is unjustified. Yet I can't shake it. Perhaps it is the fact that my mother and so many others were butchered here not long ago. Perhaps it is the three days of sleep deprivation finally catching up to me. Perhaps it is both. Perhaps it is neither. All I know is that my nerves feel frayed.

"I'm thinking I just made a huge mistake handing over my weapons," I say bluntly in a quiet voice.

"Why? They're humans, like us. They have no reason to hurt us. They're on our side," he replies.

A few moments pass as I consider what he's said. After all, he has come across more humans than I have. He and his family were the first in recent years.

"I guess," I say and hear the exasperation in my tone.

We continue to walk until we reach a room set with a makeshift table composed of long wooden slats aligned side by side. My heart leaps to my throat as the arrangement brings to mind flashbacks that echo through my mind with aching clarity. I remember eating here as a child, the setup is nearly identical.

June, Riley and Oliver marvel at what they see, at all the people in front of them. Even Will's jaw drops. I wish I felt as they do. I wish I could look on in wide-eyed wonder. But I can't. I do not feel excited in the least. All I see is the bloodshed of persons past, my people, and strangers. We are grossly outnumbered, and without my weapons, I worry I have made a mistake that will cost us our lives.

Chapter 17

Ross ushers us deeper into the dining area. With every step I take, my unease grows. I do not understand it fully. I can't explain it. I just feel anxiety swelling inside of me. When Ross finally stops in front of a table filled with five men, all caked in filth and disheveled in appearance, a tremor passes through me that cause my stomach to roll. The men spring to their feet. I flinch instinctively and take note of their appearances. I notice one of them looks as if he isn't much older than Oliver. The rest are older and rougher looking.

"Guys, this is Will, Oliver, Riley, June, and Avery," Tal introduces us.

A series of pleasantries volley around the table and Tal begins naming the men before us. But I'm unable to concentrate on names. A penetrating pair of bloodshot, heavily creased eyes is on me. The gaze belongs to the oldest, mangiest looking man among those at the table.

"Well, well, well, what do we have here," the old man smacks his lips together and says. His eyes rake up and down my body in a way that makes my temper flare wildly. Heat rips from my insides and rockets to my extremities. I feel as if I am on fire. I am trembling. My hand automatically flies to my shoulder, expecting to touch the hilt of my sword. Finding that my sheath is empty, my sword absent, fuels the fire further with panic.

"All right, dad, enough," Tal says as if he is speaking to a naughty child. His tone is mildly annoyed, as is his expression, when he looks at whom he addressed as 'dad', the same man who leered at me as if I were a side of roasted boart meat and he was a starved man. Tal's eyes move from his father to me, and he says, "Avery, please excuse my father. He hasn't seen a pretty girl in a long time. He seems to have forgotten how to behave," he finishes with a look of warning to the old man.

I do not respond verbally. I simply nod with a harsh look on my face, one that indicates that I do not excuse his father's behavior.

Ross and Tal banter amicably with the men at the table for a short time. While they do, I look at June and Riley. They seem completely at ease in their new environment, a fact that worries me beyond measure. My eyes settle on Oliver next. He is looking every which way as he examines the interior of the dining hall. He does not share my concern, and he does not seem bothered by the old man's comment or demeanor. But when my gaze travels to Will, I see that worry shrouds his features. His eyes lock on mine and his gaze becomes intense, as if he is trying to convey a silent message to me.

I do not know what he is trying to communicate. I wish I did. I concentrate on his face. But his attention snaps in another direction when more people step into the room. Three women, who are stooped, old and worn out looking, shuffle in. Their clothes are tattered and stained and in far worse condition than the men's. They enter hesitantly, taking jerky, unsure strides. I watch them and find it odd that none among them makes eye contact or so much as acknowledges anyone in the room as they shuffle along.

Though they keep their heads down for much of the time while they heft trays laden with food, occasional glances steal our way, and I swear that shock registers on the women's faces but they are afraid to say as much. Children trail after them. I count six in all. The children look as if they range in age from two to six. Another old woman lumbers inside. She is carrying an infant in each arm. I wonder who the children belong to. The appearances of the women suggest they are of advanced age and far past their childbearing years. The entire situation seems off.

It becomes even stranger when Ross calls out to the women.

"Ladies!" his voice booms authoritatively. All of the women freeze, and the children following nearly slam into their backsides as they clumsily try to make a sudden stop. The women's apprehension is obvious. It radiates from them like heat rising from the earth on a hot day. Their eyes remain glued to the ground while Ross continues. "Ladies, I'd like you to meet our new guests."

His words are harmless enough, but something in his tone shrieks through me like metal scraping metal. They carry an unspoken warning, a threat of violence that quivers in the air.

"This is Will, Oliver, Riley, June, and Avery," Ross says, pointing to each of us as he says our names.

The women glance up. Their shoulders hook forward further. They barely look at Will, Oliver, Riley, June and I. They mumble nervous hellos then quickly cast their eyes back to the ground.

Warning screams through me. I cannot pinpoint what is happening, what the reason is for the women's timid behavior. All I know is that something is not right. I decide to ask the first question that pops into my mind when I see them disappear through a doorway, out of the dining area, all the while with Ross' watchful gaze bolted to them.

"Aren't they going to eat with us?" I ask.

Ross tears his eyes from the entryway the women just slipped through then looks at me absently. "Huh?" he asks.

"The women, aren't they going to eat with us?" I repeat my question.

"Ah, no," the old man who was said to be Tal's father answers with a chuckle. "Nobody wants to look at their ugly faces while they eat. Ha!" he laughs and puffs out his chest, proud of the joke he thinks he's made.

"Dad, that's not true," Tal says tightly and shoots his father a grim look. "They just prefer to eat in the kitchen with their children." He looks at me again and offers an unnatural smile.

"*Their* children, as in those babies belong to *them*?" I ask incredulously. The words spill from me before I can stop them. My shock at his statement overwhelms me too quickly.

Tal's smile falters for a split-second. "Yes, they do," he answers after immediately regaining his composure. "Those women aren't as old as they look. They've just had hard lives."

"Yeah, who hasn't," Will shocks me by saying.

His statement surprises me almost as much as the slightly embarrassed look on his face. He shifts uncomfortably and begins a conversation about tales his parents told him about how women and men used to pamper themselves before the war.

"My father and mother shared stories they'd heard from their ancestors through the generations about all sorts of things men and women used to do when human beings ruled the planet," Will commands the attention of a small group of men from the compound. Little by little, I am getting edged out of the circle. "They would go to places called *salons* and have chemicals put on their hair, poison really, that would change its color or texture." A ripple of laughter erupts along with a series of affirmations that a few among them had heard similar accounts. "Yeah, and if that's not enough, they would go to places and have stuff injected into their faces to try to make themselves look younger."

"I remember hearing something like that from my grandpa," the old man, Tal's father, says. "Wish someone could've saved some of that junk. We sure could use it here," he says and laughs so hard he is beset by a coughing fit.

"Yeah, we could use it on the hags in the kitchen!" an unfamiliar voice chimes in. "That would make things a lot easier for us."

My insides simmer. I wonder what exactly the man's last sentence is supposed to mean. How would the women's appearances make anything easier for them? I would love to ask, but Will is still addressing them.

"The way people acted centuries ago, it's no wonder the world collapsed. Humans back then were completely crazy!" Will says.

Hoots and laughter break out all around me. The moment seems surreal. I am supremely uncomfortable and Will, who I thought shared my nervousness about the men, has officially been accepted by just about every man in the room. I try to catch his eye as he is led to the table and offered a pile of what looks to be boart meat. June and Riley sidle up next to me while Oliver is swept away on the all-male current. When they are seated, we sit and do not wait to be served. We fill a plate with meat and eat.

"I hear women used to have people suck the fat from their backsides and shoot it into their lips," Tal's father says as his gravelly voice rises above the others. He puckers his lips and forces them outward. "They would look like this and think they were pretty," he struggles to talk while holding his mouth positioned as it is which causes an eruption of laughter.

"Oh man, you look like you have a duckbill or fish lips or something,'" one of the men says.

"He does!" Will agrees and bangs the table with his hand as he doubles over laughing.

"Well, which is it?" the old man barely manages as he splutters.

"Don't matter, you still look better than those crones in the kitchen!" the man who made the duck comment says and is laughing so hard tears stream from the corners of his eyes.

Food and spittle sprays from the men's mouths and the scene becomes one marked by ugliness in all its forms. Seeing Will, gorgeous, golden Will, among them seems incongruous. I don't know what I'm more offended by, the men's behavior, their words, or the fact that Will is immersed in both, and is right at the center of it all.

Apparently, I am not alone in noticing this. However, I am alone in feeling discomfited by it.

"Will sure is popular," June says with a smile. "Everyone seems to really like him."

"Yes they do," I say and do not mask my annoyance.

"Avery, what's the matter?" June asks. "I thought you'd be thrilled to find so many people."

"Me, too," I murmur under my breath.

"Then what's the problem?" she persists and clearly heard my grumbling.

"It's everything, the women, how they reacted to Ross and Tal and the others," I start but my voice is drowned out by a roar of laughter that explodes all around us.

June's head whips to where it began. Will is getting clapped on the back.

"How are you holding up?" I try to ask her, but can barely hear the sound of my own voice. "I know you didn't want to come here," I lean in and say a little louder. I want to gauge her opinion of this place, of the people, but she seems absorbed by the noise and number of humans surrounding us.

When June's attention does not return to me immediately, I decide to keep my thoughts to myself. The possibility still exists that I am just overly paranoid due to a lack of sleep.

I eat silently and tune into the conversations around me from time to time. I remain vigilant though. I try to scrutinize every move the people around me make, try to analyze their intentions. It is draining, to say the least. I have had little interaction with humans unrelated to me, and that was limited to when I was a child of about June's age, ironically, when I lived within the walls of the compound I sit in now. I find myself wishing my social skills were as razor sharp as my battle skills.

Few questions come my way and distract me from my intensive watchfulness.

"So where's your kin, your mom and dad?" Tal's father asks. His question is ordinary enough, but it is his demeanor, the way he regards me, that gets under my skin. He examines me as if he is able to see through my clothes and lay eyes on my bare flesh.

"Dead," I offer a simple one-word answer. I have no desire to chitchat on the subject of losing my parents. And the fact that June is my sister is obvious given our many similarities even if I hadn't told Tal and the others earlier.

Halfhearted condolences are offered by the few men near me then they resume conversing with one another.

While the inquiries are scarce, the lingering stares are abundant. They last longer than curious glances. I cannot put my finger on what exactly it is about the men that has me unnerved. So they're looking at me, what's the big deal? Maybe Tal was right. Maybe the men are acting strangely because they haven't seen many women in their lives. Trying to convince myself of that is difficult.

As if sensing my inner turmoil, Will smiles warmly at me several times while we are in the eating area. He seems to be relaxed and enjoying himself. Why that irks me as much as it does remains a point I wish to examine further. I also wish I could ask Will what prompted his turnaround. If I didn't know any better and was seeing him for the first time with the men around him, I would think he'd spent his entire life with them. But I can't now, not when there is a crowd of strange men leering at me. I hope I am wrong about them, that everything is a figment of my exhausted imagination, and that being peeved with Will is encompassed in that. He looks as if he is having a good time. I wish I could say the same for myself. But I can't. I do not feel as if I have his support, and that leaves me perplexed, and angry.

I chew my meat but bitterness continues to rise in the back of my throat. Forcing myself to eat is necessary. I need to attempt to keep my strength intact. So I keep going, swallowing bite after bite, all the while I watch and listen.

When I finish, I look around and see that most of the men are leaning back, their assorted array of bellies round and full. I am still rattled by the circumstances. That feeling is compounded when the women return and clear the tables. They file out from the doorway they disappeared through and dutifully remove the metal saucers on which our food was served. As they do, they do not make eye contact or say a word. But when the women are close to me, I am able to look at them closely. I examine their skin. It looks thin and heavily creased and bears an unhealthy grayish pallor. Their complexions look as if they have not seen sunlight in many years. I purposely place my face directly in the line of vision of one of them. Her eyes flicker from my face to the table then back to me. Desperation scrawls lines around her mouth and forehead. Despair flashes in her dull irises before burning out like a tiny ember in a rainstorm.

The expression haunts me. I cannot focus on the rest of the time I spend in the dining area. When Ross speaks directly to me, I must ask him to repeat himself as I am lost in thought, trying frantically to decode what I saw in the woman's eyes.

"We had the women set up a cottage for you and your family," he says.

For a moment, my mind scrambles to figure out what he means by *cottage*. I realize he is talking about the huts in which villagers used to live.

"Thank you," I say and nod stiffly. I do not trust myself to say anything more. Without my weapons to protect us, I will not risk saying anything that might get us killed.

We are led down a long hallway and out into an open courtyard. Small structures with thatched roofs continue for as far as I can see.

"Wow," Oliver's eyes widen as he takes in the sight of it.

"Is this where I was born?" June asks me with quiet wonder in her voice. She has stopped walking while the others continue toward a nearby hut.

"Yes, this is where you were born and lived for the first two years of your life," I reply, but wonder does not shade my words. Hurt does.

We continue walking until we reach the entrance to the place we will rest for the night.

"Here we are," Ross says and grins so wide his smile turns frightening. He splays one hand out at his side to showcase the cozy interior of the hut lit by what I guess is an animal fat-fueled lantern. "You should all enjoy a night of deep, worry-free sleep. Two men will be on the wall patrolling. But don't worry, the night beasts don't live this close to the edge of the forest, and even if they did," he adds with pride, "They wouldn't be able to make it over the wall."

He did not build the wall, yet his demeanor suggests he assumes credit for it. I met the men who placed each stone by hand. They were good and decent men who walked for miles in sweltering temperatures to wash their clothes in rivers and hunt to feed the village. Women and children ate with men, and no one wore looks of anguish on their faces without illness or death as a cause. The men who built the wall were not like Ross at all.

"Thank you," Will says to Ross and clutches his shoulder familiarly. "This is terrific. We are grateful for your hospitality."

Will turns and looks over his shoulder at me, as if prompting me to add to what he's said.

"Yes," I say with a forced smile.

An irritable expression races across Ross' face like a storm cloud overtaking a clear sky. He recovers quickly, but not before narrowing his eyes at me.

"Okay then," he says and claps his hands loudly. "Have a good night and I'll see you all in the morning."

Ross turns and leaves us in the hut. The children set about inspecting a stack of sleep sacks that are in much better condition than the ones June and I had. I immediately move toward Will and tug his arm. I pull him out of earshot from the children.

"What's going on with you?" I do not waste time and demand. "I thought you were as freaked out as I am, what with the women and the weird interaction and everything," I say sharply.

"What're you talking about?" Will snaps back at me.

"What am I talking about?" I unleash on him. "Have you lost your mind? Don't you remember how that old guy looked at me when we first got here? And what about the children, *the babies*, with those old women, none of that strikes you as odd?"

I expect Will to lose his temper and shout at me. I am angry and scared and not expressing myself in a calm or rational fashion. But he does neither. Instead, his features wilt as if I've reminded him of very important points, and I begin to wonder whether *I* am losing *my* mind.

"Both of those instances were very odd," he admits then scrubs both hands over his face.

"Who do you think the kids and the babies belong to?" I ask and rein in my temper.

"That's a good question. I have no idea," he says.

"Will, I think we're in trouble here," I look over my shoulder to make sure the kids do not here me and whisper.

"Avery," Will says gently as he tips his head to one side. His pale blue-green eyes glow in the dim light. He places his hand on my forearm. His touch is so light it sends a small shiver racing up my arm. "I think not sleeping for so long is getting to you. I think it's affecting your judgment, making you a little paranoid," he says. "Let's try to get some sleep. We can talk more about it in the morning, once we've rested. I don't know about you, but I'm more exhausted than I've ever been," he says and traces a small line with his finger down the soft underside of my forearm. The sensation is so exquisite I could cry. His handsome face and mind-scrambling touch combined with the soothing tone of his voice muddles my thoughts, my memory. We have all been through so much in the last few days. Will and his siblings lost their parents. They watched them die. He is deserving of a night of rest at the very least. I suddenly feel selfish for burdening him with what may very well be paranoid imaginings of an overtired brain.

Standing as close to Will as I am and enjoying his fingertips atop my skin, I almost forget what I am so upset about. Almost.

"We'll talk in the morning," I agree. *If they don't slit our throats while we sleep*, I add in my head.

I step away from Will, away from the delightful feel of his touch, and grab a sleep sack. I unroll it beside June and, after saying goodnight to her and the others, I lay flat on my back.

My limbs feel as if they are melting into the dirt floor beneath me. Every part of me becomes heavy, even my eyelids. Much-needed sleep finds me and I drift off.

Chapter 18

I do not know how much time has passed when I wake with a start. The flame inside the lantern is so small I can barely see the inside of the hut. All I am able to make out are the shapes of sleeping bodies. I count quickly, tallying four to be sure, before climbing out of my sack and scuttling next to each of them. When I hear deep, even breathing, I am calmed somewhat.

But that calm comes to an abrupt end when the muffled sounds of cries echo through the stillness. The fine hairs on my body stand at attention. I freeze for a moment and hope against hope that my ears deceived me, that I did not just hear the strangled sound of a woman's scream pierce the night. The tortured shriek rings out again, and I know I did not imagine it. I jump to my feet, adrenaline flooding every cell in my body, and dash out of the hut.

The moon is full and the light it shines is bright. I am careful to stay in the shadows as I slip among the huts, though. I do not know what I expect to see but know that I don't want to be seen. I do not come across a single person as I skulk farther away from the hut June, Will and the others occupy, none except for the two men patrolling the wall. I glimpse them in the distance. They do not appear to be alarmed in the least.

I start to turn and head back when I see a man make his way to one of the huts. I assume he is returning there to sleep. Still, I stay and watch. He knocks at the door and another man answers. When the man answers, the front of his body is on full display. His shirt is unbuttoned and his pants are unfastened. He speaks to the man who knocked in hushed tones, then begins zipping and buttoning his clothes. He steps out and the man who knocked steps in. He closes the door behind him. I watch as the man who answered the door marches away between the huts until he is out of sight.

Beyond the door, I hear a man raise his voice. I am pulled, as if by invisible strings, toward the hut. I press my ear to the smooth wood and listen. The rumble of the male voice is accompanied by panicked pleas and then a loud slapping sound. I jump back away from the door in time to hear a female scream then sobs of misery. My hand darts out, as if of its own choice, and is on the doorknob. My heart is thudding in my chest, filling my eardrums with its fitful pounding, as I consider turning it. But the empty scabbard at my back reminds me that I am unarmed, and therefore of no use to whomever is being hurt inside the hut.

I retract my hand and ball it into a fist. I am unarmed for now, but do not intend to be for long. I search the map my mind has made of the compound, drawing on old memories as well as new ones, and begin moving toward the cabinet in which my weapons are locked. I take several steps but freeze in my tracks when the door to the hut opens suddenly.

I duck out of sight and crouch low beside a neighboring hut, out of the moonlight and swathed in sooty shadows. I hold my breath and watch as the man who entered the cabin not long ago leaves. He is buttoning his pants as he goes. He twists his upper body and barks orders over his shoulder.

"Now you keep your filthy mouths shut in there!" he warns before he shuts the door behind him.

I wait until he is gone then bolt toward the hut he just left. I open the door and nearly lose the dinner I ate hours earlier at the sight I am confronted with. Candle light flickers and casts a soft glow on the interior where four girls are nude. Shackles bind their ankles and wrists and are hooked to lengths of chain that are fastened to thick posts in the ground. One girl is crying. Blood drips from her lip and angry welts mark her body. Two appear to be no older than I am, and one looks as pregnant as my mother was when she was killed.

The room spins in lopsided circles for several turns, but it isn't until a noise behind me sounds that the spinning grinds to a dizzying halt. Large hands firmly grip my upper arms from behind. I am spun and instantly met with a vaguely familiar face, one I saw at dinner hours earlier. He is a large man with a long scraggly beard and hair to match. He was one of the five seated at the table when we arrived in the dining hall. He is crowding the doorway with his sizable frame. I would not be able to make it past him even if he weren't holding me.

"Hey there, little lady," he greets me with a kindly tone that contradicts his grasp. "Looks like you lost your way."

I squirm and feel his grip loosen slightly. "W-why are you doing this? Why are these women used like this?"

"We are growing our flock," he answers without apology. "We are rebuilding humanity."

His answer catches me off guard. I expected to hear that the women were there for the men's enjoyment, for pleasure. I'm sure they are, but they're also breeders. And the man before me thinks he is doing something noble. Hot tears blaze behind my eyelids as the direness of the circumstances hits me fully.

"Why do you have to keep them chained up like that?" I ask and feel tears spill down my cheeks.

"They are chained because they wouldn't stay if we let them roam free," he admits. "We found them wandering the woods just like you were wandering the woods. Only you came to us, like a gift dropped on our doorstep." He lowers one hand and cups my chin in his hand tenderly. My skin crawls at his touch. "So lovely," he murmurs before a rumble echoes from deep in his chest. I suppress the urge to vomit.

"You found the girls wandering through the forest alone?" I manage to ask without gagging.

"No, not all at once, at different times," he answers and strokes my cheek with his thumb. "They each had their own groups with boys and men. But we have no use for more men. We did away with them. But don't you worry about a thing," he says then lowers his voice and adds, "You're going to make a fine addition to our group of women. And so will the two little ones. They're not old enough for birthin' but Ross likes 'em that age regardless." The man licks his lips and whispers in my ear, his mouth so close his rancid breath wafts across my face. "He likes his girls real young, and pure, but I like 'em a little older, like you."

A surge of anger explodes inside of me unlike any I have ever experienced. Rage bubbles and brims and sends a memory rushing to my brain. I hear my father's voice instructing me where to kick a male Urthmen, or any man for that matter, if ever I am threatened and unarmed. The man's crotch is close. I raise my knee and launch it squarely between his legs as hard as I can.

The man's eyes widen then he doubles over clutching his pelvis. He lets go of me, and I start to run. But he regroups fast and catches me by the collar of my shirt and flings me backward, slapping me when I am in arm's reach. The blow stings like thousands of bee bites and sends me stumbling off balance. I slam into the far wall and hit the back of my head before falling to the ground.

My head is throbbing and I see a scattering of black dots in my field of vision, but I fight the compelling urge to close my eyes and submit to the darkness. I force them open and see a rock about the size of my fist. I grab it and jump to my feet, surprising him. I swing the rock as I lunge and release it. It zips through the air and hits him directly in his forehead. He staggers backward then falls to the ground.

Nature takes over. I am commanded by a killer instinct rooted deep inside of me. I see red. I want nothing more than to hurt the man who promised to hurt my sister and Riley, the man who hurt so many women, the man who intended to hurt me. I do not waste a moment. I attack. I scoop up the rock that collided with his head and straddle his chest in a single, swift motion. I hoist the rock high overhead and crash it against his skull over and over again until I am panting and covered in a fine layer of sweat. I look down at his face. His eyes are unfocused, unmoving, as is the rest of him. I search his pockets and find his keys.

I take a quick look at the women I will leave behind. I see smiles touch their features that reveal youth. Their expressions set my feet into motion. I run off in the direction of the shed holding my weapons. I run as fast as my legs will take me and do not stop until I am standing before the metal cabinet I saw earlier. I fumble with the keys, frantically trying each until I find the one that fits.

"Come on! Come on!" I whisper hurriedly as I turn the key in the lock.

When the door swings open, I nearly cry out with joy. But time for celebration does not exist for me. I have my spear, my dagger, my sword and Will's club when two men round the corner and head my way. I dart off in another direction as I see them begin to run. I drop everything except my sword. I clutch it tightly, excited to be armed again and looking forward to fighting the first man who confronts me.

These men are no better than Urthmen. They abuse women and children. They are monsters in their own right.

The first man arrives, armed. He is clutching a sword as well. He rushes me and wields it like an ax, chopping down. I deflect his labored swing easily then slice the air horizontally. The edge of my blade drags across his throat, cutting it deeply. The man's weapon clangs to the ground just as another, familiar man approaches.

I recognize Ross immediately. *Ross.* I spit his name in my mind like venom. He is the one who duped us into surrendering our weapons. He is the one who likes little girls. My body begins to tremble with fury.

"Boy, you're beautiful when you're mad," he wheezes. He is breathing heavy from running and makes the first move, hefting his blade clumsily. I sidestep his swing easily and pause for a moment, staring at him. He awkwardly attempts to slice me a second time, but again, I avoid being hit with ease.

"What's the matter?" I toy with him. "You can't handle a woman who fights back, you fat boart!"

He takes another lazy swipe, winded and red-faced. Only this time, I do not toy with him. I move in for the kill. I cleave the air with all my might, driving the blade laterally, and open him at his gut. His weapon falls seconds before his innards spill.

I turn and take comfort in knowing that Ross is out of commission, that at least the female children in the compound will be safe for the time being, and sheathe my dagger and spear then pick up Will's club. I clutch it in one hand and my spear in the other. I take off toward the hut in which June, Will, Riley and Oliver sleep. When I catch sight of our hut in the distance, I see Jay, Tal and his father standing outside. A torch has been lit. In the firelight, I see that Will has been dragged from his sleep sack. He is on the ground. Tal hovers over him with the tip of his sword dangerously close to Will's chest.

I unsheathe my spear from my back and summon every muscle in my body to be strong and precise. Then I hurl it with all my might. It flies through the night and cuts the air, never stopping until it stabs through the center of Tal's throat.

The momentum of my spear causes Tal to lurch backward. His weapon falls and he staggers a moment, stunned before he frantically tries to dislodge the object from his neck. I see it in a blur as I run full speed toward Will, see his legs cave from beneath him then his body flop back. I don't stop, though, and immediately toss Will his club. Oliver is on the ground unconscious and the girls are huddled together crying. But I cannot attend to any of them yet. Will grips his club.

"Oliver, are you all right?" he calls to his brother. But Oliver does not answer. "What's happening?" he asks.

My shoulder is touching his and I do not take my eyes off either Jay or Tal's father. "They were going to kill you and Oliver and do some sick things to June, Riley and me, weren't you?" I address the men.

Jay laughs cruelly. "We still are," he says. "What makes you think you're getting out of here?"

Tal's father licks his lips and calls for Ross and two other men.

"I wouldn't bother," I say in a voice so level and venomous it sounds foreign to my ears. "No one is coming to help you. I took care of them already."

"Liar!" Jay shouts and spittle sprays from his thin lips. "There's no way a skinny little girl like you took down any of my boys."

"Believe what you want. Your boys aren't coming. They all look pretty much like Tal looks right about now."

My words frenzy Tal's father. He moves to attack me while Jay attacks Will simultaneously. From the corner of my eye, I see that Will avoids Jay's advance and easily clubs him in the back of the head. The blow sends him to the ground and renders him unmoving. I dodge the old man's strike as well.

"Drop your sword, old man," Will advises Tal's father when he is at my side once again. The fight is now two against one.

Then the old man does something unexpected. He lowers his sword. His eyes glaze for a moment and he places his free hand over his heart. He pitches and staggers and positions himself over Oliver. His gaze shines with a sinister delight when he appears to reclaim awareness and no longer totters about. He looms over Oliver and is about to drive the tip of his blade straight through the boy's heart.

"No!" I shout and heave my sword forward. It drills through the old man's torso and he drops his weapon. Will descends on him and delivers a deadly final knock to his skull.

I rush to Oliver and place two fingers to the base of his neck. I feel a steady pulse.

"He's alive," I tell Will. But Will is standing over the old man who has fallen to the dirt floor.

"Are you okay?" I ask Oliver as his eyelids begin to flutter.

"Yeah, I think so," he says shakily.

I leave Oliver where he is. June takes my place and helps him to his feet. I get to the first man Will struck, Jay. I repeat the process I performed on Oliver, only this time I do not detect a throbbing at the base of the man's neck.

"He's dead," I say to Will. "Jay's dead."

Will drops his club and rakes both hands through his hair. He is pacing and clearly distraught. "I killed a human. I can't believe I killed a human being," he mutters. He sinks to his knees and looks as if he may be ill.

I sheathe my sword and kneel. I cup Will's perfect face in my hands and force him to look at me. "That man you killed and the men I killed were no better than Urthmen. They were monsters all the same."

Will dips his chin and leans into me, resting his head in the space between my neck and shoulder. His arms grip me, embracing me tightly. He begins to cry. I hold him where he is.

All of us have suffered. We are drained emotionally and physically. Life continues to take its toll on us with each day that passes. I wonder how high the price will go, how much we will have to sacrifice before something gives. These thoughts, and so many others, tumble through my brain. They are too much to handle. So I release them and exist in the moment I am in. I clutch Will snugly and feel our tears mingle.

Chapter 19

I lift my chin from where it is perched on Will's head and see a boy running toward us with his blade in hand. I release Will immediately and leap to my feet, recognition striking through my body like a bolt of lightning. I scoop up my sword and ready myself. The boy approaching was at the table when we first arrived in the dining hall. He'd been quiet when I first met him. Much has changed since then.

He rushes at us, all the while releasing a guttural war cry.

"What did you do?" he demands. His voice is hoarse and raw, laced with sadness and hate. "You killed them! You killed *all* my fathers!" he screams and swings his blade in my direction.

I block his swing easily and thrust my sword as our blades collide, placing all of my weight behind it. The boy pitches backward and totters for a moment.

"Drop it!" I warn him. "I'm not going to hurt you."

The boy's chest is heaving. His cheeks are red and his eyes are wild. I know he is hurting, but his pain is not my problem at the moment. Especially since his father, one of the men my blade claimed, intended to kill Will and Oliver, and enslave June, Riley and myself.

In my periphery, I see Will streak by. He is behind the boy within seconds and grabs him in a bear hug. The boy's weapon falls to the ground with a loud *clang*.

"You killed him," the boy cries and resembles a trapped mammal. "You killed them all!" He flails and thrashes for a moment, but Will holds tight.

"Your father and the others attacked us," I say flatly once the boy is still. "And I think you know that's what they planned all along. You knew what they were going to do. I defended my family

175

and me," I add and hear how easily I include Will, Oliver and Riley in my family despite knowing them for a short while.

The boy's head sags. He knows I am right.

"I'm going to let you go now," Will tells him. "But you need to be calm. No one is going to hurt you, okay?"

The boy nods feebly before Will lowers his arms. I do not wish for more bloodshed. All of us have witnessed enough. I am relieved when, once freed, the boy rushes to where Tal's body is slumped as opposed to attempting to engage me in battle again. He cries and drapes his body across him, and a small corner of my heart clenches tightly.

Will closes his eyes and slowly shakes his head from side to side. I can imagine the thoughts racing through his mind. The loss of his parents is so fresh in his mind, it is a wonder he has not fallen apart completely. I move toward him and place a hand on his back. But my hand slips away quickly when movement to my side demands my attention.

I spin in time to see a haggard face staring back at me. Scraggly lengths of wiry gray hair frame a face creased and leathered by time and elements. Watery eyes the color of soot squint at me then beyond me, to where the boy cries. The haggard face is joined by several others who shuffle and stop beside her. The women I saw earlier, the ones who carried trays of food and cleared the table after we ate, have returned.

"What happened here?" the one closest to me asks and points with a gnarled finger toward the fallen bodies. Her voice drips with what can only be described as glee.

I glance at Will then back to the woman. "They attacked the wrong people, I guess," I say levelly.

A throaty cackle breaks out spontaneously but is stifled almost as quickly as it began. Silence befalls the women. I notice the one closest to me first touch her right hand to her forehead then her belly then to her left shoulder and right. She then joins her hands so that her fingertips form a steeple and her palms are pressed together. She turns her eyes skyward.

"Thank you, Lord," she says. "Thank you for freeing us."

Some of the women nod reverently while others bow their heads. I haven't the slightest idea what is happening or why they are behaving so peculiarly. I look at the old woman who gestured with her hands, puzzled. I look to the sky and wonder what or to whom she spoke.

"Uh, my name is Avery, not Lord," I say politely. "None of us is named Lord," I add, mindful of the fact that she is old and likely mistook my name for another.

The old woman chuckles softly. The sound rumbles from somewhere deep inside her chest. It is an odd, but not entirely unpleasant, sound. "I know you are not the Lord," she says.

Her words confuse me further. I glance at Will. He looks as baffled as I am. "Okay, then who are you talking to?"

"We are talking to God," the old woman replies. "We are thanking him for delivering us from the evil that has imprisoned us for years." She speaks with a quiet respect and peace that I have never heard another speak with. I find myself wanting to learn more about God and how she helped them.

"Who's God?" I ask and feel my brows knit. "Does she live here too? How did she deliver you from, wait, what did she deliver you from again?"

"Evil," the old woman says. Her tone remains somber and humble in spite of my questions. "And God is not someone who lives in these walls. He is our Creator." She turns her eyes to the sky again. "He is up there in heaven watching over us always."

I follow her gaze to the navy sky. It is dotted with innumerable twinkling lights. I have heard the sky referred to as 'the heavens' before and often wondered about exactly what that meant. I've wondered who or what is responsible for the shimmering lights called stars and the ever-changing moon glowing overhead. Perhaps this God person is. I do not know. And while a part of me feels drawn inexplicably to the concept, now is not the time I expect to find answers.

"Right," I say to the old woman. Her beady eyes hold me, and for a moment, a strange feeling stirs in my chest, an indescribable lightness that bubbles from my belly to my collarbones. A broad smile splits the old woman's face and a look of silent satisfaction shines in her stare. "Someone needs to go and release the girls chained up in the cabin," I say and do not break eye contact.

The old woman looks away first. She turns to one of the women beside her and with a sweep of her arm and a nod of her head, the other woman shuffles toward Tal's father. She searches his belt until she finds a ring of keys. She removes it and lumbers toward the hut in which I found the girls. Another of the women who disappeared into the kitchen in the first moments we entered the compound leaves the group and goes to the boy beside Tal. She kneels in front of him and places a hand on his back.

"Oh my poor son," she says.

The boy spins. "My dad is your son?" he asks through sniffles.

A long pause stretches between them. "No," she answers thoughtfully. "You are," the woman adds in a shaky voice.

The boy's head jerks back. Confusion carves his features. "What?" he asks in a weak voice. "That's not, it's not, that's not possible," he stammers.

"Oh my child," she says. "They never told you. I know. But you are my son." The woman swipes tears that trickle down her cheeks. "Those girls the men kept in the hut, they used to be us," she says and gestures to the women with her. "We were who they created life with until we became too unappealing," she concludes and lowers her head, saying the last word with such shame I feel my own cheeks warm.

I rub my forehead and am horrified by what I am hearing.

"How long have they been doing this?" I ask.

"For as long as I can remember," the woman answers. "And it wasn't just here," she adds and limply sweeps her arm, gesturing to the surrounding structure.

Her words slither down my spine like a serpent. The women before me have spent their lives serving men, cooking for them, cleaning for them, and bearing children for them, all while enduring unspeakable abuses. Before now, the idea of something so awful was inconceivable. "All of you will come with us," I say and see no other option. They are old and slow, but I will not leave them behind to die. "We are leaving tomorrow. We are journeying out of the forest and into the world beyond to find more humans."

Gasps echo among the women. They exchange startled looks. I hear the word 'no' murmured more than once, along with the words 'crazy' and 'death.'

"We aren't going anywhere," the woman with the long gray hair says. "There is nothing out there, only death." Her comments are met with keen nods of accord.

I feel my mouth open, and for a moment I am speechless. What the old woman has said, as well as the fervent agreement, does not make sense to me. "Urthmen have been deep into the woods. They stormed the area where the river meets the lake. The forest thins here. They will come here too. It is only a matter of time," I warn the women.

But the woman with the long hair shakes her head. "No, we will take our chances here," she says adamantly. "God will watch over us," she adds and looks up at the sky.

My mind struggles to comprehend her refusal to escape before being slaughtered where she stands in the coming days. I do not understand her stubbornness. But I realize it is not my job to convince her to leave. The choice is hers. Each woman will decide for herself.

I look up at the moon and stars then back down at her face. "I hope he does for your sake, because if you stay and wait for Urthmen, you're going to need all the help you can get to fight them."

"We will die for certain if we leave," the woman replies willfully. I am not sure what she is so worked up about. I am concerned for her well-being, for her survival.

"What will you do for food?" I ask to be sure she will eat.

"I can hunt and provide for us," the young boy chimes in. His face is puffy and his eyes are red from crying. "I am staying with them and I will hunt for them."

I eye the boy. "I'm sure you can," I say and hope for the women's sake he does not possess the tendencies of the other men who ran this compound.

"But you still need to talk it over with the girls from the hut," I say. I glance over my shoulder and see Will, who has been pacing silently until now. He furrows his brow and looks at me, puzzled. I shake my head from side to side slowly then return my attention to the woman. "Talk to them," I continue. "You owe them that, at least, a say in what they do, right?" Will walks to where I can see him. He looks at me then to the boy and the women, a troubled look veiling his features.

"It will be a long time before they are right again," the old woman says. "They need calm. They will need to stay too," she says with finality.

"Just talk to them, please. Give them the option one way or the other," I say and I hear exasperation creep into my tone.

"You won't be safe here," June voices her opinion by adding.

"You won't be safe out there," the old woman counters confidently. She tips her chin high then adds, "You are walking toward certain death."

The woman's tone, though quiet, is filled with arrogance born of certainty. She is completely convinced that she is right to stay and that we are wrong to leave.

June plants her hands on her hips and tips her chin to match the old woman's stance. Her posture is defiant. "No we aren't. We have Avery, not some imaginary cloud friend," she says.

I feel heat warm my cheeks and know they are a deep scarlet hue. I am thankful for the night, for the darkness. No one can see me blushing. June overestimates me. I worry she looks up to me too much.

"I'll discuss it with the girls," the boy speaks up before a squabble ensues. "I'll tell them what choices they have."

"Good. Thank you," Will says.

"Then it's settled. You will talk to the girls and let us know in the morning what their decision is, and we need to sleep if we're traveling first thing in the morning."

"We will see you at daybreak," the woman says. She looks at June. She narrows her eyes and purses her thin, cracked lips. Clearly, she did not appreciate June's cloud-friend remark. I step in front of my sister protectively, placing my body between June and the old lady. The old lady's gaze goes to my face and she adds, "Best get inside your hut. We need to take care of our dead."

I watch for a moment, unsure of what she means by 'take care of' her dead. But when she shambles toward Tal's father's body, joined by another woman, and lifts his ankles and begins dragging him, her words become clear. She and the other woman plod down a small pathway with rows of huts on either side. Tal's father's head and body bump along unceremoniously and leave a smear of crimson in their wake. The other women remaining follow suit and drag another of the men on the floor by his ankles and haul him to an undisclosed location.

"Ugh," June says and presses her face into my arm.

"You said it," I agree.

June yawns and tries to conceal it with her hand. Her eyes are bloodshot and her skin is paler than usual.

"Let's go inside and get some shut-eye," I say and begin ushering her inside the hut we began our night in.

"I think one of us should keep watch tonight," Will grips my upper arm lightly and says in my ear.

His hot breath against my earlobe sends chills racing over my flesh. He is right, of course. I just need sleep so desperately, I can't imagine being the one to sit vigil.

I turn and face him, about to volunteer when Oliver speaks.

"I'll do it," Oliver says and I nearly weep with joy. "I've gotten the most sleep out of all of us in the last few days so I'll do the first shift."

"Thank you, Oliver," I say and resist the urge to hug him. "If I don't get some sleep, I don't think I'll be able to walk at all in the morning."

"No problem, Avery. It's the least I can do. You keep saving us all the time," Oliver says and looks away sheepishly.

"Thanks again," I add. I ignore the comment he made about me saving them all the time. I don't have the strength to argue that he and his brother would do the same for us, and retreat to the hut.

Once inside, I close the door behind me, leaving Oliver at his post. I am not surprised when I see June and Riley nestled close to one another, their eyelids heavy. Will lifts his sleep sack. He makes a production of shaking it. I look at him and wonder why he is doing what he is doing. I also wonder whether I should do the same. I quirk an eyebrow at him, and he stops and carries his sleep sack over to where mine is unrolled. He places it next to mine and lies atop it, propping himself up on one elbow while facing me. I do the same, mirroring his position.

"What was that all about?" I ask.

"I don't know," Will answers. "I guess I just don't want to sleep on something those men stepped on."

"I understand," I say. I inhale deeply. "I can't believe that there are humans in this world who harm one another. I just don't get it." I pinch the bridge of my nose then rub my forehead.

"I know. It doesn't make sense. We're all fighting the same fight, just trying to survive."

"It's true. I just don't understand. I mean, what Tal, Ross and Jay and the other men did to those women, it just, I don't know; it blows my mind. Girls around my age, chained up, naked and dirty," I say and feel a turbulent rise of anger swell inside of me. "I keep picturing their faces. Streaks were carved through layers of filth and ran from their eyes to their chins. Their gazes were hollow, haunted, as if they'd been broken," I say through my teeth. I swallow hard. "They were breeders. One was pregnant and the men kept going to them, taking them against their will. They thought they were doing something noble, that they were repopulating our species," I huff.

"Oh my gosh," Will breathes. "That's what happened."

"Yes," I answer, disgust burning hot inside me.

"And they wanted Riley and June here, too, and you," Will adds.

I cannot see his face clearly and do not know what expression he wears, but I hear the tightness in his voice. I imagine he shares my revulsion, my red-hot fury at the notion of anyone trying to harm my sister or his sister.

"The thought of anyone touching," Will starts to say but cannot finish his sentence.

I reach out my hand, hoping it will land on his shoulder, but I cannot see well enough to judge properly. When my hand lands on the warm swell of his chest, I breathe in silently, but do not release my breath. I feel the steady rhythm of his heartbeat beneath my fingertips. It quickens and I begin to pull my hand away. Will's hand lands atop mine suddenly and I feel my own heart begin to riot within my ribcage. I am still holding my breath, reveling in the feel of his large palm covering my mine. I also feel the solidness of the muscles underneath his shirt and just beneath his skin.

"When I think about what they wanted to do to you," he says. His voice startles me slightly. I was lulled by his heartbeat, enjoying the odd sensation whispering across my skin. "It makes me insane with rage," he says.

My heart stutters as my brains works to make sure my ears heard what I think he just said. He was mad about what the men wanted to do to *me*? The idea is confusing. Why would he care in the least? I am not his sister. True, I am part of his life now in a way that connects us, but I have not shared my life with him as Riley and Oliver have.

"I want to protect you," he says in a voice low and filled with tenderness.

He begins stroking the soft flesh on the top of my hand. My scalp feels as if it has shrunk and is now two sizes too small for my head.

"But I haven't been able to protect any of us so far. I haven't helped at all," he adds and laughs once. It is a quiet, self-depreciating sound.

My fingertips tense involuntarily and grip his powerful chest. "No, that's not true," I disagree with him. "You've been," I start but am suddenly breathless. "Perfect," I manage in a weak voice.

"Avery," he says my name and goose bumps race across my skin. "I admire so much about you, how well you hunt, how good you are with June, your bravery, and don't get me started about your skills as a fighter," he adds and I hear that he is smiling before I strain to see his teeth, pale against the darkness. "And you're beautiful," he says seriously. I no longer hear or see his smile. "I want to be what you are. I want to be what you need."

The tremor in his voice sends a tremor spiraling through my core. He thinks I'm brave, and good with June, that I am a good hunter and an excellent fighter, and he thinks I'm beautiful! My mind is swimming laps around a lake of happiness. I am dizzy and cold yet my insides feel as if they would rival the surface of the sun on a midsummer day. I want to tell him that I think he is beautiful, that I have never seen anyone or anything quite as beautiful as he is. I want to tell him that when he is near, as he is now, I cannot think straight, I cannot breathe properly, my entire body goes haywire and I do not know whether I am sick or losing my mind or both. But the words do not come out. Dizzying, overwhelming excitement has seized my ability to speak apparently.

"You are," I manage to choke out and hope I do not sound as crazy as I feel.

"I am?" he asks.

"Yes," I murmur.

I feel his chest moving against my hand, inching forward as he leans closer to me. His heart is drilling against it, almost matching the pace of mine. I blow out a thin stream of air and inhale again. My insides tremble the nearer he draws.

My cells are firing all at once. His face is so close I can make out the sharp angle of his jaw and the soft indentation between his nose and lips. His hot breath feathers across my face for a moment, and time seems to stand still. The scent of him fills me. He smells of sweet grass and nighttime, of sweat and musk. I want him to stay as he is forever so I can breathe him in and feel his heart beating beneath my hand.

The soft skin of his lips grazes mine as he brushes past me and presses his cheek to my cheek. I would collapse if I wasn't already on the ground, propped up on one elbow. In fact, I still think I may faint and fall to the ground all the same.

He whispers in my ear, "That makes me so happy."

The urge to grip both sides of his face and press my mouth to his overtakes me. I do not know why I feel as I do, but it frightens me. He is close, so close I can feel his pulse darting in his neck. I want to plant my lips there too. Perhaps I should. Perhaps he wants me to. I do not know what he wants. I feel my muscles begin to stiffen and I am frozen.

He leans back at bit and is facing me, his lips so close I could touch them just by puckering slightly.

"Avery," he says my name with urgency I can feel, urgency I am experiencing though I don't know why.

My heart is hammering in my ears. I am practically panting. "Good night, Will," I say and slip my hand from his then lower my body and roll on my side, away from him.

Feeling as if the ground beneath me has opened, I have the sensation that I am plunging into a blackened abyss, a void from which return is impossible. I am falling. Into what, or where, I am falling I have no idea. I cover my face with both hands as unworthiness and embarrassment pull me lower.

I hate myself for what I just did or didn't do. I feel panicked and sad, scared and excited all at once. I hear the soft rustle of Will's sleep sack and know that he is no longer right beside me. I would not need to hear it to be sure, though. I feel the coldness of his absence. I wrap my arms across my chest and place one hand on either shoulder, bracing myself against the chill that has seeped into my bones and causes me to shiver.

"Good night, Avery," Will says.

Tears heat the backs of my eyelids. I do not know why I am crying but am powerless to stop it. I allow them to fall silently until utter exhaustion grips me and pulls me under the surface of its dark and murky waters.

Chapter 20

Morning light seeps between the slim cracks in the thatched roof of the hut and I realize I have slept the night through. Physically, I feel much better. My emotions are another story entirely, however. I feel anxious and annoyed, confused and gloomy in a way that goes beyond our undetermined safety and future. It runs deeper.

This feeling is compounded when I roll over and notice that Will is gone.

Oh no! I groan in my head. What if I've scared him away? What if last night, when I froze and rolled over and went to sleep, I ruined something between us? I cannot help but believe that is the case as an endless stream of worry and self-doubt carves a channel through my brain.

I sit up slowly and scan the hut. June and Riley are still asleep. I try to stand without disturbing them, but June's eyes pop open. She sees me standing over her and alarm creases her features.

"What is it?" she asks. Is everything okay?" her eyes are bleary and her hair is squashed on one side.

"I'm pretty sure everything's okay," I answer.

"Where's Will?" Riley asks in a voice thickened by sleep. She lifts her head and props herself up on one elbow.

Their questions echo the questions swarming in my brain, yet they are asking for different reasons.

I've been so consumed by self-absorbed worry that the possibility that something happened to Will did not cross my mind straightaway. It should have. Given the dangerous world we live in, that should have been my first thought, not an afterthought. All the strange stirrings and emotions rambling around inside me have clouded my judgment.

"I don't know," I answer Riley honestly. "Stay here, both of you, I'll go outside and find out where he is," I say.

I open the door so that just a sliver of light slips in at first then carefully peek outside. I see Will and Oliver chatting and feel as if a weight has been lifted off my chest. Will glimpses me watching him and his brother. His eyes lock on mine then lower immediately. The faintest bands of pink touch his sun kissed skin. I know I have done something wrong. But I guess a part of me knew that last night before I drifted off to sleep. I feel as if my heart is being tugged to my feet slowly, torturously, and I hope I have not created a rift that cannot be mended.

I pull the door toward me and say a quick "good morning" to Will and Oliver then promptly inform June and Riley that the boys are okay.

"Will's just outside. He's talking to Oliver," I tell them.

"Whew," Riley says and flops back against her sleep sack. "Oliver was out there all night and after what happened I-I, I don't know, I was just worried." A crease appears between her eyebrows as they gather, just as June's brows do when she speaks with concern.

"You don't have to explain," I say to her. "I get it. And I don't blame you one bit for worrying." I smile at her with the same affection I smile at my sister.

"I'm so happy they're fine," Riley replies with a small smile.

I can hear the relief in her voice. I hate that her life, like ours, has been spent balancing on the tip of a razor-sharp blade where moving threatens pain identical to remaining still. No matter what we do or where we go, we are always teetering on the edge of danger, of hurt. I hope to change all that. I hope to find more people like us to band together with so that we may feel a shred of safety and peace of mind. But before we can do that, before we can go anywhere, we must leave here.

With the goal of exiting in mind, I open the door again and step outside. I clear my throat and Oliver looks at me.

"Have any of the women been by here?" I ask either of them.

"No," Will answers, and does not meet my gaze.

"Don't be so quick to answer, my boy," the voice of the old lady scrapes down the pathway like stones grinding against each other. Ropes of bristly hair in a shade that matches the steel of my blade billow in the breeze as she hobbles toward us. "I'm coming," she says then mumbles, "just takes a little longer than it used to."

Oliver grins and laughs uncomfortably. When her voice sounds again, his laughter immediately stops and his smile withers.

"Ah, you feel that?" she says and outstretches one arm. "That breeze, the scent on the wind, it means rain is coming."

"Okay," I smile and say evenly. I feel the warmth of the sun, though it has just made its appearance, and the sky is a rich, deep blue. I do not smell rain or anything unusual in the air.

"A rainstorm is all the more reason for you to stay," she wheezes when finally she is standing before us. She is winded and sweat stipples her brow.

"So I take it you're not coming with us," Will says.

"No, I am not. I thought I was clear about that last night," she adds.

"And what about the girls that were locked up, are they coming with us?" I ask, but feel confident I already know the answer.

"No. They're in bad shape. One of them is with child and is so weak she can barely stand, and the others have wounds that hardly allow them to walk across a room, much less hike across the forest," she says before adding a grumpy "harrumph."

"I see," I say sadly. The horrors those poor girls have lived through will scar them long after their bodies heal.

"Curse those men!" the old woman spits. Her small eyes are nearly black. They glisten with emotion. "But the human spirit is not easily broken. We are a strong and hearty species. What happened to them will not break them. I am living proof of that. The girls will be fine one day."

"Listen, uh," I start then realize I do not even know her name. "I'm sorry. I don't know your name," I admit.

"No need to be sorry, my child. My name is Mary," she says.

"Listen, Mary, are you sure the boy is going to do what he says he'll do, that he'll hunt and take care of you?"

"Are you asking whether he is like his fathers?" she asks and cuts to the chase.

"Well, yeah, I am," I say.

"Don't worry yourself," she assures me with the same calm confidence she spoke with the night before. "He will do right by us. And if he doesn't," her voice trails off and she stares into the distance briefly. "We can handle the boy ourselves," she concludes grimly, her voice dropping an octave, and her eyes lock on mine. An unspoken message passes from her to me. I understand just what she means when she says she and the others will "handle" the boy should he attempt any of the deeds the other men carried out.

"Are you sure?" I hesitate then ask.

Mary chuckles. "I wouldn't waste my time fretting about us if I were you. I'd be worrying about myself. There's nothing out there for humans," she levels her dark gaze at me and enunciates each word of the last sentence she spoke.

"I believe there's more out there than there is here. And I believe there are more humans than we think, out there, surviving," I counter respectfully.

"Is that what you really believe? You think there are humans out there living among the Urthmen?" she says with a frown.

"Yes," I reply with certainty I cannot explain. "And I aim to find as many of them as I can."

Before stumbling upon the compound, finding other human beings was something I only dreamed of. Then I found Will and his family. Though not all of them survived, they have been a gift, nevertheless. They made me realize I am not alone in this world with just my sister to love and protect. Will, Riley and Oliver made me want to seek out others like us. I thought that because all human beings share a common interest, namely survival, there wouldn't be a risk. Now, however, my feelings have changed. I am wary of my own species. I am undertaking this next endeavor wiser, and far more cautiously.

"God be with you," Mary says. She immediately casts her eyes to the crystal-clear sky above.

"Thank you," I say and track her gaze. I am still unsure of to whom she speaks, but accept her well wish. I am sure June, Will, Oliver, Riley and I will need all the help we can get.

"Be sure to eat before you go. After what you did for us, the least I can do is fill your belly before you march off to meet your maker," she says in her gruff tone before she turns from me and begins waddling away.

I part my lips to speak, to ask after her why she is so convinced that I will meet my demise the moment I leave the compound, but decide against it. I clamp my mouth shut and watch her go. What good would arguing with Mary do anyway? I have about as good a chance at changing her mind as she does changing mine. I agree to disagree with her and leave it at that.

I turn to face Will and roll my eyes before shaking my head slowly. He smiles at me for a moment, a brilliant smile that touches his eyes. But all too soon, his smile falters. The corners of his mouth droop and he looks away from me as if he's been reminded that he dislikes me. My insides wilt and I feel my own smile capsize. I realize I must speak to Will at some point today during our hike. Things cannot be tense between us. Too much is at stake, lives are at stake, and not just our own. Our sisters and his brother need us to function and interact together smoothly. Whatever happened between us last night has to be addressed, and fast.

After I tell June and Riley that no one from the compound will be joining us on our journey, we head off as a group to the dining area. As promised, there is food for us to eat. Turkey meat, a rare treat, as well as field greens and berries, awaits us. I eat quickly while the children chat. Will is quieter than normal, a fact that makes my belly quiver and clench simultaneously. The feeling I have, the awkwardness between us, makes me understand that I can't wait hours before Will and I discuss what happened.

"Will, can I talk to you for a moment?" I surprise myself by saying as I stand. I begin walking toward the entryway of the dining room, to where a hallway gives way to a courtyard. I walk on legs that wobble and my hands tremble in time with them. I do not look over my shoulder to be sure he is following. I hear the sound of his footsteps behind me. I don't know what I would've done if he hadn't followed. I hadn't thought that possibility through. But now that he is, I need to come up with what I will say soon or else we will just be left standing and staring at each other blankly.

I stop abruptly and take a deep breath. "Will, we can't be like this," I blurt out. "You can't be mad at me, okay?"

He rears his head slightly and his eyes widen. I can see I've caught him off-guard with my candor. He composes himself instantly.

"I'm not mad at you," he says tightly and folds his arms across his broad chest.

My eyes linger there, on the spot where my hand was pressed with his atop it, just above his heart, and heat blazes through my body. My mouth is suddenly dry and my throat burns.

"Really? It feels like you are?" I say and feel like a complete fool.

"Humph," he says and looks away. His lips are pressed to a hard line, his beautiful, full lips that brushed mine just barely.

My heart begins knocking against my chest so hard I wonder whether Will can see it from where he stands.

"Come on, Will," I say and reach out my hand. But as soon as my fingertips graze his forearm, he pulls away as if I am touching him with fire.

I drop my hand instantly and lower my eyes in shame. "Sorry," I say softly.

"Don't be. Not wanting to kiss me last night is no big deal," he says. His cheeks are red. "Just don't pretend like you like me when you don't and everything will be fine."

"Kiss you?" I ask in disbelief. He was trying to kiss me? Did I just hear him correctly?

"All right, Avery! Enough! Just don't say it. Don't talk about it again."

"But Will," I say and cannot keep myself from grinning. "I didn't know what you were doing," I admit. "I've never, you know, kissed anyone, just June, and that's on the top of her head or forehead," I start to ramble.

"I haven't either. And apparently I am so bad at it you didn't even know what was happening when I tried."

"No, no, that's not it at all. I mean, I don't know anything about that stuff, about kissing or anything," I say. "I know the basics and whatnot, but all the other stuff, all the knowing when something's happening stuff is really confusing," I admit.

My face feels as if it is engulfed in flames. I don't know what I am more embarrassed about, the fact that I'm so ignorant on the subject, or that I have admitted as much to him.

"You forget, I've been alone with June for a long time. And before that it was just the three of us, my dad, June and I. The last time I was around a lot of humans was when I lived here when I was a little girl. Since then, I've had nothing to focus on but survival."

Will's eyes lower to his feet. He kicks a tuft of weedy growth, working it with his foot from side to side. "Well it's not like I have experience either," he says in a low, mumbled voice. "I've met other people, other girls around my age. But I never wanted to, you know," he allows his sentence to linger, unfinished.

I wish he would finish. He never wanted to what? Kiss any of the girls he'd met? I want to know but do not have the courage to ask.

My stomach is cartwheeling and I worry the food I just ate will launch at any moment. That would be brilliant, wouldn't it? He tried to kiss me and I missed what was happening and as I try to patch things up I barf on him. That sounds like something that would happen to me at this point.

My stomach roils anxiously, sending worry, and bile, rocketing up my esophagus.

"Anyway," I hear his voice and my heart stutters for several beats. I swallow hard. "Let's just forget about it and get where we need to get," he shrugs and says.

But I don't want to forget about it. I want to experience what I felt last night again.

The churning stops, and instead of feeling like a sea amid a violent storm, my belly feels like a boulder tumbling to the ground below.

"Okay," I say with conviction I do not feel.

"Okay," he agrees and smiles. His smile does not reach his eyes. He starts to walk back toward the dining area then pauses and turns. He looks at me as if he wants to say something, but turns away from me quickly.

I am left standing there for a moment. My hand moves to my chest and clenches the strange ache there. I breathe against the hollow sting until I am confident I will not cry. There are enough things in this life to cry about; kissing boys should not be one of them. I roll my shoulders back and make my way back to June, Riley, Oliver and Will.

Everyone has finished eating and is ready to leave when I return. We say our good-byes to Mary and the other women who come to see us off. We head back into the forest and leave the compound, and all that occurred within its walls, in the past.

We hike for the entire morning. Trees become fewer and grow farther apart, and we are able to cover more ground in less time. The sun is high overhead when we see an end to our wooded home.

A blackened road made of asphalt appears suddenly and is thinly concealed by tall stems of dying growth.

"We made it," June says. Her eyes are round as she stares at the blacktop. "Is that a road?" she asks in wonder.

"Yep," Will answers for me. "It sure is."

On the other side of the road, squat structures with rectangle cutouts that look like eyes are interspersed. Many sag and look dilapidated. Very little of the lush greenery we are accustomed to seeing carries over into the new landscape before us. In fact, much of what we see is dirty and bare looking.

"I still can't believe we're here," June adds. Her voice is fraught with nerves. I share her nervousness. Still, I feel compelled to forge ahead.

"Are you ready?" I look to each of the children then to Will and ask.

I hear murmurs of agreement. "Okay, then let's stick to the side of the road. We'll follow the line where the pavement meets the woods."

"What happens when we run out of woods?" Riley asks.

I do not have a firm plan in place. I do not have a plan at all, in fact. "We'll make that decision when we have to," I answer cryptically. "For now, we'll just stay close to the woods."

We step from the shade of the trees out onto the street. I immediately feel hotter that I have ever felt. The sun beats down from above. Without the cover of leaves and limbs I feel exposed, vulnerable. Yet I cannot imagine retreating to the forest again and contending with both Lurkers by night and Urthmen by day.

We are not on the road long when the rhythmic patter of booted footsteps causes me to freeze. Will's eyes dart from the woods to me then back again.

"Hide," he says.

I do not waste a moment. I grab June's hand and yank her into a tangled mass of bramble. Will, Oliver and Riley are right behind me. We squeeze together and watch as an entire patrol of Urthmen march down the road we were just on. I know we should withdraw deeper into the woods but the sight before me, before all of us, holds us.

A male Urthman is perched beside a female Urthman, a rare sight. They are dressed in clothing I have never seen before. A fur lined cloth is draped across the female's shoulders. It is the richest, brightest hue of red I have ever seen and looks as if it would be soft to the touch. The male Urthman wears a similar cloth, but his is a vivid blue shade. Both are adorned with ornate gold stitching. The gold stitching matches the golden crowns balanced on their misshapen heads. The clothing and crowns do little to improve the ghastliness of their appearances, but they do give them an air of importance.

My eyes wander from their attire to their mode of transportation. They do not walk. They are sitting beside one another in a wheeled contraption. I believe it is a wagon. But my father once told me wagons were pulled by horses, an animal long-since extinct that used to serve humans.

Animals do not tow the wagon I see now, though. Human beings do.

Six humans, in all, walk atop the burning blacktop barefoot. They wear only a thin garment that covers their pelvises and are chained to the cart they draw. Their ribs are visible. Their knees, elbows and cheekbones are prominent. They look as though they have not eaten in some time. A nearby Urthman, also in the carriage, sitting on a rectangular structure right behind them, continually lashes them with a long strap of leathery looking material.

The sound of the whip cracking makes me jump. Inside, I feel as if my blood is hotter than the midday sun, boiling and about to bubble over. I have never heard of humans enslaved by Urthmen as I see them enslaved now. First, I learned of Ross and Tal's imprisonment and torture of women, and now I see this. The abundance of atrocities committed staggers me. I want to run out in front of the carriage and behead the monster whipping the humans. I want to spear the grotesque pair perched in the rear. But I know I cannot. I am outnumbered. I would be killed for sure, and June, Will, Riley and Oliver would suffer the same fate. I will not jeopardize their safety any more than I have already. So I wait and watch in horror as the cart rolls by and the patrol passes.

Once all have passed, I hear a rumble. I look through the interlaced vines and down the road and see a large truck bringing up the rear, a vehicle I have heard about and seen pictures of but have never seen in life before. My jaw drops as the massive metal machine passes.

I turn to Will and whisper, "Have you ever seen one of those?"

The expression on Will's face looks as mine did seconds ago. His mouth is agape and his eyes are pinned on the truck. He tears his eyes away from it and answers, "No," then returns his gaze to it.

I scan the faces of the children. They are all transfixed by what they have just seen. When the truck is past us and no longer visible, I am bombarded by a flurry of questions.

"What was that thing? Was that a truck?" June asks.

"Why were the Urthmen dressed like that?" Riley asks.

"Why were humans pulling them along like that?" Oliver asks.

I answer their questions to the best of my knowledge. Will helps and, together, we are able to appease much of the curiosity. With the children calm, I decide to confer with Will and form a plan.

"I think we should rest now, go a little deeper into the woods and rest. Lurkers don't live this close to the road and shouldn't be a problem," I say. "I think our best bet is to travel at night so we can move unseen. What do you think?"

"I agree," Will folds his arms across his chest and nods. "I didn't like being out there on the road in broad daylight. I felt too open, you know?"

"I do, I felt the same way."

"And you're right. Lurkers don't come this far out of the forest. Not even at night. I think we'll be fine a little further in. Let's rest now and ready ourselves for nightfall."

We inform June, Riley and Oliver of our decision. The children are hesitant at first, but prefer the idea of moving about in the dark to doing so by day when, at any given time, a team of Urthmen can simply appear and fill a street as they did moments earlier.

I lead us away from the side of the road to a small thicket of bushes. The children lie, completely concealed by the bushes. Will and I rest beside them, only partially covered.

A quick peek at Will reveals that a haunted look veils his features. He levels his aquamarine stare my way and I try to gauge what is behind it. I try to read what he is thinking. But all I see are twin pools of tropical water I once saw in an old photograph.

"What is it?" I ask Will.

Will does not answer right away. He looks off into the distance. The small muscles around his jaw work and flex. "If what we saw today, that parade of Urthmen with humans as slaves, if that's all the world has to offer, I don't know what we're doing out here or where we're heading," he says. His tone is infused with an edge of equal parts desperation and sadness. I wish I could throw my arms around his neck and tell him I know exactly how he feels and that everything will be all right. It has to be. But I can't. I am not brave enough.

"There are more of us out there," I tell him. "I can feel it in me, in my bones. They're out there. We just have to find them."

"And then what?" he asks. "What happens after we find more humans?"

"We fight," I reply. "We fight for our freedom, for the freedom of all those who've fallen before us, all those who have been enslaved. We fight for what is ours. We fight for our right to exist. We fight for our lives."

Will holds my gaze for a long while.

"I know there's hope," I tell him. "There's got to be."

I hope I am right, but after what I saw at the compound and what I saw on the road, I am not so sure anymore.

Chapter 21

Will and I nap in shifts. When I wake from mine, I see that night has fallen. As soon as my eyes focus I realize it is time to go.

"We need to move," I say to Will.

He nods and we begin waking the children. June and Riley wake first.

"Where are we?" Riley asks in the first few moments after her eyes open. She is undoubtedly groggy and confused.

"We're at the edge of the forest, near the street," Will reminds her gently.

"The street," she says as awareness and panic collide. Her eyes hurry from side to side. "I remember the Urthmen, and the humans chained to the wagon."

Will places his arm around her shoulders and brings her close. "It's okay," he says soothingly. "They're gone, and we're not going anywhere near them again, okay?"

"Okay," she says reluctantly.

"We're going to find other human beings, like us, and things are going to be fine," he tells her. I hope he's right.

"Of course things will be fine," June chimes in and gives Riley a sisterly nudge. "How can anything go wrong when the sky looks like that?" she says and points overhead.

"Ooh," Riley says as she casts her gaze skyward. "Oh my gosh, it's so beautiful."

"I agree. It's hard to imagine there are bad things in the world when something that magnificent is above for all to see."

They continue to marvel at the night sky. Though they've seen it more than once, the sky is exceptionally clear.

"The twinkly things, the stars, they look like jewels," June comments. Then she turns to me. "We've seen jewels," she gestures between the two of us. "Well not in real life, but we've seen them.

Remember, Avery? Remember when dad showed us pictures of diamonds?"

"I do," I tell her. I remember the day well. An ancient book called an encyclopedia had managed to survive the war and the carnage that followed. It had an array of information contained within its pages, most of it about places and people I'd never heard of. But it was interesting, nevertheless. "And you're right. The stars look like diamonds."

"I like the moon best," Oliver joins the conversation and weighs in. "It's bigger and brighter."

"The moon's light will help us find our way out of here," Will tells him as he grips his hand and helps his brother to his feet. His act prompts us to get moving.

I help the girls to stand as well. Together, we make our way out onto the road once again.

The temperature has dropped considerably and there is a distinct nip in the atmosphere that suggests a season change is near. I inhale deeply and feel the crisp air fill my lungs. It is different from the air in the forest. It's dustier, drier.

June is at my side and Will is behind me. We stay close to one another and move quickly. My heart keeps pace with the frenetic patter of our feet. I continue to scan the land in front of me while looking over my shoulder at regular intervals. We are alone as far as I can tell. Still, the woods on the side of the road are watchful. I cannot shake the feeling that countless eyes are minding our every move, waiting with bated breath to see what happens next. Urthmen, Lurkers, deranged humans who hold innocent women and children captive and an assortment of forest monsters have left my nerves frayed. Still, knowing that my imagination is overacting doesn't stop me from glancing that way from time to time as we go.

We continue down the long, dark road until we reach what looks like a town. Pale moonlight blanches everything in its wake, but even without the moon, I doubt anything could be done to help the landscape before me.

Rows of brick and wood structures appear and line both sides of the street. I remember learning about places such as the one before me. My dad told me they were shops. Humans once owned places of business that would sell goods and services in exchange for stuff called *money*. Money once controlled the world. It is hard for me to imagine paper and coins controlling anything. Especially since those who'd had plenty of it died just the same as those who had not. Their money had only delayed the inevitable slightly, and bought them suffering at the hands of abominations along with it. Money fell to extinction along with humanity. As far as I know, it holds no value at all. And the places where it changed hands, the shops, bear the appearance of its elimination.

Broken windows stare at us like lifeless eyes as we pass, and torn awnings flap quietly in the faint breeze that stirs. Piles of debris are clustered as far as I can see—stones, rocks, bricks and other material I cannot identify. Heaps of rubbish arise from the pavement and look like mangled metal corpses. They are covered in a lumpy, dry-looking substance the color of dried blood. They resemble the truck that passed when the Urthmen marched by earlier, but without wheels or the ability to move.

"This place gives me the creeps," June says and shivers. She wraps one arm across her body.

"Me, too," Riley says. "What is all this stuff? Where are we?"

"I heard stories about places like this. I think this used to be a town," Will tells the girls.

"It's really scary, this town place." Riley comments.

"I know, it is," Will agrees and drapes his arm across her shoulders reassuringly.

"Do you think Urthmen live here?" Oliver asks. I hear the edge in his voice, the nervousness. I feel it too. I wondered the same thing. But I suppose if Urthmen did live here, we'd be dead already.

"No, I don't think so," Will answers. "These buildings are just shells. It doesn't look like anyone or anything has been here for ages."

The metal heaps and storefronts are covered in a sooty layer of grime. The forest was never filmed in such muck. All that I am seeing is foreign and gloomy.

"Have you ever seen a place like this?" I ask Will.

"Uh-uh. I've only seen the forest," Will shakes his head and says.

"Me, too," I say. "This place is awful," I add. "It's so depressing."

"I know," he agrees as we come to a turnoff.

"What do you think? Should we go down this road?" I ask Will.

"Yes," he surprises me by having a finite opinion. "Anything to get away from these buildings and all the other junk around here," he adds and curls his upper lip in disgust.

We make our way down a new street. I immediately notice that the layout is different. Houses, not buildings, line the lane.

"Oh wow! Houses," I hear Will whisper excitedly. "I've always wanted to see one of these. Haven't you?" he does not wait for my response and continues. "My parents used to tell us stories they'd heard." His head swivels as he looks from one house to the next. Childlike awe replaces his guarded expression. "All the things humans had, stuff like rooms and furniture, running water and tubs they bathed in, and lights! Lights inside the walls! Can you imagine!" he says and even in the dim light provided by the moon, I can see his translucent blue-green eyes dance with wonder.

My stomach feels as if millions of bubbles are bouncing and bursting. His excitement is infectious. I feel my own interest pique.

"Haven't you dreamed about what they look like inside?" he asks me

"Yes, I have," I admit and the vision I imagined since I was a child reappears in my mind's eye. Soft, plush material beneath my bare feet, *carpeting*, I believe my father called it, and walls that shut out the cold and heat just as the cave did, only the hard, coldness of it is missing, replaced, instead, with comfort and warmth. I always picture soft colors similar to the forest only less vibrant, more soothing. I envision all the luxuries I heard about: a soft, cozy bed to sleep in, water piped inside that runs both hot and cold, chests that run by power that keep food fresh. All of it sounds too magnificent to be true. Yet seeing the houses now as I do, I realize it was true once, long ago.

"You want to get a closer look?" Will nudges me lightly and asks.

"No, Will, we can't," Riley protests.

"Yeah, I don't know about that," Oliver adds.

"Come on," Will tries. "This might be the one and only time we ever get a chance to do it."

"I would kind of love to see the inside of a house," June says quietly.

"Me, too," I confess.

"Then what are we waiting for?" Will asks. "Let's go," he says as he looks all around then dashes off toward the house nearest to us.

Worry niggles at the back of my brain. But I disregard it. I am carried on a wave of pure curiosity that I cannot resist. I take June's hand in mine and follow after him. Oliver and Riley are not far behind.

Will is at the front door before we are even on the front step. He tries the handle and finds that the knob turns easily, it is unlocked. He steps inside.

Sallow light illuminates a narrow pathway and pushes against the darkness within. I scan the immediate area, terrified and inquisitive simultaneously. I spy a stout, cylindrical object in a windowsill to my immediate left. I go to it, wondering, dreaming it is what I think it is.

"Will," I murmur. "Look." I urge him to join me. In the time I wait, I cannot resist. I feel it, instantly noting the waxy substance beneath my fingertips confirms what I suspected. "A candle," I say as I wrap a hand around it. Something gritty coats it, but it's too late for me to worry now. I slide my other hand beside it, and as I do, I bump a compact item that is lightweight. I lower the candle to the sill right away, my curiosity provoked beyond any familiar threshold. I fumble with the packed little thing my hand hit, straining my eyes to see that I am holding a thin cardboard cover. One side is smooth while the other bears a coarse strip. I slide my thumb along a ridge on the side opposite the coarse strip and lift a flap. The cardboard opens like a book, only inside, I don't find pages. I find slender sticks. "A matchbook," I manage breathlessly.

"What?" Will asks incredulously. "No way! Let me see." He is beside me within the space of a breath, his solid arm brushing mine with every move he makes. My body is at odds over which is more exciting, my recent discoveries, or Will's proximity. "Wow," he says as he manipulates the pocket-sized treasure. "Think they work?"

"There's only one way to find out," I turn my head toward him and challenge.

My pulse darts against my throat as I wait, anticipation goading it along.

"That's right," he says and tears a stick from the folder. "Here goes nothing." He flips the book and slides the bulbous tip of the stick along the grainy strip on back.

To my delight and his, a spark flashes before the entire head is aglow.

"Wow!" Riley exclaims.

"Cool!" Oliver agrees.

"Amazing," June adds.

"I know, right." Will agrees, his eyes riveted to the flame.

"I can't believe it," is all I can say.

I watch as Will brings the flame to the wick of the candle and a soft glow haloes it, bathing the room in warm light.

"Oh my gosh," I can't help but gasp once I am able to see the space around me more clearly.

All around me I see items I believed were fabled, the stuff of legends and bedtime stories parents told their children. In the room to my left, a couch, similar to the one we had in our hut at the compound when I was a little girl, faces a cushioned chair between which a table sits. The floor is covered in what I assume is carpeting. I would like nothing more than to remove my boots and socks and walk atop it barefoot, but I do not know what chemicals remain embedded in the fibers. Everything seems to be covered in a chalky, white film. I do not know what the film is composed of and do not intend to find out.

"This is crazy," Will says as he looks around the room with the couch and chair, all the while holding tight to the candle. "Can you believe this? It's real. The stories our parents told us are real." I hear hope in his voice. His hope makes me smile and feel my own surge of optimism. "And it's not even that dirty," he adds and points to the fine coating covering everything we see.

"I know," I reply, smiling.

"People, human beings, used to actually live here, maybe even kids our age," he says and sounds as if he is struggling to contain his enthusiasm.

To my right is another room.

"Will, come this way," I wave him toward me. "Come on. Let's look in here."

He obliges and lights the way inside. Cabinets that appear to be made of wood hang from the walls, and another table and chair are set up close to the exterior wall. A window is in front of it. I imagine a family sitting there, eating their fresh food and talking while enjoying the outside through the comfort and protection of a pane of glass. I stare at the dark world beyond the glass.

My eyes continue to scan the room. Oddly, I see a bowl with fruit sitting atop the counter just below the cabinets. Fruit does not last long in the forest after it is picked. It certainly wouldn't endure centuries of chemical fallout and war. They would have rotted, turned to dust and blown away long ago. My eyes follow the line of the countertop and freeze on a bowl with a mushed substance inside. I move toward it and reach out a hand. I touch the bowl. It is warm. Seeing the fruit then touching the bowl and finding it warm sends a trill of awareness down my spine that raises the fine hairs on my body. The situation narrows into razor-sharp focus.

"Someone is here," I say as chills speed over my skin in waves. "We need to go, now!" I whisper urgently to June, Will, Oliver and Riley.

We turn and begin scrambling toward the door. But immediately the sound of footsteps echoes and freezes the blood in my veins.

"Oh my gosh," June says in a hushed, frantic tone.

"Go! Go! Go!" I urge everyone. But before we make it to the hallway at the end of which the only known exit lies, we hear a voice.

"Wow! Humans are in my house!" the voice says and then makes a soft chuffing sound through the two asymmetrical holes below his eyes.

A miniature creature with a misshapen head, disproportionately larger than his stubby body, ambles toward us. His lidless, black eyes are wider and clearer than I have ever seen on any other Urthmen, and his nearly transparent skin seems thinner. It displays the vivid entanglement of veins spanning his entire head like a web more readily. Perhaps it is because he looks to be a very young one.

"Shh!" I shush him.

"I can't believe it!" he says and claps his stumpy hands together excitedly. As he does so, the black line of his mouth contorts into an expression that displays small, pointed teeth, making him appear even more monstrous.

I make a mad dash to him, figuring that where there is one there is more. I clamp one hand over his mouth and hold the other against the back of his head. He tries to scream.

"Be quiet!" I tell him, but the clatter of footsteps racing down the hall means it is too late.

I let go of him and draw my sword. Will grips his club. The children scurry behind us as we prepare to fight.

"Mom! Dad!" The young Urthman shouts.

Two Urthmen storm into the room, one is male and the other is female. In the instant I glimpse them, an idea flashes through my mind, streaking like lightning in the sky. I collar the young one, bring him within arm's reach of me again and place my blade against his throat.

"Stop where you are," I order the pair.

Both stop instantly. Their cloudy eyes dart from him to my blade then to me. They widen considerably, a feat I have never witnessed an Urthman perform.

"Please, don't hurt him, human. He's just a child," the male says.

A child implies human origins. The thing my blade is pressed against is nothing more than a young slaughterer of my species.

"I have seen plenty of children slaughtered by your kind," I say in a low voice that sounds foreign to my ears. "It never seemed to bother you, taking their lives,"

"We didn't do anything to you," the female cries out, her voice shrill and pitched high, similar to a distressed woman's voice. "Please just let our son go," she begs.

"Son," I mumble the word with disgust. My mother may have had a son growing inside her womb when she begged and pleaded for her life and the life of her unborn baby. But mercy was not shown to her. It is a word that is absent from their vocabulary. I have seen many sons struck down in my lifetime. The creature before me is not a son; he is not a human being. He does not deserve such a title. He is nothing more than the offspring of a murderous pairing in a murderous species.

Sweat collects between my shoulder blades and trickles down to the small of my back. My forehead is slick and so are my palms. My pulse is thundering in my ears. I lick my lips and look at Will. The children are out of harm's way, close to the front door. His eyes lock on mine, but his expression is indecipherable.

"Both of you come over here slowly," I order them. I watch them closely as they cautiously slide their feet forward until they stand by their offspring.

"Please," the male begs. "Just leave. We won't tell anyone you were ever here."

He is trying to convince me he is civil. What a joke. I know better than to believe such nonsense.

"You expect us to trust you?" I ask him in amazement. "You would bludgeon us to death the second we look away," I say and a crazed laugh passes between my lips.

"No, we would never do such a thing!" the male pretends to be indignant about what I have said. "We are not soldiers. We are not like the others who overtake villages. We're ordinary beings, parents."

"We live here in peace," the female adds and attempts to augment her cadence with a soothing lilt.

"You're lying," I shake my head and say. They are trying to mess with my mind, trying to sway me to believe they are tame, obliging citizens, that I misunderstand their role. Well they are not fooling me. I know better. "You are murdering liars, all of you!"

"Avery, let's just go," Will's voice floats through the ether and wraps itself around my heart.

"What?" I ask him, dumbfounded.

"Come on, these people aren't looking for trouble. We can just leave." A pained expression dominates his handsome face.

"Are you crazy? You're calling these creatures *people*?" I am beyond shocked. They have managed to get to him, to penetrate his defenses, despite watching both his parents die at the hands of their kind just days ago. "You actually expect me to trust them after what you saw them do, after what you lived through?"

Anguish gathers his features. His shoulders slump forward and his pain is evident. "These beings did not kill my parents," he says in a trembling voice. "*They* didn't do it," he says and points to the three Urthmen. "I don't want to be like the monsters that killed my mom and dad, and if we kill them, we are no better than they were."

I can't believe what I am hearing. For the briefest of moments I am speechless. Bile burns up the back of my throat as his position gels in my mind. Will is not on my side. He does not see things as I see them. I swallow hard and speak with calm I do not feel. "Will, we have to kill them," I tell him levelly. "You're thinking of them like humans, like they are the same as we are, but they're not." Memories of my mother's death, and the deaths of his parents, come flooding back in a cold rush. "Think about it. Remember what they are and think about Riley and Oliver. Think about June and I."

The female and the young one start to make a sound similar to crying. "Avery, I can't. That's not me. It's not us," Will says.

The word 'us' succeeds at momentarily jumbling my thoughts. I begin to focus on what he meant by that. But my thinking rights itself quickly. What he meant by his choice of words is irrelevant. Our lives are at stake. We cannot let the Urthmen live.

"If we don't do it, they will get help and hunt us down," I tell Will.

"We won't, I promise!" the male says, his voice bordering on whiny and pathetic.

"Shut your mouth!" I warn him.

"Avery, don't do this," Will continues to try to sway me away from what I know is the right thing to do. Something between regret and apology flashes in his eyes.

I know they have to die. Just because they have behaved in a mildly human fashion does not make them human. They are hardwired, genetically altered and programmed, to hate and hunt humans. My sister's life rests on me ending theirs. I clutch the handle of my sword in my hands and grip it tightly. I swing it in a wide arc and am about to slice it laterally and be done with it when Will's club rattles to the floor with a *bang*. I halt my blade mid-swing and freeze. He steps in front of me and places his hands in front of his chest in surrender.

"Avery, this is a family. They are not soldiers," he says meekly, fixing a penetrating gaze on me. "Having compassion is what makes us human, it makes us better. You can't do it. Remember what you are."

I gaze into the bottomless depths of his aquamarine eyes. I see innocence. I see warmth and empathy. But sadly, none of those qualities serve us now.

"No," I tell him. "If I draw upon compassion, as you're telling me to, it does *not* show my humanity. It makes me a fool."

"Please," he begs.

"We won't tell. You have our word. On our child's life, we swear we will not tell the others that we saw you," the female promises. My eyes linger on her, searching for a shred of truth to her words. I see nothing, just the face of a vicious predator.

"Avery, look at me," Will says and diverts my attention away from the female Urthman. "I'm begging you, don't do this. If you do you are no better than they are, and I don't want to be a part of it,"

His last sentence lands like a slap across my face.

"Of what? Of me?" I ask and narrow my eyes at him, stunned that he would even utter such a thing.

"Of this, of what is going on right now," he answers. "I can't travel with an executioner," he says finally.

He is talking about me. He will see me as an executioner if I kill the Urthmen, our enemies for centuries. I feel as if I have been slapped and punched in the gut.

With an unsteady hand, I lower my weapon. My mouth is dry, my temples pound. Will issued an ultimatum and I caved. I compromised principals that have kept me and my sister alive since we were born. Kill or be killed was my father's motto where Urthmen were concerned. There was no maybe. Every cell in my body shrieks at once that what I am doing is wrong. I feel it in my bones, in the lifeblood that pumps through me.

Reluctantly, I back away from the three and out the front door. "You better make good on your promise and keep your mouths shut," I mutter as I leave.

"We will," the male Urthman says.

"Thank you so much," the female says.

I sheathe my sword and all of us run out into the street. As soon as our feet touch pavement, I hear the piercing peal of bells echoing though the silence. The high-pitched sound persists. I twist and look over my shoulder at the front of the house. I see the male's form filling the doorway. In his hand he grips a club. The female squeezes beside him. She, too, is brandishing her weapon.

"Humans!" the male screams louder than I ever imagined a creature could call. His voice rips through the night. "Humans are here!" he persists.

Doors of neighboring houses begin to open and torch wielding Urthmen spill from them. Shock registers on Will's face, shock and understanding. He knows as well as I do that letting the three Urthmen, the male and female and their offspring, live was a mistake that could prove fatal. But time does not exist to assign blame. We take off running. We are being pursued in the open by dozens of Urthmen who will kill us if we are caught.

I realize in that instant that my life, as well as the lives of those I love, will likely end tonight.

Chapter 22

"Run faster!" I scream to Will, Riley, Oliver and June. I grab June's hand and jerk her forward, in front of me. "Come on, come on!" I urge Riley and Oliver too. They must remain where I can see them, and we all need to get as far away as fast as possible. We flee from where Urthmen are approaching.

"You think we're stupid, don't you, humans?" I hear the male Urthman whose home we were just in call out after us.

His inhuman voice no longer sounds civil, and it certainly does not sound pleading. It has returned to what Urthmen always sound like, a voice that is tinny and grating and slices at my eardrums like innumerable blades. And it taunts us.

"Don't look back!" I tell the children when I see Oliver screw up his features and glance over his shoulder. "Just keep running!"

Cruel laughter erupts between the male and female. "You thought we would just let filthy humans run free in our town! Ha! You will be dead long before the sun rises!" the female cries.

Rage wells from a cavernous reserve, inundating every cell in my body as it overflows.

A dark recess deep within me, hidden and coiled tightly like a venomous snake, beckons me to run back and do what should have been done in the first place. But I must deny it. I must deny an inherent part of me that demands their blood be spilled. Instead, I press on. I sprint away from the male and female.

We run along the blackened street. The glow of the moon has faded, its light hidden behind a bank of clouds. We cover a lot of ground and pass numerous cross streets. I feel my blood throbbing against my skin in time with my speeding heartbeat. My flesh struggles to contain it. I pump my arms and pant as I race. But before long, I notice the children slowing.

"I can't," I hear June gasp as her grip on my hand goes slack. "It hurts too much."

One hand flies to her side and clutches what is undoubtedly an aching stitch that has developed. Even in the thick, sinister darkness, I can see that she grimaces. I hate that this is her reality now, running, always running for her life.

"No, June. Keep going," I encourage her despite the fact that my entire body is hurting and trembling also.

My breathing is labored. My arms and legs sting unbearably. Each sears with fatigue.

I peek over my shoulder, slowing only slightly as I do, and see torches are still advancing. Anger crops up inside of me, and it is not earmarked for the male and female Urthmen exclusively. I am angry with Will as well. I listened to him, even though I should not have. I allowed my feelings for him, as confusing as they are, to cloud my judgment; to cause me to deviate from what I know is right. And now we are paying the price for my clouded judgment. As I run, I vow to never let it happen again. My feelings must never interfere with the safety of my sister and I.

"Turn here," I tell our group between choppy breaths as we come upon a turnoff street. Everyone does as I have told them to, including Will.

When I round the corner and make my way down the side street, I steal a look over my shoulder and see that some of the torches that glow eerily in the void have stopped moving. Only a few are following us as far as I can tell. I am tempted to breathe a sigh of relief. But a sinking feeling in my gut prevents me from doing so. I know that Urthmen do not easily give up. They do not retreat. They kill.

I try to force their deadly nature to the back of my mind when the pitch-back darkness becomes disorienting.

"Will, I can't keep going," Riley says. Her voice is thin as she barely manages to speak between breaths. She has slowed considerably and is jogging now.

Will rushes to her side and places an arm around her waist for support. "I gotcha," he says. "I'll help."

"No, I'll slow you down," Riley pants dejectedly.

"No you won't. I'll carry you if I have to," Will tells his sister.

As mad as I am at him, I admire his dedication to his sister. Unfortunately, carrying Riley would slow Will almost as much as her lethargic trot is slowing him now. I need to come up with something else, something that will buy the children time to catch their breath.

Another cross-street catches my attention. I almost missed it smothered in the oily shadows that coat the area. An idea forms in my mind.

I do not have time to think it through and time is running out. I do not know how much longer the children have before complete exhaustion claims them and they collapse. I must act now. I must go off on my own.

"Take the kids and keep going straight," I tell Will. "I'm going this way," I say and point back in the direction we came from.

"No!" Will whispers so loudly his voice borders on a normal volume for speaking.

"Shh!" I shush him. "Do you want them to hear you?"

"Sorry," he says quietly. "But you can't go off alone. We need to stay together."

"We can't. The kids are tired and slowing. The Urthmen will be on us in no time if I don't do this," I say.

"We can make it. I can carry Riley, trust me," Will says.

A bitter huffing sound escapes my lips. Frustration, fear and fury plow through my body as one. "Trusting you got us where we are now," I mumble under my breath and feel my upper lip curl over my teeth. I can't believe I allowed the words to fall from my lips, no matter how quiet they were. I am angrier than I originally thought.

Will does not respond to my comment. Perhaps he did not hear me. I cannot tell. I cannot see his face clearly through what feels like layers of impenetrable darkness. I only hear his voice echoing. "Come on Avery, I can do it. Don't you believe me?" he tries to persuade me by saying.

I feel something in me stretch so far that it thins and threatens to snap. "No, Will, I don't," I growl. "And from here on out, I call the shots. Take the kids and go, now," I say in a tone that does not leave room for argument or compromise. "I'll catch up and find you," I say just before I turn back and speed my pace, slapping the soles of my shoes against the pavement loudly so that I all but guarantee I will be heard and pursued by Urthmen.

I move down the side street and instantly see an old, broken down car we passed moments ago. I crouch low and duck behind it, waiting for the torch wielding Urthmen to make their appearance. I hear the tapping of their boots as they approach and dread tiptoes down the length of my spine. But it is coupled with something else, an entirely different sensation. Ire and hate boil together and gurgle beneath my flesh. I am frightened, yet a part of me eagerly anticipates the impending confrontation. I yearn to vent my wrath. I have a score to settle.

I unsheathe my spear from the scabbard at my back. I ready myself to act, gripping the weapon so tightly it bites into my palm. The footfalls draw nearer. All of my emotions converge and bombard me at once. I worry I will hyperventilate from overload. Outwardly I am still, as poised as a wildcat just before it pounces.

I see the torches. There are three of them, and they are close. They light paths that make the Urthmen's presence known long before their arrival. But I have an advantage. Their light glows on them, not me. I see them, and judging from their actions, they do not see me. I watch them through a busted out window in the car. Their black eyes glow with fiery light and make them look even more grotesque than they already look, a feat I thought impossible.

Just as they are about to pass, I stand slowly, quietly. I think of my mother, of Will's parents, of Riley and Oliver, Will and June, of myself and all the others who perished at the hands of the mutant species that reigns over the planet, and I launch my spear.

The sharpened tip pierces the air and carves a path through the inky darkness and rockets straight into the back of one of the Urthmen's heads. I bend down in time to hear the familiar sound of a female Urthman's voice scream out in pain. I raise enough to carefully peer out through the broken window once again. I see that one has fallen, the female I presume, and the other two spin around, looking in every direction.

Their hideous faces are etched in confusion. They search for the source of the attack and one makes his way toward the car. I watch him and wait.

My muscles twitch from holding my crouched position for so long, and with expectancy. He begins to walk to where I stay. I scuttle around the car holding my sword firmly and close to my body. When he comes around, I spring to my feet and drive my blade through his midsection.

His mouth opens wide and he emits a strange groaning sound. The section of his shirt my blade entered becomes tinged in an expanding pool of garnet. I retrieve my sword and watch as the Urthman wobbles and staggers backward a few steps. He looks down at the wet spot on his shirt that surrounds a gaping wound. I do not waste time. I take advantage of his shock and kick him. He topples over and crashes to the ground. When he is flat on his back, I plunge my blade in the center of his chest to ensure he does not get up.

My head whips from side to side. I see the final Urthman. He has stopped and is coming toward me. His small, black eyes bore into my skull and I recognize his horrid face as well as his clothing. It is the male from the house Will and I were at with the children.

My insides simmer. I am seething. I do not know who I am more furious with, me or him.

"They're over here!" the male from the house screams.

I hear the shrill voices of more Urthmen. The sound is distant and is changing direction. Still, his bloodlust compels him. He cannot seem to help himself. He charges me, swinging his club wildly. I drop to one knee and dodge the flurry of swipes intended for my head in a single, swift, lightning-fast motion. When I pop up to an upright position, I slash the space in front of me and open him from his waist to the middle of his chest.

Gore spills from him. He drops to his knees. I look upon his wretched face and see every Urthman that has come before him and will come after him. My mother's face flashes in my mind's eye shortly thereafter. I let him bleed while I recover my spear. When I return, what little color the Urthman had has seeped from him. I spit on the pavement beside him.

"Filthy monster!" I say. Then I twist my blade to one side and slice the air horizontally. The razor-sharp edge of my sword meets with his neck. There is a brief pull, resistance right before muscle and bone yields, and his head tumbles from his shoulders and rolls to the ground below.

My breaths are short and shallow and my entire body trembles, but I do not have a moment to spare. More Urthmen are coming. I must go. I take off in search of June, Will, Riley and Oliver. I backtrack, retracing every step I took to lead the small search party after me, not the others. In the distance, I see four shapes, human shapes. I tear after them, testing my leg muscles again. They hear my hurried footfalls charging their way. They all turn, and June sees me first.

"It's Avery!" I hear her whisper. The joy in her tone is clear. I wish I could hug her. I wish I could pull her tight and tell her everything will be all right. But we are far from all right.

"Turn in here," is all I say when I jog up beside them. I guide them into an open field.

When we are deep within and concealed by tall grass, I say, "Down! Everybody get down."

Everyone drops to his or her knees before lying flat on their bellies. Only our heads are raised as we watch for movement on the street between the high blades.

"Are you sure this is a good idea?" Will whispers.

I cannot believe he has the audacity to question what we are doing, where I've decided to place us, when the very reason we are hiding is his fault.

"No!" I answer heatedly. "I'm not sure this is good idea!"

Bitterness spikes my words. I did not plan to sound as hostile as I did. But I am fuming. The demand on my body has been great. All of us have been taxed to our limits, and wouldn't have been had Will let me do what needed to be done back at the house.

June interrupts my stewing. "Thank goodness you're okay," she says and gives me a meaningful look. Her expression reminds me of one my mother used to make when she would advise me with her eyes to pay attention or knock off whatever misbehavior in which I was engaged. I assume June is indicating the latter and would prefer it if I keep my resentment under wraps.

"Yeah," Will agrees. "I'm so glad you're all right."

"No thanks to you," I mumble under my breath.

"What's that supposed to mean?" Will asks with genuine shock. This time he heard me.

"It means exactly what it means," I snap.

"You're mad at me?" Will asks. He jerks his head back to punctuate his surprise. He looks injured. I would be bothered by how I am making him react if he didn't almost get us killed. We may still die. The night is not over yet. Urthmen are still after us. We are, by no means, safe.

"That's right," I retort. "I am furious and you know why."

"Uh, no, I don't," Will says and matches my tone.

"Guys," June tries to interrupt our bickering. But I hold my hand up at look at her sharply.

I return my gaze to Will. "Oh, so you still don't see that we should have killed the monsters back at the house? You don't get that from what's happening now, that *everything* that's happening now is because of that?"

Will's cheeks blaze. He looks as if he has been slapped. "I don't want to be like them," he says and I hear the faintest crack in his voice.

Under any other circumstances, I would hate myself for making another person feel as I've undoubtedly made Will feel. But our lives are at stake. We may all die because he stopped me from killing the three Urthmen when I had the chance. I accept my portion of the responsibility. I do. I was mesmerized by his aquamarine eyes and the flurry of silly, lightheaded reactions that teem inside me whenever he's near. I listened to him.

"We don't have the luxury of moral high ground. We need to survive. Period. Nothing else matters," I say and shake my head. "But rest easy and know that you succeeded, Will. We aren't like them at all. We are being hunted, they are not. They will live through the night, we probably won't. I hope you enjoy your moral high ground while it lasts," I say.

"Avery," June closes her eyes and cringes at the spitefulness of my words. Truth be told, I cringe a bit too. I have never been so mean in all my life. And even though it is warranted, it still does not feel good.

"I'm so sorry, Avery," he says and lowers his head.

"Don't be," I say levelly. "Learn from it. And if we survive somehow, I call the shots from here on out."

His face is somber when he nods in agreement.

June opens her mouth to speak. I brace myself for her to defend Will, but her lips clinch shut and her eyes leave me. When they do, they round and remain unblinking. Her jaw drops open but she does not make a sound.

"June?" I ask concernedly. I follow her line of sight and immediately see what she sees. My breathing hitches and dread shakes me to my very core.

Bright light shines and tunnels through the darkness. And it is not alone. Several other beams accompany it along with a thunderous rumble similar to the one I heard when the truck passed earlier in the day, only louder. I rise slightly and peer through the willowy reeds. I see three enormous trucks barreling down the road. An Urthman is situated in the cab and is behind a large, circular object that projects the light. He is directing it all along the roadway, sweeping it from side to side. I duck quickly when the shaft of light skims past my head.

"That thing is like a portable sun. What's powering it?" I panic.

"I have no idea," Will answers.

I lift my chin and stare once again at the trucks. Without warning, they swerve off the road and begin barreling through the field in which we are hiding.

"Oh no," I breathe. "No, no, no!" I gasp. "Run!" I scream to June and the others.

We bound to our feet and attempt to scurry away.

Suddenly, the light is all around us. We are bathed in it as fully as if we were standing out in unfiltered sunlight. A truck is roaring behind us, nipping at our heels like a Lurker, while another advances from the side. Urthmen spill from the vehicles, they pile out in staggering numbers. I realize running is futile.

I shove June behind me. Will does the same with Riley then Oliver. Oliver is unarmed. I pull my sword from its sheath and clutch it in both hands. I watch as Urthmen file through the tall grass, tramping a path through the growth until they are before us.

The realization that I have failed Oliver, Riley, Will, and June sinks in my chest like a stone, taking me down with it. I feel as though I am being pulled into the earth itself. My blade is heavy. My arms and legs are spent. A high pitched ringing resonates in my ears so loudly it drowns out the growl of the trucks and the shouts of the Urthmen swarming all around us. I have failed us. We will die within seconds, here, in the grayed and dirty landscape that was once home to our kind.

I swipe the sweat from my brow and look from side to side. We are grossly outnumbered. But I will not die without claiming lives before I fall. I will fight to my death.

When the first beast makes his way toward me, I strike him down, opening him up across his waist. Judging from the stunned expression on his face when I swing, I gather he expected me to willingly surrender my sword. He expected wrongly.

As soon as I withdraw my blade and attempt to swing it again, the Urthmen descend on us. A blow lands against the back of my skull. A scattering of multicolored dots glow in my field of vision. They are slowly replaced with murky blotches that fill in until all I see is utter blackness.

Chapter 23

Ice-cold water rains over my head and body, splashing against me so that it bites my skin like countless bee stings.

"Wake up, human!" A tinny voice shrieks through the void like metal striking stone.

The icy blast and the voice combined bring me back to consciousness abruptly. I jerk my upper body upright. My eyes snap open and my head swivels. I can barely see, but what I make out conjures dread and pure hatred, two emotions that shake the bones in my body and nearly shatter my soul. Urthmen, unmistakable in all their horrific nastiness, are before me.

"No, no, no, no," I try to scream but my words come out as little more than muffled, incoherent babble.

My vision is groggy and jumbled, yet I see them, a mess of dark shapes blurring together. But soon that mess focuses to a machete-sharp point, along with an ache in my forehead that is equally knifelike. The intense pain, coupled with my vision, confirms that I am alive. Impossibly, I am alive and conscious.

Consciousness brings with it not only the perception of intense pain and stinging cold, but also the realization of my predicament. My eyes scan the space before me. Cavernous stone, wet and gray, surrounds me on three sides, while metal rods fill the fourth from the ground I lie upon to the low, rocky ceiling. I am in a dark and chilly chamber corroded with tree roots, spider webs and bars.

Bars cover the entrance to a shadowy tunnel, the only apparent way out. And the four hulking Urthmen I saw as soon as my eyes opened are still holding dripping buckets, posted just beyond the bars.

My heart begins to patter frenetically. The harder it pounds, the more my head throbs. I am imprisoned. I do not know where I am or how I got here. All I know is that I am caged. I feel an immediate flash of anger when I look to my left and see my sister. She is conscious too. Caked blood mats her hair. She has raised her body so that she is on her hands and knees. Her frail body shivers and she heaves several times as if she may vomit.

"June," I try to form the word from my lips but my mouth is uncooperative. Her name is absorbed by the atmosphere. "June," I try again. This time my voice is stronger. It has graduated to a raspy whisper.

June's head tilts toward me. Her movement is slow and labored.

"Avery," she murmurs in a barely audible voice. "You're alive."

Even in her weakened condition, I still hear the relief in her tone. But I doubt she is even a fraction as relieved as I am to see her, to hear her voice and know that she is alive. Seeing her gives me a reason to survive, to fight.

"Are you oaky?" I ask her softly and ignore the Urthmen at the bars.

"I-I think so," she answers in a shaky voice. "But I don't feel so good."

"What? What do you mean?" I say and stand slowly.

The small act is met with skull-shattering jabs behind my eyes, but I do not care. June needs me. I can feel it. I promised her long ago that as long as my heart beats in my chest, I will find a way to get to her, no matter what. The distance between us is minimal, my sacrifice insignificant.

I breathe deeply against the pain and regret it instantly. The fetid, sour stench of death permeates the air around me. I gag involuntarily. Twinges ricochet around my head like spearheads exploding into my brain. The effect staggers me. I grind my molars and pant, using every ounce of might to push against it, to push the pain to a remote place inside of me. I focus on June. I envision her as she was not long ago when we went to the meadow filled with wildflowers. We both fell asleep on that hot summer morning. But before that, June lay, her clear face the picture of peace while her golden tendrils fanned out around her head and coiled around stems. I can see her clearly in my mind's eye, smell the flowers and feel the sunshine on my skin. It's as if a gentle breeze, perfumed with the sweet smell of grass and earth and a vague combination of flowers, blows and replaces the foul odor of rot and a heated glow encroaches on the darkness. I can almost feel the warm swath of sunlight heating my skin, ridding me of the aches and chills that have settled deep in my pores.

I place one foot in front of the other. My legs are unsteady as I make my way toward her. The small area spins for a moment but I will it to stop. I grip the rough wall for stability. As soon as I am close to her, I drop to my knees and place both hands on her shoulders.

"Oh June," I say and hug her tightly.

She twists and sits up sluggishly.

"Don't," I tell her. "Don't move if it hurts."

I know she hears me, but she does not listen. She turns into me despite my warning and slips her arms around my neck. The movement makes her wince and I wish I could find and personally kill the beast responsible for her injuries. They all look similar. It would be a nearly impossible task, but one that I would relish in if given the chance. I silently pledge that if we survive by some inexplicable and extraordinary stroke of luck, I will kill them. I will kill them all. I will watch the Urthmen fall if it takes me a lifetime to see it through. They will pay for what they have done to my mother, to Will's parents, to June, and all of humanity.

As I hold June close to my chest and try to calm her trembling form, I examine the cave further. I see Will, Oliver and Riley. They are dripping as I am. We have all been awakened with frigid water.

"Will," I call to him. "Are you all right?"

"I'm okay. You?" he replies.

"I'm fine," I answer. "Riley! Oliver! Are you guys hurt badly?"

"No too bad," Oliver says. "My head hurts and is fuzzy, but I think I'm okay."

"Me, too," Riley adds in a weak voice.

"Where are we?" Will asks. The confusion scrawled across his features mirrors mine.

"Looks like some kind of underground prison," I say. The gravity of my words seizes me in an ironfisted grip. We are locked up awaiting a fate that can only be awful.

With nothing left to lose, I release June and stand. I ignore the complaints of my muscles and joints and fly to the bars. I grip one cold, metal rod in each hand.

"Hey! *Hey!*" I shout at the Urthmen standing nearby. My voice sounds rough and primal. It wells from a place in me that wants to protect my sister and friends, to survive. The conversation between the Urthmen stops and they train their beady eyes on me. "What are we doing in here? Why are we caged?" I demand. "Why didn't you just kill us?" I scream, launching question after question at them.

I know they are stunned by my outburst. I can see it in the slight tick of the expression of the Urthman closest to me. But his shock, as well as the others' shock, is short lived.

He closes the distance between us in the time it takes me to blink, moving with swiftness I thought Urthmen incapable of, and swings the object he holds. My knuckles are smashed with his bucket before I have time to react. Without warning, wood clashes with skin and bone. I cry out in agony. Blistering pain rockets from the joints in one hand halfway up my arm.

"You filthy monsters!" Will shouts when I drop to my knees and clutch both hands to my chest. In my periphery, I see that he lunges at them, sticking his arms through the bars to try to grab them. But I am hurting too badly to try to stop him. His attempt to defend me could get him hurt too, or worse.

The Urthman closest laughs at him. "Shut your mouth, human! All of you shut your mouths!" the Urthman orders. "You'll find out what you need to know soon enough," he says and another cruel snicker escapes him. "And I wouldn't get used to it here. You won't be here much longer." Laughter erupts among them and continues until I feel as if my eardrums will explode from the horrid sound. Will charges at them a second time. I reach out a smarting hand and stop him.

"Don't," I manage through my teeth. "It's not worth it. They're not worth it."

He mumbles something inaudible under his breath and stares down the Urthmen with the ferocity of a wild animal. Rage radiates from him. I feel it. It glows like an ember. I brim with a similar fire. But for the time being, there is nothing either one of us can do about it. We are trapped, prisoners of Urthmen.

The firestorm inside me is tempered briefly when June's face is before me.

"Let me see your hands," she says softly.

"They're fine," I say.

In truth, I think bones have been bruised badly, at least two. She will see as much if she glimpses them. Swelling has already begun, and attempting to bend the ones I suspect are injured results in stabbing pain. I hug her. "What happened to us? How did we get here?" I ask. My face is buried in her hair. I wonder whether my words are muffled when she does not respond right away

"We were taken by Urthmen. Details don't matter at this point, do they?"

Her words, the expression on her face, both unite and chill me to my core. She is right, of course.

"No, I guess they don't," I agree.

"I remember being hit in the field," Will says. His voices echoes through the cavernous hollow in which we are being held. "I have a knot on the back of my head," he says and rubs his hand up the nape of his neck to the top of his head. He groans. "Oh wow, it's tender." He pulls his hand away and looks at it. Flecks of dried blood dot it.

Oliver mimics his brother's actions. "Me, too," he says with a scowl.

"My head hurts in the same place," Riley adds. "And I have a huge lump. Ouch!" she cries as she touches the back of her head.

"Looks like we were all taken the same way: a nice blow to the back of the head," Will says with disgust.

"I remember being swarmed and hit, then everything went black," I say.

I no longer embrace June, but she remains near, her small frame curled against mine. The meager warmth from her is a comfort. So is her scent, though it is tinged with dampness, and blood.

"Why do you suppose we're here?" Will asks. "I've never heard of anything like this, have you?"

"No, never," I confess. "I've only known them to kill, immediately, like it's something they can't help but do."

"I know. That's all I've known my entire life. This," he says and splays his arms at his sides. "Whatever is going on here, it's bad."

I agree with Will, but I do not dare say as much in front of the children. I think that whatever is to come will be far worse than anything we could possibly imagine, worse than our most terrifying nightmares.

Approaching footsteps add to my sense of impending doom. My head whips toward the bars and the sound. Six more Urthmen approach. They wear what resembles metal melted to fit their bodies like skin, and dread slithers down my spine.

"Open the cage," one orders the Urthmen posted beyond our cage. "It's their time."

"Our time for what?" June turns to me and asks. Her eyes are wide with fright and her voice trembles.

"I-I don't know," I reply.

The Urthman that bashed my knuckles with his pail fumbles in his pocket for a moment and retrieves keys. Once he finds them and unlocks our cell door, he opens it.

"Let's go," one of the armored Urthmen barks and gestures for us to leave the cave.

Worry howls through my core like a bitter wind, freezing every muscle in place.

"Move now!" he screams when I don't move right away. But his tone, added to the metal he wears and the deadly looking blade he carries, sets my limbs into motion. I do as he says and walk out. June follows. She slips her hand in mine and squeezes. Will, Oliver and Riley are right behind us.

Three of the six Urthmen are ahead of us. They begin walking. Their armor rattles and clacks as they march. Deep-seated intuition warns that perhaps it is a death march, and we are the guests of honor.

"Keep going, straight down the corridor," the Urthman continues to instruct us. He and the other two with him pick up the rear.

I have no clue what is happening or where we are being led, just that we have to follow. I try to glance over my shoulder to gauge Will's reaction to what is happening and see that it is no different from mine. He looks equal parts scared and confused. His eyes roam the hallway. There is nothing to see, but there is a faint buzz in the air I have never experienced before, an excitement that resonates in the atmosphere and is palpable. And it is more than the nervous energy radiating from us. Terror does not charge it. It is something else entirely. I find myself panicked by what generates it.

Soon, the faint buzz swells.

As we walk, what began as a weak hum transforms. It surges around the walls of the tunnel. Growling and rolling like a hungry beast, it echoes and grows louder the longer we walk. By the time we are midway down the corridor, the sound is a deafening roar. Even the walls vibrate. I have never heard such a commotion. Thunderous cheers, clapping, and stomping, all merge to create a rumble that shakes the earth beneath my feet.

I cannot hear my thoughts by the time we reach the end of the tunnel and stand before a cage with a closed door on the other side of it.

One of the Urthmen unlocks the door to the cage. "In," he snaps.

Will, June and I exchange confused and horrified looks. We hesitate.

"Get in now!" The Urthman bellows and begins shoving us inside. Once we are all in, he slams the cage door shut and locks it with just us inside.

"Oh my gosh," I breathe. My heart is hammering so hard it pummels my ribs. "What's happening?" I scream. My voice is shrill. It echoes the utter panic I feel.

"Shut up, human!" the Urthman who unlocked the gate booms. "You'll find out soon enough!" He cackles then steps away. When he reappears, he is holding an armful of objects. I see my sword. He throws it at me, then tosses a large blade to Will before passing smaller ones to the children.

"Why are you arming us?" I ask. I am more confused than I have ever been in my life.

None of the Urthmen responds. They back away and head back down the tunnel, except two. Two remain with us, each holding a bow and arrow.

Noise ebbs and flows like a tide lapping against a shoreline all around us. The cause of it remains unknown.

Will nudges me. His shoulder rests against mine and he looks at me. "I don't like this," he shouts over the rumbling.

"Something very bad is about to happen," I yell back to him.

"What's happening, Avery?" June asks. Her eyes plead for me to tell her.

"I don't know," I reply honestly.

As soon as the words leave my lips, the door in front of us falls open, taking the far wall of our cage with it. Bright light blinds us. I squint and raise a trembling hand to my brow.

"Out now!" one of the Urthmen armed with a bow and arrow barks.

"What? Where are we?" I ask and know fully that I will not receive an answer.

"Go!" he shouts. I glance over my shoulder, and immediately see that arrows are pulled taut in their bows. "Out now, or we'll fire and kill you where you stand!" he roars a final time.

My body lurches into action. I stumble but regain my footing quickly. My movement spawns a plume of dusty particles to kick up. When the cloud clears, I look down and realize I am standing on pale sand. The light-colored sand and the intense brightness distort my perception. But I am able to see Will, June, Oliver, and Riley when they are beside me. They all scramble and move closer to me. I look around and my jaw drops.

A roar erupts all around me, the same roar I heard in the tunnel, only much louder. The sound is earsplitting. And now I see the source of it. Tiers of seats begin at ground level and rise high into the sky. Urthmen fill the benches, though most are on their feet shouting, stomping, pumping their fists, and flailing animatedly. There must be thousands of them. And their attention turns to us. We have entered an arena. The roar, the screaming and chanting, all of it is for us. The crowd is calling for our blood to be spilled. They are calling for our deaths.

Chapter 24

"This can't be happening," June cries and wraps her arms around my waist, squeezing so tightly it almost hurts. She is crying and shaking. I feel like doing the same. I hold her tightly with one arm and clutch my sword with my free hand.

The cheering is quickly replaced by boos and jeers. I feel an object strike my temple. I touch my hand to my head. A slimy substance coats the spot that was hit. I sniff my fingers. The matter is foul, like spoiled food. I look on the ground and see that a rotten tomato sits at my feet. More moldy and decomposing produce is launched at us. Several pelt my body. But I am less concerned about the putrid fruits and vegetables hurled our way than I am about the humans I see lying in the sand in the distance.

They do not move, and an expanding pool of crimson surrounds them.

Riley begins to hyperventilate. "I-I-I can't breathe," she gasps.

Will draws her close. He rubs her back. "Don't look," he tells her and guides her face toward his midsection. "Breathe in through your nose until your belly fills then blow out through your lips."

The moment is surreal, listening and watching Will comfort Riley about her panting when we are on display in what can only be described as a coliseum similar to the ones I'd learned about in ancient textbooks. I feel as if I am in a dream, the worst dream my brain could possibly conjure.

The nightmarish sensation multiples tenfold when I see two Urthmen saunter from a doorway, grip the humans by their feet and drag them away, leaving a trail of blood behind as the only reminder of their existence.

My gaze is pinned on the scarlet streaks until one of the largest Urthmen I have ever seen steps from the shadows across from us. Even though he is not near, it is plain to see that he towers and likely doubles my height. Clad in armor from head to toe, he clutches a long thick sword unlike any I have ever seen before in one hand and a shiny shield in the other. He begins walking toward us.

I want to scream, to run, to do something, anything, but I am paralyzed by fear.

The promise of bloodshed quivers through the air like the strike of a finely honed blade, and awareness makes me shudder. The gargantuan Urthman is headed for us. We are armed and expected to fight him as entertainment for those in the arena.

An Urthman dressed in an ornate, brightly colored costume steps to the center of the round surface we stand upon. A hush befalls the crowd.

"For our next event," he begins. "We have this ragtag group of lowly humans. They killed four of our brothers and sisters in the residential area of Elmwood just hours ago." More booing ensues and is accompanied by a slew of words I have never heard before. I assume they are terrible judging from the hateful expressions on the faces of those screaming them. Taunts and hissing continues until the Urthman at center stage motions with his hands for the crowd to be still. "Let's see how they handle the Undefeated Champion of the World, a brother who needs no introduction, with more than three hundred kills, please put your hands together for Throm!"

The beast that loomed has made it to where we are. He raises his arms and the crowd erupts, cheering. Up close, I can see Throm clearly. His oblong head bulges on one side. His eyes are black, but rimmed in ruby-red, and one hangs markedly lower than the other, lending his appearance an aspect of fright that nearly matches his imposing height. He does not have a nose, just holes that are larger and deeper looking that any other Urthman I have had the misfortune of seeing, and his mouth is little more than a cruel slash across the lower half of his face. He rears his hear back and the slash widens to reveal jagged teeth that resemble rows of sharpened arrow tips, and I feel my heart stop mid-beat.

Throm throws his meaty arms in the air again. One holds a blade and the other a shiny shield. The crowd explodes in a frenzy. They are jumping to their feet and cheering. The noise level rises to the point I fear my ears will bleed. But bleeding ears would be a welcome occurrence next to what Throm has in store for us.

"Kill them!" a female Urthman screams, her voice beating out the others.

Throm looks to her and nods. He rolls his head from side to side, his thick neck cracking as he does. Veins protrude from it and run the length of his stubby neck which seems to immediately give way to broad, rounded shoulders. He is a mountain of a being, composed of heaps of thick muscle. And his gaze zeros in on us.

"Get behind us!" I scream to the children. Will and I stand shoulder to shoulder, though I am certain there is nothing we can do to defend ourselves against Throm.

Throm advances with speed that betrays his size. My insides plummet to my feet when he is just about on us. I grip my blade with both hands, the ache of bruised fingers suddenly irrelevant, and swing my blade. Throm instantly moves his shield and blocks my swipe with ease. Will makes a similar attempt only to have his blade connect with Throm's shield as well. Only this time, Throm raises his shielded arm high and brings it down against Will's body. Will careens through the air and lands hard on the ground. I try to attack, slicing the air with my sword in a pitiful attempt at stopping Throm. My blade meets the armor at his back and causes no damage. I grit my teeth in frustration. The mammoth Urthman is a coward, wrapped in protective metal to prevent any harm from coming his way. Fighting him is like fighting a steel wall.

I shuffle to my side, careful to keep my body between Throm and the kids, just as he attacks. He hefts his oversized sword and hacks the air laterally. I try to deflect it, but the angle he attacks from is elevated. That and his overwhelming strength cause my stance to falter. His razor-sharp edge slices the flesh at my forearm.

I howl out in pain and the crowd cheers wildly as my blood dots the white sand below. "Throm! Throm! Throm!" they chant in unison.

I ignore the sting of my cut and lunge at him. I cleave the air and meet his shield. As my body is outstretched, Throm wastes no time and lances the span between us. The tip of his blade drags across my stomach.

I immediately feel a warm gush flow from the wound. Blood seeps from it and wets my shirt. Seeing this, the audience becomes frantic with feverish delight. Their chaotic excitement fills the space.

My vision doubles and becomes bleary. The noise surges and returns in intervals and I fear I will fall. From the corner of my eye, I see Will leap from the ground and charges Throm. Oliver joins his brother, and Riley and June follow. I want to scream for him to stop, for all of them to stop, but all I can focus on is the sudden weight of my sword. I look at it; follow the silvery line of it until my gaze lands on an image of Throm with his blade held high over his head and June just below it. He is about to cleave her in half.

The sight jolts me into action. With a war cry, I pitch my arms forward, driving my sword high, into his raised arm. My blade only reaches his wrist, but severs his hand from that point. The hand, along with his sword, crashes to the sand below. June races behind me, and Throm howls out, a bloodcurdling sound that shrivels my intestines.

Every Urthmen watching is on his or her feet. They boo and hiss. When Throm spins toward me though, they clap and seem to regain some of their enthusiasm, but not for long. Will leaps onto Throm's back and struggles for a moment before his blade is at the beast's throat. He slices it open and both he and Throm fall to the ground.

Utter silence blankets the audience when Will stands and Throm does not. I scan hideous face after hideous face and see that each is frozen in shock. A flurry of activity nearly kicks up a sandstorm at the edge of the arena floor across from us. Within no time, doors open and a half-dozen Urthmen charge from them. They are not as big as Throm, but are covered in armor and intimidating, nevertheless.

A stream of tears spills from each eye and down my cheeks when I look at them then to my wounds. I know we will die, that we will not overcome the odds. Still, I raise my sword. My strength is draining fast and blood seeps from my cuts.

"I'm sorry," I say to Will then turn to June. "I love you, June. I'm so sorry I failed you."

June drops her sword and runs to me. She is sobbing when she says, "Good-bye, Avery. I love you, too."

"Kill these humans!" the announcer who introduced Throm says. At his urging, all six of the Urthmen take off toward us.

In my periphery, I see two Urthmen leap from the stands to the arena floor. Dread courses through my veins and pumps in time with my chaotic heartbeat. I assume the Urthmen intend to aid those headed our way, and that we will not even make it until the six advancing descend on us. They wear hooded cloaks and as they draw nearer, I see them pull their robes from their bodies then grip their chins and peel the skin from their faces. June shrieks and buries her head in my torso. My eyes dart from the pair that jumped from their seats to the others approaching. I don't know who I should be more afraid of.

When my gaze returns to the two who shed their cloaks, I see that what they pulled was skin, just not their own. Human faces are revealed. Both appear to be around my age. One is tall with dark skin and equally dark eyes, and the other is pale like me with sandy colored hair.

The blonde boy pulls two objects from a leather strap at his waist as he runs toward the impending conflict. He aims both at the Urthmen. A loud popping sounds from both devices. I flinch and instinctively cover June's head. Peeking, though, I see two of the six Urthmen fall. Elation twirls in my gut. I am glad to see them die. My eyes are pinned to the two humans that sprang from the stands. My gaze moves to the large man with the dark skin. He holds a sizable mallet. He swings it with ease and slams it into the head of another Urthman, whipping his head back with a loud *snap*. The blonde boy yells, "Now!" and the dark-skinned man drops the mallet and pulls out another contraption. Additional popping sounds ring out, and two more Urthmen crumple.

Everything happens so fast. I am dizzy from blood loss and shock, from fear and adrenaline. Grotesque faces grimace all around me, a macabre sight that chills me to my bones.

Will and I should be taking cover, but with a hostile crowd and no other way out, I doubt cover exists at this point. Instead, we huddle together, Will and I use our bodies to shield the children.

"Are those guns?" Will shouts to me and asks.

"I don't know," I answer, though it looks as if that is exactly what the one guy is using. It doesn't seem possible that they would have guns. From what I was told, there hasn't been a working gun in the hands of any creature for more than a hundred years.

"Whatever it is they're using is stopping the Urthmen," Will replies.

As soon as the words leave him though, the blonde boy holsters the weapons. They appear to be malfunctioning and he is forced to use two daggers he pulls from sheaths on either leg when the final Urthmen standing is upon him.

The crowd waits with bated breath for the blonde to fall. But as soon as the Urthman is close and swings his sword, the blonde ducks. When he springs up, he rams his daggers beneath his armor and turns the blades. The dark-skinned boy with him fumbles with a device in his hands, and before long, a thunderous explosion booms and rocks the ground beneath my feet.

"Oh gosh! What's happening?" June screams.

Riley is crying and Oliver's entire body quakes. In the distance, I see that the far wall, near the place where the six Urthmen charged from, has crumbled. The outside world is visible.

The Urthmen in the stands clamber as panic and confusion sweeps through the stadium.

"What do we do?" Will asks.

"We need to get out of here! Come on kids!" I grab June's hand and look around. All I see are Urthmen clustered together and bumping into one another. Chaos has overtaken the entire arena. I look away from them and search for a way out.

As I do, I notice the blonde boy is racing toward us. He reaches us quickly and grips my arm. "Let's go, now! There's no time to waste!" he shouts. He tugs me toward the gaping hole in the stadium wall. I do not know who he is or where he came from. All I know is that right now, he has a plan to get us out of the stadium in which we almost met our demise. He clutches my hand, and I let him lead me, all of us, out into the brilliant daylight.

Chapter 25

I struggle to run. The gash at my stomach complains at my every movement, but staying in the arena and being slaughtered by Urthmen is not an option. Instead, I cling to the hand that holds mine like a lifeline and allow myself to be led through the hole blown in the wall.

Once outside, I am drenched in sunlight. Warm rays kiss every inch of my exposed skin and heat the clothing I wear. A cool breeze gusts and feels as if it is blowing straight through me. The effect of the conflicting sensations would be pleasant were it not for the fact that blood continues to flow from my midsection.

I try to continue, but it is an effort. "I-I don't know if I can keep going," I say. My voice sounds thin; even I can hear it. It echoes how I feel.

"Come on!" Will urges me. "Don't give up now! We have to keep going!"

Slightly muffled and distorted, Will's words sound as if they are echoing from the end of a long tube. I place my hand atop the wet spot on my shirt then pull it away and look at it. My palm, along with every other finger, are coated in bright red. "Oh no," I say and feel my legs begin to give out from beneath me.

A dizzying rush of color, the pastel blue of the sky, the soft gold of the sunlight and the rich green of the trees in the distance, rushes at me in a kaleidoscopic jumble. I start to falter. Darkness teases in my peripheral vision and I feel myself fall. But before I hit the ground, strong arms circle my waist and grapple me, settling me to a seated position gently.

"Whoa there, I gotcha," a voice says. My eyelids flutter. I fight against the dark tide pulling me down, tempting me with oblivion. Between my eyelashes, I spy short hair similar in color to mine. Straight, sandy-blonde wisps with a scattering of pale streaks cover

228

his forehead. "Come on, stay with me," the voice echoes from nothingness, towing me toward it. "What's your name?" it asks.

"Avery," I hear myself barely form the word. "M-my name's Avery."

"I need you to open your eyes okay. I need you to look at me," the voice continues.

Frantic voices sound all around me. I am vaguely aware of a young girl crying. The voice, the soft, musical voice rings through the air and wrenches me, connecting every synapse in my brain until I realize the young girl crying is June.

"June," I mumble.

"June is here," the voice says. "And she needs you."

At those words, I force my eyes open. My gaze is met with a pair of brown eyes dressed with long, dark lashes.

"Hey, welcome back," the eyes crinkle ever so slightly at the edges. I lower my gaze and see a jovial half-smile. His expression seems absurd given the circumstances, yet I am hypnotized by it. "I'm Sully, and that's my friend Jericho." He thumbs over his shoulder to the tall, dark-skinned man I saw in the arena.

"And I'm Will," I hear Will chime in. "Now can we please get out of here?"

"Hi Will," Sully says, but his eyes do not leave mine. "We'll go as soon as she's able."

"There are Urthmen headed this way!" June cries out.

"They're out of the building, preparing to attack," Will adds urgently.

I know I should look to the depraved beasts headed our way as everyone but Sully is, but I can't. I'm incapable of looking away from him for fear I will lose what little calm I cling to.

"Jericho," Sully says, his eyes still locked on mine. "You ready?"

"Yes I am," Jericho replies, his voice so deep and rich it is mesmeric.

I jerk slightly, ripping my eyes from Sully for a split-second and try to twist to see what Jericho is doing, but doing so causes pain so intense it knocks the air from my lungs. Confirming what I worried was true, my heart pounds and blood leaks from my wounds vigorously. My gaze returns to his face and I decide to keep them there.

"Oh don't worry about what he's doing," Sully says calmly when my body faces him once again. "He has something for the

Urthmen they'll never forget." An edge of humor tints his words. I do not see anything funny about being pursued by Urthmen. "I'm going to lift your shirt and get a look at your wound, okay?"

I nod in agreement and feel the wet fabric of my shirt peel away from the slash. "Ouch!" I protest.

"Sorry," Sully says. "Okay, it's not too bad." Deep golden eyebrows, gathered in concern, betray his words though. "But the bleeding needs to be stopped. You're losing too much blood." He lowers my shirt and trains his gaze on my face.

"How are we going to stop the bleeding?" Will asks.

"First, we have to get out of here," Sully answers, and again, his eyes remain on me. "Jericho, now would be a good time."

At his words and at the sight of approaching Urthmen, Jericho tinkers with a square device with odd knobs. He adjusts one and a thunderous explosion rocks the ground beneath me. Sharp and quick, the deep-bass bang is immediately followed by a sound similar to heavy rainfall. Pressure builds against my eardrums. I topple over and land against Sully's solid chest, ears ringing faintly. I stiffen and try to right myself, the vague noise in my ears only adding to an already agonizing experience.

"I gotcha, don't worry, Avery," Sully says in a voice that is low, almost intimate. I don't know why, but I am soothed by it. A hand cups my elbow, Sully's hand, and guides it upward. "Slowly, okay. Take it slow," he advises me.

"Oh Avery," June says and slides my free arm over her shoulders.

I am flanked by June and Sully as we start moving again.

"That should keep those cowards busy for a little while, but they will regroup soon; make no mistake about it. We need to move fast," Jericho says.

I strain my eyes and turn my head to see that the Urthmen who haven't been blown to pieces are scattering from a cloud of sand and strewn debris. They run in the opposite direction, away from us. The scene is marked by chaos and confusion. A chilly, satisfied smile tugs at the corners of my mouth.

That smirk falters when Sully encourages me to walk by beginning to do so himself. Reluctantly, I look away from the mayhem and I take several clumsy steps. My strength has been sapped and searing pain ricochets from every angle. Awareness that I will not be able to continue only adds to the pain. "Go. You guys go ahead," I urge everyone after sliding my foot forward only to experience excruciating twinges and a gush of my lifeblood seeping from the cut at my stomach. "I can't," I say in frustration.

But before I can say another word, Jericho steps between Sully and I and scoops me up like a child. "You will not stay behind, Avery," his deep voice rolls soothingly. Powerful and capable, his arms are hoops of thick steel. They hold me high off the ground and I realize he is not much smaller than the Urthman who injured me in the arena. His rich, dark skin is scarred, but his eyes, nearly the same color as his skin, are clear, pristine. They radiate a kindness and warmth that makes my own shine with tears.

"Thank you," I whisper and my voice cracks.

"I'll carry her, Jericho," Will says. His face is etched in stone, a strange, unfamiliar expression clouding his features.

"Uh, I think we'll move a lot faster with him carrying her," Sully says to Will.

A tiny rumble of laughter resonates and seems to echo from somewhere deep inside Jericho. Will huffs and mumbles something I cannot hear. Jericho does not wait any longer or debate. He runs, his long, muscular legs covering ground quickly with their elongated stride. Over his shoulder, I see June is being carried by Sully and Riley by Will.

We run for what seems like forever. The jarring and bumping makes blood rush from me faster, and pain unlike any I have ever felt branches from my cut. Jericho slows then stops after he crosses an expansive piece of property at the edge of which a barn sits. Sully opens a wide, wooden door and we hurry inside.

The interior of the barn is decrepit. An entire upper level has collapsed atop stalls and cobweb covered shelves sag as if bearing the weight of heavy snow rather than silken threads.

"Set her down over here where the light is good," Sully says and points to a location I cannot see.

Jericho places me on what feels like a pile of dried grass. It is stiff and prickly, but at the same time soft and comfortable.

"All right, Avery, I'm not gonna lie, this is going to hurt." Sully's voice is laden with what sounds like guilt.

"What's going to hurt her?" Winded and flushed, Will is coated in sweat. He can barely catch his breath to speak when he appears at my side.

"Don't hurt my sister, *please!*" June joins Will and stands beside him. Her hands fly to her mouth when her eyes land on my torso. "Oh my gosh! Avery!" she gasps.

Will's eyes widen as well.

"I won't mean to hurt your sister, but I have to do something to stop the bleeding. If she keeps bleeding like she is, she'll die." Sully is blunt with June, a fact that makes me bristle. I do not know why. She needs to know the truth. Still, my instincts balk at his forthrightness. "Here," he tells me and brandishes a flat stick. "Bite down on this as soon as I start. I'll be right back."

Sully leaves me for a minute and meets Jericho near the barn door. They riffle through a bag until Jericho holds a tube of something and Sully holds a large, hooked needle and a spool of thread.

The overwhelming stench of blood, *my blood*, smoke and rotting wood pollutes my lungs and makes me gag. Desperation and panic rise within me. I wonder what it is that Sully plans to do to me. He told me it would hurt, that I may need to bite down on a short plank of bark as a laboring woman would. Both have my heart hammering away painfully, like strikes of a sledge hammer.

"It's okay, Avery. Everything's going to be fine," Will tells me. But his words have little effect on the ice chips charging through my veins.

June places her head on my shoulder. Rubbing her cheek against the fabric of my shirt she whispers, "Please be okay, Avery."

Her words wrap around me and encircle my heart, melting it. "I'll be fine, June. Good as new." I square my shoulders and sit up as best I can, feeling compelled to live up to her high expectations of me.

But when Sully returns, the woozy, sick feeling returns. He holds a tubular container of liquid. "First I'm going to clean it, then I'm going to sew it up."

I take a breath, expelling it quickly. "Okay," I say reluctantly.

He hands me the stick. "I'd take this now if I were you."

A quick glance at Jericho reveals that his head is cocked to one side, his expression compassionate. He frowns and says, "It won't help the pain, but it will give you control."

His honesty is appreciated. I slip the fat stick between my teeth and know there's no turning back. Part of me feels foolish with my mouth wide and the stick lodged in it sideways, that is, until the first drop of liquid touches my flesh when it is applied with a white, fluffy swatch of fabric.

The moment the wet fabric swabs my skin, a sound rips from me that I didn't think myself capable of making. Burning, stinging pain shoots from every direction around the open cut. I cry out against the wood in my mouth, my back teeth gnashing against it. Sweat stipples my brow, yet I am cold and my body trembles. The sting is followed by the sensation of something sharp being inserted along the edge of the wound. I inhale sharply and clench my abdominal muscles against the twinge. It continues, the torturous stab of the hooked instrument passing between the upper and lower portion, then tugging it together, closed.

I start to feel as if I won't be able to endure the pain any longer. I close my eyes and try to envision a peaceful, painless experience. They are few, but they exist in my memory. I draw upon them, calling to mind when June and I were at the river not long ago. She was upset because I'd unintentionally insulted her. To redeem myself and remind her that the magic of littleness was not lost on me, I began bouncing and splashing, scooping handfuls of water and slapping my palms up before the water returned to the river. When my hands collided with the water and smacked it, droplets sprayed in every direction. At first, June had rolled her eyes at my antics, but before long, she couldn't resist and joined in. We stomped and flopped and splashed in the water until our bellies hurt from laughter. Carefree, even if just for a short time, we had fun. We got to act our ages.

Recalling that day makes me forget the smarting around my wound. It temporarily diverts the discomfort.

When I open my eyes, I am focused and feel as if I am better able to govern my pain.

My gaze scans the faces in the room. Oliver looks green, as if he may vomit at any minute. I have to say, I share his feeling to some extent. Keeping my mouth partially open and grinding my molars against the wood leaves me feeling queasy in addition to the slew of other horrendous sensations I am wrestling.

Will is beside Oliver. His suntanned skin has blanched somewhat and his arms are folded across his chest. His expression softens considerably when he catches me watching him. I quickly look away and turn my gaze to June. Sweet, innocent June's face is puffy and pink, her eyes red-rimmed from crying. She smiles feebly as soon as she feels my eyes on her and I force one of my eyes to wink. Riley does not look much better. She alternates between sobbing and sniffling. The children have been through too much already. Seeing this only adds to their many ordeals and burdens minimally.

"Avery, you're doing great," Sully says gently.

My eyes are drawn to him. He looks up from what he is doing and I am amazed by how nimble his hands are. Long, slender fingers continue to move agilely even when he is not watching them. "Last time I did this for Jericho, he cried like a baby." I open my jaw and allow the wood to drop. I smile at him and his eyes lower to where he works.

"How do you do that?" I ask of his ability to sew through flesh and bring it together as it was before.

"Sully can fix anything, even people," Jericho says. His voice flows like a mighty river when he speaks, surging with truth and loyalty.

I wince briefly as the needle pricks through my flesh yet again, losing my concentration. "What about the guns? Those were guns you had at the arena, right?"

Sully nods absently, his gaze fixed on an intricate knot he is fashioning.

"Where did you find working guns?"

Before Sully answers, Jericho says, "I told you, he can fix anything." He beams with pride, much like a father would at his child.

"Whatever he said," Sully says and arcs an eyebrow mischievously. He moves on to the cut on my arm. He cleans it and begins stitching it as well. "I learned a long time ago to just agree with him. No one ever wants to get on his bad side."

Jericho chuckles. It's a hearty sound that fills the barn.

I look down and see that my largest wound is closed and the next is well on its way to being closed as well.

"Wow, that's amazing!" June gushes. "Thank you!" she says and throws her arms around Sully's neck.

"My pleasure," he says and watches me over June's shoulder. Then to himself, he says, "Just a few more here, and done."

My sister releases him and wipes tears that have spilled over her lower lashes.

"I can't thank you enough," I say. "What you did for me, it's, I don't know, just incredible." I fumble for the right words. No one has ever done anything for me as momentous as what Sully just did. He healed my broken body. I doubt a simple "thanks" is sufficient.

From the corner of my eye, I see that Will's brow is furrowed. The small muscles around his jaw are flexing and his posture is tense.

"Isn't it incredible, Will?" I ask so that he knows I am okay, that there is no need to worry any longer. But his stony demeanor does not change. In fact, it hardens when he glances at Sully.

"Yeah, Sully is terrific," Will says without the slightest bit of enthusiasm or sincerity.

I narrow my eyes at Will, searching his face for a reason for his suddenly sour mood. I am all better now. He shouldn't be concerned. But he is.

"Listen, Avery, I know you're still in pretty bad shape, but we need to get out of here. Urthmen don't stay gone for long, not when they've been humiliated as they've been today," Sully says. One side of his mouth tilts and forms a half-smile. "They'll find us if we stay." His smile wilts and his expression becomes serious. "Think you can run?"

"Uh, I think so," I answer honestly. Sitting up, I twist. The stitches pull with every movement. But compared to the pain I felt before, this new discomfort is trivial. "I can run. My life depends on it." I slide from where I sat and stand. I still feel shaky.

June approaches me cautiously and hugs me so lightly I can barely feel her willowy arms circling me. "I'm so glad Sully fixed you. We're lucky to have met him," she says quietly.

"Ah, you keep complimenting me, you'll never be able to get rid of me," Sully teases.

June's cheeks blush and her mouth twists to one side. For once, she is speechless.

"We're not looking to get rid of you," I shock myself by saying. I don't blush, which is all the more shocking. Instead, I meet his gaze and stare directly into his eyes.

Colored a deep, dark-brown hue that matches winter trees at twilight, I see something in them that lures me. His eyes are rich with secrets and loss, pain and sadness. They communicate darkness that transcends the color of his irises and delves to uncharted depths. I cannot explain why, but I feel compelled to ease that ache in him, and a little scared too.

Sully smiles a broad, almost defiant smile, though I am at a loss for what exactly he is defying. "Good," he says.

"Great. We'll have that to look forward to," Will says in the same inflectionless tone he used before.

"What's the matter, Will?" Riley asks. "Why are you so grumpy?"

Embarrassment flickers across his face before a tight smile stretches his lips. "Grumpy, why would I be grumpy?" he asks.

"I don't know." Riley shrugs and appears baffled.

"We need to leave," Jericho says. We've been here too long."

"Ready?" Sully asks me.

"Ready," I say.

He slings a backpack over one shoulder and leads the way out of the barn. I take June's hand and follow him. Will, Riley, and Oliver are close behind us, and Jericho picks up the rear. We venture out into the brilliant daylight. I do not know where we are going or what the future holds, all I know is that we've found two more humans. Sully and Jericho risked their lives to save us. I would've died if they hadn't acted. The debt I owe them is great, and owing another is unfamiliar. But for now, I cannot think about repaying them. That will come later. All that matters now is that we survive, one moment at a time.

Chapter 26

I move as fast as possible, running despite the constant tug at my waist.

"Where are we going?" I ask.

"We live about three miles from here," Sully answers.

"You live here *with Urthmen*? How do you not get caught?" Will asks and does not temper the incredulity in his tone.

Unbothered, Sully replies, "You'll see."

Even though I am not looking at Sully's face, I can hear that he is wearing a half-smile when he replies to Will. Neither says anything further and we continue to run.

June is ahead of me. Lengths of coiled gold trail behind her, glistening in the warm, buttery sunlight. She pumps her arms as her legs work and her feet take turns hitting the ground. Watching her streak across the field, I am reminded of how fast she is, and how beautiful she is.

My throat tightens inexplicably. I swallow hard against the lump that has gathered there. June deserves better than the life she lives, all of us do. Peace is what we crave most, peace and a semblance of normalcy. We do not have either. Instead, we are fleeing for our lives; *where* we are fleeing to remains the question. Only Sully knows. Somehow, I doubt it will be as picturesque as the scenery before us.

The landscape is far different from where June, Will, Riley, and I first entered from the forest. Even though I am running, I am not oblivious of it. Covered in lush grass with full trees interspersed intermittently, low hills roll as far as I can see. The vibrant green stretches, reaching until it meets the horizon line. There, a vivid blue sky greets it. It is hard for me to imagine the earth I run on is the same place I arrived at yesterday. It is harder to imagine that creatures as vile as Urthmen reign over space so lovely, especially after seeing how they entertain themselves.

I push the arena, and the sight of humans being dragged with a trail of blood in their wake, to the back of my mind. It will haunt my days and nights for years to come. Urthmen, always Urthmen, are responsible for my nightmares, both when I sleep and when I wake.

We continue down a gentle slope that drops to a roadway lined by stout, closely spaced shrubs. The bushes are not much taller than Will or Sully. Jericho would have to crouch to be concealed by them.

"Now what?" Will asks.

"Shh!" Sully shushes him and holds up his hand.

A rumble sounds in the distance, the crackle and crunch of something heavy rolling over gravel. Faint at first, it grows nearer quickly. Sully's head snaps in the direction of it.

"Everybody get down," he says. "We've got company coming." His eyes are hard but his mouth curves upward on one side to what resembles a partial grin.

A roar and crunch, familiar to the one I heard days earlier, swells. Vehicles are approaching. My heart shoots from my chest to my throat. My skin is suddenly cool and clammy and my breathing becomes short and shallow. But they are not a result of the weather or running, and they are not a result of my newly stitched wounds. The threat of being caught again is too awful to bear.

As if intuiting my quiet panic attack, Sully lightly grips my upper arm, careful to avoid the stitches on my forearm. "You won't be taken in again," he says, his voice low and gravelly.

His touch is a ribbon of fire that curls its way up my arm and blazes through my core, and his gaze is fixed on my face. Beyond him, I see Will. He is watching us; his eyes pinned on me as well. I shift uncomfortably, uncertain of what is happening, why they both watch me so intensely. But the crunch of wheels on gravel, an approaching vehicle, demands everyone's attention.

"Ah, here come our guests," Sully comments grimly as he parts a portion of the bushes so that I can see.

Thin limbs laden with prickly spines block much of my view. Still, I am able to make out that a convoy led by a wagon is passing.

I feel June edge up next to me.

"Oh my gosh," she gasps as she peeks from beside me. "Not another one!" Her hands fly to cover her mouth.

I follow her line of vision and suck in a harsh breath. "I can't believe it."

The scene before my eyes is revolting. Six humans, caked in filth and wearing little more than cloths to cover their hips, are affixed to the cart with thick leather straps. Almost as revolting as the sight of humans pulling the wagon is the crowned monster perched atop it. His small, malformed head with closely set eyes the color of boart dung, and wide holes where a nose should sit, bobs along.

The features are similar in appearance to how every other Urthman looks. However, this particular Urthman possesses a dramatic difference. Thick, blubbery lips bounce as the wagon jostles him. They resemble twin tube-shaped animal skins stuffed with moss or another spongy substance. His mouth looks a lot like that of the gilled creatures that reside in lakes and streams. On them, it is commonplace. On the Urthman, the oversized lips look absurd.

But his lips are not the only strange aspect of his appearance. As he moves closer, I see him clearer and notice another. Shiny clothing crusted with a glittery substance I have never seen looks as if it will burst at the seams, his swollen belly straining against each article. Bloated legs and bulky arms end with hands and feet that look inflated.

The crown-wearing Uthman holds a whip in his meaty hand, flicking it sporadically across the backs of the humans. They flinch when the whip bites their skin. Each lash leaves behind a red welt. Swollen and bleeding, the welts cover raised, discolored flesh on their upper bodies.

Though I saw a similar scene unfold when we first arrived at the edge of the forest, my eyes still struggle to process what I am seeing, that the image before me is of humans pulling the Urthman's cart like beasts of burden. My mind can't seem to catch up and reconcile the view.

I look away, unable to watch the abuse any longer. I see Sully. His lips are pressed to a hard line and the color has drained from his face.

"What is that?" June whispers to Sully and points to the Urthman.

Sully laughs bitterly. "That's a well-fed Urthman," he says through his teeth. "See that crown on his head?" He points to golden wreath on the Urthman's head. "That means he's royalty."

"Royalty?" June scrunches her features.

"Yup, that means he's *really* important," Sully spits resentfully.

June's eyebrows look as if they will disappear into her hairline at any moment.

"I know," Sully says when he sees her surprised expression. "Seems ridiculous that one particular Urthman is special, right?"

June nods. "So being special means he gets to beat the humans pulling his wagon?" she asks, her eyes wide and shining with tears.

"Dammit!" he snarls

My pulse quickens. He raised his voice louder than a whisper.

"Humans pulling that fat boart's cart like animals, like Urthmen are above them!" Sully says and does not keep his tone quiet. He reaches to the holster at his waist and retrieves his gun. From his pocket, he produces bullets and begins loading them into the open chamber of the gun. He repeats the process with his other gun.

"What're you doing?" Will asks him, echoing my exact thoughts.

"What does it look like I'm doing?" Sully snaps.

"Whoa, calm down," I say softly.

Ignoring me, Will continues. "You can't do anything, Sully. There's about twenty Urthmen in that convoy, and she's hurt." He jabs a finger in my direction. "And we have little kids here. We can't risk it."

In a swift, single motion, Sully reaches out a hand and grabs Will. For a split-second, I worry he will strike him. But instead of fighting, he twists Will's head toward the cart. He opens the bushes and says, "See that down there? You see them? Those are people, humans, *our kind*. Our brothers are being used like animals." He releases Will's head. "You're damned right I'll risk it. If it were you down there, or your sister or brother, wouldn't you want someone to 'risk it' to save them?"

Will's jaw works from side to side. His eyes are smooth, turquoise stones. His gaze slides to Sully. "But we are outnumbered."

One side of Sully mouth slants upward. "Jericho, toss one into the ten Urthmen at the rear of the convoy."

"With pleasure," Jericho replies with a wicked grin. He digs into a satchel attached to a long strap that crosses his chest. He pulls out a rectangular package and throws it over the bushes and into the procession.

The line of Urthmen stop and look toward us. Sully stands and aims a small metal device at them and depresses a button at its center. The package detonates and a blast rocks the world around me. Limbs careen through the air and rain from the sky, landing all around us with gory *thud*s.

"I think their numbers just shrank," Sully says with impish cheer just before he takes off toward the Urthmen.

Will looks from Sully to me. His expression is hard, but tenderness sparkles in his gaze for the briefest of moments, sending a wave of flutters pulsing through my belly. "Stay here," he says to me and pleads with his eyes.

He dashes off after Sully and Jericho, and my fluttering stomach plummets to my feet.

"No, no! What're they doing?" June asks me, a deep crease forming between her eyebrows. "Why are they going?"

I worry that they're charging in to their death. Hot tears scald the backs of my eyelids. I feverishly blink against them. "They'll be back," I say. My voice cracks. "I hope," I add.

I turn my attention back to the scene on the street. Dismembered legs and arms litter the road along with fragments of other body parts that I cannot identify. A few heads are intact and roll down the road. Sully immediately fires into the crowd. Three Urthmen fall before they even raise their clubs. The remaining seven swarm and he squeezes off another five shots. Three more fall. Confusion and mayhem ensues and I panic thinking I've lost track of Will and Sully. Jericho rises like a mountain, among the beasts. He grabs the first Urthman he sees and picks him up over his head. The Urthman squawks, a horrid, shrill sound that claws at my ears, just before Jericho slams him into the side of the carriage. Bones crack loudly. The Urthman slumps to the ground in a broken, lifeless heap.

Jericho turns and yanks his mallet from a sheath at his hip. He swings it in a wide arc. It connects with the head of a nearby Urthman, sending him flying to the pavement with half of his skull missing.

Seeing the carnage all around them, the two remaining Urthmen in the convoy drop their clubs and raise their hands in surrender.

The Urthman with the crown watches, wide-eyed, his fatty lips parted and jiggling. His pasty skin is flushed to an unhealthy shade of magenta. "What is the meaning of this?" he demands, spittle spraying in every direction. "You must defend your prince! That is a royal order!"

The surrendering Urthmen do not respond.

"This is treason! You will be punished! I am Prince Neo and I hereby accuse you of treason!"

"We surrender," one of the Urthmen says.

Sully approaches them, his gun aimed between them. "There is no surrendering," he says. I hear two loud *pops* and both fall. He then leaps onto the cart. He slowly walks to the portly Urthman.

"So, you're a prince?" he asks, his voice dripping with malice.

"Yes, and I can give you wealth beyond your wildest dreams. My father is King Leon. He will pay you whatever you want. Name your price."

"Money, huh," Sully says and scratches his chin with one of his weapon-wielding hands. "Hmm, that's some offer."

"I know it is, especially for a human. But I can arrange it."

A long pause passes between them, I start to believe Sully is considering Prince Neo's offer. The notion nauseates me.

"See, I don't want money from your father or you. I only want one thing."

"Anything! Land, food; name it and you'll have it!"

Sully lowers his head and makes a clucking sound with his tongue. When he lifts his chin, he is unnervingly still.

"Nah, I don't want any of that," Sully says through his teeth. "All I want is your life," he adds with icy certainty before two more pops ring out and I see Prince Neo collapse to one side.

Excitement rings through me with the clarity of a bell tolling. It resonates through my core and vibrates to my fingertips and toes. I am glad to see him die. If that makes me as bad as an Urthman then so be it.

Not everyone shares in my happiness to see the prince fall, however. A quick look at Will reveals that he is among those who do not. He stands eerily still, a troubled expression veiling his features.

"Let them go!" Sully shouts and recaptures my attention. "Free our people." His voice echoes down the street, resounding with truth and righteousness through the cavernous hollows of my being. Goose bumps cover my skin. A part of me feels like clapping, applauding everything Sully has done until now. When Jericho unsheathes a machete from his thigh and hacks at the leather straps until they break, tears stream from my eyes freely.

"You're welcome to join us," Sully approaches one of the newly freed men and says. But the man doesn't respond, and his eyes dart from side to side.

In fact, all of them are wild-eyed. They babble and wander, mumbling incoherently to one another. Frightened and cagey, they resemble injured animals.

As soon as the last of the six is loose, they run off, rambling incomprehensibly.

Sully lowers his chin to his chest. He holsters his guns and shakes his head slowly then rakes his fingers through his hair. I resist the urge to run to him. I can feel his disappointment, his frustration.

"Their minds are broken," Will says. "They'll wander around aimlessly until they get themselves killed. They'll be dead before the day's end. We just risked our lives for nothing."

Anger flashes across Sully's face. For a moment, he looks every bit as deadly as he did when battling against Urthmen. "No," he says, his tone so calm it is threatening. "We didn't risk our lives without reason. Those men will live and die free, as every human should, not live and die chained to a cart like an animal." He looks to Jericho who nods solemnly in agreement. He then turns and begins walking back toward the bushes, toward June, Riley, and Oliver; toward me. "Let's go," he says and does not look back.

I realize in the brief time it takes him to close the distance between us that I am honored to fight alongside him. He represents all that I have been taught, all that I am and will ever be. I realize that like June, Will, Riley and Oliver, Jericho and Sully are my future.

Chapter 27

We travel for several more miles after Sully killed the convoy of Urthmen, crossing the street and remaining hidden by the trees that line the other side. While we do, the scene continues to replay in my head over and over. I search my heart for regret or remorse for what happened, even though I did not do the killing. But I come up empty. Maybe I am not better than the Urthmen as Will implied when I was about to kill the family of them back in town. Maybe he is right. Maybe I am a monster. If being a monster means wanting to live for more than just a day, to try to secure some kind of future for my sister and I, then I am every bit a monster. I want more than today, I want tomorrow, and many days, months and years thereafter. I want a life. I want to live. I wonder whether Will understands the difference between surviving and living.

Several times while we jog along, Will's eyes meet mine. His expression is always the same: troubled. He's likely seen more death and gore in the last week than in his entire life. Seeing his parents die at the hands of Urthmen has scarred him, of that I am confident. How could it not? All the other carnage only serves to further widen the aching chasm that has been opened within him. He did not approve of what Sully did earlier. He'd made that plain enough. I enthusiastically approve, but I still feel bad for Will. The wound of his parents' deaths is still fresh. I try to convey to him with my eyes that I am sorry for his pain. There isn't much I can say in front of everyone else. Preserving Will, Oliver and Riley's privacy is important to me. They can share what they want with Sully and Jericho when or if they want to. It is not for me to determine that for them.

"Where are we going?" June asks Sully and distracts me from my brooding.

"We are going to the place where Jericho and I live. But listen June, and everyone else," Sully addresses not just my sister, but all of us. "You need to do exactly as I say. The next turnoff will take us to the edge of a heavily wooded area. As soon as we get in there, everyone needs to follow my orders, okay?"

June agrees first, followed by Oliver and Riley's mumbles of approval.

"Avery, are you good with that?" Sully asks me directly.

"Yep," I reply stiffly after a quick glance at Will.

Will's upper lip is lifted higher than usual. He shakes his head slowly, as if disgusted.

"How about you, buddy? You good with that?" Sully addresses Will.

"Do I really have a choice?" Will snaps.

Amusement dances in Sully's dark eyes. "You always have a choice. Just this one is either listen to me, or be blown to smithereens," he says with a wink. "Choose wisely."

Will is left with his mouth agape, a question or angry comment burning somewhere beyond it. Not waiting for it, Sully shrugs and turns from everyone. He continues leading us until the line of trees and shrubs we follow gives way to thicker clusters of growth.

The sun is not as high in the sky. I am hungry and exhausted. I would love nothing more than to eat and rest in a safe place. But we are out among Urthmen, in their territory. I doubt such a place exists.

We cross a small seasonal stream, swollen with water and leaves. Once we are across it, we are immediately swallowed by an abundance of thorny bushes and brush. Branches, crisscrossed at every turn, threaten to gouge our eyes and undergrowth tugs at our pant legs. Trees grow larger the deeper we delve and canopy our path, filtering much of the sunlight. Wherever it is we're headed, I doubt any Urthmen would bother to look. The landscape is downright hostile. More than once, I hear June say, "Ouch!" and assume that, like me, she is getting pricked by spiny burrs and limbs.

As if the thorns aren't enough, a riot of tangled vines slithers at our feet, waiting to trip us as we plod along. Sully and Jericho, of course, move easily, gracefully even.

Fortunately, the bushes and undergrowth start to thin and walking becomes a little easier.

"Okay, everybody stop," the bass of Jericho's voice pours from him like heated honey. He freezes, his massive body eerily still as his eyes sweep the surrounding area. He points to something I do not see at first. When I strain my eyes, though, I realize it is a nearly invisible wire about chest height. "You see this?" he asks us. We lean in and look. "This line leads to explosives. Animals indigenous to this area pass beneath or around it easily, but it is rigged to trigger those explosives when something heavy, like an Urthman, walks into it."

"Each of us has to step under it carefully, then wait for further instruction," Sully chimes in. "There are more like this one throughout the woods."

June slips her small hand in mine. It is clammy and cold.

"Don't worry, sweetie, you'll be fine. We'll go together and just wait for Sully or Jericho to tell us what to do next," I tell her.

Will expels air from his nose loudly. I snap my head toward him and tip my chin while furrowing my brow, as if to ask what the matter is. He rolls his eyes and frowns. I guess he is not a fan of Sully and therefore not happy about following his orders. I would prefer not to be blasted to bits as the Urthmen were in the convoy. I hope Will shares my wish to stay in one, whole piece. He gestures for June and I to go before him. I nod and turn my body sideways then dip my head and upper body beneath the wire. June does too. We repeat this process about ten more times, navigating an intricate labyrinth of lines, until I see a white clapboard structure with sooty streaks smudged from the upper windows to the roof. The paint is peeling and weeds have grown over the first-story windows, but I can clearly see that it is a house. Beside the house, two vehicles are parked. One is a truck and the other is, if my memory serves me correctly, a camper. I have never seen the latter, only heard of them and seen creased and faded images. Regardless, both appear to be in decent shape. They do not resemble the cars I saw lining the streets when we first ventured out of the forest.

Next to me, June's grip on my hand tightens. "Whoa, is that a house?" she asks.

"Ah, home sweet home. Well, kind of," Sully steps up beside me and says. His shoulder brushes mine and heat spirals from the point of contact, twisting down my arm and spreading through me like fire.

"This is where you and Jericho live?" June asks.

"Yep, that's right," he replies and takes a step back causing our arms to touch again.

"And there aren't any Urthmen in there?" she asks, her brows gathered in concern.

"Nope." Sully shakes his head.

"You sure?" June persists.

"I am," Sully says confidently.

"Wow, you have your own house," June marvels.

"Everyone should have a place to call home, one that isn't under constant attack," he says earnestly.

"What must that be like?" I hear myself say without thinking.

"What, you never had that?"

"I guess we did for a while," I say absently. "But the monsters that come out at night in the forest found us, and once they find you," I allow my voice to trail off, but Sully finishes my sentence.

"They never stop," he says and a chill races up my spine.

A pause spans for several beats. Will has taken Riley and Oliver to relieve themselves with Jericho covering them. I am alone with June and Sully.

"So you rigged this place with all the wires and explosives?"

"That's right. Knowing this place is equipped with trip wires and bombs helps me sleep at night."

"Sleep," I say ruefully. "I miss that."

Sully grips my upper arms and turns me so that I face him. His expression is intense as his piercing eyes bore straight into my soul. "Tonight, you will sleep, I promise you that. Everything will be okay." He holds me with both his hands and his gaze, but oddly, I do not feel nervous or uncomfortable. To my surprise, I am calm. It has been a long time since anyone has taken care of me in even the slightest way. Sully has saved my life three times; first in the arena, second when he stitched my wound, and third when we came upon the convoy. Being saved is foreign to me, but pleasant all the same.

"She needs it, Sully," June says softly and breaks the powerful eye contact. "Avery is the best fighter there is. She's killed boarts, Urthmen, spider-monsters, crazy humans who wanted to use her to breed more humans, and a bat. And that's just in the last five days." June frowns. Her eyes well up with tears. "She saves everybody all the time. She needs sleep. She needs someone to take care of her for once."

Hot tears singe the backs of my eyelids. They appear suddenly, along with June's stark observation. Her words have touched a nerve I did not anticipate was so raw.

"Wow," Sully says and releases my arms. He turns his attention to June. "Sounds like your sister is something special, not that that surprises me or anything; I knew she was the second I saw her in the arena." He pokes the tip of her small nose. "And as long as she's with me, I'll give her a break, okay? I'll take good care of her."

June looks as if she may explode. Emotion is fairly bursting from her. Her eyes are wide and a grin stretches across her face. "Good," she says. Her single word is so laden with excitement I have trouble suppressing my own smile.

"Come on." Sully reaches out a hand to her. "Let's go inside. I'll show you around."

The soft swish and rustle of leaves and the snap of twigs means Will and his siblings are back.

"Whoa, you have a truck and a camper?" Will says as soon as he sees the parked vehicles. "Do they work?"

"I've rebuilt the engine and transmission. As far as I know, everything works. Only problem is, we don't have gasoline."

"Gasoline?" I ask. "What's that?"

"It's the liquid that was used to run vehicles in the past. But it's scarce now. What little is left is fiercely guarded by Urthmen," Sully says. "We'll talk about all that tomorrow, though. Come on. Follow me around back so we can go inside."

We file behind Sully, June leading the way, and follow him around the side of the house, past the camper and the truck to the back of the house. But to my surprise, he does not climb the short, rickety looking flight of steps. Instead, he begins separating long, reedy weeds until a door, placed flush against the earth, appears. He pulls a key from his pocket, unlocks a padlock looping through two metal hoops and opens the door.

"Wow!" June exclaims.

"It's an old bomb shelter," Sully tells her just before he turns and begins descending a ladder. "Come on down."

June does not hesitate. She climbs down immediately. I follow, then Will, Oliver, Riley and Jericho come afterward. Jericho shuts the door behind us and engages a lock from the inside.

I expect to be submerged in darkness. But peculiar, ashen light fills the space below me. It intensifies when I am standing on a hard floor. My eyes scour the room and I stop mid-breath when I see rectangular screens with pictures within them. The picture changes continually, and appears strangely familiar.

"What is," I start, but I cannot form a sentence. I am riveted by the image, transfixed by what I think I am seeing. "Is that the wooded area we just came through?"

Sully smiles slyly. "It is."

"So those are," I begin, but I dare not utter the word.

His dark eyes brim with anticipation. "Go on," he urges me as if we are the only two people in the underground bunker.

"Picture boxes," I ask more than I say.

Picture boxes are the stuff of legend, they are fabled stories Will and I heard as children and now share with our young siblings. Never in my wildest imaginings did I ever believe I would see one for myself. I thought they'd always be objects my mind's eye conjured. But here they are, in Sully and Jericho's lair, and right before my very eyes.

"Picture boxes, televisions, they're both just names, but yes, that's exactly what they are." Sully's words snap me out of my trance.

It is all so surreal, so magical. I swallow hard then ask one of the many questions blazing in my brain. "But how are we seeing the woods we were just in?"

"Cameras," Sully answers and I feel my jaw drop. I know I must look like a buffoon, standing as I am with my mouth agape. But I am flabbergasted. Cameras are devices used long ago that transmitted live images for digital recording or viewership. Until today, I considered them even more elusive than the picture box.

Another question plagues me, one that involves both the picture boxes and the camera. Long ago, a power source was necessary to keep things like them functioning. "What's powering the camera and the picture, uh, I mean televisions?"

The children's heads bounce between Sully and I, in awe, as they follow our interaction. Now, they are watching him, waiting for his response. I am too, as it turns out.

"Solar power," he answers.

"What's that?" June asks.

"Well, it means we use the sun's rays to power a generator that powers the television and the cameras."

"Whoa, cool!" Oliver exclaims.

"Wow," Riley adds.

"How did you learn to do such a thing?" June asks, her voice quiet and reverent.

"He knows how to fix things," Jericho's voice rumbles like distant thunder and sends our attention his way. A small chuckle rolls from deep in his chest. "I told you before, Sully can fix anything." He shrugs his enormous shoulders and flicks his hands to the sides.

"The technology existed long before the War of 2062. I just gathered materials along the way and tweaked them," Sully says matter-of-factly.

"What about the guns?" I ask, intrigued beyond measure. "How did you get them? And what about the bullets?" I fire the questions in rapid succession, my mouth working in time with my brain.

The corners of Sully's mouth hook upward to a sneaky smile. He narrows his eyes at me and again, a playful glint gleams in his eyes. "I rebuilt the guns from old parts I found through the years. As you can imagine, I found a lot. Urthmen are dumb as stumps. They wouldn't know what to do with any of the stuff I came across, so they left it, right Jericho?"

"That's for sure," Jericho agrees.

"As for the bullets, well, I got lucky with that one. Years back, I found a bullet press in a bomb shelter, completely intact. All I needed to do was search for scrap metal to make the jackets and formulate the propellant."

"The what?" I can't help but ask.

"The stuff inside the actual bullet," Sully answers.

"*Okay*," I reply and do not hide that I am confused.

"It's really not that big of a deal. I find sulfur, charcoal, and saltpeter."

"Salt who?" I stop him again. "Now you've totally lost me."

Sully laughs. It is a pleasant sound. "Now that's even less of a deal than the other stuff. Salt peter is harvested from decomposed manure. It's also found in caves, but manure is easier to come by."

"Manure? You mean poop?" June asks and is barely able to keep from giggling.

"Yep," Sully nods with a naughty expression on his face. "I mean poop, old animal poop to be exact, but poop all the same."

June and Riley are overcome by a fit of giggles. Even Oliver can't resist and joins in. I smile and so does Jericho. Will, however, is not amused in the least, a fact that is not lost on Sully. He frowns and looks between Will and I. I shake my head slightly and close my eyes. Will watched his parents die and is now responsible for his two siblings. Laughing at the word "poop" is not at the forefront of things he needs to do.

"Does anyone else live here with you two?" I ask and steer the conversation back to the host of questions rattling around in my head.

"Nope, just Jericho and I," Sully answers.

"We have freed many humans, but none have stayed," Jericho adds.

"No one ever stays and fights. They all want to hide and live," Sully says.

"Well we're not going anywhere. We're with you. We want to fight." I hear the words spill from me; know that I have spoken for all of us when it is only me who feels that way. I cannot imagine jeopardizing June's safety, or Will, Riley and Oliver's for that matter. Yet, I cannot imagine leaving either. The life we led was no life at all, running and hiding, living in constant fear of how we would defend ourselves when the time came, and it always would. Finding Urthmen in the forest was not some random improbable occurrence we could chalk up as an isolated incident. It meant that the moment we feared had finally come.

I know that Will is displeased by what I have said. He looks at me harshly, as if I have either gone mad or betrayed him in some monumental way.

"We," Will says emphatically and points among he and his siblings, "Would like to live in peace."

I part my lips to speak, but Sully beats me to it.

"There will be no peace until we kill them all."

His words resound in my bones, in every part of me, for they are words that express my exact sentiments. As long as Urthmen live, we will be hunted, and we will never live freely, in peace.

"And we are now in big trouble," Sully emphasizes the word "we" as Will did. "That fat Urthmen we killed in the convoy was the king's son. As soon as word gets out, which I am sure it has already, Urthmen will flood this area in search of us."

"There's a king?" Oliver asks.

"Yes, King Leon rules the world. He's the leader of the Urthmen," Will replies.

Will balls his fists. Rippling muscles flex and bulge down the length of both arms as he does. His anger is barely harnessed; bubbling beneath the surface of his skin so volatilely it is practically visible. "Did you know that fat Urthman was the king's son beforehand, before you decided we were going to attack?"

"No, not when we bombed the convoy." Sully answers. "I knew he was royalty because of the crown, but I didn't know it was King Leon's son until he told me as much, and by then it was too late. If I'd known the convoy was carrying Prince Neo, I would've thought twice. I never would have jeopardized all of us like that. Now they are going to come here. Even with the wires and cameras, we're not safe here."

At his words, June immediately rushes toward me and wraps her arms around my waist. I do not groan about the soreness the contact causes. She is frightened, and for good reason. Once again, we are holed up in an unsafe shelter. True, this one has sophisticated technology that may give us advance warning. Some Urthmen would likely be killed in the process, but not all. The ones that survive would pursue us.

The gravity of what has happened, of what will happen, crystallizes fully. But I am too fatigued to wrap my mind around what needs to be done. I am tired, so very tired. Being captured and caged, then winding up in an arena where I was slashed by a behemoth Urthman more monstrous than any other, and witnessing the fall of Prince Neo and his minions has taken its toll on me. I am drained on all fronts. Exhaustion sinks it teeth into me and devours me completely. My legs feel as if they're made of spongy moss and my arms feel like stone. My body wavers. I feel as if a dense mist has settled all around me, dizzying me, disorienting me.

"Avery? Avery, are you okay?" I hear June. She sounds as if she is calling to me from a great distance. I am aware that she is right in front of me. Her feather-light arms encircle my waist.

"Avery, can you hear me?" Will's voice is near, so strong and sure it rips me from the hazy fog descending on me.

"Yeah," I say and hear the thickness in my voice.

"Are you okay?" Will asks. I hear the concern in his tone. He reaches out and cups my elbow in is hand.

June moves to my side and watches me with wide, concerned eyes.

"I'm, I don't know. I'm suddenly wiped out," I admit.

"I'm here for you," Will says, urgency lacing his words.

"You need to lie down," Sully tells me. "Come on. Come with me. I have a cot you can sleep on."

"A cot?" I ask with surprise. "Where did you," I start. "I mean, how did you ever get a cot?"

The narrow collapsible beds, like so many other items in Sully's possession, are things I believed extinct long ago.

"Oh I'm just full of surprises," Sully replies with a wicked arc of one eyebrow.

"I bet you are," Will mumbles under his breath as his grip on my elbow tightens marginally. I feel an unnamed emotion pulsing from him. Is it anger, frustration, or something else entirely, I wonder. "Come on, Avery, let's follow Sully and get you comfortable. You need to sleep if you wants those cuts to heal," he says and draws me closer to his body. His scent surrounds me and I feel heat blaze up my neck and color my cheeks.

With Will's help, I am led deeper into the room to the far corner where a metal contraption with a thin pad atop it sits.

"I'll get you a blanket," Sully says. He disappears and returns with a length of darkly colored fabric. "Make yourself comfortable."

I sit on the bed, suddenly self-conscious that a roomful of people are watching me, waiting for me to lie down and go to sleep.

June pushes between Will and Sully who hover over me. "Rest, Avery. Please. I need you to get better," she whispers close to my ear.

"I'll be fine, June. Don't you worry." I poke the tip of her nose and force a smile across my lips. I can tell it convinces her as she returns the smile with one of her own. "I love you," I add.

"I love you, too," she says. "I'll stay close by."

"I'll take care of her," Will assures me with a knowing look.

I meet his gaze despite that I am blushing. I appreciate his offer to look after June. Ordinarily I would protest and insist that I'd do it. But I am too tired. "Thank you," I tell him.

June slips her hand in Will's hand and leads him away. Oliver and Riley follow along with Jericho. I am left with Sully.

"Rest up, Avery," he says and pats my shoulder lightly. A metallic scent, tinged with a mild, charred smell likely caused from the house he lives beneath, mingles with the scent of grass and spice lingers in the wake of his touch. It comforts me for reasons I cannot explain. Perhaps it reminds me of the way my father, a man who could fix and find many things, smelled, or perhaps it is because Sully saved my life more than once today. Either way I am grateful for him.

"Thank you, Sully," I say as he is about to walk away.

"What for?" he asks without turning.

"For saving my life," I reply.

He spins and faces me. His dark eyes glow with a fire that knocks the wind from me. "You would have done the same for me, I know you would have."

"Yes, I would have," I say after a pause.

"Then you have nothing to thank me for," he says right before he walks away and joins the others.

I ponder his words for the briefest of moments before sleep beckons me like a long-lost friend, welcoming me with warm, open arms. I allow myself to be cradled by the velvety abyss and quickly fall into a deep sleep.

Chapter 28

My eyes open to the sight of a room awash in ashy light. Briefly startled and unsure of where I am, I bolt upright and whip my head from one side to the next. I see June's face peek around Will, who's standing sternly with his arms folded across his chest, and am flooded with relief.

"Avery!" she exclaims before she hurries toward me. She throws both arms around my neck and squeezes tightly. "Oh thank goodness you're okay!" She steps back and looks at me.

Smiling, I tip my chin and say, "Hey you." My voice is hoarse and unfamiliar to my own ears. I clear my throat. "Of course, I'm okay." I feel half my mouth turn upward and imagine I am smiling the way Sully does. The thought makes me feel giddy and guilty simultaneously.

The guilt is emphasized when I look past June and see a familiar gaze trained my way.

Wearing a peculiar expression on his face, Will watches me. His brilliant blue-green eyes slice through the gray light and shimmer like twin turquoise gemstones. The sight makes my breathing hitch and I wish I could read what is behind them, what exactly he is thinking.

"Hey! Look who's awake!" Sully's voice echoes from a corner of the room I cannot see and strikes like a bolt of lightning through my core. I watch as Will's features collapse and his bright eyes become overcast. When Sully's head pops up from behind a pile of miscellaneous metal parts, I nod goofily in answer.

Will glances in Sully's direction with his eyes narrowed and his jaw set. When he returns his attention to me, he asks, "How are you feeling?" just before he approaches.

He closes the distance between us and stands before me. Reaching out a hand, he strokes my cheek with the back of his hand, sending my pulse skyrocketing. The gesture is gentle, so tender it borders on affectionate. My racing heart stumbles clumsily at his proximity, at his touch, just as it always does, and heat creeps up from my collar and warms my cheeks. Words escape me. I know he's asked me a question, yet I seem to have forgotten both what he asked me and how to speak.

"I'm okay," I answer when words finally find me and hope he does not hear the breathlessness in my tone.

Will lowers his chin and stares at me hard as if to scrutinize my response.

"Really, I am. I'm fine," I say and feel my blush deepen.

"I'm so glad. I was really worried about you."

"He was," June adds. "He was a nervous wreck the whole time you slept."

"How do you know that?" Will twists and asks June with a brow arched.

"It's not like you're good at hiding your feelings, Will," June says. "I mean, come on. You were practically pacing the whole time. You might as well have had *I'm so worried about Avery* written across your face." She giggles and I spy a faint hint of pink tint Will's cheeks.

"Hmm, I was pretty worried," he admits.

My insides begin fluttering wildly. "I'm sorry for worrying you, and you know, June and, well everybody," I fumble. I cringe at how idiotic I sound. He just said he was worried about me, no big deal. I was sliced open in two places by an Urthman.

"You don't have to apologize for worrying me," Will starts. I feel his long, slender fingers wrap around my hand. Reflexively, my gaze drops to where his hand touches mine then moves slowly back to his face. He watches me intently. "I worry because," he starts but is interrupted by a familiar, booming voice.

"Who's apologizing in here? It better not be Avery," I hear Sully say just before he becomes visible.

Will slides him a glance from the corner of his eye and his expression tightens. In a low voice, he says, "What timing."

"Hey there! Glad to see you're up. You're sitting. That's a good thing. How's your belly feeling, the stitches, that is?" Sully asks. He walks over to the cot and stands beside Will, smiling. He places a hand on Will's shoulder as if they are the oldest of friends. Will looks as if he is seconds away from jiggling his shoulder and shaking off the hand, and I do not know why, but I feel bad for both of them. Sully for Will looking as if his shoulder has just been slathered in boart droppings and Will for being interrupted while trying to communicate some important point to me.

"My belly is sore, but not too bad," I say. "And my arm is pretty much the same."

Much to Will's relief, Sully drops his hand from Will's shoulder. He leans over me and picks up my arm and examines the stitches. "Looks pretty good, if I do say so myself." His touch is like fire burning dried leaves. It sweeps up my arm and blazes like a brushfire. "No new blood, that's a good thing, right?" he says with a wink. "Now let's take a look at your stomach."

He is about to reach for the hem of my shirt when Will speaks. "Why do you need to look at it?" he snaps. "She said she's fine."

"I need to look at it to make sure it isn't getting infected and that the stitches are holding," Sully replies evenly. I think the edge in Will's tone is lost on him until he adds, "Take it easy there, handsome. I'm not trying to get a free peek at her belly button or anything." He gives me another jaunty wink.

Incensed, Will's upper lip tightens over his teeth until he catches me watching him. His features soften and he watches Sully's hands as they roll the edge of my shirt halfway up my torso.

His fingers nimbly dance along the line that used to be a considerable split. His brow is furrowed and his mouth is a hard line, yet his eyes sparkle with merriment, as if he is privy to a joke the rest of us cannot hear. Part of me desperately wants to be let in on the joke, to share with him that intimate knowledge that drives the wicked glint in his eyes and the sly smile that rounds one cheek. But the fact is that I know nothing about Sully, and I do not know what to make of him just yet. All I do know is that he saved my life, along with the lives of my friends, sewed me up and kept me from bleeding out. He is obviously gifted when it comes to repairing and restoring technology once believed to be defunct, and he is fearless to a near-fault. Beyond that, I am in the dark, save for something else I've observed about Sully, an aspect of his personality that concerns me deeply. He seems to have a negative effect on Will.

I do not know why but since teaming up with Sully, Will has been brooding and oppositional. The last thing I want is to cause a rift between us. Will is an indelible part of me now. I cannot imagine one day passing without looking upon his golden, glorious face. Just knowing that he is seeing my bare flesh now, despite being grotesque and wounded as it is, makes my insides quiver. And he is not alone in seeing it. Sully joins him. Though looking in more of a clinical capacity, Sully has my shirt hiked up to where my ribcage begins to show. The constant sensation of his fingertips grazing my sensitive skin combines with his mischievous grin and the impish spark in his gaze and makes my head spin.

But despite the strange and conflicting feelings storming inside me, shame and self-reproach are present too. Until just a week ago, I had never seen another human being that I wasn't related to in many years. Now, there are five that I intend to travel with. Exhilarating and daunting at the same time, I do not know how to act. Especially since there seems to be friction brewing between Will and Sully.

I shift uncomfortably and clear my throat again. "So how does it look?"

"Everything I'm seeing looks great," Sully answers. His eyes wander from the wound and skim the rest of my exposed flesh. A small smirk steals across his lips, and a strange heat fills me. Will does not see Sully's small act, a fact that I'm thankful for, and he does not see the ribbon of warmth that slowly wound its way from my chest to my limbs. I worry that if he did, he would have punched Sully dead in his face. Perhaps *I* should have done just that. I doubt I would have had the strength, though. My arms, and legs for that matter, feel as if they've liquefied.

"So she'll be fine?" June asks.

"Yep," Sully says and pulls the hem of my shirt down. His knuckles graze the length of my midsection and I feel as if a stream of fire trails behind them. "The stitches on her belly look good. They're holding the cut closed just as they should. She just needs to take it easy for a little while and she'll be good as new in no time." He pinches one of June's cheeks and I see a squeal welling just beneath the surface of her skin. I know how she feels. A squeal is begging to leak from me, too.

"Hear that, Avery? You have to take it easy," June says. The laughter in her tone is evident.

"I don't know about that," Will chimes in. "Our Avery here doesn't know the meaning of *take it easy*, do you?" he says playfully and places his hand atop mine.

The contact of his warm hand resting on mine feels like thousands of tiny, light pinpricks are occurring at once. My scalp feels two sizes too small and a chill whispers up my spine.

"Is that right?" Sully asks and quirks a brow.

"Oh yes!" June comments.

"Well I'll just have to stick right by her and make sure she listens, won't I?"

"We all will," Will says sharply. His hand grips mine momentarily before relaxing then his thumb sweeps across the top of my wrist. I want to close my eyes and savor the feel of his rough fingertip stroking the soft skin there, but Sully watches me. His gaze drops to where Will's thumb works and I shrink inwardly. I tense. Will's thumb stops moving and he withdraws his hand. My hand feels cold. I look at it then look up. Everyone is watching me, waiting, but for what I have no idea.

"So, uh, what's the plan?" I finally say. "What do we do now?" I look between Will and Sully.

"What do you mean?" Sully asks, a mysterious look flickering across his face.

Will looks taken aback. I wonder why both of them are behaving so peculiarly.

"We need to start getting people together to grow an army, right? We can fight back, on a small scale, but we can fight and start the war to take back planet Urth," I say.

The stiffness in Will's posture loosens marginally, as if he is relieved. I find it odd that a person so against standing our ground and battling Urthmen should look so thankful for my proposal.

"I think you're getting a little bit ahead of yourself," Sully says with a soft chuckle. "There aren't many humans running around out there, in case you haven't noticed."

"I found you and Jericho, didn't I?" I say defiantly and am not sure why.

Sully holds my eyes with his as he scratches his chin thoughtfully. "It would take years to round them up much less rally them to fight," he thinks aloud. "The only place where there's a large human population is in the underground city, and they have no interest in fighting."

A large human population living in an underground city! The notion sounds too good to be true!

"Come on, Sully! You expect us to believe there's an underground city?" Will laughs mirthlessly. "That's a myth. No such place exists."

"No, it's real," Sully says with conviction.

"Thousands of people living together underground and Urthmen haven't found them, yeah, okay," Will huffs with certainty that borders on arrogance.

Hearing our conversation, Oliver and Riley join us. Jericho leans against a wall with his arms comfortably folded across his chest.

Sully stands and addresses everyone. "Mock all you want, but I know it's true. I grew up there," he stuns me by saying. "I was kicked out when I was thirteen because I wanted to do exactly what Avery wants to do. I wanted to fight. I wanted to lead a revolt against the Urthmen regime. I made so much noise about it I was asked to leave. So please, don't tell me it isn't real."

I steal a glance at Will. He looks as shocked as I feel. In fact, after a quick glance around the room, I see that everyone wears the same expression, except Jericho and Sully.

"You mean to tell me thousands of people live together safely?" I ask and feel the corners of my mouth falter, tears welling in my eyes. The idea of it is all that I've wanted, all that I've dreamed of for June. And Sully claims it is real, that he has been there.

"More than ten thousand if you want to be more precise. But that was before I left."

My jaw comes unhinged. "More than ten thousand," I gasp.

"Yep, and they're just content to live there, to hide is more like it, and grow their food hydroponically with their livestock on hand. I guess you could argue they have everything they need, you know, if you think living like rats in a sewer is a life worth living. I didn't." Sully stares off toward an unseen place only he sees. "I couldn't take existing in hiding, knowing eventually we'd be found, and that other people in the world were dying." He swallows hard. "I mean, Urthmen are dumb, but even if they take decades. I'm sure they'll find the underground city. One of the humans will slip or a solar panel will be discovered."

"I had no idea," I murmur.

"No one does, unless they've lived there as I have. But it's not some great place like you think it is, especially when I would go out on supply runs and see the suffering in the streets. I'd go back down and shake my head, wondering why we were so content to just *be*, you know, to just lie down and die about everything."

Sully's arms are folded across his chest. His fists are balled tightly and I can see the rage flaring like firelight in his dark eyes, rage and regret.

"So how did they manage to avoid the Urthmen?" Will asks.

"The city is in the desert. Nobody journeys out into the middle of the desert without a reason. And even if they did, they wouldn't see it."

"I don't understand," Oliver says.

"This place, the city, it was the most elaborate underground shelter ever built. Some say it was designed centuries ago to house intel on foreign countries, kind of a spy files city. It is literally the size of a small city. But as soon as the first bomb fell and the war officially started, the files were cleared out and the President, along with the entire government, was sent down there."

"Who's government? What are you talking about?" Will asks, his brows gathered.

"Ours," Sully answers. "We are all descendants of Americans. Our ancestors were from shelters."

My mind spins in circles as it struggles to process what I've heard. Reeling, I ask, "How do you know all this?"

"I learned it in history class."

"History class?" I ask incredulously. "You went to school?"

"Yeah, all kids did in the underground city, which is called New Washington, by the way," Sully says offhandedly.

I reach out and grip Will's arm for support. He immediately wraps an arm around my shoulders and I feel the hardness of his thick muscles flex and he safeguards me from falling. "I can't believe this. Schools, New Washington, all of it, it's like a dream," I mumble incoherently.

"It's not a dream, trust me," Sully says and his gaze examines Will's arm draped over my shoulder protectively. I squirm, but Will does not let go.

"So you know exactly what happened in the war, how the world came to be this way," I ask more than state.

"I do," Sully answers. "If you really want to know, I can tell you about it."

"Please, tell me. Tell all of us what happened," I say in a voice far stronger than I feel.

I gulp hard against the lump of dread that has collected in my throat. Sully has information, answers to so many questions that have plagued my brain since I was old enough to understand the condition of the human species. And now, all of those questions are about to be answered. I hope I can handle all of it. I hope I can handle the truth.

Chapter 29

"It started in 2059 when a terrorist organization composed of religious fanatics called Jaish-e-Al-Queda overthrew several governments in the Middle East in a coordinated, multi-country coup," Sully begins.

"A coup?" June asks?

"A takeover is what a coup is, and in this case it was violent," Sully answers. "So America learned of this and sent the military to a place known as Pakistan to guard their government from being removed from power. See, our government knew Pakistan was the only country in the Middle East with nuclear capability of firing on America," he continues to a rapt audience.

The room is still, as if everyone waits with bated breath for him to keep going, to share with us what set our current situation into motion.

"While the military was over there, here, the people were freaking out. They knew World War III was coming, that the religious fanatics didn't care if they died as long as they killed us first. They believed that in the afterlife they would be rewarded for killing evil Americans."

"Oh my gosh," I gasp. I've never been given insight into the original cause of the war. I only knew that it happened.

"This war was going to be the end of the world as far as all of North America was concerned. Underground shelters were built all over the county as more and more people panicked. The underground city was redesigned for the President and Joint Chiefs of Staff so he could keep a working government in the event that the worst-case scenario came to pass.

"What America didn't know was that while they were so busy worrying about a nuclear holocaust, Jaish-e-Al-Queda had operatives in Iran, one of the countries they overtook, who worked alongside scientists and created a weapon known as Anthricin, a hybrid of the highly toxic protein *ricin* found in the seed of the castor oil plant and *anthrax*, a disease caused by bacteria found in spores."

"Wait, what?" I stop Sully from going on. "What does all that mean?"

"Biological weapons," he says and I feel the hairs on the nape of my neck stand on end. "After a few years of experimenting, Jaish-e-Al-Queda had in their possession bacteria and viruses that would cause widespread sickness and death among humans and animals. They eventually loaded Anthricin into rockets and launched them with the intent to kill."

"That's what caused the Urthmen to be the way they are and the Lurkers and the spider monster and that enormous bat you killed when we hid in the tree," June turns to me and says in one breath. Her cheeks are rosy but the rest of her is pale. I move from Will and envelop her in my arms. Her heart patters madly against my midsection.

"It's okay, June," I whisper in her ear. "This is history. Sully is teaching us about the past."

In truth, I am sickened by what I am hearing. The idea that human beings, regardless of where they lived and what ideologies they held, intentionally killing one another is unconscionable. *What for* is the real question: Power? Money? Greed? Control? I can't imagine anything worth killing another of my species for other than the protection of my sister, or myself. And now the people present are added to that list. This religion of which Sully spoke, was it worth ending the entirety of civilization? The members of Jaish-e-Al-Queda must have thought so, and were stark-raving mad in my opinion.

Will's voice, smooth and steady like water flowing over rocks in a slow-rolling river, returns my attention to the here and now, to the future. "The humans in the underground city, New Washington, they are descendants of survivors of the attacks?" he asks.

"Pretty much," Sully answers. "But this group, Jaish-e-Al-Queda, they didn't start in North America. The first rocket loaded with their biological weapon was launched at Israel, their fiercest enemy. As soon as that happened, Americans took cover. Rich and powerful people had space reserved in the underground shelters. The rest were left to wait."

"Why didn't we do something? Why didn't America fight back?" I ask.

That fiery glow undulates in Sully's eyes when his gaze lands on me. Is it pride that lights the fire or something else entirely? I wonder. "The American government did. They fired on Iran first. But Jaish-e-Al-Queda got wind of it and, before the country was obliterated, launched their missiles here."

"There was no turning back once that happened," I say slowly, the gravity of what humans, my American ancestors, experienced knocking the air from my lungs. "The people who weren't in shelters, their fates were sealed."

Sully nods somberly. "Those who weren't killed in the first few days went mad as their bodies deteriorated slowly, transforming them, mutating every cell inside their bodies."

"The viruses did what they were supposed to do," I say, my voice barely a whisper.

"And it affected every living creature. I guess one of the countless things Jaish-e-Al-Queda misjudged was how quickly their weapon would spread. Everyone on the planet who was exposed became infected, but not all died. The ones in the underground shelters were okay. But above, they changed into something else, something monstrous."

"Early versions of Urthmen." I complete Sully's thought.

"Exactly," he says.

A stunned hush befalls the room. We heard the stories from our parents, but for some reason, hearing Sully recount it as he does gives us a better feel for it, more of a firsthand account. His words are chilling. Our origins are simpler to explain. The Urthmen are another story entirely.

"The President and Joint Chiefs launched nuclear weapons and destroyed the rest of the world knowing what had happened in Israel after the biological weapons detonated. Reports came in about creatures. America and Canada were the only places where nuclear bombs did not fall."

"So North America really is the only place where life exists?" June asks. I hear the tremor in her voice, the fear. We'd been taught that North America was the only inhabitable place on the planet where life was supported, but we never knew for sure. We'd only heard stories passed down from generation to generation. Somehow, hearing him verify those stories, I feel more terrified and isolated that I did before.

"No one knows for sure, but that is what is believed. That is what's taught in school," Sully answers.

"The President and his people went underground. I get that. But what happened afterward, after years passed?" Oliver asks.

"I'm sure you heard some of it from your parents. The stories have been told for centuries. But I'm guessing it was much worse than what any of you heard."

"Why is that?" Will asks. The trace of an edge returns to his voice. "Why would our parents or family withhold the truth from us?"

"As I said, it's just a guess. I don't know that they did or didn't. I know if I had a kid I wouldn't feel comfortable telling her how our ancestors were torn to shreds by mutant versions of their own species when they came up after more than two decades of being holed up."

I hear a pair of startled gasps. I assume one was from June and the other was from Riley.

"See what I mean?" Sully says to Will without the slightest hint of arrogance. "They heard filtered versions. They don't know that the President and the others thought they'd destroyed every living thing in the world and that whatever altered beings, if any, existed, they'd be long dead before they surfaced. They thought they'd reclaim the planet and everything would be fine. They were wrong."

Sully does not speak dramatically. He shares his knowledge offhandedly. Perhaps that's why his words are so haunting. I wrap my arms around June more tightly to combat the chill that's settled deep in my bones despite the pleasant temperature of the room.

"How do you know the same hasn't happened to the people of the underground city?" Oliver asks concernedly.

"I don't," Sully says bluntly. "Not for a fact at least. But facts or no facts, I'm pretty sure everyone's fine and things are still humming along down there," he adds and his eyes shine with what I suspect are unshed tears. He blinks and looks to his feet for a moment then continues. "Those people, my kin, they could live forever down there, right under the radar of those mutant monsters. They've got livestock and indoor food growing capabilities."

"But the President and everyone down there after the war, didn't they have all that stuff too?" June asks.

"They had what they thought would carry them for more than two decades, and they had guns. They thought that when they ran out of supplies, they could come up then return."

"Wait a second. Didn't their guns do anything against the monsters when they came up?" Oliver asks.

"At first, yes. Heavily armed men and women were able to fight them off for a while. But they soon found out they were outnumbered. As their ammunition dwindled so too did their numbers. They were slaughtered shortly after their ammunition ran out.

"The offspring of the warped monsters were in their teens at the time and had more intelligence than their parents. They were what Urthmen are today. They led their older, diseased family members, and they destroyed every modern weapon they found, knowing that without them, humans couldn't beat them. They knew they had the survivors outnumbered and would eventually kill off the entire human race. And they nearly succeeded. There aren't many of us left."

"But why?" June asks, tears streaming down both cheeks. "I know what they did, but I don't understand why. Why did they hunt humans then? Why do they hunt us now?"

"That, June, is the one question teachers and history books do not have the answer to, not a finite one they agree on. Some say the potent combination of the two viruses altered more than just the DNA of affected people, that it changed their brains and gave them a bloodlust.

"Others say they resented humans that were unchanged, hated them with such passion that they became murderous, motivated by the purest of jealousy. But those are just two of the many theories. No one really knows. Only the original ancestors of Urthmen held the answer to your question, June," Sully says.

I feel as if a frigid thread has made its way into my veins, into my lifeblood, and has instilled cold in me that will never warm. I heard a milder version of Urth's history, just as Sully thought, And I suspect everyone in the room save for Jericho and Sully had the same experience, for we all bear the same troubled expressions. Being reminded that the first Urthmen were humans whose DNA was scrambled by a senseless attack perpetrated by other human beings still staggers me. Knowing the details compounds the shock I feel with a thick layer of disgust.

"I want to go there," June releases me and says. She turns to Sully. "I want to go to New Washington. Can you take me there?" She swipes tears from her face with her fingertips.

"It's probably long gone," Will says gently.

"No," Sully disagrees sharply. He looks June directly in the eye. "New Washington lives on now as it did during those first two decades after the war, only better, more efficient."

"You said yourself you don't know for sure if it's still there," Will counters but without condescension.

"I said I don't know for a fact. But I know my city. And I know it's there. I feel it in my bones," he says with confidence that is inspiring. "June, if you want to go there I'll take you. But I won't stay down there. I can't be underground, cowering, while other human beings are up here being slaughtered."

"Uh, she's not going anywhere, Sully. Not without me agreeing first," I say. The words fly from my mouth of their own accord, reflexively like breathing. June is my sister, my responsibility, not Sully's. He may be a new addition to our clan, but he is, by no means, in charge.

Amusement twinkles in his eyes, only this time I do not find it charming. "Okay then Avery, do I have your permission to take June to the underground city I grew up in?"

"No," I answer immediately, defiance carving into my tone. "You do not. My sister stays with me."

"Oh Avery, I'm afraid you misunderstand me. If she wants to go, we all go to New Washington, together." Sully's words are like a slap to the back of my head, unexpected and disorienting at the same time.

"What?" is all I manage to say.

"We're not safe here, you know that, right?"

"Uh no, we seem okay to me, what with all your cameras and wires and gadgets, and guns," I say and sweep my arm, gesturing to the piles of equipment and miscellany he has.

"It would seem that way. I get that. But we killed a prince today, the Prince of Planet Urth."

"We didn't kill anybody. *You* killed Prince Boart-Boy, whoever he is. Not us," I remind him.

"And you would have done the same in my position," he fires back.

He is right, of course. I am stuck, at a loss for words temporarily. My insides grow hot, thawing the iciness from earlier. "Fine. You're right. I would have," I concede. "But that's not the point."

"Neither is who killed him. The fact of the matter is he's dead, and Urthmen, stupid as they are, know that one of their own didn't take him out. A human did. And which humans made a big old spectacle of themselves at a very public place?"

"We did," I roll my eyes as his point gels.

"Precisely," Sully says with barely restrained triumph.

I realize in that moment that we do not have a choice in the matter. We must leave. June, Will, Oliver, Riley and myself must journey with Sully and Jericho out into the unknown. We must find the underground city, New Washington.

Chapter 30

I look among Will, Oliver and Riley for an answer, for some form of confirmation that they are or aren't on board with venturing off in search of the underground city. The children appear to be more than willing to go. But Will is a different story.

The muscle at the side of his jaw is working continuously. Hard and unreadable, his features betray nothing.

"Will, what do you think about all this?" I ask him.

The only way I know he's heard me is when his eyes finally rest on me. And even then, they reveal nothing.

Sully's eyes dart between us, and he claps his hands together loudly. "How about I give you two a moment to hash things out?"

"Thanks," I say to Sully absently.

Sully joins Jericho and they disappear behind a mountain of supplies. With them out of earshot, I turn to face Will.

"Well, what do you think?" I repeat my question.

"Sounds like it doesn't really matter what I think."

His words land like a slap across my face. They sting and I was unprepared for them. "Will, I never—" I start but he interrupts me.

"Never what, meant to ask me whether I want to go off with these two guys, who, by the way, we know nothing about?"

"No that's not what I was going to say—"

"Well it doesn't matter now I guess. Ask me, don't ask me. You call all the shots now. You said so yourself," he huffs and tosses both hands in the air.

"Will," I say gently. "It's me. What's going on?"

"I know I almost got us killed. I know my actions at the house are what got us caught and landed us in the arena, but that doesn't forfeit my right to decide for myself, or at least be consulted before life-changing plans are made." His tone is less angry, and I understand what he is saying. I never meant to make him feel as though I'd stripped him of having a voice in what we do or where we go.

"I'm sorry," I say plainly. Judging from the stunned look on Will's face, I can see he is taken aback.

"What?" he asks, his face scrunched in confusion.

"I'm sorry I made you feel as if a mistake surrendered your right to be involved in your destiny."

His shoulders slump and any hostility I sensed seconds earlier seeps from him. He rubs his forehead then scrubs both hands over his face.

"We don't have to go if you don't want to," I say and lightly touch his forearm.

He lowers his hands from his face slowly, but not before he clasps a hand over mine, holding it in place. "Yes we do," he says and meets my gaze. His eyes are the sky and land merged, paled by light so that they are a translucent blend of blue and green. My breath catches in my chest as he holds me with them. "Yes, we do," he says again.

"The children will be—" I start to say.

"Not just for them, but for us too. We could make a life there."

The intensity of his words and the gleam in his eyes suggest that there's more to leaving than simply finding a safe haven to hide from the monsters who roam that planet, that maybe the opportunity to actually live rather than exist is real.

A quiver races from my chest and passes through my stomach at the notion. Envisioning life without the constant worry and tension of ever-present danger seemed like a dream before today. As hard as it is to imagine, I find myself yearning for it too.

But with that yearning comes the continual niggle at the back of my brain. Living secretively in an underground utopia, as magical as it sounds, does not erase what is going on in the rest of the world. It does not make me immune to the plight of my species.

A calling beckons me, ringing through my core like the toll of a bell, and I know what must happen.

"Yes, that is true," I tell Will as my eyes well with tears. "So I take it you want to go?" I sniffle then ask him.

"Yes, I do. I want to go to New Washington," he replies, his eyes shining.

Without warning, Will closes the distance between us and embraces me tightly. I feel his heart pounding against my chest, keeping time with my own frantic heartbeat, and I am lost in his scent, his warmth. Time and planning cease to exist. Wars and monsters, danger and death, all of it falls by the wayside as I inhale his rich, musky scent. My arms reach out and match the ferocity with which he clutches me. I am dizzy, giddy with an inexplicable joy so filling it borders on sadness. I feel as if I am floating, suspended above my own body on the wings of a mighty bird. And I am not afraid. In fact, I don't want to come down. He lowers his chin, dipping his head so that his lips hover just above mine. His hot breath feathers against my mouth, only this time, I am ready. I know what he intends to do and I will let him. He inches close, our hearts drilling in sync.

"So are we going, Avery?" June asks.

I snap my head in her direction, her voice anchoring itself to me and yanking me back to reality. My hands fall to my sides and I step away from Will, embarrassed, though unsure why exactly. "Uh yes, we're going," I answer.

"Yay!" June cheers. "Riley, Oliver, we're going!" she calls out to the others.

A lively eruption occurs among the children followed by a buzz of excitement that is palpable. I look at Will to see whether he can feel it to, but his eyes are cast downward. I want to reach out to him, but as soon as my hand rises from my thigh, Sully's voice fills the room.

"I hear we're going," he says.

"Yep, looks like we are," I nod.

"Any idea how we're getting there?" he asks.

I can't tell whether or not he's joking. One eyebrow is cocked and he smiles his perpetual, crooked smile, but I'm still unsure.

"Sully, you're joking, right?" I ask.

"No, not at all."

"What? Come on!" I say.

"No really, I mean, we can walk. It'll probably take us about five years to get there. Of course, we'll either starve, be eaten or killed by Urthmen before then, but I'm willing to try!"

I shake my head, trying to right my thoughts. Surely I didn't hear what I thought I just heard. He is obviously just teasing me, isn't he? I wonder.

"Come on, enough already." I glance at the kids. Their moods have deflated substantially. "Cut it out, you're scaring the kids."

"What do you mean? I'm just being honest," he replies.

"Sully, stop it, all right. It's not funny. You have the truck and a camper. We won't have to walk," I look toward the kids and smile halfheartedly.

"True, I do have the camper and the truck, but you're forgetting one crucial component: gasoline. As in, I don't have any. And without gasoline, those vehicles don't operate."

My jaw goes slack and I do not blink. Part of me contemplates slapping Sully right across his arrogant face. But I don't. Instead, I close my mouth and swallow hard then grind my molars. "So you got my sister and Riley and Oliver excited over nothing?" I lean in and smile, talking through my teeth quietly

"I said I'd be happy to escort June there," he replies in little more than a whisper, and with that twinkle of amusement I found charming before, but now find grating.

"You gave them hope and now you're taking it away," I narrow my eyes and practically growl.

"Has anyone ever told you that you're beautiful when you're mad?" he murmurs.

"Has anyone ever told you I eviscerated the last person who said that to me?" I reply in the same tone he used and watch as he takes a step back. "Gasoline," I return his attention to our conversation. "Where do we find it?"

"It's guarded by Urthmen, but that's the least of our problems."

"Why is that?"

"Do you have any idea how dangerous it would be to take a vehicle on Urthmen roads cross-country?" he asks.

"Maybe you should have thought of that before you let us believe we could have a semblance of a life."

Sully's head rears back as if I did decide to slap him. His eyes are wide and devoid of laughter. He looks almost remorseful.

"What?" I ask him. "What is it?"

"Nothing," he answers quickly and looks at his feet.

"No really, what is it?"

"It's just that, it's what you said. You and June haven't ever had any sort of life."

"We haven't. We've always been on the run, even when we lived at the cave or at the compound. We were constantly threatened," I admit.

Sully and I are practically nose to nose. Consumed by anger and disappointment seconds ago, I forgot we stood in a roomful of people.

"Is there a problem?" Will interjects and reminds us both that we are not alone.

"Nope," Sully says and his face returns to its usual inscrutable expression.

"We just have to work out a plan to get some fuel and we'll be on our way," he says and slides a glance at Jericho before returning his attention to me. "Looks like we're going on a road trip. Is everyone in?"

"I'm in," I say.

"Me, too," Will adds.

"Count me in," June claps.

"And me," Riley cries out.

"Let's do it," Oliver chimes in.

I look to Jericho who stands with his head bowed and his hands clasped over his belly. "Hey," Sully calls. "How about you? You coming with us?"

"Of course! Did you think I'd let you go off and get into trouble without me?" Jericho lifts his eyes and says with a hearty chuckle.

"All right then, I need everyone to huddle up," Sully waves us all toward him. "We need to formulate a plan to get gasoline," he begins when everyone circles around him. I hang back a moment and watch Riley and Oliver, Will and June, the people I love, and feel my chest tighten. I will miss them. They belong in New Washington. They deserve to be safe and happy. They deserve the life they always dreamed of. But I do not. Another fate awaits me, one less peaceful, one far more complicated.

I will go with them to the underground city, and I will try to convince the people there to fight. If things are as good as Sully says they are I doubt anyone will join in my crusade and I will leave without Oliver, Riley, and Will. I will leave June, too.

We know what we have to do as a group, and now I know what I must do as an individual as well. I have not shared the conclusion I've reached with anyone, not Will, not even June. I fear that saying the words aloud might break me, and I sincerely doubt my voice would hold if I tried. My chest clenches at the thought, at the expression on everyone's face when I announce what I will do. I am glad I will have many days to work myself up to it, to steel myself. Still, as I watch June talk excitedly with Sully, offering her input, her silvery-blue eyes sparkling with something I have never seen in them before—true hope—I worry that even with time to prepare, my revelation will not get any easier. I also fear that she will never forgive me. But I hope someday she does.

Until now, hope has been a futile emotion I barely allowed to breeze through my brain in passing. All I could do daily was try my best to be courageous, to survive. Neither June nor I would have ever dared to anchor ourselves to it as we have now, since Sully shared with us news of the underground city. But all that has changed.

Hope is what I am banking on for June's future. Hope is all that motivates me; hope of a better life for June, hope for safety and stability, and hope for a future that includes more than just existing from one day to the next, but actually living and embarking on new experiences.

I hope June is happy one day and that she is able to reconcile with my decision to leave if that is what comes to pass. I hope she finds it in her kind and decent heart to forgive me, her last living blood relation, for leaving her to defend the people of Planet Urth.

The End

About the Authors:

Jennifer and Christopher Martucci hoped that their life plan had changed radically in early 2010. To date, the jury is still out. But late one night, in January of 2010, the stay-at-home mom of three girls under the age of six had just picked up the last doll from the playroom floor and placed it in a bin when her husband startled her by declaring, "We should write a book together!" Wearied from a day of shuttling the children to and from school, preschool and Daisy Scouts, laundry, cooking and cleaning, Jennifer simply stared blankly at her husband of fifteen years. After all, the idea of writing a book had been an individual dream each of them had possessed for much of their young adult lives. Both had written separately in their teens and early twenties, but without much success. They would write a dozen chapters here and there only to find that either the plot would fall apart, or characters would lose their zest, or the story would just fall flat. Christopher had always preferred penning science-fiction stories filled with monsters and diabolical villains, while Jennifer had favored venting personal experiences or writing about romance. Inevitably though, frustration and day-to-day life had placed writing on the back burner and for several years, each had pursued alternate (paying) careers. But the dream had never died. And Christopher suggested that their dream ought to be removed from the back burner for further examination. When he proposed that they author a book together on that cold January night, Jennifer was hesitant to reject the idea outright. His proposal sparked a discussion, and the discussion lasted deep into the night. By morning, the idea for the Dark Creations series was born.

The Dark Creations series, as well as the Arianna Rose series and the Planet Urth series, are works that were written while Jennifer and Christopher continued about with their daily activities and raised their young children. They changed diapers, potty trained and went to story time at the local library between chapter outlines and served as room parents while fleshing out each section. Life simply continued. And in some ways, their everyday lives were reflected in the characters of each series.

As the story line continues to evolve, so too does the Martucci collaboration. Lunches are still packed, noses are still wiped and time remains a rare and precious commodity in their household, but it is the sound of happy chaos that is the true background music of their writing. They hope all enjoy reading their work as much as they enjoyed writing it.

Books by Jennifer and Christopher Martucci:

The Dark Creations Series (A YA paranormal romance series)

Dark Creations: Gabriel Rising (Part 1)
Dark Creations: Gabriel Rising (Part 2)
Dark Creations: Gabriel Rising (Part 1&2)
Dark Creations: Resurrection (Part 3)
Dark Creations: The Hunted (Part 4)
Dark Creations: Hell on Earth (Part 5)
Dark Creations: Dark Ending (Part 6)

The Arianna Rose Series (A paranormal romance series)

Arianna Rose (Part 1)
Arianna Rose: The Awakening (Part 2)
Arianna Rose: The Gathering (Part 3)
Arianna Rose: The Arrival (Part 4)
Arianna Rose: The Gates of Hell (Part 5)

Coming Soon:

Planet Urth: The Underground City (Book 3)

The Planet Urth Series (A YA science-fiction/dystopian series)

Planet Urth (Book 1)
Planet Urth: The Savage Lands (Book 2)

Thank You So Much For Reading Our Book!

We deeply appreciate your readership and would love to hear from you!

For information about upcoming releases (or just to say hi!) please visit our website at http://darkcreationssaga.com or our Facebook page at http://on.fb.me/1dlUUF5

Thank you again for reading!

Love,
Jennifer and Christopher Martucci

Oh, One Last Thing Before You Go...

When you turn the page, you may be given the opportunity to express your thoughts on Facebook and Twitter automatically. If you enjoyed our book, would you take a second to click that button and let your friends know about it?

If they get something out of the book, they'll be grateful to you, and we will be, too!

Thank you so much!

Love,
Jenny and Chris